the narrows

m. craig

PAPERCUT PRESS
Olyphant, PA

PAPERCUT PRESS

Copyright © 2011 by m craig

Cover and interior design by Nim Ben-Reuven

Editorial work by Elizabeth J. Byer

ISBN-13 978-0-9837844-0-1
ISBN-10 0-98378-440-10

Published by Papercut Press
517 Burke Byp
P.O. Box 388
Olyphant, PA 18447

Printed in the United States

to my mamaeche,
for bringing me into this world
and putting up with me ever since

dragon shriek ripped through the calm espresso air of Stein's café on Christiania Street. The soft strains of chatter lulled as a few coffee drinkers paused their conversations to glance over at the barista, who shoved a mess of black bangs under her bandanna and tightened her grip on a ferret-sized fire dragon. She pressed dusty coffee grinds into the filter and tugged on the dragon's spiny neck until a stream of flames spewed from its mouth and heated the machine's charred bronze pot. Mumbling a curse, the barista gritted her teeth against the dragon's reptile squirms and plunged its snout into a steel container of bear's milk. Fluffy frothing sounds came from the coffee bar until, in one quick, practiced motion, the barista yanked the dragon back, flicked it into a cage hanging from the ceiling, and slammed the door shut.

"Escape from in there," she snapped. Little dragon-bite scars dotted her hands from years of making espresso. She poured the steamed milk into a mug and clunked it onto the counter. "Bear's milk latte," she called. The dragon, along with four others, sprang into frantic flight, smashing their bodies off the bars and making the cage swing widely on its chain.

"Cut it out!" the barista growled, spinning around and threatening the creatures with a glass of water. The winged amphibians settled onto their prison perches, clung to them with their filed-down claws. As the cage's lurching slowed to a sway, one of the monsters shot a breath of fire at the barista. Another fixed its gaze on Sim, who was sitting alone three tables away. Her dark hair fell in waves onto an open newspaper, but she looked at the street outside, as if lost in a daydream. With a jerk, Sim glanced at the dragon's rust-red face and scaled body, its pointed joints and paper-thin wings. The things were creepy. But they made amazing coffee. The cafés on the other side of the Brigantine River used magic dust to fuel gadgets that heated water into steam and brewed a bitter sludge that tasted like earwax. The coffee in the Bikeway Narrows, like everything in that tiny and isolated part of the city, was different.

Sim looked away from the fire dragons and back out the window, where locked-up bikes and rusty wheels covered the fence guarding the front of the café, along with an iron dragon that struck a clawed pose near the door. The coffee at Stein's cost one sol, equal to one gram of magic dust; a third of what it cost in Greater Terresin and five times better. In the middle of the café a chandelier made out of beer bottles and candle stubs dripped a spiral galaxy of wax onto the center of a long communal table, where coffee drinkers lost themselves in newspapers or books, or argued politics and social theory from their mismatched chairs. Sim sat next to the overstocked bookshelves, which had spilled their burden onto the floor in high stacks of hardcovers, at a small table made from a cross section of an old oak tree.

A handful of regulars seemed to frequent the coffee shop as often as Sim did, but she never talked to them. She was separate, awkward, still new to the city. She had found Stein's a week ago, on her second day in Terresin and her first day in the Bikeway Narrows. The memory of the night she had run away wrapped around Sim's thoughts, blurring the words of her newspaper. She couldn't help but wonder how she'd ended up in this strange place, so far away from everything she'd ever known. And as much as she didn't want to think about it, her mind went back once again to the night that haunted her.

The train station's platform was dark and empty. Translucent globes with fairies trapped inside them dotted the stationhouse's back wall, shedding a little light onto the murky tracks. A ruffling sound came from the platform's far end.

"Think you can steal from us and get away with it?" a man's voice said, followed by the sound of a kick and a grunt. "Hold him tight, boys."

Adrenaline set Sim's ears ringing. She pulled a wand out of her inner coat pocket—a wand that wasn't hers, that she had no clue how to even use; a wand that was the reason she'd been forced to run. But holding it in front of her made her feel braver, somehow, so she kept it there and clutched the smooth wood as she stepped down the dirty platform toward the noises. Five men were huddled in a circle. Two of them were restraining a guy in quester's clothes: knee-high leather boots, a wide belt with a sheath hanging from the side, leather bands around his forearms.

"I'll teach you to choose your quests more carefully, boy," the middle one said. He swung back his arm and planted his knuckles into the quester's nose.

They were going to kill him, Sim realized in a flash. Any rational person would have crept back into the shadows and hid until the thugs had left. But Sim didn't have time to think rationally. She shook her wand and delivered an attack spell at the man's back. She didn't know how she'd done it; she felt like raw fear was streaming from the center of her body, down her arm, and out of the wand in the form of a lightning bolt. The other two men spun around to face her, but Sim sent a bolt at each of them before they could react.

The two men who were holding the quester dropped him to the ground. "Magicweaver," one growled under his breath as he pulled out a dagger. The other had a gun, powered by magic dust. He pulled the trigger and sent a red bullet of energy at Sim, but she flicked it away with her wand, sent a bolt at his chest, and then at the other's just as he was reaching his arm back to throw the knife.

Sim blinked. The night air was cold. A chilly breeze blew through her open jacket. The quester was on the ground, cradling his stomach. Around him, the five thugs littered the platform in various states of incapacity. Sim tucked her wand back into her jacket. A train whistle howled through the night. There was no time to see if the men were still alive. Sim grabbed the quester's sword by its heavy hilt and dragged it back to him.

"What are you doing?" He moaned as she tried to shove the sword back in its sheath.

The train creaked to a stop. Sim's heart skipped a beat. She couldn't miss it; if she missed the train, they'd catch her for sure. The doors flew open and she flung the sword inside. Gasps of pain grumbled out of the quester's slightly parted lips. Sim grabbed his leather wristbands and dragged him across the platform and into the car. Her shoes scuffed against the compartment's hardwood floor. Sim grunted, leaned her weight back, and gave him one last good yank. The quester's boots slid into the car just as the iron doors snapped shut inches away from their rubber soles.

"Tickets?"

The train master hovered above them in his red suit and cylindrical, gold-trimmed hat. He looked down at the quester with an expression that made Sim worry he'd kick them off the train. Her hands shook as she searched through her pockets.

"Here," she said, handing him the slip of paper.

"And his?"

"The bag on my belt," the quester mumbled without opening his eyes.

Sim unbuckled the dirty canvas pouch and shifted through a handful of potions until her fingers grazed the folded ticket. The train lurched forward. Her hand was still shaking when she held out the quester's pass, but Sim did her best to make her gaze defiant. The train master frowned, probably disappointed that he'd have to let them ride, and handed the tickets back to her.

"Take a seat, please," he said, and stepped over the nearly unconscious quester.

The quester was heavier than he looked. Sim dragged him to one of the booths and pushed him against the window. She pulled his legs out of the aisle and sat next to him, holding onto his bicep to make sure he didn't slip out of his seat when the train hit especially violent bumps. He looked about twenty, with dark hair and a scruff on his chin that was on the verge of becoming a beard. His bottom lip was swollen and split open, his left eye already turning from bright pink to deep purple. Sim held a handkerchief under his nose until the blood dried around his nostrils in a dark maroon crust. Eventually he blinked his eyes open, pulled out a green potion, and swallowed it in one gulp. For a full minute he stared blankly at the back of the seat in front of him, and then jumped and looked over at Sim.

"Who are you?" he asked, his back against the window.

"I'm Sim." She breathed, still shaken from everything that had happened.

The quester scanned his eyes around the empty car and then laughed. "You saved my ass, didn't you?"

"I guess so."

"Awesome." He smiled and grimaced from the cut on his lip. "Thanks for that, Sim. I'm Cader."

They shook hands.

"What brings you out to this remote part of the exurbs?" he asked.

"I grew up here," Sim said carefully. "I'm going to Terresin. Moving there."

"Oh, really? To what part of the city?"

"I'm not sure yet," Sim said after a pause.

Cader frowned at her and narrowed his eyes. "You don't have a place to stay, do you?"

"I'll find one."

"Listen, you should just stay at my place. There's room for another person. You'd have a whole room to yourself. If you hate it you can always find somewhere else to live. It's the least I can do, after you helped me out back there. I owe you a lot more than that."

"I don't want to be any trouble—"

"Things happen for a reason, you know?" Cader said with a grin. "There was a reason that you came onto that platform when you did, a reason that those men chose the train station as the place to jump me. We can't just ignore the synchronicity behind all of this. Besides, the house is huge. Half of the rooms aren't even being used. And I can help you find a job. I know people."

"You're sure it wouldn't be a problem?"

"Not at all. And that was amazing what you did back there on the platform, by the way." He glanced at Sim's plain servant's dress. "Are you a quester in disguise?"

4

Sim shook her head. "No. The moment took me over, I think. I have no idea how I cast those spells." The wand pressed into her ribs. She hoped he wouldn't ask about it. "Why were those guys after you?"

"They stole a lot of money from someone, and then I was hired to steal it back. They weren't too happy about it. Don't know how they tracked me down, though. I must be getting sloppy. Time to head back to the city and reboot, for sure." Cader's eyelids started to droop.

"You should sleep," Sim said. "I'll wake you up when we get there."

Cader nodded and leaned his head against the window. Sim herself couldn't have slept if her life depended on it; not with all that had happened that night, and the incredible uncertainty that lay before her.

Sim turned her attention back to the paper she was reading. It was better not to think about where she'd come from, better to think about something else. Pulchra was sending more troops to Siccor, the article said, where monsters were leveling towns along the country's northern border. The soldiers had started to call the things "ogres," from the Siccorian word for oozing.

Sim finished the story with a sigh and looked up to catch the stare of a girl who was sitting at a table nearby, the same newspaper held before her in a neat fold. Her eyes were the color of moss and dark honey, with eyelids that drooped in a way that made her look either bored or slightly sleepy. She wore an old black T-shirt with the neckline cut low and the sleeves torn off. Sim held the girl's gaze for a moment longer and looked down, blushing. She locked her eyes on a coffee stain that had left a ring around the middle of the headline, and wondered what she'd done to attract the girl's stare. No one ever noticed her. Sim stood and took her mug to the dish bin, using the action as a cover to glance across the room again. The girl had gone back to reading.

A racket arose from the dragon cage. The screeches and rattling iron caught the attention of a few customers sitting at the coffee bar, but most of them seemed not to notice. Other baristas were better at keeping the dragons placid. This one held her hands up in exasperation and then, in one quick movement, grabbed a glass of water and doused the cage. The dragon shrieks stopped. A girl near the bar jumped up and flicked water from her arms.

"No more espresso drinks, folks!" the barista yelled, with an exaggerated shrug. Spinning around, she threw the glass at a wall behind the counter and turned away as it smashed to the floor.

The guy working the cash register glanced up at her. "Dude, you need to clam down," he said, shaking his head.

"Fine." She waved a hand at the dragons. "You deal with them." She stomped outside and squatted against the bike fence, glaring out at the street. The fire dragons quivered in a heap at the bottom of their cage. Water dripped from their claws and wing bones. Sim placed her mug in the bin and looked up at the girl's table again, but it was empty. She was gone.

The barista was still brooding when Sim walked past her and onto Christiania Street, where summer sunbeams warmed the shoulders of the young people walking together in twos or threes, hiding their eyes behind dark sunglasses and sharing stories of debauchery from the night before. They wore leather boots, tank tops, and jeans that had been cut short against the summer heat. Their hair would have earned them confused or judgmental stares had they been in the small town where Sim had grown up, but their nonconventional cuts fit the Bikeway Narrows, where nature was slowly reclaiming the old edifices of what had once been a vibrant industrial neighborhood. A chrome track bike swerved around Sim, nearly hitting her. Its angry rider glared over his shoulder through brown-tinted goggles and then continued on with a shake of his head. Like an idiot, she'd been scanning the sidewalk instead of watching where she was going, hoping to catch sight of the girl from the café, not even sure why she was so curious about this random person.

Across the street from Stein's, overgrown vines stretched between a small vegan bakery and a rotting three-story. Sim pulled the plants aside and stepped into the smell of hot vegetable death. The alley was like a giant compost heap. Trash peeked between the weeds and crumbled chunks of brick crunched under Sim's boots. She stepped toward the Old Wall, an imposing stretch of masonry that towered over the shorter buildings of the Narrows. Its top walkway was lined with pillars and gaps, where archers used to sit and wait for approaching enemies. Now the bikers strolled along the path and sat in the grass patches growing between cracks in the mortar. No one ever came back here, to the space at the bottom of the wall where Sim liked to hide her cruiser even though everyone else left their bikes out in the open.

Sim pedaled past Stein's, past a whiskey well called the Blue Carnation, and past a closet of a book shop. She left Christiania and glided up to a small shop that sat in the middle of an abandoned block of apartments. Hardly anyone ever went down this street, just two blocks away from the bustle of Christiania. Sim leaned her bike against the shop's brick wall and pushed into the old-books, grease, and must smell of the Incubator. Even after a week of Sim's intensive cleaning, the shop was still dusty and cluttered. Twisted handlebars and bicycle frames were piled against one wall, broken grandfather clocks lined another. There were screws and cogs and tools everywhere. As far as Sim could tell, the shop used to be a grocery store. She'd spent two full days throwing away old cans of food and blackened loaves of bread, and another day pulling old shelves out onto the curb, where they'd been quickly spotted and claimed.

Azzer appeared from his workshop in the back just as Sim dropped her bag behind the counter. He was older than most of the people in the Narrows, with a graying lion's mane of hair and small bright eyes that were bordered by tiny wrinkles. He had to be at least six feet tall and, since Sim was a bit shorter than average, he towered above her in a way that was often intimidating. But his voice was soft and his smile genuine. Cader knew him through questing acquaintances, and had gotten her a job at the new fix-it shop just as he'd promised.

"You can finish cleaning the front of the shop today," Azzer said, getting straight to business. "Those boxes need to be unpacked, and everything cleaned. I have a lot of work to do in the back. We're just about ready to open. Two more days, maybe. I have some inventions that are very nearly finished."

"Anything exciting?"

He tilted his chin up and narrowed his eyes. "It's all exciting," he said with a grin, and turned from her. He disappeared behind the maroon curtain hanging between two floor-to-ceiling bookcases, which separated the storefront from his workshop in the back.

It wasn't long before dirt marked a black line beneath Sim's short fingernails and dust spotted the black jeans she'd bought the day before. Pants that were loose around the ankles would get caught in her bike chain and ruined with grease, so she had bought a pair of the tight- fitting jeans that everyone in the Narrows seemed to wear. The days were starting to get hot, though, and once she made more money she'd have to head back to the thrift shop on Christiania and get some shorts.

Sim stood and stretched her neck. She'd been unloading boxes for hours now, taking breaks in between to clean the shop so that the work wouldn't get monotonous. For as long as she could remember, she'd always been cleaning for someone. At least Azzer was nice, even if he was a bit strange, and he paid her well. Sim threw her dust rag onto the counter and pried open a box full of books. She piled them on the counter, and paused when the title of one caught her attention. *Brewery Basics* was stamped across the cover in simple, bold letters. The table of contents listed chapters outlining how to set up a microbrewery and brew small batches of beer.

"Take it."

Sim jumped. She put the book back on the counter and grabbed a rag.

"I was just looking at it," Sim explained. "I'm almost finished. I just have to put the rest of these books away."

Azzer ran his hand over the book's cover. "Brewing is illegal, you know," he said, staring at it.

"I know. I—"

"Got a lot of good memories from this book," he interrupted, and then glanced up at her. "Made me a lot of money, too."

He held it out to her.

"You really don't have to—"

"Just don't get caught. And if you do, don't say you got it here." His clear gaze held hers, adding weight to his words.

"I won't," Sim said and took the book from him, frowning because Azzer didn't seem like the type of guy who would break the law, even if he had set up shop in the Bikeway Narrows. "Thanks," she added.

Azzer nodded. "You live on the other side of the river?" he asked. He was gazing out the window at the buildings across the street.

"Yeah." Of course she did. Everyone did.

"You should be heading back, then. It isn't safe to bike back too late. You can finish in the morning." He opened the front door and flipped down a kickstand that he'd bolted there to serve as a doorstop. Sim slipped *Brewery Basics* into her bag, made sure it was closed tight, and stepped around the clutter behind the counter.

"Good work, Sim," Azzer called after her as she rode away.

"Thanks!" she yelled back over her shoulder.

Three friends were riding ahead of her when she got to the street that ended at the bridge's onramp, the path that everyone took to get back into Greater Terresin. A girl with a fauxhawk and low, curved handlebars led the way until the three riders got to the bridge, stood on their pedals, and zipped up the incline so that Sim was left happily alone. The once-bright-red steel of the Narrows Bridge was now faded to a sickly pink. Its iron supports with their splotchy rust patches jutted out of the river like the dead fingers of a frozen mechanical giant. Carriages were too big to cross the bridge, and no one was crazy enough to walk through the fourteen blocks of abandoned factories that buffered the Bikeway Narrows from the Brigantine River. Because of this, only bikers and brave souls with skateboards ever went there.

A feeling of heavy clumsiness settled into Sim's legs. She struggled up the bridge, gasped for air, and tried to ignore the burning in her thighs. Five people passed her before she reached the bridge's apex and flew down the other side. But the biking didn't get any easier after the bridge: Greater Terresin, with its speeding hired drivers and oblivious pedestrians, was hostile to bikers. The whole ride home, Sim had visions of smashing into an opening carriage door and crumpling into traffic, getting crushed under the wheels of a roaring truck. But she wouldn't let a little danger daunt her. She made it back to the quiet, leafy roads leading up to Kailash Street and the three-story red-brick house that looked as if it belonged on a hill somewhere in the countryside, not squashed between boxy apartment buildings.

The first week at Kailash had been a time of uncertainty and hesitation. The sky had been black when Sim and Cader had gotten off the train and emerged onto the sparkling, billboarded streets of Central Terresin. Sim had followed Cader in a daze as he walked through the crowded sidewalks, away from the shops with high windows and brightly lit displays toward darker, quieter city streets. "I know it's far," he said, "but it's safest to walk. We're almost there." By the time they had arrived, Sim was so tired that she went straight to the room he said could be hers and collapsed onto the bed.

The soft scent of frying dough had gently roused Sim from her dreams the following morning. She'd never woken up to the smell of pancakes. Her stomach growled, but she stayed in place, casting her eyes about her new room until she was convinced that she wasn't still dreaming. Dusty sheets covered most of the furniture, but the room was large and bright. Sim fought the urge to stay in bed until Cader came to look for her. On the train he'd told her that his roommate Kai was a Munian immigrant, an absolutely amazing cook, and that she could be bossy, but that Sim would learn to ignore it. Their third roommate was Prudence, who had been gone for the past three months and was still off questing somewhere in the Hinterlands.

"Finally," Kai said when Sim made her way down to the kitchen. "It's nearly noon." Kai turned to face her, hands on her hips. She was thin, almost waifish, with a guarded expression set behind her thick-framed glasses. On the counter behind her was a series of tubes, beakers, and ring stands with different colored potions swirling through them. The huge kitchen took up nearly half of Kailash's first floor. The stone counter with the potion-brewing equipment stretched along the length of one wall. Another wall held a shelf lined with tiny vials and mason jars filled with dried herbs. Kai studied Sim from behind her glasses and then turned back to the stove to flip the latest batch of pancakes. "Those are for you," she said, pointing a spatula toward a covered plate. "Cader's already left."

"Thanks," Sim said, noting Kai's accent. She talked like the Munian dignitaries who would go to Nogron's fancy parties, whom Sim always tended to avoid because they were more pompous and proper than any of his other guests. The accent sounded out of place in a kitchen, but Kai looked at home standing over a stove.

Kai came to sit with her, and Sim grasped for something to talk about.

"So Cader said that you're from Munia."

Kai looked up at her. "Yes?"

"That's cool."

Kai raised her eyebrows and dug into her pancakes.

"You're a potions master?" Sim asked, eyeing the equipment laid out on the counter.

"I'm hardly a master," Kai said with a snort. "The magic's in the plants. I'm glad you brought that up, though. You'll have to help in the garden if you're going to be staying here."

"Yeah, of course. That would be great."

Sim focused on her breakfast until it was finished. Kai took their plates to the sink and then brought Sim to the back yard, where spiraling towers dotted the patch of land behind the house like wisps of dark green smoke. The tops of the highest spirals reached just below the cone roof of the house's highest turret. Beds of vegetables covered the ground between the spirals, and rose up, in steps, to a fence at the back of the lot.

"Each vertical plot has at least twenty different herb species," Kai said proudly. She pointed to the thick mother spiral at the center of the garden. "That one has over a hundred. Most of those prefer the shade, so it doesn't need to be as thin as the others. It's a system that they've perfected in Munia."

"How do you—"

"Tubes of dirt or water—it depends on the plant type—form the structure for each spiral." Kai pulled back a handful of a plant that smelled like mint, showing a copper pipe with the top fourth of it sliced off to expose just enough dirt for the plants to sprout. Holes drilled into the sides of the tubing allowed the herbs to grow sideways as well as vertically. Kai glanced at Sim and continued. "They're complicated, but don't worry; you won't be dealing with them."

Weeding. That was the chore she had been assigned to supplement her rent. Sim hated it, but she didn't dare say so. She didn't know where she would go if Cader and Kai told her to leave. She pushed her bike against the back of the house and went to the cucumber bed. Her knees sunk into the moist grass surrounding the wooden planter and her fingertips grew cool as they became coated with earth. She pulled out one tiny green shoot after another until the whole bed was clear of them.

"How was work?" Kai asked when Sim pushed her way into the kitchen.

"It was fine. Azzer should be paying me soon, so I can start giving you rent."

Kai nodded and dropped a handful of leaves into a boiling pot. Sim went to the sink and wrinkled her nose against the bitter smell coming from the stove.

"What are you working on?" she asked.

"Sleeping potion." Kai threw in a sprinkle of little black seeds. "It takes a whole day to brew."

"Do you know when Cader will be back?"

"It depends on how many orders he has."

Cader had only one condition for Sim about living with them: She was never, ever to speak a word about the potion business he and Kai ran out of their kitchen. Sim was sure that the whole thing was illegal, and that Cader was probably selling the potions without the proper permits. She was sure he'd love the brewing book.

Sim left the kitchen, walked through the small foyer with a staircase that led to an upstairs hallway lined with seven bedrooms, and fell onto the couch in the living room. She lost herself in a novel until she heard Cader come in through the back door.

"What's up?" Cader said when Sim rushed into the kitchen. He was sitting at the table with the notebook he used to keep track of his potion sales.

"I have a surprise for you. A book." Sim grinned.

Cader put down his pen and raised an eyebrow. "Okay. Let's see it."

In the time Sim had been reading, Kai had switched from concocting potions to fixing dinner. She turned from the stove, pushed up her glasses, and glanced from Cader to Sim. "What's going on?" she asked Cader.

"I think Sim is trying to tell me that I need to become more educated."

"What?" Kai said.

Sim slid the book across the table. Cader's face froze for a moment as he read the title and then his eyebrows and jaw stretched away from each other.

"Where did you get this?" he asked, skimming the book's index.

"What is it?" Kai stepped toward them.

Cader put his hand over the title. "It's nothing you'd be interested in."

Kai's eyes narrowed and she looked from Cader to Sim again. "You two are up to something."

"Not yet," Cader said with a smirk.

"Really?" Sim said. "So we're going to try it then?"

"Are you kidding? Of course we are."

Kai jumped and made a grab for the book, but Cader rose to his feet and lifted the brown leather-bound tome out of her reach. "This is awesome. We can do it in the basement."

"Do what in the basement?" Kai demanded.

"Nothing. And don't you go snooping around," Cader said, suddenly stern.

Kai stepped away and stood there for a moment, examining Cader's face. She groaned and turned back to the stove. "Fine. Don't tell me. I don't even want to know. Just keep it to the basement."

"Oh, we will," Cader said, flipping through the pages.

"And don't think I haven't noticed that you've been letting that animal back into the house."

Sim glanced around the kitchen, but Drangs must have been elsewhere. She had been hoping that Kai wouldn't notice her and Cader's new pet.

"I'm going to start getting everything that we need tomorrow," Cader said softly.

"I can help tomorrow night. I'm working now, remember?"

"How is it?" Cader asked. He'd been so busy the past week that they'd barely seen each other.

"I like it. Azzer's really cool."

Cader nodded. "Awesome. I knew you'd like the Narrows. Prudence likes to hang out there when she's around." He flipped through the book and stopped at one a page displaying an annotated diagram. "This'll be so easy. Except for the calibrating. We'll have to figure that out when we get to it."

"Azzer might know how," Sim offered. "I can ask him to teach me."

Cader looked up at her with a flash in his eyes. He grinned. "Well, isn't that convenient?"

"I guess it is," Sim said, and went to find Drangs before Cader could lecture her on fate and synchronicity, which she could now sense coming before he even opened his mouth.

"Looks like Kai's going to let Drangs stay in the house," Sim said as she left the kitchen.

"Huh. We'll see about that," Kai said.

Cader smiled at her. "Told you she would."

II

An angle grinder sent a sharp whine to the front of the Incubator as it bit into a piece of metal, and then softened to a purr when Azzer must have activated some sort of silencing gadget. The shop had just opened for business the day before and no one seemed to know about the Incubator yet. Sim sat behind the counter on the edge of a stool, staring across the room at a tattered map of the known world. Colorful fanged dragons and sharp-nailed monsters loomed at the map's blurred edges, a symbol for the Hinterlands, wilderness that had yet to be civilized and carved out into states. The monsters were a reminder as to why so few ventured into the unknown. Outlined in gold were the Enchanted Nations: Eridos, Munia, Branium, Elm, Tridea, Volvox, and Pulchra. The countries scattered throughout them were bordered by black lines—Siccor, Ogbond, Sangua, Coveland, Nierra, and the Maria Islands—the Ancient Kingdoms, where kings ruled instead of councils and laws were upheld by swords instead of courts. Sim was sure that Nogron was out there somewhere, looking for her. Maybe she should have left Pulchra and gone on to one of the Ancient Kingdoms, where it would definitely be more difficult for him to track her down.

And maybe it hadn't been such a good idea to take that brewing book. She had wanted to thank Cader for getting her the job, but she never thought he'd actually go through with building a brewing machine. All week he'd been hunting down parts and putting everything together down in the basement. Prison. They'd go straight to prison if they got caught, although she wasn't so sure that would be any worse than what would happen if Nogron ever found her. But Sim had nowhere else to go. And working at the Incubator allowed her to earn money without filing any government paperwork. This new life allowed her to be practically invisible.

In an attempt to distract herself, Sim focused on the fuzzy ball of energy at the center of her chest and began to pull magic out of the air. She ran her fingers over the rough metal and rust of an old pair of handlebars that were missing their grips. One side of the bars curled up toward the ceiling, as if she was molding putty, but with her mind instead of her fingers. The metal slowly pinched together in some places and ballooned out in others. Sim had never understood how she was able to do this—to imagine something and then make it happen in real life. Shifting things, as Sim liked to call it, had always been an outlet for her troubled mind. She felt like she had back in Locklawn, when she would run off by herself to the center of the woods and just stand and listen to the rustling leaves and gurgling water and chirping birds streaming toward her all at once as if she were at the center of the universe. A calm sense of peace settled into her being as she was reminded that there was more to the world than met the eye. If nothing else, Sim believed in that. She had to. She felt it. The other end of the handlebars pulled upward and split apart to form crooked iron branches. Sim flattened out leaves and stretched the metal so that soon it looked like a small bonsai tree was growing out of the wooden counter. Its trunk was as gnarled and convulsed as Sim's unsettled mind, its branches reached in all directions as if they didn't know if they should grasp the ground or the sky.

"Hey."

Sim jumped, nearly knocking over her stool. She caught one of its legs and set it upright before looking up to meet the striking gaze of the girl standing on the other side of the counter. Her eyes were gold or brown or green—somewhere in between. They held Sim's, and she felt a flood of energy concentrate in the middle of her torso, just above her stomach. Sim looked away. It was the girl she'd seen yesterday at Stein's.

"Didn't mean to sneak up on you," the girl said with a smile. "But you were pretty into..." A look of surprise came over her face as she glanced down at the handlebar bonsai tree. "How did you do that?"

"It's nothing." Sim grabbed the sculpture but it slipped out of her hands and fell to the floor with a clatter. She snatched it, shoved it under the counter, and tried to compose herself.

The girl narrowed her eyes. "Okay," she said with a shrug, and then went to the shelves beyond the bikes to look at the tools and gadgets.

Sim wiped down the already clean counter and glanced up at the girl. She was relaxed, standing with one hip cocked out and her hands on her belt. There was something about her, either the way she was standing as if she didn't have a care in the world or the way her oversized shirt hung on her narrow shoulders. This girl was untouchable, special somehow. Sim wondered what her name was, and how she could ask her without seeming weird.

"You hang out at Stein's, right?" the girl asked, still looking at the shelves.

"Yeah, sometimes," Sim said, trying to sound casual. "It's a good place to read."

"It usually is," the girl said quietly, as if distracted. Still scanning the books, she added, "I didn't even know this place was here."

"We just opened, actually."

"What exactly is it?" Her eyes scanned the grandfather clocks, the old mail sorter that now held a growing collection of rolled-up maps, the three cruisers that still needed to be oiled and tuned. "A thrift shop without any clothes?"

"Um..." Sim hadn't really thought about it. And Azzer hadn't really talked to her about it. "We're a fix-it shop, but we sell old things, too. Gadgets, questing gear, that sort of stuff."

"That's really cool."

"Is there something you're looking for?" Sim immediately regretted that she'd turned to business so soon, instead of trying to draw out the conversation.

The girl looked over her shoulder. "I could use new bike lights," she said with a small smile. "It's really horrible biking around here at night without them." She walked back to the counter as Sim grabbed two lights off the back shelf: a bright white one for the front, to light up the Narrows' potholes, and a dimmer red one for the back, to be seen from behind by the carriages that drove in Greater Terresin at night.

"These are the best ones." Sim put the two copper-cased gadgets onto the counter. They had dials to control the intensity of brightness, and the light itself was a crystal set into the center of a concave, polished mirror.

"They don't need magic dust," Sim explained. "I'm not sure exactly how they work, to be honest, but that's what Azzer said. Something about those stones set into the casing."

The girl frowned. "Azzer?"

"Oh. He owns the shop. Makes the gadgets."

She nodded and brushed her bangs out of her eyes. "You're sure they don't need any magic dust at all?"

"That's what he said."

"That's really awesome." The girl ran her fingers over the lights. A bright circle shone against the back wall, even in the daylight, when she flicked it on. "Well, they work."

"They should, as long as there's enough magic in the air for the stones to absorb."

"Yeah, but that should never be a problem in the city, right? I mean, there's so much magic that just occurs here naturally. That's why Terresin was built here in the first place."

"Right." Sim nodded, though she had no idea what the girl was talking about. She sounded confident enough for Sim to agree with her. There was an awkward pause, and Sim scrambled for something to say.

"How much?" the girl asked.

"Forty sols for the pair."

The girl grinned. "I knew it was too good to be true." She slapped down some bills. "But if they don't need dust, then I guess it's worth it."

"Thanks," Sim said. "Just bring them back if you have any issues and we'll fix them for you."

"Yep. I'll see you around." The girl raised her hand. She grabbed her bike, swung open the door, and, as if it were an afterthought, turned back to Sim. "My name's Wood, by the way."

There was a pause again, and Sim blushed and blurted, "I'm Sim."

Wood smirked. "Well, I'll see you around, Sim."

"See you around."

The bell on the Incubator's front door rang as it shut behind Wood, and Sim was alone again, left to wish that she had been able to think of something intelligent to say. She wondered whether it would be weird for her to go to Stein's right after work. There was something about this girl that Sim couldn't quite describe or wrap her head around. All she knew for sure was that she wished Wood hadn't left so quickly.

"You look happy for such a glum day," Azzer said when he came out from his workshop. He knotted his bushy eyebrows and tilted his head down as he frowned out the window. "Hope it doesn't storm," he added in a grumble.

Sim snapped out of her daze. "I like gray skies."

Azzer went behind the counter and dropped a handful of bike locks onto the back shelf. They didn't run off of magic dust either, or have the stones that made the bike lights work. The locks were just plain old "U"s of metal, with plain old keys to lock them.

"You can stow the extras here," he said. "Just make sure one's displayed...." He paused and then stood, holding the tree in his hand. "Did you do this?"

"Yeah." Sim's heart skipped a beat and her cheeks reddened. "I'm really sorry. I know I was supposed to be working on—"

"You used magic to make this?" he interrupted, and looked up at her. Sim nodded.

"You have a talent for it." He frowned again and pursed out his lips in the way he did when he was considering an idea. "Keep practicing," he said, placing the tree on a shelf in the bookcase that Wood had just been looking at. "Maybe I'll have you work on some things once you get the hang of it."

For a moment thoughts of Wood shifted to the back of Sim's mind. "Get the hang of what?"

Azzer turned to her and locked his tiny blue eyes with hers. "Magicweaving. You have a knack for it. You did that without a wand—I can tell by the energy of it." He glanced back at the tree. "By the way it shifts when you look at it out of the corner of your eyes…It's a great talent to have, Sim. You don't have a wand, do you?"

"No," Sim lied. Only magicweavers, questers, and the wealthy had wands or other magical amplifiers.

"Interesting."

Sim got slightly uncomfortable, because she wasn't a magicweaver and it felt wrong to let Azzer assume that she was. But she wasn't sure how to correct him.

"Here, work on this," he said, putting an old watch on the counter in front of her. "You can keep it once you're finished, but you have to figure out how to fix it on your own. That's the best way to learn."

He turned and went back to his inventing space, and Sim was glad for it. She started to pull the watch apart, but soon got frustrated with its tiny parts and intricate workings. She paused to stare at the ceiling and let her mind dwell on the new person she'd met, and how she may have finally, finally made a friend. The watch was still broken by the time Azzer was ready to close up the shop, so Sim promised to figure it out at home, slightly embarrassed that she'd let herself get so easily distracted. Azzer waved away her apologies, and she quickly swept the front room and went outside to slide the dirt and tiny metal bits off the dustpan and onto the street. The grit caught in the wind and was swept away in a dirty gray plume, highlighted by the late afternoon's golden sunlight.

By the time Sim got back to Kailash, the sky had turned dusk blue and Kai was finishing up a spicy-smelling dinner. Sim sat in the living room, peering down into the gadget and trying to wind a cog with a tiny pair of tweezers. The work was enough to distract her from thinking about Wood, but her thoughts went instead to the night she had run away. The wand was still hidden in an inner pocket of her jacket, thrown on top of an old chest with the rest of the clothes she'd been wearing the night she had fled Nogron Mansion. Sim left the watch and brought the wand down to the living room. She'd planned on searching through the overstuffed bookshelves to find out something more about it, but ended up lying on the couch and just staring at the thing. She ran her fingers over the wooden handle, where someone had branded a crest with three mountains and a setting sun. Sim could make something of herself if she learned how to use it. But her thoughts kept drifting to the night of Nogron's summer ball, to that brief moment that had changed her life so drastically.

* * *

17

At the time, Sim hadn't considered why Nogron would ask a timid servant girl to steal the ceremonial wand of Sir Leonidas Lightshield, a governor and famous statesman. The party was already well underway and Nogron's ballroom was packed full of businessmen and politicians dressed in elegant black tuxedos and long, graceful gowns. Jaylenik had just tripped her, on purpose, and Sim had splattered frosted cookies all over the back of Leonidas's suit jacket. Instead of yelling at her, the tall, blond gentleman had taken Sim's hand and helped her up, making it easy for Sim to slip the wand out of his holster and into her own pocket. He had turned away and was taking off his jacket. Sim had her hand wrapped around the wand and was about to bring it up to Nogron's private office. But something stopped her. She turned back to Leonidas and held the wand out to him as if he'd dropped it.

His jaw fell. "How did you—you should be dead." He blinked and swallowed to regain his composure.

"What?"

Acting quickly, Leonidas placed a hand between Sim's shoulder blades and led her out to the back patio. He threw his frosting-stained jacket onto a stone bench and refused to take the wand when she offered it again.

"It's yours," he said in a whisper. "It belonged to your mother."

"My mother doesn't know how to cast spells."

"You're Silvia's daughter," he insisted. "If you weren't, you wouldn't be able to touch the damn thing."

"But—"

"I'm not going to stand here and explain the intricacies of a blood bondage spell," Leonidas snapped, annoyed. He frowned and stepped away from Sim. "But you're her only daughter, the only living being who could inherit her wand. The spell must be broken, now that you have it...." Frown lines appeared on either side of his mouth as he sneered. "Of course Nogron wants it. This is too much, even for him...."

"You aren't making any sense—"

"I can't be implicated in this. Nogron has too much sway. It has to look like you stole the wand and kept it for yourself. That's the only way."

"But I—"

"There's no time to explain," Leonidas said, taking her shoulders in his hands and hunching down to her height. His eyes were wide with fear, and Sim couldn't help but decide right then that she had no choice but to listen to him, even if she wasn't sure what was going on.

"You need to get out of here." His voice was barely more than a whisper.

"Leonidas?" A woman called from the house. "Are you out here?"

He glanced over his shoulder. "Yes, just a minute!"

He grabbed his coat and searched through the pockets until he pulled out a folded wad of sols.

"Take the money," he said, his voice now calm and full of the persuasive ease of a politician. "Nogron will be too distracted tonight to even notice that you're gone. You really only have two options: Run, and use the wand to unlock the secrets of your life, or go give the wand to Nogron and see how he repays you."

For a moment Sim held Leonidas's gaze. She'd learned years ago not to trust Nogron.

"Where would I go?"

"Terresin." Leonidas's eyes shone with relief. He pushed the money into her hands. "Go to the city. Take the train; that's the fastest way. There should be one more leaving for the city tonight. Be sure not to miss it. And be careful. Lay low. There's no knowing what lengths Nogron will go to find that thing."

Laying on the couch in Kailash's living room, Sim continued to study the wand. It looked so plain. Sim didn't understand why Nogron would want it so badly. She should have made Leonidas tell her more. She shouldn't have just listened to him and run away, when she didn't even know if she could believe a word of what he'd said. If he was telling the truth, then everything she'd ever known about herself was a lie. His story would at least explain why Sim's mother had always seemed to hate her so much. It would almost be a relief to know that that woman hadn't really given birth to her. Leonidas had implied she could use the wand to get answers, but he'd also warned her to lay low. Sim wasn't even sure that she wanted to find out more about this woman who was supposedly her real mother, who sounded to be very much dead, anyway.

"Where'd you get that old thing?" Cader said from behind her.

Sim sat up straight with a jolt and looked over at him. She instinctively hid the wand under her hands.

"That's not what you used when you kicked ass back on the train platform, is it?"

"It's nothing."

"Don't worry," he said with a laugh. "You don't have to show it to me if you don't want to. Those wands were pretty standard back in the day, when the Academy was still open and Pulchra was sending explorers out to start to map the Hinterlands. That's the crest of the Royal Academy of Explorers on the handle there. Those wands are a bit rarer now that the school doesn't exist anymore, though."

"What happened?"

"The government ran out of money to fund expeditions, so there was no reason to train new explorers. Questers ended up taking their place. We're mostly contracted out independently, but the government will hire us too sometimes, for less politically appealing jobs."

Sim frowned back down at the wand.

"You know, if you're interested in questing, I can try to get you a spot at the Battle House."

"Battle House?"

Cader laughed. "I always forget that you grew up in a small town. Battle houses train wannabe questers in sword handling, archery, defense—all of that good stuff. You'd have to start there if you ever want a chance at getting a quest."

"Yeah," Sim said with a shrug, even though she'd never lifted a sword in her life. "What do I have to do?"

"Well, it's hard to get in, but I should be able to get you a spot as soon as someone leaves. I'll let you know when it happens. Anyway, I came to tell you that dinner's ready. You should come and eat."

Sim nodded, and left the wand on the table next to the watch, which still wasn't even close to being repaired.

Cader slowed before they entered the kitchen and said, in a quiet voice, "The brewing machine should be ready in a day or two."

"I'll ask Azzer about the calibrating tomorrow."

"Awesome." Cader grinned and went straight for the kitchen, leaving Sim to turn her thoughts back to the wand. The Royal Academy of Explorers. She could start looking into that and see what she found out. Sim thought about it all through dinner, nodding and smiling at Kai's gossip about the people who went to pray at the Veldindor Devotional she attended every morning, but not really listening. Sim helped Cader wash the dishes when they were finished, and then brought the wand back upstairs to her room, to tuck it away in the bottom drawer of her dresser. It wasn't worth it. Poking around for answers would only make it easier for Nogron to track her down. Besides, she was here now, in Terresin, starting a new life. The last thing she wanted was to dwell any more on her old one.

Watches were the worst. Every time Sim thought that she was close to fixing the thing, it would fall apart in her hands, or she'd screw the back on only to discover that it wouldn't wind. Her fingers felt too big and clumsy, and the pieces too small to manage. Azzer had spent the morning showing her how watches worked, but little details kept slipping from her mind. Sim could tell that he was starting to get frustrated with her, and she was beginning to worry that he might ask her to leave. He'd reached the end of his patience after she'd lost one of the watch's hands, and had to call to him to see if he could find her another.

"Here," he'd said shortly, grabbing an old bike from a pile against the wall and slamming it down in front of the counter, either because if its weight or his agitation. "Clean this. I think you can handle that. They all need to be wiped down."

The cleaning was brutal work; someone had wrapped the entire bike in duct tape and dusty patches of old glue and thread clung to the frame after she pulled off the tape's top layer. It wasn't long before her fingers were starting to go numb from the scrubbing. But the work was enough to distract her from the nervousness that had set her on edge throughout her whole bike ride that morning. She couldn't figure out how to approach Azzer about the calibration, especially now that he was in such a bad mood. She was afraid—that he'd get mad, or maybe that he'd tell her she wasn't talented enough to do it.

"I'm sorry I had to spend all day on this," Sim said quickly when Azzer came up to the front again and she'd only gotten through two bikes. "That tape was really hard to get off. There were a few customers, so we sold some stuff, but it was pretty slow."

"Looks pretty good." Azzer ran his finger over the bike's smooth black top tube. "What sold?"

"A pair of goggles and some typewriter keys. Someone came in and looked at those fountain pens you made. I think he'll end up coming back for one."

Azzer nodded. "I need your help with one more thing before you leave." He put a chrome dagger sheath on the counter. Three blue stones were set into its center and delicate braising decorated each side where the metal halves met.

"It's a compressor sheath," Azzer explained. "They allow questers to carry around their longswords without the holster getting in the way when they bike. It would be impossible to make such a thing without magical energy. Those blue stones absorb energy straight from the air and channel it through the gadget to make it work, like I was telling you the other day. I just have to calibrate the settings first...." He peered at the stones and slipped his magnifying goggles over his eyes. "Hold it so I can have my hands free."

Sim took the sheath and focused intently on what she was doing, determined not to mess anything up again. Azzer lifted his head with a snap and stared at her. His large eyes blinked from behind the convex lenses. He glanced over at the bookshelves, where he'd put the tree that Sim had made.

"What did I do?"

"Nothing. Sorry. Actually, I'll hold the sheath and let's see if you can calibrate the stones."

Sim frowned at him. "Me?"

"It's not difficult." Azzer's voice was deep, but reassuring. "I'm positive that you can do it. You just need to know what a thing is for, and what you want it to do. Keep that in mind and direct your energy into the device. Feel for the stones. You don't actually have to cast a spell; you just need to give a little...push. Like a shock. The magic's in putting the thing together. But only those in tune with the energy within themselves can calibrate the stones so that they connect with the gadget. Do you see what I'm saying? Put a little of your energy into it. That's all."

"Okay." Sim was willing to try, and there was no disagreeing with him. Sim stared at the three milky blue sapphires and tried to picture a long blade disappearing into the small sheath. Because it felt like the right thing to do, she placed a fingertip onto each stone. A tingling feeling rose up in her chest. For the briefest moment the stones glowed bright blue and somehow the sheath became even more solidly real than the other three-dimensional objects around it. Sim blinked and the gadget looked normal again.

"Did I do it right?"

Azzer pulled his goggles up to his hairline. "We have to test it, don't we?"

He went to the umbrella stand he'd put in the corner, pushed aside a few wooden canes, and wrapped his hand around the hilt of an old longsword. Orange splotches of rust stained the rag he ran over its dull edge. He glanced at Sim. The sword's blade was three times the size of the sheath. There was no way it could fit. He pulled his arms wide apart, the sword handle in one hand and the sheath in the other, and brought them together. Sim held her breath a little at the moment when the sword should have stopped in the sheath, and then laughed a sigh when the blade kept going in until the hilt stopped at the sheath's opening.

Azzer grinned. "Guess you did it right."

He paid her and Sim went straight to Stien's. It felt good to leave the shop with a fold of sols in her pocket and the sense that she might actually be good at something. Like she was in control of her own destiny. Stein's took on a different ambience at dusk, when the candle stubs in the beer-bottle chandelier were lit and big mason jars full of tangled strings of lights hung above each table. The café used magic dust only for lighting, as far as Sim could tell. Blaring harmonica music streamed from the hand-crank record player, which the baristas and regulars would take turns winding up.

Sim looked up from the book she'd brought to read and fought the urge to attempt a silencing spell on the phonograph. She'd just have to wait until the horrible song was over until she could get back to *Saffron and Pulchrina*. Kai had practically thrown it at her when Sim said that she'd never read it. Apparently it was the most important book of Pulchran literature—an old story that chronicled the beginning days of the nation. Sim was surprised to find that she liked it. She'd expected the writing to be dense and archaic, which some of it was, but the love story between *Saffron and Pulchrina* kept her riveted.

A warm breeze danced into Stein's, scraping circles across the worn wooden floor. Sim glanced up to see who was entering, and watched as a grizzly-bearded dwarf stomped inside. His dirty sneakers scuffed quick steps up to the register and he lifted onto his toes so that his nose was just above the counter. The dwarf looked up at the barista. She was bent over, checking to make sure that she'd put enough grounds in the coffee press. The dwarf waited while she poured in the boiling water. At the espresso machine, a guy barista glanced at the dwarf and then yanked on a dragon's neck until it screamed steam. The girl working the register turned around. She jumped, and smiled to cover her surprise.

"Can I help you?"

"Can I have an application?" the dwarf asked, in a felty low voice, his words as rushed as his footsteps.

"What? Oh. Sorry. We're not hiring," she said almost as quickly, with a little laugh at the end.

The dwarf mumbled something under his breath and turned to leave, pulling the brim of his hat down over his forehead. The barista watched him walk out with a slight frown on her face. The guy at the espresso machine shrugged, raised his eyebrows, and looked back down at the dragon he was working with. Sim stared at the door, where the dwarf had made his quick escape.

"You saw that too, huh?"

Sim nearly jumped out of her seat. It was Wood. She was sitting behind her. The backs of their two couches were pushed together. Sim turned so she could see her better.

"The dwarf?" Sim asked, wondering how she hadn't noticed that Wood was sitting so close.

Wood nodded and shifted so that she didn't have to crane her neck. "That was so rude."

"She could have been nicer about it," Sim agreed.

"She could have been honest."

"They're hiring?"

"They've been looking for someone for a week now." Wood shook her head and stared at the door. "They just don't want dwarves working here." She sighed and looked back at Sim. "Anyway, what's that you're reading?"

Sim lifted her book and Wood's eyebrows shot up. "*Saffron and Pulchrina*? That's a great read," she said. "It's so important to understand how this country was founded, even if it is just a myth." She smiled and added, "And it's one of the best love stories ever."

"It's good so far," Sim agreed, fighting an inexplicable, annoying blush. "What've you got?"

"Nonfiction. A book about battle houses in the city and quester culture. It's fascinating. The best houses have orb rooms that transport questers into an illusionscape that mirrors all different parts of the Hinterlands. It's a meditative transportation: They can battle to the death, but no one gets killed. Imagine that."

"Sounds like fun," Sim said.

Wood shrugged. "You need to be invited into a house, though. It's pretty inbred. But you get to travel all over the world."

Sim was about to mention that Cader went to a battle house, but thought better of it. She didn't want to imply that she could get Wood an invitation. It was a conversation to be saved for later.

"I'd love to go to a few of the Ancient Kingdoms," Sim said, changing the subject. "I think I will, as soon as I save up enough money."

Wood's face lit up. "Me, too. I can't wait. It's always been my dream to go to places where magic isn't so readily available. Life is so different out there, where there aren't any gadgets or charms or running water even. Things like those bike lights I got from you—which are great, by the way—would never work there. Not enough magic in the air. That's why I love Terresin, and I'd totally come back here after, but it's important to see other parts of the world. Have to finish school first. Get a degree. Then I can do whatever I want." She raised her eyebrows. "Maybe I'll join a battle house."

"No loans to pay off?"

"My parents are paying. I'm lucky. I'm thinking of doing something with questing. It's just so interesting."

"I'll have to borrow that book when you're finished."

"Sure." Wood seemed happy that Sim had asked. She narrowed her eyes and said, "Sim, right?"

Sim nodded, and Wood continued, "Well, let me know what you think of Saffron and Pulchrina when you're finished. The ending's the best part."

"They live happily ever after?"

"You'll see. Don't want to ruin it for you."

Sensing that Wood wanted to go back to reading, Sim left it at that. She did her best to focus on nothing but the creamy pages and midnight words in her lap. When she finished her coffee two chapters later, Sim stood with a stretch. She decided to get a refill.

"One sol," the barista said after she filled Sim's chipped mug. She'd been laughing with one of her friends who had come in, talking about a rock band they'd seen play the night before. Sim paid and brought her coffee over to the thermos of whiteflower milk, a creamy white nectar that came from tiny blossoms grown and processed right there in the Narrows by a group called the Whiteflower Collective.

As she walked back to the couch, Sim studied a painting that hung on the wall behind Wood, who was facing the milk bar. In the painting two young lovers whispered to each other through a wall, both of them androgynous to the point where it wasn't clear who was the boy and who the girl. Wood sat cross-legged, staring down at the book in her lap. Out of the corner of her eye, Sim saw Wood glance up at her and then back down. Sim pretended not to notice. A smile crept across her face when she sat down. She couldn't help it. No one in the Narrows ever paid any attention to her. If a girl like Wood wanted to talk to her, that meant she finally had to be doing something right.

"Does that shop of yours fix shoes?" Wood asked after Sim had sat down.

"Azzer can fix anything." Sim shrugged. "That's what he says at least."

"I'll have to come by again, then. I completely wore out the soles of these awesome boots I have from walking all around campus last semester."

"Where do you go to school?" Sim asked, and she soon found that as long as she asked Wood questions about her life or views Wood was happy to answer, and the conversation could keep going for as long as she liked. Sim was fascinated by the college sophomore who had a passion for books and came from a family in the exurbs. She was a-religious and antiwar. She thought that dwarves deserved more rights, and that there was something about the Narrows' factories that was silently malicious. Sim wasn't sure what to make of her. All she knew was that she loved hearing her talk. She could sit there for hours and listen to her ramble on about anything.

III

The tomblike air in Kailash's basement was more musty and dank than Sim remembered. The last time she'd been down there was when she'd been exploring the house and happened upon the cruiser that had quickly become the key to her freedom in the city. As soon as Cader had seen her dusting it off among the herb spirals, he told her about the Narrows and said he'd try to find her a job there. Now the shallow sound of her breathing got lost in the basement's shadowed depths. She was reminded of her adolescence, of the days before Jaylenik Nogron had become a spoiled priss, when they would sneak around Nogron Mansion together, looking for mischief. Back then Sim had worried about getting caught by one of the older servants, or, worse, by Lady Nogron herself. This present fear-fueled excitement was different, though; stronger. They were breaking the law, and if they were caught, the punishment would not be a slap on the wrist and an order to scrub the kitchen floors by hand.

The brewing machine's swirling tubes, steaming pipes, and esoteric dials made it seem like they were alchemists, and not brewers or outlaws. As he was building the machine, Cader would occasionally ask Sim to see if she could find a certain part or tool at the Incubator, and Azzer happily lent her whatever she asked for. Unsurprisingly, Cader had been amazed by the idea of magical stones that could erase the need for magic dust, and it hadn't taken him long to track a few of them down and modify the book's instructions to set them into the brewing boxes. Sim's job had been simple: All she'd had to do was put the brew mix into the machine and calibrate the boxes, just like she did with the gadgets at the Incubator. Leftover cups of barley, yeast, and hops crowded the workbench, the remnants of Cader and Sim's experiments in perfecting their recipe. They'd added a slew of Kai's herbs—bodhi, orris, sage, and sorrel wood—as their secret ingredients. The whole decanter was a good five strides long, with a spigot at one end that streamed a sea-colored liquid into the white beer bottles Cader had gotten for them. Five days before, Sim had put the bottles into the boxes she'd calibrated, and now the Kaianide was ready. Kaianide—the name of their beer, because Cader thought it was funny and Sim didn't really care.

Cader's bony knees jutted out from the frayed ends of his cutoffs as he squatted in front of the workbench and rolled up the crumpled green tarp he'd used to cover the box. Sim fought an urge to shush him. But even Kai, who was in the garden just beyond the basement's high rectangular window, wouldn't be able to hear them. Cader was sure of it. He'd also hung clear-violet crystals from the box's edges, to muffle any magic that was working inside of their wooden panels. If the Guard did come by, the brewing charm would be undetectable.

Brass latches from the Incubator clicked open under pressure from Cader's thumbs. He caught the box's loose panel in his palms and eased it to the floor. Sim tiptoed over to him and dropped to her knees on the dirt floor. She shifted back to sit on her heels and cocked her head to the side as she gazed into the box. Three rows of white bottles sat in the bluish shadows. The little light that came in from the garden window caught on the bottles' curved edges and gleamed back at Cader and Sim.

"Well, it didn't blow up," Cader said.

"Looks okay," Sim agreed.

"I wish I could do a cooling spell." Cader reached out a hand and wrapped his long fingers around two of the bottles' necks. He placed them lightly on the workbench and stretched up to his feet. "We'll have to hide them in the fridge and try it later. Warm beer is never good."

Sim stood and took one of the brews into her hand, turned it around and shifted it from one palm to the other. Cader had his fingers interwoven in his hair, probably thinking about how they could hide the beers so that Kai wouldn't notice them.

"I can do a cooling spell," Sim said. Jaylenik Nogron had liked her water ice cold, always, no matter what, so it was a spell that she'd been required to know. One of the older maids had taught it to her, after sneering and saying that ignorance was never a valid excuse for being lazy.

"Can you do it without a wand?" Cader sounded slightly surprised, and Sim was mildly offended. He and Kai must have thought she was worthless; Cader had his healing practice and the Battle House and Kai had her strange earth magic, or whatever it was that she did with the herbs and potions.

"I think I can. Don't be surprised if it doesn't work, though."

"Can't hurt to try." Cader handed her the bottle.

Sim pushed away thoughts of how embarrassing it would be if she forgot how to cast the spell, and concentrated fully on the beer in her hands. Her mind became saturated with thoughts of ice and shivers. She remembered the night when her mother had kicked her out of the house. She'd been walking home from work alone, as she always did, and hadn't thought twice about walking along with the strange man who'd come up to her, asking for directions. He'd stayed with her until the path was just about to leave the woods, and then grabbed her arm and pushed the point of a dagger to her stomach. He promised to kill her, right then and there, if she didn't give him all of her money. Her mother had been furious; she'd thought that Sim was lying, that she'd spent the money on something for herself instead of handing it over for rent. And she'd kicked her out for good.... Sim cut away the memory of her mother's peaked eyebrows and angry sneer, and focused solely on the numbing cold that had seeped into her bones that night when she'd slept in the old abandoned house near the treeline, the night before Nogron had enlisted her to steal Leonidas' wand. And then she pictured the beer in her hands feeling the same way, believed with her entire heart that it actually was. Sim opened her eyes. The bottle felt exactly the same as it had before. She sighed through her nose. She should have known better than to even try.

"I can't do it," Sim said with a shake of her head. She pushed the beer into Cader's hands and went toward the steps. He caught her bicep to stop her.

"Sim." He grabbed her hand. His was clammy and hot. He let her go. "It worked," he said.

Sim frowned and looked down at her palms. When she touched her fingers to her cheeks, a shiver ran through her shoulder muscles. Her hands were ice cold, along with the beer. Cader put the Kaianide on the workbench and pulled an old bottle opener out of his back pocket.

"Now," he said with a smile. "Let's see how we did."

He snapped off the cap and let it fall to the floor. A swirling white mist spilled just over the brim, and gyrated inside of the bottle's neck like a tiny ghost tornado.

"Cool," Sim said. "Is that a good sign?"

"I think so."

The mist was gone after a few more moments.

"I'll go first," he said.

"Wait."

Cader looked up at her, the bottle halfway to his lips.

"What if we did something wrong?"

"That's why I'm going first." Cader smiled again.

"But—"

But the beer was already pouring into his mouth. He held it there with his cheeks slightly puffed, swished the liquid around, and swallowed. He followed this with another sip.

Cader laughed and opened his arms. "See? I'm fine," he said with a shrug. He held the bottle out to Sim, and raised his eyebrows in a question. After a pause, she took it. The Lady Nogron had her own cache of liquors, which Sim had mixed under her careful supervision, but she'd never seen a beer before, let alone tried one. The brew was bitter and light. It had little bubbles that tickled her throat when she swallowed and traces of spice from the herbs that they'd stolen from Kai for the recipe.

"Good, right?" Cader's eyes gleamed the way they did when he won an argument with Kai. Sim took another sip and smiled. The beer was good. Really good.

"What the hell are you doing?" An angry voice rang out above them.

Sim gasped, sucking beer into her lungs, and doubled over in a fit of coughing. The steps pounded under Kai's feet.

"How long have you been creeping on us up there?" Cader asked.

Kai ignored him and grabbed the bottle out of Sim's hand.

Sim rasped one last long cough and wiped away the tears burning in her eyes.

"You okay?" Cader asked her. Sim nodded, afraid that the coughing would start again if she spoke. She kept her breaths shallow and short. Kai didn't seem to notice. Her eyes were wide and angry behind her thick-framed glasses.

"What the hell is this?" she demanded.

"It's beer, Kai," Cader said slowly.

"This is what you two have been up to down here?" Kai threw the bottle into the darkness beyond the workbench. It clanged off of something metallic and then shattered on the floor. Kai's eyes went to the brewing box.

"Get rid of it." Her hands were on her hips, her face tilted up toward Cader's. He leaned against the workbench casually, standing in front of the beer but attempting not to look like he was trying to protect it.

"We're going to sell it and make some extra cash," Sim said.

Kai's head snapped toward her and Cader gave her a look that said it would have been better to keep her mouth shut.

"Are you serious?" Kai demanded. "You do realize that it's illegal to brew alcohol? Illegal to sell it? Illegal to consume it?" She looked to Cader and continued, "If we need more money, I can just have my father send it. You know that. This is absolutely unnecessary."

"We're going to be careful," Cader assured her.

"You'll be careful when you're throwing it all into the river," Kai said. "Do you have any idea what will happen when you're caught?"

"We won't get caught," Sim said quickly.

"You will. And I'm going to be dragged down right along with you because of this inane, childish, thick-headed endeavor." The only sound was Kai's quick and angry breathing. "If you don't get rid of it, I will."

"It's two to one," Cader said. "And you know Prudence would side with us if she was here. We're keeping it. We'll be careful, and we won't get caught. We need the money, Kai. You know we do. We can't keep asking your father."

For a moment Kai's expression was frozen, as if Cader hadn't said anything at all. Her breathing slowed. She blinked and took a step back. "I don't want to have anything to do with this," she said, putting her hands up in front of her like a shield. "I don't want to hear about it, I don't want to see it." She gave Cader one last glare, shifted it over to Sim, and then pounded back up the steps. Little clouds of dirt plumed off the wooden framework with each aggressive stomp.

"Well, I'm glad we got that out of the way." Cader sighed deeply and shook his head and arms, as if he could fling away all of the negative energy. When he stopped, he took the second bottle in his hand and held it out to Sim with a smile.

"We know it tastes good," he said. "Now let's see if this stuff works."

Rock music murmured out of a discrete venue called the Dragon Spine every time the bouncer pushed open the front door. Sim leaned against a lamppost across the street and looked up at the imprisoned fairies buzzing around inside of a dirty, luminescent fishbowl. It was cheaper to capture fairies than to use magic dust for light, though all of that would change soon, according to the news. But the news only reported what the governors said, and the governors tended to lie. One of the little creatures was lying at the bottom of the bowl with her arms crossed under her chin, gazing back down at Sim with eyes the color of the full moon.

So that Kai wouldn't be mad, Sim had agreed to go to Veldindor Devotional with her that morning. It had been horrible. The church was dim and quiet and Sim couldn't understand the strange chant language of the priests, even though she'd been forced to go to devotional throughout her childhood. She had sat and stood and kneeled along with Kai, and pretended to be praying when really she was daydreaming about the day before, when Wood had come into the Incubator again.

"What did you think?" Kai had asked, as they walked home with bags full of vegetables from the market next to the church.

"It was a lot bigger than the devotionals I used to go to."

"You really should go every day, you know. Every morning. Unless you're sick. It's better if you get into a routine."

"I think it's better for me to pray on my own," Sim had lied, and hoped that Kai wouldn't ask her to go again. There was something about the Veldindor devotees and their preoccupation with holiness that made Sim slightly uncomfortable. She fit in better into Cader's world, where people seemed to live by their own rules, even if they weren't always good ones.

Now, standing in the creamy light, Sim did her best to look causal, like she belonged in this remote part of Lower Terresin, a half-hour walk from Kailash, in the opposite direction of the Bikeway Narrows. A silencing spell covered the whole street, so that Sim hadn't heard the sounds of breaking beer bottles and drunken laughter until she and Cader were right on top of them. He'd left her at the streetlight, said that he had some potions to sell, and disappeared down a nearby alleyway. While she waited, Sim watched the drinkers go from dive to dive. Cader had explained that the Terresinian Guard could easily be bought and convinced to overlook the prohibition law, but only if people were quiet about their business. In Lower Terresin, this meant that bars congregated on lowly trafficked, narrow streets. The borders of the silencing spell served to wall in a slice of the city where people were free to do as they pleased—like the Bikeway Narrows, but somehow seedier. Sim was sure that the red lights hanging in half of the windows on the street weren't just for decoration, and that the stumbling, sallow women wearing heavy eyeliner and scant clothing were not there looking for a good time.

The Dragon Spine didn't seem to be so bad. Three lanky girls laughed together as they ignored the line that had gathered outside the bar. With their giggles, bony limbs, and shiny hair, they strutted up to the bouncer. Their smooth backs were bare even though the night was cold, and they all wore gold pumps that were charmed to glimmer every time they took a step. The backless shirts were in fashion now in Greater Terresin, but Sim thought that they looked ridiculous, like satin bandannas with neckties.

At Cader's insistence, Sim had had to get new clothes for the meeting. They both had to look the part. Actually brewing the beer was only half of the game. She wore her tight black jeans and a V-neck T-shirt, and the new leather boots and vintage leather jacket she'd bought. Kai would have to wait for the rent. Cader lent her a thick leather wristband with some symbol on the front of it and Sim bothered Kai for the dark eye charcoal that she herself never found an occasion to wear. If Kai had known that they were going out not for fun, but to meet a potential distributor for their beer, Sim was sure she never would have handed it over.

Sim eyed the bouncer, who was as tall as the door and had long dreadlocks that hung over his bare chest. A thick leather belt hung loosely around his hips and a tattoo of a nautical compass marked the space between his shoulder blades. He was a quester, without a doubt. Sim was getting good at picking them out. When the next song came on, he nodded and bounced to the beat. Sim hoped that he was as good-natured as he seemed.

Finally Cader reappeared from the alley. His face was set in an annoyed frown. "Come on, hurry," he said.

"Everything okay?"

"Don't worry about it." Then he added, in a mumble, "That took way longer than it should have."

Sim headed toward the back of the line. Cader glanced back at her. "Where are you going?" He gave her a look. "Please, Sim."

He pushed her ahead of him. His black sneakers snapped at her heels. Sim had never seen him this on edge—not nervous, but mean. She wasn't sure if the situation was making him anxious, or if he was playing a part that she ought to mimic. This whole world was so new to her—the bouncers, the alcohol, the music. Sim felt like she was free-falling, riding a wave and praying to the fates that it wouldn't pull her under. The sturdiness of her boots gave Sim that extra bit of self-assurance she needed to throw up her chin and wear a confident scowl. But it was all a mask, nothing more than a defiant mask.

The bouncer glanced at Cader and then smiled down at Sim, who tried to keep her face expressionless.

"Trying to cut the line?" the bouncer said, slow and good-natured. "The bar's too full to let anyone else—"

"We're meeting someone downstairs," Cader said, his voice a bit more quiet than usual.

The bouncer laughed and pushed the door open. "Well, why didn't you just say so in the first place? Go on in, then."

The front room shifted under a dim, rouged light cast from bowls of red fire hanging from the ceiling and torches that bordered either side of the bar. The air was steamy, even though the dancing was in a dark room in the back and fewer people were in the front, where couples sat together on bar stools and whispered secrets in shadowed corners. Two guys were kissing on a long bench that ran along the blackened front window. They were both young and built, their bodies like sculptures, their hair perfectly molded into matching, pointy fauxhawks. Next to them was a guy wearing sunglasses and a strange golden gadget earring. Sim had no idea what the gadget did, though it looked like something that might come into the Incubator for a repair. The earring, along with the pocket watch that hung around his neck and his brown leather vest, marked him as a frequenter of the Bikeway Narrows. Sim had never seen him before, but she felt an instant connection to him. The guy was chatting with a short-haired, dark-skinned girl whose lips glowed purple in the dim light. Her leg was strewn over his, and his arm cupped her shoulders. They were both oblivious to the couple next to them. On their other side, one of the girls with the glittering shoes leaned over to look at the kissing guys. Her face scrunched in disgust. She grabbed her friend's hand, and pulled her back toward the dance floor.

"I can't believe they would just do that in public," Sim heard the girl say as she pushed past her and Cader. "So disgusting."

Cader frowned at them and then slid into an empty spot in front of the black marble slab that served as the bar. The bartender was a few years older than Cader and had short hair and a trim black beard. Muscles rippled under his loose long-sleeved shirt, cut low to show off his hairless chest, as he poured drinks with a few quick movements. Cader caught the bartender's attention and ordered two shots. They seemed to know each other. Sim wondered if it was from the Battle House, or because Cader was a regular here, but she didn't dare ask. From then on she decided to keep her mouth shut.

With deft movements that showed he'd done the same thing hundreds of times before, the bartender clanked four shot glasses onto the marble in front of them. He turned over a black bottle with "Fire Whiskey" marked on the label, above a maroon dragon that was spewing flames from its throat. When the shots were full he pulled two beers from underneath the counter, snapped off the caps, and pushed the bottles toward them. "Here ya go, Cader. On the house."

Four shots and two beers. Sim had still never really drunk anything other than the three Kaianides she'd had with Cader, but she convinced herself that she'd be fine. The bartender glanced at Sim, nodded, glanced back at Cader, and then jumped right into the next order, never stopping for a moment.

Cader grabbed a shot and gave one to Sim. Her fingertips tingled from the whiskey that had spilled over its edges. Cader raised his shot and Sim did the same. Grinning, he held his free hand over the two glasses and snapped his fingers, creating a blue flame that ignited the alcohol. The fire rippled down the sides of the glass and onto Sim's fingers, so it looked like she was holding a small fireball. The fire licking at her skin felt soft and subtle, like grazing her hand over fleece.

"Prudence taught me that one," Cader said, still smiling. "That's the limit of my magicweaving abilities. Except for healing, but that's different."

Sim clanked her flaming glass against his and watched as he threw back the shot. She did the same. Her tongue and gums burned even though the whiskey barely spent any time in her mouth. Her eyes watered and her throat was on fire. Cader scrunched up his face and slapped his empty shot glass onto the bar.

"Shit," he said, shaking his head and rubbing his stubble. He picked up another shot and Sim did the same, even though she could still barely breathe from the last one.

"That's it, Sim!" He slapped her on the back and chuckled.

Already Sim could feel the alcohol swimming in her stomach like a burning tide pool. It wasn't a bad feeling. Fire ran through her veins, warming her body. It tickled her fingertips and crackled lightly at the edges of her mind. She'd have to be careful not to drink too much more. The song changed to one that was high-pitched and quick-beated. Sim bounced on her toes and looked back at the jumping bodies in the back room. "Let's go back," she said, surprising herself. Dancing had always intimidated her.

"Later," Cader said. "We have to meet this distributor first."

Beer in hand, Cader pushed past a tall guy with a black mohawk and headed toward a glowing red doorway. In the stairwell, the upbeat song mixed with loud heavy-metal music from the basement. Bright strobe flashes lit the bottom of the steps. One second Sim could see Cader perfectly and the next everything was black. She blinked and a garish light washed over the stairs again. Steam filled the bottom half of the basement and evaporated upward in smoky spirals shaped like dragons, devils, and monsters. To the right was another bar, long and black. Cader turned from it and headed toward a platform where a DJ violently bounced his head to the rock beat, directing the dancers on the floor in front of him. They spun through the smoke demons, scattering the shapes with their thrashing arms and swinging heads. Sharp spikes made of bone jutted out of their shoulders and elbows. With a sickening drop of her stomach, Sim realized that the dark, gleaming spots on the bone and the sticky wetness beneath her boots had to be fresh blood.

At the edge of the dance floor was a tiny walkway, just enough space for Cader and Sim to walk through and not to get pulled into the mass of mutilation, where the dancers pounded air and flesh and the stone walls as if they were all the same. No one seemed to mind; they were in a common trance, running in circles, bodies slamming together, exulting in their pain. Sim gasped when she caught a glimpse of a face that had been spelled—purposefully mutilated—to look like a dragon's. Drawing her eyebrows together, she set her face in a scowl. Otherwise she was sure her fear would have been blatant. Even though part of her was afraid of getting pulled onto the dance floor, another part wanted to jump in and enter the trance, to become one with the shifting mass where everyone moved to the same violent beat, simply because she did fear it.

Cader entered a narrow hallway, dark so that Sim could only see his silhouette. She trailed her hand along the hallway's damp stone walls until, with a jolting abruptness, the blaring music was muffled to background noise. For a heartbeat Sim was sure she'd gone deaf. Then she and Cader emerged into another dimly lit room and she realized that there must have been a muffling spell cast just before its entrance. Instead of fire bowls or strobe lights, candles lined the stone walls and wooden bar. Wax spilled down the bronze candleholders and pooled onto the bar and tabletops, and onto the stone floor beneath the candelabras. Sim shook her head to clear the ringing in her ears. The room looked like a tomb with curtained booths built into its walls. An obese, bald albino man sat at a table in full view of the hallway. His pink eyes looked over Cader for a moment, went to a double-edged axe leaning against the wall next to him, and then lingered on Sim.

"This one," Cader said, heading toward one of the booths. He pulled back the curtain and slid onto a long velvet seat. After a deep gasp of air, Sim followed and closed the curtains behind her. Her breath caught in her throat. She'd expected a man. The distributor's striking blue-green eyes were lined in black, her hair cut short and shaved on one side. She was probably in her late thirties. Piercings ran up her ears and one formed a U under the center of her nose. Tattoos colored her arms. She was wearing a black button-up vest with nothing underneath. A silver watch or compass—Sim couldn't tell—peeked out from one of her pockets. She sat up straight with her arms resting on the table and her hands folded in front of her.

"It's about fucking time," she said.

"Are you Acheron?" Cader asked.

She nodded. "You're Cader?"

"Yes. This is Sim. Sorry we kept you waiting."

Sim glanced up and met Acheron's gaze. She knew it would make her seem weak, but Sim had to look away. A tattoo of a snake eating its own tail rung around Acheron's arm just below her elbow. A blue god with six arms danced below it, followed by three solid lines, each with a break through its middle.

"It's fine," Acheron said. She looked back to Cader. "How do you know Prudence?"

"We've quested together."

Acheron cocked her head. "You don't wear the marks of a quester."

"The marks of a quester?" Sim asked, not quite following.

"It's nothing," Cader said quickly. He looked at Acheron. "I choose to keep my body pure."

Acheron seemed to be impressed. "Respectable," she said with a little laugh. "You follow the way?"

"I do."

Acheron leaned back in her booth and eyed Sim again. "Who's the girl?"

"An accomplice; our calibrator. She can be trusted."

Acheron's gaze took in Sim, who did her best not to move. Pursing her lips, Acheron looked back to Cader and said, "All right. Let's see it."

Cader took three Kaianides out of his bag and lined them up on the table. For a moment Sim worried that the albino man might get angry if he found out that they'd brought their own beer. But the curtains were thick, and closed. Cader looked at Sim expectantly. This was why he'd brought her along: She was there to cast her cooling spell and impress Acheron.

"It's okay to cast spells here?" she asked, her mind going to the albino man once again. Her stomach was still swimming from the fire whiskey and her head was dizzy.

"That's what these booths are for, aren't they?" Acheron said.

"It's okay," Cader said.

They were both getting impatient. She was wasting their time.

Another deep breath helped to clear her mind. Sim cupped her palms around the bottles and focused on them. Turning her hands icy cold, she cast the spell that she'd done half a dozen times in the past two days. This time was different: Either because she was getting used to spell casting or because of the fire whiskey, Sim didn't feel drained at all after she chilled the beers. She felt the energy leaving her body, but it instantly replenished itself.

Cader took one of the bottles and his mood brightened in a flash. His confidence returned. He took off the caps and smiled at Acheron. "I think you're going to like this."

"I'll let the brew speak for itself." The bottle rested on the edge of her lips. Her charcoal lids slipped down over her eyes and her head tilted back. She poured the Kaianide into her mouth, let it fall over her tongue. She swallowed, opened her eyes, squinted them at Sim, and then took another sip.

"You're right," she said, putting down the bottle. "It's good. And original."

"We have more," Cader said with a grin.

Sim iced four bottles, and Acheron slid them under the candleholder that was nailed to the stone wall. They all drank, faster than usual, but not rushing, either.

"How long does that cooling spell last?" Acheron asked Sim.

"A few hours," Sim said, even though she had no idea. It wasn't like her to lie, but she felt as though she had to. And, apparently, she was good at it.

"It's rare to come across people who can cast their own spells these days," Acheron said. "It's too bad. We're all turning into mindless cows."

"It was different before?" Sim was getting more comfortable with each additional sip of her beer. She wanted to get the woman to talk, to hear what she had to say. Acheron's life was as mysterious and intriguing to Sim as the marks on her arms.

"Of course it was." Acheron took a long sip of her Kaianide. "Just twenty years ago—not even—everyone in Terresin was able to cast their own spells. Nothing came pre-charmed, or had to be plugged into the magic-dust grid. Magic dust was only used out in the country, where there wasn't enough natural magic to cast spells without a good wand and a strong talent. But now magic dust's being pumped into the country and charms are being used in the city."

"Everything's turned on its head," Cader said. "The city's changed a lot. Used to be a more magical place."

"Yes, there's less magic in the air now," Acheron said, staring at the candle against the wall. "More difficult to cast spells because they pulled so much magic out of the air to turn it into dust for their charms. And to pump it out to the rich men in the hills."

Sim gave her a questioning look. "Why would they do that?"

"Why not? Whoever controls magic controls everything," she explained. "If, instead of casting spells, people have to earn magic dust to activate charms or power gadgets, then they're forced to work more and more. Forced to work in dead-end jobs for shit that they don't even need."

"It's all about power," Cader added. He was tugging nervously on one of his ears.

Acheron glanced at him. "We're getting to the point where no one can do anything for themselves. That cooling spell you just did would have been child's play twenty years ago. But now everyone's forgotten how to do it."

"The prohibition's a part of it," Cader said. "Keeps people scared, reminds them that the Guard is in control. And you can't pre-charm beer. It has to be brewed by someone who can calibrate."

Acheron sighed. "But we do what we can, right?"

Cader held up his beer bottle to hers and clanked them together. Acheron emptied hers and slid it to the end of the table. It was only her second.

"All right," she said. "I'm in. You know the deal?"

"I do," Cader said. "You can take the rest of these with you if you want."

"I don't carry product around. But thanks." She looked at Sim, held her eyes. "I'll see you."

"Definitely."

Cader held out his hand, she shook it, and did the same to Sim. Acheron met Sim's eyes once more and then was gone, leaving them alone in the booth. Sim slipped to the other side of it, to sit across from Cader.

"That went really well," he said with a smug smile. "I think she liked you."

"Liked me?"

Cader raised an eyebrow.

Sim blushed and said, "Oh. Well. I—"

"We should get going," Cader interrupted. He put the rest of the Kaianides back into his bag. "I don't like hanging around here for too long, especially not downstairs. Weird vibes."

Sim nodded. "Agreed. Let's go."

Upstairs, the bartender was standing in the entrance as they were leaving. He stepped outside and moved sideways so that Cader and Sim could pass. "I'm sorry," he said to someone standing on the sidewalk. "You know you can't do that here. I gave you a warning."

"Give us a break, Atif." It was one of the pair of guys with the fauxhawks who had been kissing at the bar before. His face and chest were red. "As if you've never been with a man before."

"I don't know what you're talking about," Atif said with a shake of his head. The bouncer's hefty arms were crossed over his chest. He looked from the two guys to Atif with a raised eyebrow. Atif glanced over at him. "Yelling lies isn't going to get you back in here."

"Fuck this place," the guy yelled. He grabbed the other's hand and strode down the sidewalk.

"They aren't my rules," Atif, yelled after them. "You know they aren't. I have to follow—"

The guy held up his middle finger, raised on an arm that was extended upward as high as it would go, and Atif gave up.

"Let's go, Sim," Cader said, and she realized with a jolt of embarrassment that she'd been staring at the whole thing. She turned away quickly, but not before Atif turned back to them and caught her gaze.

"I'll see you around, man," Cader said to Atif with a raise of his hand.

"Yeah, see you," Atif said, frowning. With his head tilted toward the ground, he punched the door open and stomped back into the club. A streetlight buzzed with the sound of fairy wings on glass. Sim paused and stared up at it with drunken anger. She felt herself drawing energy from the air into her center until her heart felt crackly and powerful. She flung her hand toward the streetlight. To her surprise, the glass cracked. The bottom half of it fell to the ground with a shatter. Fairies flew around Sim's head, too quickly for her to get a good look at them, and zipped like shooting stars above the buildings and out of sight.

"Damn, Sim," Cader said, spinning around to face her. "What the hell are you doing? I told you we have to be discrete. You know what that means?" Glancing around to see if anyone had noticed, he put a hand on her back and rushed her down the street.

"It's wrong," Sim said.

"I know it is, but that doesn't mean you can go around breaking every streetlight in Terresin. Pick your battles."

Cader didn't stay angry at her for long. Sim could tell that he agreed with her. He was just afraid of getting caught. And with the Kaianides still in his bag, she couldn't blame him. She herself hardly cared; her sense of danger had been dulled by the beer and whiskey running through her veins. She felt powerful, free. She would have broken every streetlight in Terresin, if she weren't sure that Cader would never invite her out again if she did.

Ten minutes took them out of Lower Terresin and into the strangely deserted streets of the downtown area. The sky crackled and blinked. A roar ripped through the canyons between the impossibly high towers. Huge, glowing billboards powered by a constant supply of magic dust lit the street with a soft glow. Fairies would never be used to light this part of the city, where the people who actually mattered would see them and have to deal with the brutality of enslavement. Sim stopped thinking about it, distracted by a tugging feeling at the edges of her mind. She turned to study a person-sized ad for a three-patty cheeseburger and remembered that the signs here were charmed to grab the attention of whoever passed. This was one of the many reasons she avoided this part of the city; she did her best to ignore the photos of carriages and pheromone perfumes and gold-plated wands. But there was no way to walk downtown without being aware of them.

Next to an ad for an engagement ring with a marble-sized diamond, someone had spray painted a stencil of two male Guard members embracing each other with a kiss. Sim smiled; at least someone had something meaningful to say. But the happy feeling didn't last long. Even with Cader walking beside her with his tall and certain strides, a sense of dread perched on Sim's shoulders. There should have been more people out on the sidewalk, even this late at night.

"Where is everyone?" Sim said, but Cader seemed not to have heard her. Electricity crackled through the air. The sky flickered occasionally, like the inverse of a light that was about to go out. The clouds behind the purple towers shifted from gray to dirty orange.

"That's so weird," Sim said, hugging herself. Her voice was amplified in the humid air and their footsteps sounded louder than they ever had.

"It happens sometimes," Cader said. "More than usual lately."

"The sky where I come from never looked like that."

"I think it's a city thing. The lightning's the worst part. Hits someone every time. Five people died during the last storm. That's why no one's out. We should hurry."

"When was the last storm?" Sim asked. They passed the blank front windows of a kitchen-gadget shop. Copper instruments—charmed mixers, heaters, blenders, and choppers—filled the dark store behind the reflection of Sim and Cader walking by.

They sky growled again.

"Two weeks ago," Cader said. He looked up at the towers, and Sim sensed a soft feeling of anxiety emanating from him. "Come on, walk faster," he said. Sim searched Cader's face for a trace of worry, but he looked calm. It must have been her own fear that she'd sensed. She quickened her pace to keep up with him, so that they could get to Kailash before the lightning struck again.

IV

im had found Drangs among the dumpsters wedged between a grocery and a fancy Munian restaurant a few streets away from Kailash. She'd been walking back from buying a toothbrush and soap with part of what was left of the money Governor Lightshield had given her, when she'd heard a soft, persistent mewing coming from the alley. Sim had taken a few steps in and squatted down to see what was making the sound. With a happy gurgle, a tiny unicat had darted out from under the dumpster and jumped into Sim's lap. She had stroked his turquoise fur and he'd nuzzled his head against her jaw, tickling her neck with his little white horn. Even then Sim had known that Kai would never allow an animal in the house, and since she'd only been staying there for three days, Sim wouldn't dare ask if she could keep a pet. But he'd followed her home and stayed around the periphery of Kailash until Cader eventually noticed him, named him, and snuck him inside.

Now, it was Sim's first day off in a week and she was nuzzled into a big armchair in the foyer with a hot mug of Kai's tea cupped in her hand and a napping Drangs curled up at her side. Sim was already on the third chapter of *A History of Magicweaving*, which had just outlined the difference between spell casting and magicweaving: Anyone could learn how to cast spells, but only certain people were born with an innate ability to shift the elements. Magicweavers were usually prevalent along certain family lines, almost as if the trait was genetic, but it also wasn't that uncommon for someone to be the first magicweaver in their family, which made the ability seem to be more of an innate talent. Sim was about ready to brew herself another mug of tea, when the doorknob started to jiggle. Sim looked up with a frown; it was too early for Kai to be coming back from her daily Veldindor devotional.

A key clicked in the lock and a tall girl with short, messy black hair stepped into the foyer. She wore a duffle bag strapped across her chest, and loose-fitting khaki pants that were held snug against her shins under high leather boots. Her sleeves were rolled up to her elbows, showing the colorful tattoos on her forearms. Patches of grime dirtied her clothes and bluish bags had formed under her eyes, as if she hadn't slept in days. She swung the duffle bag over her head and dropped it onto the floor.

"Who the hell are you?" the girl said, and put her hands on the wide leather belt that hugged her hips. Her eyes bore into Sim's.

"Ah—I'm—I'm Sim," she stuttered. "I live here."

The girl flicked her hair out of her eyes and continued to stare at Sim without blinking. Sim's gaze shifted to the sword hanging from the girl's belt. This had to be Prudence.

"Kai should be home soon," Sim offered.

"For how long?" Prudence asked.

"What?"

"How long have you been living here?"

"Oh. Three months."

Prudence grabbed her bag and hoisted it up onto her shoulder with much more ease than Sim would have expected from someone with such a slight frame. "If you see Cader, will you tell him I want to talk to him?" she said as she walked past Sim and went to the staircase.

"Sure," Sim said to her back.

"Thanks." Prudence stomped to her room and closed her door hard behind her.

So this was the girl that Cader and Kai kept talking about. Sim couldn't figure out why Prudence immediately seemed to hate her so much. It could be that she was just tired from her journey back. That had to be it.

Sim had finished five more chapters and two more cups of tea when Kai came pushing through the door with her arms full of groceries. "Prudence is back," Sim said, putting down her book. Kai's eyebrows rose and her face lit up. Sim took one of the bags from her and followed her into the kitchen.

"Where is she?" Kai asked.

"Upstairs. She's been there for a while."

"She's probably sleeping." Kai nodded.

Sim leaned forward against the counter, staring at the arugula that had spilled out of Kai's canvas bag. "Do you think she's okay with me living here?"

Kai stopped unpacking and looked up. "Well, it's not up to her, is it? Why would you even ask that? I'm sure she's fine with it." Kai took out three potatoes and added, "You just have to get used to her, Sim. And give her some time to get used to you. Pru's not so good with strangers."

* * *

The sun was blazing. No trees grew in this part of the Narrows; nothing but endless lines of lifeless factories and warehouses bordered the street. For the fifth time in the past five minutes, Sim snapped open the wooden box Azzer had given her and checked the little compass set into its center. Runes lined its outer ring, but they didn't help her at all, since she had no idea how to read them.

"Just calibrate it," he'd said. "And intend the compass to point you to where you want to go. I would imagine that you'd have to picture the place clearly, but other than that it should be easy."

Sim could've killed him. The compass's arrow had taken her around countless turns, making it impossible to retrace her route, before pointing her directly west for twenty minutes. Five times already she'd checked the reddish stone that was set into the back of the gadget to make sure that it wasn't cracked or worn down. Maybe Azzer had accidentally put an old rock into the compass instead of one of his magical gems. Sim was losing any hope of ever reaching the Narrows Bridge. The road ended at a sprawling, two-story factory. She had to go left or right, but the arrow pointed straight ahead. Sim snapped the box shut and dropped her bike onto the asphalt. The streets were empty. No one ever came out here. A tingling feeling pricked at her skin, as if she were trespassing on holy ground.

Sim swayed with a sudden wave of dizziness. Warm sweat coated her palms when she ran her hands over her scalp. The warehouse before her had windows that were still intact, and painted black so that the sun couldn't get in. Sim ducked underneath a large gash in the fence surrounding the building and tried to convince herself that the anxious feeling in her stomach was from the heat. The heavy metal door had no padlock on it, but only opened a few inches when Sim tugged on the handle. She propped one foot up against the wall and heaved backward with all of her weight, until a loud creak echoed through the cavernous building. Cool warehouse air rushed outside and enfolded Sim's burning skin. The darkness welcomed her. Sim stepped inside, eased to the floor, and leaned her back against the wall.

Harsh daylight streamed in from the open door and illuminated metal shipping containers that were stacked two or three high and blocked off the rest of the warehouse from Sim's view. As she pulled herself to her feet, she realized that the vast room wasn't as dark as she'd first thought; the paint on the windows was semi-translucent and allowed a dim gray glow into the building. Her footsteps echoed on the high concrete walls, but other than that an eerie silence surrounded her. Chalky white bird droppings streamed down from the tops of the containers, caking over a thick layer of dust. Sim followed a path through the boxes until she came to a doorway, dark against the rest of the wall. The heat hit her again when she stepped out onto the warehouse's roof, back out in the glaring light. The twin pink arches of the Narrows Bridge peeked above the factories to the northeast.

"Thank Veldindor," Sim mumbled. She calibrated the compass, reaching inside of herself and sending her energy into the gadget. She felt the soft, pulsing energy of the stone and enmeshed river thoughts with the calibration, wished with all of her being that she would get there. She begged the compass to work, shut her eyes tight, and opened them. The arrow pointed east, and stayed in place like a regular compass when she turned in a circle. She clicked the box shut, went back through the maze of shipping boxes, and paused by the door, preparing herself for the heat.

"What are you doing here?"

Sim jumped and squinted into the darkness. "Who's there?"

"I should be asking you that." It was a girl's voice. She stepped closer to Sim, slowly, gracefully, until she was standing just at the edge of where the light reached. Her hair was deep red, almost brown, and hung in thick locks over her bare alabaster shoulders. Black eyeliner trailed lines past the corners of her dark eyes, which were staring at Sim with a strange expression that was somewhere between disbelief and fear. She was too slight looking to be dangerous, but her glare was intense.

"I'm sorry," Sim said, taking a step back. "I didn't know that anyone lived here." When the girl continued to stare at her and didn't respond, Sim added, "I was lost and wanted to get out of the sun." Sim frowned at the shadows covering half of the girl's body. A fuzzy white bird was perched on a piece of leather armor strapped to her right shoulder.

"Is that an owl?" Sim asked, moving closer.

"Are you some dumb explorer?" The girl pulled away. "No one comes here. The bikers keep to the wall. They know better than to wander." The girl's hands were on her hips, her chin thrust slightly upward. The owl's yellow eyes glowed at Sim.

"I'm not exploring, I'm..." Sim held out the compass. "I work at a fix-it shop. The compass took me here."

The girl frowned down at the gadget and then up at Sim. "That's impossible."

"Look, I was just about to leave—"

"Wait," the girl said quickly. "Don't come back here. It isn't safe. You're lucky I found you."

"Why?"

The girl's eyes were cold, but not toward Sim. "You're better off not knowing. You should stop coming across the bridge at all, but if you won't then keep to the wall. Stay out of the west side of the Narrows." The girl met Sim's eyes directly. The owl spun its head around to stare at Sim as the girl turned and melted into the shadows.

"Weird." Sim hurried outside and yanked the door shut behind her. The compass took her east, back through the factory desert, and then north to the slowly moving Brigantine. The Narrows Bridge peeked above the factories long before Sim got to the river's edge, where she had to dismount her bike and walk through weeds until she got back to the main road that eventually led to Christiania Street.

Azzer was at the front of the shop when she got back. He was rearranging the bookcase, probably because there were no customers at the moment and he couldn't stand to be idle. As Sim walked into the shop, he forgot about the books and walked over to the counter.

"You did it," he said.

"Yeah, it took me all day." Sim dropped the compass in front of him. Her clothes were soaked with sweat and her face hot from the start of a sunburn.

"You'll get better at it," Azzer said, tipping his head up a little. He didn't seem to know what to make of Sim's negative attitude. She looked away and started working on a watch that wouldn't wind.

"This," Azzer said, pulling the watch out of her hands, "is child's play. It's just a machine. It's useful, it's great. It doesn't need magic dust to work because it gets energy from the swinging of your wrist. But it only marks the time. Any dwarf or drone could fix this. You're much more talented than that, Simetra." Azzer put the watch down and crossed his arms over his chest.

"What?" Sim hated it when he used her full name like that.

"Calibration is the first step to connecting with the magic that's around us. It's the first step toward becoming a magicweaver."

"So?"

"So, you can't fix gadgets until you can calibrate them. Gadgets like this compass—" he picked it up and held its face toward Sim, "are tools for setting people free. Everyone should have access to them. You can be different, Sim. I can tell there's something different about you. You could be one of the few magicweavers who actually help people."

Sim frowned at him, not knowing what to say.

He turned from her, frustrated. "Bread and circus games, Simetra. That's what this is all about. It doesn't matter what crap they feed people or what empty distractions they shine in their faces. Keep the masses fed and entertained, and all is well. Don't you see it? Wands allowed anyone with money to learn magicweaving, but then magicweavers simply rose to the upper ranks of society. Ordinary people still suffered. The rich still exploited and manipulated everyone. Then the great Nogad Nogron came along, with his mass-produced, magic-dust-filled gadgets and the whole world was turned on its head."

Sim's spine prickled at the mention of Sir Nogron's name. She was silent, not wanting to say anything that would let Azzer know she'd been so close to a man whom he seemed to have such strong opinions about.

"It was revolutionary," Azzer continued. "Nogron found a way to actually extract magic from nature and concentrate it into a physical form. All you had to do was buy his dust and pour it into one of his gadgets, and it would work like magic. Indeed, it was magic. Just without any conscious thought. Then he came out with his charmed carriages, and everything was set in place. A mere thirty years later, and we use magic dust as our currency instead of gold and everyone has at least one of Nogron's gadgets in their homes. But nothing's changed, not really. The masses are still exploited, but now it's in a more subtle, sinister way. They can't even see it."

Sim's head was starting to spin. It was impossible to follow Azzer when he went off like this. "So what does any of this have to do with me learning how to calibrate?" she asked, trying to bring him back.

"Circus games, Sim. People are blinded by the shiny gadgets, the useless shit that they slave away for at their meaningless jobs." He held up the compass again. "This is different. Gadgets in and of themselves aren't bad. Gadgets that liberate people, that are made to last and be repaired, that are created in a way that makes people's lives better, that's what this shop is about. We can put real, meaningful tools into the hands of ordinary people. We can do it without exploiting people in the Hinterlands, without destroying forests and oceans, without forcing people to work themselves sick. We can fix the things that people already have so that they don't have to buy new things all the time. The self-printing books, the air coolers, the automatic blenders: all of that useless shit that people spend their magic dust on—it's all worthless. We can change that. But I can't do it alone. I need your help. I need you to learn how to calibrate. Do you understand?"

Sim nodded, even though she didn't have a clue. "I do. That makes sense. I'll try to learn."

"I'm working on a new device that should make it easier. It could be finished within the week, maybe." Azzer glanced over the work that was laid out in front of Sim, and sighed. "I should get back to it, actually." He smiled and added, "Well done, Sim. Well done."

Sim murmured a "thanks" and grabbed up the watch again, until she got distracted by her thoughts and began staring at the wall across from her, wondering if Wood would be at Stein's after work. The door opened, springing Sim out of her daydream.

"Space out much?" Cader said, walking in with his skateboard wedged under one arm and a large brown box under the other.

"Cader?"

"Don't look so surprised to see me." He laughed. "I just wanted to thank Azzer for the brewing book."

Azzer pushed aside the curtain and stood just in front of it, examining Cader and then the box.

"Oh," Sim said, forgetting that Cader only knew Azzer through an acquaintance and that they'd never actually met before. "Azzer, this is my roommate Cader. He's the one who built the brewing machine. Cader, my boss, Azzer."

"Nice to finally meet you, man," Cader said, sliding the box onto the counter and propping his skateboard up against the wall. He stuck out his arm and shook Azzer's hand. Azzer nodded and pulled up the box's top flaps to look inside. He took out a beer and glanced at a large grandfather clock that stood between the map of the world and a fireplace that they never used.

"Two thirty," he mumbled, then snapped his eyes up toward Cader. "Drink one with me?"

"Of course." Cader pulled out three beers and shot Sim a look. "I took them straight from the brewing box, so you'll have to ice them."

"You can do a cooling spell?" Azzer asked.

"I had to know it for my last job."

"That's the second surprise of the day," Azzer said, taking his cold beer from Sim. "Number three would be if you kids actually know how to brew."

"You gotta try it," Cader said with a smug grin. He took a swig of his own.

"Hm." Azzer nodded once, forcefully almost, after a big swig. "Not bad for your first batch. Needs more hops."

"I like it wheaty," Cader said with a shrug.

Azzer shook his head. "More hops."

"We were talking about trying new recipes next week," Sim said.

"Just be careful. Already told you that."

"The Guard actually seems to be getting more lax these days." Cader slid onto a stool that Azzer had pulled out of the corner for him. "There must be something else monopolizing their attention."

"Gangs, probably," Azzer agreed.

"Can't be bothered by us drinkers." Cader laughed. "I'll tell you what, though. It wasn't so easy to track down those gems for the brewing boxes. Half of the people I talked to had no idea what I was asking them for, and most of the others just laughed at me."

"But you got them?" There was a glint in Azzer's eye.

"Yeah. I mean, you just have to know the right people to ask, the right places to look."

Sim watched them talk, paying just enough attention so that she would be able to enter the conversation if they demanded it of her. They didn't, though, thankfully. Cader went to the back of the shop with Azzer to see an invention he was working on, leaving Sim at the counter with the broken watch.

"Ride home with me?" he asked when he came back to the front, since it was time for Sim to leave. Azzer handed her a fold of sols.

"Sure," she said, and immediately regretted it. But she wouldn't have been able to explain herself if she had insisted on going to Stein's.

Cader's skateboard jumped over potholes and weeds, leading the way to the bridge. Sim pedaled at her fastest just to keep up with him.

"I need to come here more often," he said, facing her. "Who said this 'hood is just for bikers?" He popped the front of his board onto an old rusting trash can, slid its nose along the can's rim, spun, and landed flat on his wheels. He climbed the bridge with his right leg kicking out behind him in full, constant strokes. Halfway through, he switched to his left without missing a beat. And so they went, all the way back to Kailash.

Sim leaned her bike against the back of the house and did some weeding while Cader went inside to meditate. Finished, she pulled open the back door, stepped into the kitchen, and stopped. The screen door slammed behind her. Prudence was leaning against the counter, wearing an old military jacket and tight black jeans and eating a bowl of cereal. The longest layers of her short black hair hung just below her ears in uneven locks.

"Hey," Sim said.

Still chewing, Pru tilted her head up a bit to see beyond her bangs. She swallowed and opened her mouth just as Kai burst into the kitchen.

"That's Prudence," Kai said, then slapped her forehead. "Oh, right, you've met." She looked at Pru. "Why didn't you tell us you'd be coming back? People were starting to say that you were dead."

Prudence shoved another spoonful of cereal into her mouth and shrugged. "It was a last-minute decision. Who said I was dead?" Her voice was slightly raspy, as if she'd smoked too many cigarettes.

"Just some idiot that Cader brought over one day. Where did you go?"

"A lot of places."

"You weren't fighting in that ogre war, were you?"

Pru stared at her for a moment. "Does it matter?"

"Well, you can't just—I mean...how long are you staying for?"

"Not sure. Look, we still have our deal, right? I'm not looking to stay here for free. I never have."

"I know," Kai said, her frenzied manner subduing. "I know. It's just...I was just worried. The things I've been hearing about those ogres...It's good to have you back, Pru."

In two steps, Kai was wrapping the crossed-armed Prudence into a hug. Being a good head shorter, Kai placed her ear on Prudence's shoulder and held her for a moment. Pru seemed surprised. "Missed me?" she said. "You're loosing your edge, Kai."

"Whatever. You know what I mean." Kai stepped back. "You still have that ugly jacket, I see."

"Ah, there's the edge." Prudence untangled her arms and shoved her hands into her pockets. She looked down at her jacket. "I like it." She glanced over at Sim.

"Oh!" Kai moved into the space between them and grabbed Sim's hand, leading her over to the counter. "Right. Sim. Cader found her."

"Found her?"

"It's a long story—"

"I have to get going, actually." Prudence moved toward the door. "Have to get ready for the Battle House."

"Sim's coming with us," Cader called from the living room, where he was in a headstand. His meditation room upstairs was going through a cleansing and filled with a heavy, sweet-smelling smoke.

For a moment Pru looked slightly annoyed, but she pulled her lips to the side of her mouth, nodded, and left the kitchen.

"Leave in ten minutes?" Cader said as she passed through the living room.

"Twenty." Pru skipped up the steps and yelled down, "This hallway smells like crap, Cader."

"It's bobbinroot!" he yelled back.

"You're going to the Battle House?" Kai asked, frowning at Sim.

"This is the first I've heard about it."

Kai laughed, raised her eyebrows high, and turned to the potion she was brewing. "Well, good luck. Anyway, I can't believe Prudence is back. I was sure she'd be gone for good this time. We'll have brussels sprouts tonight, since she'll finally be eating with us. They're her favorite, I think. Unless it's changed. It does, sometimes."

"You ready?" Cader stood in the doorway, smiling at Sim with a glint in his eyes.

"I don't know—"

"There's no backing out. I got you a spot. The house is full, and they're really hard to come by. I only got you in because some guy left on a quest."

"I'm going to suck so bad," she moaned.

"Everyone has to start somewhere," he said with a shrug. "Get dressed. Something comfortable. This won't be easy. But the things that are worth it never are."

The clatter of combat training rang off of the Battle House's wooden floors and high ceilings. Master Keisenheart was standing before a wall that had a menagerie of weapons hanging from it: longswords, daggers, scimitars, axes, longbows, shortbows, and crossbows. Keisenheart's hands were behind his back, his feet spread wide. He was directing a line of sword-wielders in a set of drills. Beyond them was Master Videria, a lithe woman in her late thirties who kept her jet-black hair held back in a braid and used her icy blue eyes as an aid to discipline. She was yelling at a boy who wouldn't stand up perfectly straight while taking aim. Her arms waved in quick snaps, pointing to the students who were doing it properly. The very sight of her made Sim nervous. Finally there was the silent, brooding Master Throop, who had shoulders wider than Sim would have thought possible and could lift the heaviest axe in the house as though it had no weight at all. He was talking quietly to a student who wore a confused expression but kept nodding as if he understood what Throop was saying. Cader explained all of this to Sim in their first five minutes there. Five minutes. That was all the time she had to get her bearings.

Prudence had changed into clothes similar to the ones that Sim had first seen her in: loose-fitting black pants, high leather boots that clung to her shins, a black shirt with a broad brown belt hugging her waist, and wrist-guards on both arms. Her sword handle stuck out of its scabbard. Intricate knots were brazed into it, but Sim didn't dare ask for a better look. She did her best to make it seem like she wasn't even there, so that she wouldn't get in the way. For whatever reason, she desperately wanted Prudence to accept her. But her housemate seemed ambivalent.

"Cader!" Atif, who had been jumping rope along a side wall, jogged up to them with the rope hanging from his hand. He took Cader's hand in his, and they embraced each other quickly, with smiles. Atif glanced at Sim and raised a hand in recognition; he remembered her from the Dragon Spine. He looked back to Cader. "I was hoping you'd come today; I need some real competition."

"Well, here it is," Cader said with a laugh.

Atif stepped back when he noticed Prudence. "Hell, Pru. I didn't know you were coming back to Terresin. I thought you would have been finished off in Ogbond for sure."

Pru frowned at him.

Still smiling, he put his hands on his hips and shook his head. He looked at Sim. "You're lucky to be living with these two; they have a lot to teach."

Sim smiled back, not knowing what to say.

"You're not the one who's been saying I'm dead, are you?" Pru asked, as if she already knew the answer.

"I—" he started, searching for an explanation. "I—well, I heard—"

"I think we've wasted enough time talking," Cader cut in. "Let's suit up and head to the orb room."

"Is she ready for that?" Pru asked, motioning at Sim.

Cader scratched his head. "She's probably not bad with a bow," he said.

"Has she ever orbed in before?"

"No, she's never been here before. Okay. Maybe you should work with Master Keisenheart today, Sim," Cader said with a look of apology.

Dread filled Sim's chest. She glanced over at the militant line of sword-wielders, all in perfect step with one another. She swallowed and said, "Yeah, sounds good."

"I have a partner," Atif said. "I'll go see if he's up for it." And he ran back to where he'd been jumping rope.

"You can watch if you want," Cader said to Sim as they headed toward the weapon wall. "You learn just as much from watching."

"Only if you know the basics," Pru disagreed.

"I'll work with Keisenheart," Sim said. She went toward the area of the Battle House where sword practice was held before she even thought to ask them what the hell she'd actually be doing. It was too late: Cader and Pru were already suiting up for the orb room, and Sim would have been more embarrassed to walk all the way back to the other side of the house just to ask them how she should introduce herself. So she stood off to the side of Keisenheart's line, and the longer she waited for an appropriate time to announce herself, the more awkward the whole situation became.

"Okay, good," Keisenheart said at the end of the drill. "Faster next time."

Everyone caught their breath and Sim was about to walk up to him and ask what she should do, but he beat her to it. "Can I help you with something?" he asked, his sharp blue eyes almost glaring at her.

"I was wondering if I could work with you today," Sim said quickly.

Keisenheart ran a hand through his short, graying hair and nodded over toward Cader and Prudence. "You're with them?" he asked. She couldn't force a word out of her throat, so she nodded, instead.

"Okay, fine," Keisenheart said with a sigh. "But you most certainly can't do drills in that. That much should be obvious; look at everyone else. Go put on some armor, find a suitable sword, and jump in. Don't interrupt."

He turned back to his students, who had all been staring at Sim. They were all armored, but Sim hadn't noticed until right then. "Okay," Keisenheart said with a clap. "Back to it. From the beginning. Faster this time."

There was just enough room at the end of the line for one more person, between a lanky guy and the wall. Sim stepped into place, her hand clutching a sword that was heavy and slightly awkward, and her shoulder chafing under a cuirass that was too big. The tall guy was visibly annoyed that he had to share space with her. Without even giving Sim a glance, Master Keisenheart yelled to the line to switch drills, and in unison everyone started to swipe, jab, and duck. Sim stood there like an idiot, watching them. Her neighbor nearly stepped on her when he went back to his place after his duck.

"Watch it," he grumbled. Sim mumbled an apology and moved closer to the wall.

"Next set!" Master Keisenheart yelled, right when Sim was just starting to get the hang of the one they were doing. She jumped right into the routine, watching the lanky guy and following his motions as he did them. Block, duck, kick at the feet, jab. They went into their second repetition, but Sim didn't do any better. Everyone could see that she didn't know what she was doing. Part of her wanted to leave the line, take off the armor, and wait for Cader and Pru outside. But she stayed, convinced that leaving now would only make her look more foolish.

Over and over, in her head, Sim told herself that she could do it, that during the next repetition she'd nail it. Cader had insisted that this positive thinking would work. But it didn't. Of course it didn't. Sim was so distracted by telling herself that she was doing fine and would get it perfect the next time that she hit the dull blade of her sword against the wall. It sprang from her hand and slid into the middle of the empty space between Master Keisenheart and the line. Sim froze, and a few of the other students stopped as well. The most well-trained ones kept going through the drill, pretending not to have noticed.

A scowl on his face, Keisenheart strode to the sword, snatched it up, and marched over to Sim. "Come over here," he said, not trying to hide his impatience. "Next set!" he yelled over his shoulder. He led Sim to a corner where a bunch of worn staffs leaned against the wall.

"Never lose your sword," he said, pushing it into her hand. "You lose your sword and you die."

He reached past her to pull a small blade off the wall. "The sword you're using is too heavy for you. Take this." Sim took the handle of the almost childish sword he'd picked out for her. Keisenheart continued. "Now I'm going to teach you three basic things: swipe, block, jab."

He went through the motions slowly, keeping his eyes on Sim's to make sure she was paying attention. "Try it," he said when he was finished.

Sim did, but she was so nervous that she forgot to start in the attack stance that he'd shown her at the very beginning. Keisenheart yelled at her for getting her footwork wrong, sighed, and looked over to his other students. "Stay here," he said. "Keep doing what I just showed you and pay attention to the details, especially where your feet are."

He left Sim to practice the embarrassingly simple drill all by herself, out in the open where everyone could see her. She clenched her jaw and started. She was determined to get it down perfectly. The sooner Keisenheart saw that she got it, the sooner she'd be able to rejoin the line. Sim faced the wall, so that she wouldn't have to see everyone watching her, and started. For the next half hour she did the same thing over and over again, not taking a break, ignoring the burning in her muscles. In her mind she could see herself doing the whole thing perfectly, but the image refused to translate into her movements. She felt utterly unable to control her body, frustrated that her arms and legs and hips refused to obey her thoughts. Hot tears filled her eyes. She was glad that she was facing the wall and no one could see them.

Cader came up to her and stood nearby, waiting for her to finish, but Sim wouldn't stop. She did the same basic moves again and again, punishing herself. "Hey," he said after a minute. Sim finished the repetition, and then let the sword fall to her side. She needed water. Her whole body was numb. "Maybe you should take a break?" Cader said. She could see the embarrassment, the pity in his face. Sim frowned her tears away.

"I need to practice," she said.

Cader looked uncomfortable. He nodded. "Well, Pru and I are taking a break. You can join us if you want, and then we were going to do long-distance."

He was only suggesting archery because it was easier. Sim swallowed, deciding to pretend that the whole embarrassing craze she had been stuck in moments ago had never happened. She took a deep breath and forced a smile onto her face.

"Bows?" she asked him, raising an eyebrow.

Cader seemed relieved. He smiled back at her. "Bows sound great."

Sim put her sword back and followed Cader to where Pru was sitting with a skin of water. Keisenheart didn't even notice that she'd stopped her drill; he was snapping at one of his students for moving too slowly.

Neither Pru nor Cader mentioned the fact that Sim had been ostracized to the corner and thrown out of Keisenheart's battle line. She was glad for it. She just wanted to forget that it had ever happened. Pru held the water skin out to her, and Sim drank from it deeply. She wiped the sweat off her face and neck with a towel she'd brought, wondering again what craziness it was that had brought her there, and knowing the answer even though she pretended not to. It was for Wood. It was for the slightest chance that Wood might be impressed when Sim told her that she was on her way to becoming a quester.

V

im's biceps burned as she cruised through the Mondran Quarter, where white-robed devotees of the goddess Mondra tended to live and congregate, isolating themselves from those who believed in other gods. Sim was stopped at a long red light, leaning forward on her handlebars and gazing at the carriages speeding through the intersection. Even her bike-toned legs were sore from the Battle House exercises. Just in front of her, a young woman pushed a baby carriage across the street. Three small children followed behind, dressed identically in white saddle shoes and knit sweaters. The mother didn't give Sim a glance; Mondrans hardly ever acknowledged nonbelievers. The light turned green and Sim stepped up onto her pedal, pumping her legs until she was riding along with traffic, sometimes a little slower, until she reached a broad, empty road that ran along the river. Heavy patches of broken glass forced Sim to ride in an S curve, leaning to the left and then the right, shifting her center of gravity. Sim noted that it was strange that there was so much glass around, but didn't really think much of it. An instant later Sim slammed on her breaks and swerved sideways. Her left boot slid along the glass-covered pavement and the edges of her tires skidded until she stopped just before the bridge's stone archway. Sim dropped her bike with a clatter. Her boots crunched as she took two steps toward the bridge and stared at the glistening onramp. The sunlight caught on hundreds of sharp points and edges that covered the entire path. Sim put her hands on her hips and waited for her heart to stop skipping. A breeze blew her hair into her face, cooled the heat in her cheeks.

Though she wasn't sure exactly why she was doing it, Sim grasped the wind with her mind. She remembered the fierce gusts at the top of a high, treeless hilltop. She remembered the day when she and Jaylenik had been caught in a thunderstorm while playing in the woods, and had to cling to each other as they ran back to the mansion so that the wind wouldn't blow them sideways. Sim poured her heart and mind into the magic until it swirled and grew brighter. She was a tiny sun burning bright at the center of the universe. Raw power coursed through her being. Her clothes flew around her body like a wild pennant and her hair swirled about her head. A shimmery glow bordered the left side of the bridge as the glass flew off the bikeway in a crystalline waterfall.

Sim released the wind and faltered from a wash of fatigue. She took a deep breath, and then two more. Her bike had blown two feet away from the force of the gust. The solid sound of boots hitting pavement echoed on the empty street. Prudence emerged from a niche in the bridge's archway and headed toward Sim, walking her track bike beside her, an unlit cigarette dangling from her lips. Her hair was even more of a wild mess than usual. She snapped her fingers to conjure a flame, took a drag, and shoved her hand into a pocket.

"You almost blew me into the fucking river," she said.

"I'm sorry, I—"

A smile crossed Pru's face, and Sim knew she was kidding.

"Not a magicweaver, huh?" Pru said.

"I don't know how I did that."

"But you did it."

"I—that thing you do with your fingers, to make fire—Cader did it before...."

"Magicweaving," Pru said with a nod. "Some people are better at it than others." Pru swung her leg over her handlebars and slid one of her boots into a toe strap. "You coming or what?"

"Who do you think put all that glass there?" Sim asked as they pedaled up the steep incline.

For a moment Sim thought she wasn't going to answer, but then Pru said, "Maybe the Mondrans, maybe the Guard. Probably the Mondrans. The Narrows have been off of the Guard's radar for years. Too much other shit to worry about. But I never thought the Mondrans would go this far."

"You think the Mondrans did this?"

"They're not really fond of bikers going through their neighborhood."

"Do you think they'll do it again?"

"Who knows?"

Then they made it to the steepest point of the bridge, where Sim fell behind. It was too hard to talk there, anyway. They rushed down the other side, past three bikers, and toward a few questers who were waiting beneath the archway on the Narrows side. All three of them were wearing questing outfits. Pru would have ridden right past them if they hadn't been blocking the way.

"What's up?" Pru asked, obviously annoyed that they'd made her stop.

"Did you see that wind?" one of them asked.

"I felt it."

"It had to be one of you who did that," said a guy who was sitting on the crossbar of his yellow frame. "How'd you do it?"

"We didn't," Pru said.

Sim, who had been about to explain what had happened, shut her mouth and tried not to look confused.

"You must have, unless there was someone else over there?" The guy took off his goggles and pulled them back over his forehead. "We just wanted to thank the person who did it. It's not every day you get to meet—"

"There's no one to thank."

"Then who—"

"How the hell should I know?" Prudence leaned forward and gripped her handlebars. "Look, man, we need to get to work. If you find the guy, thank him for us, too."

He seemed to buy it, or didn't care enough to let the confrontation with Prudence escalate. He nodded and studied Sim suspiciously, as if he was trying to remember her face, then he apologized and moved out of the way. As they rode off, Sim heard him talking to his friends about the Mondrans, and how they'd crossed a line.

"You should keep that trick of yours to yourself," Pru said when the group was far behind them and they were surrounded by nothing but abandoned factories. "Don't tell people anything they don't need to know."

"Okay. But why?" Sim said.

"It can get you into trouble," Pru said. "Do what you want, but I wouldn't tell anyone."

"No, I won't."

Sim didn't know who she would've told, anyway.

Work dragged on forever. More customers were coming to the shop now that the news of the Incubator's opening and Azzer's magic-dust-free gadgets had spread through the Narrows. Questers came looking for utility belts and magical maps. Poets came in to have their typewriters repaired. Others came with broken headphones, cracked goggles, bikes that needed their parts adjusted. Azzer did most of the repairs himself, and left his tinkering and inventions for after closing time. When there were no customers, Sim calibrated firestarters and treasure boxes. The steady flow of work should have kept her happily distracted, but she kept checking the moonfaced grandfather clock and counting the hours until she'd be off and free to go to Stein's.

Wood was waiting for her on the stoop of the apartment building next to the shop. A book dangled from her hand and her tank top was rolled up so that her stomach could get some sun. Squarish sunglasses shielded her eyes and her hair was pulled off of her face in a braid that ran from her forehead to her ear. Sim kept her gaze on the street.

"Hey, girl," Wood said with a smile. "I would've come in, but I didn't want to get you in trouble for chatting on the clock. Figured I'd just wait for you here." She sat up, pulled down her shirt, and threw her book into her bag. "Feel like hanging on the wall? I know a great spot, and we can grab a six-pack on the way."

"Sure," Sim said, stifling a smile of her own. "Lead the way."

Wood hopped down the steps and grabbed her bike, a red-framed roadster with ten speeds and drop-down handlebars wrapped with gleaming cherry tape. She stepped onto her pedal and they started toward Christiania. Sim noticed that she tended to stand up on her pedals when she rode, pumping quickly and then coasting along. She glanced over her shoulder at Sim. "Anything interesting happen today?"

"Work was kind of boring. But...Did you hear about the bridge?"

"Of course I did. It's crazy right? Makes you wonder what the Mondrans might do next. Maybe it was just some kids playing a prank, though. Hopefully nothing else will happen."

"I don't know....There was a lot of glass. It looked like the whole bridge was covered. I don't think kids could've done that."

Wood frowned over at her. "You saw it?"

Sim nodded. "I was so mad when I stopped at the arch and saw that there was no way over here. I don't know what happened: I sort of just grabbed onto the wind and made it blow all the glass off. It's crazy, right?"

"You did that?"

Sim could sense that Wood's eyes were wide with surprise behind her dark lenses.

"Please don't tell anyone, Wood. I promised my roommate that I wouldn't talk about it. I'm not even sure why it should be a secret, but I believe her."

"I won't tell anyone if you don't want me to. But still, Sim, that's—Controlling the elements is magicweaving in its purest form." She looked over at Sim with a grin. "That's kind of awesome."

They sat with their backs against a stone ledge, sipping on Bongo Tree Lagers while they watched the bikers strolling past them. Four more beers perspired at Sim's hip, and she wondered nervously if it would be vain to do a cooling spell if they got warm. She didn't want Wood to think she was showing off. They had to sit close so that the beer and both of their bodies could fit in the shade of a tree that reached its branches over the walkway. Their bare shoulders pressed together lightly, their bodies separated by nothing but the thinnest sheen of clammy sweat. Sim tried to ignore the heat that pulsed through her chest at Wood's touch, and to keep her shallow breaths long and even. She imagined that they weren't touching at all. That was the only way she could deal with it.

"Fuck the Battle House," Wood said with a flick of her hand and a look of scorn when Sim told her how humiliated she'd been the day before. It felt strange to talk about her feelings so openly.

"I thought you said you wanted to join one."

"I want to study questing culture; that's different. You don't have to go to a battle house to be a quester. It's awesome that your roommate got you into one, but if they're going to be such condescending assholes then maybe you should just quit."

"I guess you're right."

"You should get out of that place while you still can. Then you can hang out with me more."

A group of four friends, still in the middle of their conversation, looked down at Sim and Wood as they passed. "Judgmental row," Wood said under her breath, with a raise of her eyebrows. "But I guess that's what people come up here for: to see and be seen."

Sim wasn't bothered by it. The thought of people looking down on her clothes and deciding whether they liked her look or not was so absurd to her that it put her outside of the situation. Sim was somewhere between being comfortable in her own skin and not caring at all about what random strangers thought. That's what she told herself, regularly.

The stone walkway was hard and uncomfortable. Sim put a hand on either side of her hips and lifted herself up to move into a different position. Her arm grazed across Wood's, pulled away, and met it again when she settled back onto the path. Sim glanced up to find Wood grinning at a guy who was walking past them. He slowed his pace and turned up the sides of his scruffy beard into a matching smirk. He held Wood's gaze for a long moment and then looked away.

"Who was that?" Sim asked, frowning after him.

"Adrian. He works at a bar down the street from Stein's. We hook up sometimes."

Sim didn't know what to say, so she stared straight ahead at the two girls walking past them. Her heart knotted up like a sore muscle, just for a beat, but Sim ignored it.

"He's kind of a tool," Wood added. She dismissed the thought of him with a shrug and took another sip of her beer. Sim wanted to ask her why she hooked up with him if she didn't really like him, but decided that it was none of her business. Wood reached across Sim to grab another two beers. She pried off the tops with her keychain and handed one to Sim.

"Anyway, there's this guy at the bookshop who I'm way more into. It's probably not a good idea to get with coworkers, though."

"No, probably not," Sim said with a shrug. "But whatever."

"Yeah, we should just do what we want. Live out our desires. That's what this place is all about, right?"

"Yeah. Definitely."

"I mean, there are always other guys. What about you? Any men in your life?"

Sim frowned, fighting a blush but not knowing why. "Nope." She forced a smile. "Not right now, anyway." There had been boys back at Nogron Mansion: nasty peasant boys who would throw rocks at birds and always get into fights with one another. Some of the scrawnier ones had tried to get Sim to go back into the woods with them, back where no one would see and they could do whatever they wanted. But she always said no; she always had an excuse not to. She eventually kissed one of them behind the dragon stables. At the time, Sim had been glad to get it over with, to have finally been kissed. After a while they left her alone, realizing that she was never going to go any further, and not caring enough to try and convince her. It became easier to just avoid the boys, instead of thinking about what she was so afraid of.

"Well, I don't see why. You're really pretty. But you're smarter than I am. Guys suck. Sometimes I wonder why I bother."

"Then why do you?"

Wood laughed and gave Sim a look.

"Oh." Sim forced a grin. "Right."

They watched the people go by, talking occasionally, until their beers were gone and the sky was getting dark. For the summer, Wood was working at a bookshop on Christiania that Sim had passed a hundred times but had never gone into. Since they got off at the same time, they made plans to meet each other at Stein's again the next day.

Cracked steps wound down a tower notched into a bend in the wall. "You should come by and say hi before work tomorrow, too," Wood said as they crept down them. Rusty torch holders lined the staircase between long, narrow windows that let in just enough light to see where the next few steps were. "I have a book you should read." She pressed her hand up against the inner wall to keep her balance.

At the bottom of the steps a mess of empty beer bottles spilled out from a deep niche that had probably once held a store of shields and arrows. Other brewers would come and get the bottles when they needed them, knowing right where to look and relying on the consistent thirst of the Narrows bikers for their supply.

Sim and Wood were walking next to each other now, through the damp tunnel that led to the street. Their voices echoed off the walls, merging with chatter from other groups. In the darkness they were nothing but silhouettes, occasionally illuminated by the sunlight that streamed in through cracks in the stones.

"I think I'm going to head to the bookshop and help close," Wood said when they got out of the tunnel. "See you tomorrow?"

"Yep," Sim said, her heart sinking a little.

The bike light strapped to Sim's handlebars skipped a creamy circle of brightness over the dark street. There were no streetlights off Christiania, where worn statues of muses cradled oil globes that burned bright in the Narrows night, dancing in the spaces between the trees that clawed at the road with their roots. She'd decided to take a new way home, closer to where she'd met that strange girl who had told her to stay away from the factories west of the Narrows, but not so far that she would get lost in the vortex of the factory maze.

An orange glow lit the end of the block just ahead of her, where three cages holding burning fireballs levitated at the edge of the sidewalk and shone flickering light onto a group of chatting girls. One girl stood on her tiptoes and grabbed a ring on the bottom of the cage, pulling it down closer to her as if it were hanging from an invisible elastic cord. With her rouged lips wrapped around the filter, she stuck a cigarette between the grates and inhaled. A puff of smoke escaped from the sides of her mouth. She examined the ember and turned away, letting the cage float back up into place as she rejoined her friends. They stood before a large front window, charmed dark navy so that passersby couldn't see into the bar.

Sim pulled on her breaks to slow her bike. One of the girls was wearing a bronze-buttoned military jacket like the one Prudence had. The girl's long dark bangs hung in her eyes, her hands were shoved in her pockets, and a cigarette hung from her lips. Sim rolled closer. It was definitely Prudence; she was facing the bar's tall, wooden doors. The jacket, leather boots, and the thin, slouching figure were sure signs that this was her roommate. Sim stopped just behind where Prudence was standing and opened her mouth to get her attention, but then hesitated. A girl with shoulder-length blonde hair stepped outside, spilling dance music into the quieter night air. A surprised smile sparkled on her face. She raised her hand in a wave and stepped over to Pru.

"Can I have a cigarette?" the girl asked.

Prudence slid her pack out of a pocket and flicked open the top. The scanty rows of white cylinders fell together as she tilted them toward the blonde, who drew one out and leaned forward to light it off Pru's. Pru jerked her head back. She lifted her hand to the unlit cigarette and snapped her fingers together so that a flame sparked to life and hovered above her thumb. The blonde smiled.

"I'm impressed," she said, and lit up with Pru's fire. Prudence didn't respond.

"We were having a heart-to-heart last time I saw you," the girl said, taking a step closer to Pru so that there was only an inch between them.

"I'm sure we were." Prudence stood up straight and turned away.

The girl's cheeks reddened as she started to ramble about Prudence's jacket, saying how she liked it. "What was the story behind it again?" she asked, her lips curled into a fake smile. "Someone gave it to you, right?"

Prudence pulled her cigarette out of her mouth, ashed it, and looked around. Her eyes found Sim. A cloud of smoke billowed from her mouth as she held Sim's gaze with her own.

"Excuse me," Prudence said while the blonde was still in midsentence. "There's someone I need to talk to. Sorry."

With two quick steps, Pru flicked her butt into the street and was standing in front of Sim, staring at her with grateful eyes that questioned why Sim was there.

"You coming inside?" Her voice was slightly lower than usual and her brow furrowed, though not quite angry.

"What is it?" Sim asked.

"A bar."

Sim's throat seized and kept her from answering. She felt like she was standing outside of a gateway to another world, one in which she knew none of the language or customs. One in which she would surely make a fool of herself. She'd heard people talking about this bar before. The Geraldine. She knew what type of bar it was.

"Come on," Pru said under her breath. "I'll buy you a beer."

Sim nodded. She brought her bike up onto the sidewalk and leaned it against the building, trying not to look nervous.

"You don't want to get stranded in the Narrows at night, Sim," Pru snapped, grabbing the handlebars away from her. "Be careful with your shit." Wheeling the bike with her left hand, Pru glanced around and then slipped into the darkness between the Geraldine and the purplestone next to it. Sim followed, stepping into alley air that smelled of rotting garbage and puke. Broken glass crunched under Sim's boots. She only went a few steps in.

A pile of garbage bags rotted in a heap at the middle of the alley. Pru lifted one of them, felt its weight, and then placed it carefully on top of the bike. She grabbed two more bags to cover the front wheel and frame, and then squatted next to the bike with her hands hovering over the garbage. When she was finished the bike was impossible to spot.

"Can you teach me that?" Sim asked. She took a step farther in.

With a short sigh, Prudence stood, straightened her jacket, and brushed her hands on her jeans. Once she'd fixed her hair, she gave Sim an annoyed look and slid past her, out of the shadows and back into the firelight, where the blonde was still working on her cigarette. She took it out of her mouth and studied it as they approached the building, and then glanced up at them as Prudence pulled open the door and led Sim inside.

The music was good—an upbeat rock that was just loud enough so that it would be hard to listen in on conversations. Sim was reminded of her brief visit to the Dragon Spine, but this bar was nothing like the Lower Terresin club. Girls of every shape, size, and color were packed around the bar. There were a few guys here and there, most of them dancing wildly with two or three girls, the rest hiding their faces in their beers and looking slightly lost and uncomfortable. The space was a lot smaller than Sim had imagined it would be from the outside. It was just the bar, a few tables at the front, and a few more at the back.

The soft skin of strangers rubbed against Sim's bare arms as Prudence led her through the crowd. Some of the girls looked at Sim with an open, grinning, look-you-up-and-down interest that caught her off guard. Others ignored her entirely. It seemed like all of them had their eyes on Pru, at least for a moment. Unsure of herself, Sim tried to keep her eyes there, too. Or on the walls. They were covered with art nouveau posters, fliers from local bands, and sprawling graffiti. A spray-painted stencil of a naked woman riding a bike commanded the wall next to one of the bathrooms. Her hair flowed long swirls behind her and onto the door, stopping at a sideways "W" or "M," turned as if the letters were a joke and they were all just "E"s.

"Let's stand here," Prudence said, and moved to an open space toward the end of the bar. Sim slid behind three girls with brown beer bottles, each of them uniformed in white wifebeaters and loose-fitting jeans. Between guitar riffs, Sim caught a slice of their conversation: They were complaining about girls who brought guys to the bar with them. One girl leaned back so that her shoulder pressed into Sim's. Sim pretended not to notice.

The bartender had her hands full with all of the girls waiting for drinks, but she came over to Pru almost as soon as she reached the bar.

"Hey, Pru," she said with a grin. She glanced at Sim and then looked back to Prudence. "Going for a newbie tonight?"

"She's just a friend," Prudence said. "And she's straight. Sim, this is Candace."

Sim smiled at her and raised a hand. Not even ten minutes in the place and she was already labeled as an outsider. But at least now she knew that Pru didn't have any wrong ideas about her.

"It's my pleasure, Sim." Candace smiled and then looked at Pru with open disbelief. Prudence ignored it. "We'll each have a Bongo Tree," she said.

Chuckling, Candace nodded and turned away from them. Behind the bar there were twenty or so beer bottles lined up, each of them with a bright, well-designed label. Except for the one on the end, which was all white.

"They have Kaianide." Sim said. "I didn't know that Cader distributed them here—"

"He doesn't," Pru said quickly. But Candace, returning with their Bongo Trees, had already heard her.

"You know about Kaianide?" she asked. She put the two bottles onto the bar and snapped off the caps. The beer fizzed as the metal lids clanked onto the counter. The conversation behind Sim continued, but she was already bored with it and tried to tune it out.

"I brew it," Sim said.

Candace's eyebrows shot up. She looked to Prudence. "This one's a keeper, Pru— beautiful, talented, and dangerous." She winked at Sim and went to the other end of the bar to serve a girl with a jet-black mohawk and mirrored aviators. Prudence glowered. Sim wondered why she was in such a horrible mood—even worse than usual.

"You shouldn't go around telling people your business. That's what I was trying to tell you this morning," Pru said. "Keep it to yourself." Pru didn't seem terribly worried, but her tone was serious. She was starting to sound like Kai, with the way she was telling Sim what to do all the time.

"She seemed nice." Sim shrugged.

"Candace can be trusted," Pru said with a nod. "But you never know who else is listening. Anyone looking for an extra sol will sell you out to the Guard in an instant. The less people who know, the better. Most people aren't nice."

Sim pressed her lips together and then took a long swig of her Bongo Tree. Pru really was starting to sound like Kai.

"I don't mean to boss you around." Prudence took a drink. "But this city can be brutal. You have to watch your back or bad shit will happen to you. It's better not to find out the hard way."

"I guess you're right," Sim said.

A peal of laughter erupted from the front corner of the bar. Sim followed Pru's annoyed glare to a group of girls with long, shiny hair, fancy tops, and lime-green mixed drinks. They were stroking one another's arms, leaning in together, now dancing. Prudence was right: It was better to be safe. Sim wanted to change the subject. "So who was that girl outside?" Prudence frowned deeper, and Sim wished she'd thought of something else to ask.

"Just some clingy—she's no one." Prudence shook her head. She studied the label of her Bongo Tree, spinning the bottle slowly, trailing one edge of it along the top of the bar. Sim looked around again, careful not to set her eyes on the wifebeater girl behind her. A girl with a black unicorn tattoo wrapped around her bicep pushed her hand into the wall, against the front spokes of the bike stencil. She balanced herself as she leaned forward to kiss a girl with long blonde hair and big, thick-framed glasses. The girl with the tattoo took her free hand and slid it under the other's shirt, wrapped her fingers around her waist, returned her embrace. They were caught in a dizzy balancing act between what was appropriate for a public space and what their mutual desire ached to express. But only Sim seemed to notice. Most people were happily drunk by then.

"A shot for each of you," Candace said, grabbing Sim's attention. She slapped two small glasses onto the bar and streamed a glowing purple liquid into them.

Prudence grinned. "My favorite," she said.

"And there's more where that came from. You know I like to see that smile." Candace laughed and cocked her head toward Sim. "And this one needs to loosen up."

Pru's grin deepened and Sim noticed for the first time that she had dimples. "More might be in order," she said, raising an eyebrow. "It's this one's first time here."

"Really?" Candace slapped another shot glass onto the bar. "Well then in that case, I'll be having one too."

Before Sim had time to be embarrassed, Prudence had raised her shot in a toast.

"Welcome to the Geraldine, honey," Candace said.

They clinked their glasses together and threw their heads back. The toxic-looking purple liquid chilled the back of Sim's mouth. She stifled a cough and grabbed her throat when it turned burning hot. She looked up at Prudence, who was laughing at her.

"What was that?" Sim coughed.

"Knew you'd like it," Candace said, and then she was off to serve the other girls.

"Ice fairy nectar," Prudence explained. "It's from where I grew up. You can only find it in the North. The fairies spell it to ice your throat."

Sim swayed a little in her seat.

"And burn your stomach," Pru added with a grin.

"You're from Siccor?"

"Used to be."

For the first time since they had come into the Geraldine, Sim caught Prudence subtly glancing around the bar, taking everything in, examining everyone who was there. Occasionally her eyes would linger, but never long enough for Sim to figure out who it was she'd been looking at. They went outside again and Pru talked to one of the girls while Sim sat on a wooden planter near the door. Sim stared off, pretending not to care that she was just awkwardly sitting there, and waiting for Prudence to acknowledge her again while the other girls kept giving her curious glances.

"You're good to get home, right?" Pru said, turning to her suddenly.

Sim frowned and then realized that Pru wanted her to leave, now that she'd fended off the blonde girl.

"Yeah, of course," Sim said, standing. She hesitated for a moment and then rushed toward the alley without looking back. Pru's cloaking spell kept making Sim's eyes turn away from her bike, until her hands finally found the grips and pulled it upright.

"I see you haven't taken my advice."

Sim nearly jumped out of her skin. A silhouette leaned against a dark doorway she'd passed on her way into the alley. She caught her breath when she realized it was the same girl she'd seen in the factory, almost a week ago.

"What the hell?"

"I didn't mean to scare you," the girl said without a trace of an apology in her tone.

"Okay." Sim started to push her bike toward the street, but the girl stepped in front of her, into the dim firelight at the mouth of the alley.

"I need to talk to you," she said.

"Who are you?"

"My name is Lilith. I'm a strix." She looked like she'd just admitted to being something vile. Her face was guarded, as if she expected Sim to hate her for it.

Sim shook her head. "What's a strix?"

Lilith sighed and rolled her eyes. "You're a magicweaver. I'd assumed you must be a quester. The questers know."

"I'm not either of those things."

"You can calibrate a magicweaver's compass but you're not a magicweaver. Right. I'm not an idiot."

"What exactly do you want from me?" Sim asked, getting slightly defensive at the girl's tone.

"Nothing. Forget it." Without saying anything more, Lilith shoved past her and disappeared into the shadow of a dark alley.

"Hey, wait!" Sim called after her, but she was gone, again.

Sim had a bad feeling for the entire ride home, like she was being watched. It was just paranoia, and embarrassment at being so awkward at the Geraldine. But she never had to go back to the bar again if she didn't want to. The happy drunkenness numbing her temples made it easy for the awkward feeling to dissipate. Sim enjoyed the bike ride in the dark, aware that biking drunk was dangerous but not really caring. She was only a little tipsy. She'd be fine. Lilith. The girl's name was Lilith. Sim was sure she could find that factory again, if she tried. Even if she didn't remember exactly where it was, she did remember exactly what it looked like, and she was sure that Azzer wouldn't mind at all if she borrowed that compass. Something about the girl piqued Sim's interest. She had an inexplicable sense that Lilith could tell her something that she needed to know.

The next morning Sim sat on the couch in the living room, losing herself in *Saffron and Pulchrina*'s fateful thrust into forbidden romance, in an effort to forget about her own empty love life. Heavy boots stomped up the front steps and across the porch. The door snapped open and Pru stepped in, stumbling as if her legs didn't quite work right. A black hood was drawn up over her head, hiding everything but the profile of her nose and a mess of dark bangs. She yanked off her aviators and threw them onto a table near the door.

"Oh," she said, pausing when she realized that there was someone in the living room. Tiny pink veins colored the whites of her eyes, and her face was paler than usual. "Hey."

"Hey."

Pru sank into the couch beside Sim. The smell of alcohol and cigarettes clung to her short, messy hair. A moment of silence tensed up Sim's back. She wondered if she should ask Pru what had happened, or if she'd be crossing a line. Pru pulled the paper off a bagel she'd gotten from the corner deli and bit into the toasted whole-wheat bread with cream cheese and a tomato sandwiched between it. She kept her gaze set on the floor, and Sim pretended to go back to reading her book.

"Good night?" Sim asked a minute later. She couldn't help it.

Prudence snorted a laugh. "Yeah, I guess," she said between mouthfuls.

There was an air of mischief, or promiscuousness, that hovered around Pru: the way she leaned her upper back against the lower part of the couch and put one foot up on the coffee table, the way her lips hardly moved when she chewed. Sim hid behind her book and decided not to ask any more questions.

"Ugh, why does my coffee taste like cigarettes?" Prudence said. She slapped the cup onto the table and buried her head in her palms. Her hood fell down onto her back and her hair stuck out between her fingers. She rested her elbows on top of her legs and stared down at the ground between her knees.

"I need to stop doing this," she mumbled. "I should have just come back with you."

Sim lowered her book. At first she thought Pru was talking to herself, since she was still gazing down at her boots.

"Stop doing what?"

Pru shot her a frown. "What do you think?" She blinked and shook her head, and Sim knew that she hadn't meant to snap at her.

"I don't know why I do it." Pru's raspy cigarette voice made it sound like she was about to cry. "It's like I'm searching for something, but I don't know what it is. I see a girl I'm attracted to, and the next thing I know we're making out and then we're going to her apartment or wherever. There's never any real sort of connection. It's always physical, and in the end it's always the same: I wake up and I run. Sorry," Pru said with a slight look of embarrassment. "I don't mean to put this on you. It's not your problem."

"It's okay," Sim said. "I don't mind. What do you think it is you're searching for?"

"I don't know." Pru stared at her coffee as if it would give her the answer. "Something real," she said finally.

"What do you mean?"

"A connection; I want a real connection with someone."

"You're searching for love," Sim said, and earned a dark glare from Pru. The glare softened again when she realized that Sim was being serious.

"I don't know. Maybe." Pru picked up the coffee and took another sip, swallowing it with an expression that was worthy of a tequila shot. "I doubt it."

"Maybe it takes time to have a connection with someone. You could try letting something develop."

Prudence stared blankly ahead, her mouth opened ever so slightly. A look of vulnerable confusion softened her features.

"What is it that you're so afraid of?" Sim asked, without even thinking.

"I don't know," Pru whispered. This was her, the real her, with the mask of toughness and cold ambivalence pushed aside just for a moment. Sim realized with a shock that Pru was just as confused as she was. They were stuck, through no choice of their own, and would remain stuck until fate came along to shove them into a violent shock of change, so that they could be wounded and heal and become people who were totally new and yet totally the same. Like phoenixes, born out of fire.

Drangs pranced into the room and jumped onto the table. Kai's recent attempts at training him to stay off the furniture were failing horribly. He looked at Pru with wide eyes and little cooing mews. She flattened down his hair and held the bagel out to his mouth. He started to lick the cream cheese off it. The moment had passed, and Sim was glad. She wasn't sure how much more of Prudence's self-loathing she could handle.

"I need to get some sleep," Pru said, pushing herself to her feet. She grabbed her coffee cup. "Thanks, Sim," she mumbled without looking at her. And then added, "Night."

"Wait, Pru?" Sim hesitated. Pru looked back at her, eyebrows raised. "Do you know what a strix is?"

Pru's eyes darkened. "Why would you ask me that?"

"I—" Sim stumbled, confused by Pru's strange, almost angry expression. "There's this girl who came up to me in the Narrows. She said she was a strix, and seemed to expect me to know what she meant. She said that a quester would know."

"You're sure she said strix? What else did she say?"

"That was it. She left when I told her I didn't know what she was talking about. The first time I saw her, when I was in the west testing out this gadget for Azzer, she told me to stop going to the Narrows."

"You saw her twice?" Prudence frowned deeply at Sim's nod and scratched the side of her head. "And she didn't try anything?"

"What do you mean?"

"She didn't attack you?"

"No, I wasn't worried about that at all. She didn't touch me."

"She can't be a strix," Pru said, though her gaze remained troubled. "That's impossible. Maybe she was messing with you."

"But what's a strix?"

Pru shifted her eyes to the wall, frowning. "Can we talk about it later?"

"Yeah, sure."

"Cool." Pru went to the steps. A minute later Sim heard the shower turn on in the bathroom. She closed her book and wondered if Pru would ever actually explain anything to her.

VI

The red tinge of a sunburn spanned across Wood's nose and cheeks. She turned a page of her book and pushed her bangs off her forehead and into a cowlick. Sweat beaded on her neck and shoulders. Fans and air-cooling gadgets only worked with a steady stream of magic dust, so Stein's had neither. The magic-dust grid of Greater Terresin didn't extend to the Bikeway Narrows, and no one had the magic to spare for something as trivial as cooling the air. Instead everything slowed, and the Bikeway Narrows became even more estranged from the quick-moving world of Greater Terresin.

"I can't stand this." Wood threw her book on the table and fanned herself with her hands. She narrowed her eyes at Sim and then leaned toward her. "Ice my coffee?" she whispered, pushing her mug forward.

"I don't know." Sim glanced around. "I shouldn't—"

"No one's going to notice. Please, Sim? I'm about to faint from this heat."

Sim nodded and bit her lip. "Okay." She wrapped her hands around Wood's mug and shut the café noises and coffee smells out of her mind so that she could focus on the energy in her chest and icy thoughts from her past. The magic flowed into her body and out of her palms in a tingly wave. Sim took her hands away and put them on the back of her neck. A shiver ran down her spine from the sharp change in temperature.

"Ugh, I love you." Wood grabbed the coffee, put it up to her cheek, and then drank it in gulps. "You're the best."

"Come here," Sim said. She glanced around to make sure no one was looking and put her hands on Wood's face, just under her ears.

"That feels so good." Wood closed her eyes and put her hands over Sim's. She leaned closer and guided Sim's fingers down onto her neck. A giddy feeling fluttered in Sim's stomach and she fought the sudden urge to pull away.

"I'm sorry I'm so sweaty and gross," Wood said, leaning back in her chair. She held

Sim's hands on the table and wiped her sweat off them.

Sim swallowed. "It's fine," she said.

"It's crazy how you can just do that."

"I'm going to ice mine, too." Sim pulled her hands away and cast the spell on her own coffee. She felt that she was being awkward, but didn't know how to stop.

"If you've got it, you gotta use it," Wood said, cocking her head. "No shame."

"I know. I just think that Prudence was probably right when she said—"

"Yeah, yeah, I know: Be subtle and secretive. But how did you deal with it when you were growing up?"

"It was never a big deal. There were a ton of spells I had to do for Jaylenik, the girl I worked for. She was too lazy to do anything for herself. I'm a pro at waterproofing thanks to her. She was really sensitive about her dragon-leather boots."

"She sounds like a bitch."

"She was." Sim clenched her jaw. "She is." Even though she hadn't seen Jaylenik in months, the very thought of her still hardened Sim's heart with a solid hatred.

"Well, it's a good thing that you got away from there. It was really brave of you to just run away like that, without having a plan or anything."

Sim stared down at the table. "It wasn't brave. I didn't have a choice."

"You always have a choice. It was so easy for me to move to Terresin for school. Like the road here was paved with gold. I was living in this huge, inbred bubble of privilege before I found the Narrows. You'd hate it, Sim. It's so boring. But it's not so bad now that I know how to break free. Anyway, we should get to work. See you here after?"

"You know it."

"Yes!" Azzer yelled, and a loud crash came from the back of the shop.

A pair of charmed headphones slipped out of Sim's hands and scattered its pieces across the cluttered countertop. Azzer burst through the curtain, almost at a run.

"I did it," Azzer said, coming up to the counter with his eyes sparkling. "It was so obvious the whole time! When you're trying to augment vision you can't just create an instrument and calibrate it; you have to make sure it self-calibrates to each individual. Of course."

"Wait, what? Azzer." She waved a hand at him to remind him that she was there. "I have no idea what you're talking about."

A smile brightened Azzer's face. He took a step back. "I think you might be impressed." He lifted his hands, holding a pair of goggles with tinted lenses and a belted leather strap.

"Haven't you always had those?"

"These aren't ordinary goggles, Sim." Azzer looked down at them admiringly. "Words can't do them justice. Try them on."

Sim hesitated. She'd told herself that she wasn't going to test any more of his gadgets, not after the compass incident. But she set her jaw, took the goggles, and pulled them over her eyes. Their glass was dark like sunglasses, but other than the shaded room, everything looked normal.

"I don't think it's working—"

"You have to calibrate it. Each time you put them on you have to activate them with your own energy."

Sim looked at him. "But then only people who can calibrate will be able to use them."

"Just try them out."

Immediately Sim could feel that the goggles were different from anything Azzer had ever made before. A bond opened between her and the gadget, so that her energy was constantly flowing into them and their magic constantly flowing into her. It felt strange; the goggles became a part of her, just like her fingernails or teeth.

Sim opened her eyes to a world full of color. Azzer glowed yellow, with a pulsing rainbow belt where he kept his tools. Everything in the shop took on a new dimension. The compasses and headphones and treasure boxes glowed in indigo, magenta, and violet. The pocket watches and leather gloves and old bike wheels—things that didn't need calibration—stayed as they had always been, though now they looked colorless, lifeless. At the beginning of the day Sim had set up a bookshelf to display Kai's potions, which Azzer had agreed to sell. Behind the goggles they looked like tubes of neon with smoky light seeping from their cork stoppers, probably from the potent plant magic held in Kai's herbs. The tree that Sim had sculpted when Wood had first come into the shop glimmered with colors somewhere beyond violet.

"It's a trip wearing them in here, isn't it?" Azzer said with a laugh. "Like being on pixie pollen. Come on, let's go outside; it'll make more sense out there."

Sim tiptoed behind him, walking slowly so that she wouldn't get overwhelmed by the assault on her vision. But Azzer was right: Everything was calmer outside. They went across the street. The Incubator looked like a glowing circus sandwiched between dark apartment buildings. Some of their windows shimmered with a light blue glow. Thin red latticework, like flimsy fences made of red light, guarded a few of the doors. Azzer smoothed his hair back and slid a pair of bronze goggles with clear lenses over his eyes.

"Masking spells," Azzer said, pointing to one of the windows. "That's how the dwarves have been making it seem like this place is deserted." He saw Sim looking at one of the red fences and added, "Those would be alarm charms. You can see the gadget glowing there in the upper corner of the window."

A shock of green light streaked across the air just above them. Sim stumbled back. "What was that?" she breathed.

Azzer laughed and clapped his hands. "Magnificent," he said. "They're picking up the long-distance charms, as well. You can send messages or charms as far as you want to, so long as you have enough magic dust. But I'm surprised to see a long-distance charm all the way out here....You see, every spell that's cast or charm that's activated leaves behind a magic trail. That's what these goggles are showing us."

"How do you take them off?"

Azzer's excitement faded a notch. "I thought you'd want to experiment with them more."

"I do. But I don't want to break them on you."

"They're yours. You get to have the first pair."

Sim started to protest, but Azzer held up a hand to stop her. "In return, you can play with them and let me know what you find out. You're more in touch with your magic than anyone else I know, and I can't just give them to anyone off the street. You felt the connection stay open, right?" Sim nodded, and Azzer continued, "I'm hoping that you can direct the goggles to show you other things, or to control how much magic you see, depending on how much energy you put into them. I need you to explore that for me."

"Okay," Sim agreed, though she still felt hesitant. There had to be a reason people couldn't usually see magic trails. She wasn't sure if the goggles were a good thing or not.

"Just be careful not to drain yourself."

"Right." Sim closed her eyes and drew her magic back into herself. A strange feeling sucked at her mind as the connection broke apart, similar to the way her ears felt when they were under water and then suddenly came up into the air. Sim pulled the goggles from her eyes and put them up on her forehead.

Azzer had done the same, making his bangs stick straight up. "Back to work," he said with a laugh.

"Back to work," Sim agreed, following him back inside.

She was about to put the goggles away, but stopped and narrowed her eyes at the headphone parts strewed across the counter. She pulled them over her eyes again. As soon as she calibrated the goggles, the different parts of the headphones glowed in different colors. Some pieces had two or three colors glowing from them, and some had only one. When Sim put a red, yellow, and blue cog onto a blue spindle, the cog turned blue and the colors of the other pieces shimmered and changed. There were more blues now. Sim attached a yellow and blue dial to the cog and spindle, and watched as it all turned blue. The colors shifted again. It was like a puzzle. She was finished in ten minutes, holding a pair of headphones, which glowed bright indigo, in her hands.

"Azzer!" she yelled, still staring at the headphones, hardly believing what she'd just done.

Clanking and shifting sounded in the back room, and Azzer reemerged with the bronze goggles over his own eyes. He looked to the headphones and smiled. "I don't think we're ever going to look at the world in the same way again, Sim."

Sim smiled back and nodded. "I guess not." For the first time she felt the fuzzy satisfaction of knowing that she was present for the beginning of something important. She couldn't quite wrap her head around the thought, but suddenly the tiny Bikeway Narrows and Terresin, encased in its stone walls, and even all of Pulchra, felt new and bigger than it ever had. Adventure. And she didn't have to take a step to find it.

"Whiteflower milk latte," Sim told her favorite barista, the dark-haired girl who had no issues with yelling at customers to shut up when they got out of hand over a silly political argument.

"Sure thing," she said. Her words lilted with a slight Siccorian accent, so that she skipped the "h." The dragon screamed and the whiteflower milk frothed. At the espresso machine stood the silently brooding beast-man—that's what Sim liked to call him in her mind, since the dragons never seemed to give him any trouble. He was quiet, straightforward, and didn't feel the need to engage in meaningless chitchat with the customers. He was a poet, maybe. Sim wasn't sure. After hanging out in the same café for months, she still didn't know the employees' names. It was easier to pretend that she didn't care.

The smell of hot coffee calmed Sim's nerves as she scanned the tables. The café was quiet at the moment, with the awkward writers scribbling in their notebooks and the illustrators calmly inking sketches on the backs of old fliers and everyone else pouring their attention into either books or zines. Wood was sitting at the end of the long communal table, her bangs hanging in front of her face and her attention absorbed in a thin pamphlet.

"Whiteflower milk latte," the beast-man said, just loudly enough for Sim to hear. He slid the drink onto the counter, gingerly switched dragons, and started on the next order. Sim smiled down at her mug. A fairy danced in the foam, drawn in the delicate dark lines of crema. It was impressive, but Sim was too distracted to tell him that she thought so. She walked slowly toward the empty seat across from Wood, who flung her bangs out of her face and scribbled something.

"Working hard?" Sim asked, standing across from her. Wood looked up with a slightly annoyed expression, and then smiled when she saw who it was.

"Oh, hey." She put her pen down and ran her fingers through the long part of her hair. Her eyes settled on the goggles hanging around Sim's neck. She grinned and raised an eyebrow. "New look?"

"Azzer gave them to me." Sim put her latte on the table and sat down in the chair.

"I like it. They look good on you. As long as they're not hiding those beautiful eyes of yours."

"Thanks." Sim blushed and ignored the compliment. "They're—" She looked around to make sure that no one was listening, even though Azzer had never told her to keep his new invention a secret. "They actually allow you to see magic as it's working. Like neon streams of light. I've hardly used them yet, but they make fixing gadgets so much easier. I wish I could show you."

"So then do!" Wood laughed and held out her hand. "What?" she said when Sim paused.

"Well, you have to calibrate them yourself or they won't work."

Wood's face fell. She laughed and raised her eyebrows to cover her disappointment. "Seriously? But hardly anyone knows how to calibrate. He'll never be able to sell them."

"I know; that's what I told him."

Wood leaned back in her chair and looked away with a frown.

"I'm sorry," Sim said, scrambling for something that would make her feel better. "I shouldn't have even brought it up. It's really not even that big of a deal—"

"But it is, isn't it?" Wood snapped her gaze back to Sim. "The best schools in Pulchra teach kids how to calibrate when they're in elementary school, when it's still so easy to learn. But those are all private schools. My parents aren't poor by any means—my dad's a healer in the town where I come from and they're paying for me to go to college now—but there's no way they could have afforded a fancy private school where I could have learned how to calibrate."

"At least you get to go to college," Sim said softly. "And you won't have to borrow from the banks."

"I know." Wood threw out her arms in an exaggerated shrug. "I shouldn't be complaining. And yet I can't help but feel like I've been cheated."

They were quiet while Sim frowned down at the fairy in her latte and Wood glared off at the wall again.

"Anyway, I have to pick classes for next semester." Wood turned back to her pamphlet. Large stars already marked the margins next to classes that she'd been considering. "I really wish I could take one of these magicweaving classes. Then I could learn how to calibrate and spell cast. But my parents refuse to get me a wand. And they'll only pay for tuition while I'm in school, so all the money I make at the book shop has to go to rent."

"I have a wand," Sim said. She'd nearly forgotten about it. "I'm not using it. You can have it."

"Really?" Wood scrunched her eyebrows up and together.

"Yeah." Sim shrugged and wondered what she was getting herself into even as the words slipped out of her mouth. She scratched at the spots of wax that had dripped from the chandelier above them. "Someone gave it to me. It's literally just sitting in my drawer. You'd be putting it to good use."

"Wands are a lot of money. I wouldn't be able to—"

"You can pay me back when you're a successful magicweaver," Sim said with a smile.

"That would be so awesome, Sim, I can't even begin to..." Wood shook her head and beamed. "That's really, really nice of you. I have to register for classes next week so—"

"So I'll bring it to the Narrows tomorrow and give it to you then."

Wood squealed and hit the table lightly with her palms. The latte cups at Stein's were wide and shallow—perfect for Sim to hide behind, pretending to sip at her drink when she was really covering a content smile. But in the back of her mind she wondered if it was really a good idea to give away the wand that Sir Nogron had enlisted her to steal, the very wand that was the reason she had had no choice but to run away from her old life. But she was sure it would be fine. No one would know that it had belonged to Leonidas Lightshield. Cader had said that explorer wands were common.

"Awesome," Wood said, writing in her notebook. "So then that takes care of my Monidy and Remidy afternoons. I'll schedule everything else around that. I can take ancient Munian literature or the economics of magic dust. What do you think?"

Wood leaned forward to push the pamphlet toward Sim so that she could read about each class. Their knees pressed together under the table and energy tickled Sim's body so that her chest felt like it was inflated with helium. She pulled her leg away and sat back farther in her chair, pretending to focus on the class descriptions.

"Munian literature for sure," Sim said.

"Definitely. I would never take an economics class."

As much as Sim tried to listen to Wood's explanation of why economics was the bane of humankind, she was distracted by thoughts of what she'd just done, offering to give away that wand. But she had told Wood that she could have it and now there was no going back. Sim took another sip of her latte and smiled at whatever Wood had just said. It would be okay. This would bring them closer together: They'd be better friends now and they'd have another excuse to hang out. Sim let the happy energy bubbling up from her stomach overshadow that little itch of worry, and the whole thing was easily forgotten.

* * *

The wand was still in its place in her bottom drawer, now buried beneath a bundle of her old clothes. The wood was smooth to the touch, and just slightly gnarled at the end, where it fit perfectly into Sim's hand.

Cader was leaving his meditation room just as Sim was on her way downstairs. "Whatcha got?" he asked. His face was calm and his eyes clear. He was on a high from standing on his head for so long. There would be no hiding anything from him.

"It's nothing," Sim said, but handed him the wand anyway.

"Ah, that wand again. How exactly did you get your hands on it?"

"It's a long story," she said. They stared at each other for a moment and then Cader grinned. His dimples were deep and his eyes sparkling.

"Okay," he said with a short laugh and a shake of his head. "No explanation needed. I'd keep it close, though. That's a pretty sweet amplifier." He gave it back to her and went toward the steps: Baking smells from the kitchen drew Cader like a magnet. Sim sighed as she followed behind him, though she wasn't sure why she felt so relieved.

"Keep your fingers out of there," Kai snapped.

"I just want a little," Cader whined, to annoy her.

"Heading to the Narrows?" Prudence asked when Sim passed the living room. She was sprawled on the couch, wearing ripped black jeans that looked like she'd owned them her entire life. A half-read book hung from her hand and reading glasses perched low on her nose. Pru was never awake this early. She glanced up at Sim. "Care if I ride with you?"

Sim's response caught in her throat.

"I just need to grab some things," Pru added.

"I can wait," Sim said quickly. "Yeah, let's head over together."

Prudence folded down the corner of her page and threw the book and her glasses onto the coffee table. "Meet you in the back."

Kai appeared from the kitchen and stood in the doorway between the foyer and the living room. "Where are you two off to?" She pushed her clunky frames up her nose and then said to Sim, "I thought you didn't have work until later today."

"If you had a bike you could come with us," Prudence said with a small smile as she hurried past Kai and ran up the steps toward her room.

"I would kill myself if I got on a bike," Kai yelled at Pru's back. She turned to Sim, looked at her for a moment, and then went back to the kitchen.

"I made breakfast bars," Kai said, reappearing with a tray in her hands. "You can take some with you." She held out a plate of mud-brown, green-speckled rectangles. Shimmering protection charms buffered a centimeter of the air around each bar, so

77

that they wouldn't stick together.

"They're the best," Cader said from the kitchen. "Take a bunch or I'll eat them all myself."

"Shut up, Cader."

"What? I'm being serious."

"I want some!" Pru called from up in her room.

"One's good for me," Sim said, taking a bar from the top. The charm felt smooth and staticky. She slid it into her bag, between a book and a few tools from the shop.

Kai followed Sim through the kitchen and stopped at the back door. "Are you sure you don't want—"

"I love these," Prudence said, and grabbed a handful of the bars as she passed her. "Thanks, Kai."

With a swirl of smoke, Prudence dispersed the protection charm and bit into the sludgy hunk of nutrients. "Did you get some?" she asked Sim, her mouth full. She shoved her aviators over her eyes.

Sim nodded, and Prudence stopped at the bottom of the steps to turn back up to Kai with a smile. "Thanks, Kai. You're the best."

"Don't cause any trouble," was Kai's stoic response. She turned from them and shut the kitchen door behind her. "Don't you have something to do?" Sim could hear her saying to Cader.

"Nothing but spend time with my favorite person."

Prudence grabbed her bike and swung her right leg over the handlebars, which were low and straight like those on most of the bikes in the Narrows. She stepped onto her pedal and moved toward the walkway on the side of the house. Sim hurried to keep up with her.

"That's the thing about those cruisers," Prudence said. Once they were out on Kailash Street, she circled back and around Sim so that she was riding beside her. "They're so slow."

"I know. But it's better than nothing. And I get to sit up straight."

"You should try to find a road bike. Cader can probably find one for you if you ask him."

Pru took the lead, turning down streets that eventually took them through the Mondran Quarter. Since the bridge incident, Sim had been keeping her ears perked for any talk of Mondrans, and from what she could tell they weren't so different from followers of Veldindor, except that they thought Mondra to be the one and true goddess and they allowed the rules of her scripture to dictate everything from when they prayed to what they ate. The main road through the quarter was quick and dangerous, with carriages parked on both sides of the street. Mondrans were everywhere, crossing the road at the middle of the block, hurrying into shops, and gathering in unisex throngs outside of their temples. The men wore loose, bleached pants under their robes, and white shoes. Pointed, felt hats rested on their heads even though the air was warm. The women wore long robes with white stockings and ivory pumps. Their hair was cut to the shoulder, slightly curled, and covered with lace.

From behind round eyeglasses, a man stared at Sim in her brown shorts and baggy button-down with an expression that made her feel not quite threatened, but extremely uncomfortable. Usually the Mondrans wouldn't even look at outsiders.

A truck was double-parked on the road in front of them so that it took up half of the street. Grunting dwarves hauled bags of flour across the sidewalk and into a small bakery. Pru glanced over her shoulder as they glided into the open lane. A driver behind them laid on his horn, angry that he had to slow down. She went to the side of the street again, in front of the parked truck, and Sim rushed to do the same. The carriage sped up so that it was next to Sim, and then slowed so that it stayed beside her. At first she thought the carriage was turning right, and then realized that it wasn't turning at all but was trying to shove her off the road. The speeding bumper was inches from her leg. Sim swerved to the right. Her front tire smashed into a parked carriage and sent her flying off her saddle. Somehow she managed to hit the carriage sideways, her shoulder breaking the impact. Sim tumbled onto the sidewalk and gasped to catch her breath. Prudence stood in the street, one leg on either side of her frame, her arms flailing around her in wild anger, cursing at the carriage driver, who was stopped at a red light.

The driver leaned over the passenger seat and stuck his head out the window. He was middle-aged, but the anger etched onto his face made him look ancient. He pushed his fuzzy white devotional hat back on his head and in a heavy accent he said, "Stay off the road. Next time I'll run you over."

"You're gonna fucking kill someone," Prudence yelled back.

"Your kind aren't wanted here. Go away." The driver disappeared back into the car.

Pru's jaw was clenched and her brows lowered over her eyes. Her hands were balled into fists at her sides. She grunted in anger and turned to Sim, who was picking up her bike and rolling it back into the street.

"You okay?" she asked Sim.

"Yeah." Sim leaned over her frame and examined it; there were no apparent issues. Her shoulder throbbed, but she'd be fine.

"Good. Let's go."

Sim followed her, wondering why she was in such a hurry. The carriage was still stopped a few yards ahead of them. As she pedaled toward it, Prudence unsnapped the black pouch that she kept on her belt. A short sword, its length hidden by a de-sizing charm when sheathed, appeared in Prudence's hand. She gripped the handle and sat forward on her saddle.

The first slash was quick and easy. Prudence leaned over the side of her bike and sank the blade into the carriage's rear tire. Air hissed out of it. Prudence was slashing the front tire before the driver could even react. Then she was past the car. Sim could see the Mondran frowning at her as she flew past his door.

"Hey! What the—" A stream of angry slurs came from the car window. The door clicked open. Prudence turned around to face the driver with a glare. She flipped him off and then she and Sim raced forward. There was no way he could catch them without his tires, but they still didn't slow down until they got to the bridge. In silence they climbed the high incline, and then flew down toward blocks and blocks of reddish factories that eventually led to the little wedge of a neighborhood that was the Bikeway Narrows.

"You'll never guess what happened to me on the way over here," Sim said to Wood as she eased into the seat across from her.

Wood narrowed her eyes and cocked her head. "Ran into a wild dragon?"

"Funny," Sim said, and launched into the story about the Mondran carriage driver.

"Wow, Sim," Wood said, looking worried. "You're lucky you didn't get hurt. You're okay, right?"

"My shoulder hurts a little," Sim admitted. "But it'll be fine. I'll have Cader heal it when I get back."

Wood nodded, and frowned up at Sim. "It's getting to be ridiculous, this feud between the bikers and the Mondrans."

"I know," Sim agreed. "I just don't get it. The most direct way to the bridge is through the Mondran Quarter. It's not like we do anything to bother them. We're just riding through."

"It makes sense once you understand Mondran Culture."

"Really?" Sim asked. She hated this feeling of being ignorant. But she couldn't pretend to know something that she didn't have a clue about.

"The Scriptures of Mondra say that it's wrong to wear flashy clothing, or to dress immodestly. When Mondran children see bikers riding through in shorts or tank tops or bright colors, they start to question their parents and their beliefs, and the parents get pissed."

"But it's so hot out!" Sim laughed. "Of course we're going to wear shorts."

"They don't wear them. They deal with the heat because they believe that they'll be damned in the afterlife if they dress immodestly."

"Seriously?"

Wood nodded. "That's their religion. It's easier for them to follow it if they're closed off from the rest of the city. And they are, mostly: No one but Mondrans ever goes to the Mondran Quarter. No one has a reason to. Except for the bikers riding through to get to the Narrows Bridge. I wouldn't be surprised if they tried to close down the streets to stop the bikers, except they won't do that, of course, because the Mondrans ride around everywhere in their carriages. It's the ultimate sign of wealth for them."

"That's crazy," Sim said. "The streets belong to everyone."

"I agree. That's what I argued in a paper for the class I took on it last semester. But it's not going to change how Mondrans view outsiders."

"I guess we'll just have to deal with it then, and so will they." Sim opened her bag and rummaged inside. "So, I didn't forget..." This was a bad idea, a horrible idea. She never should have brought it up. She put the wand on the table. It stayed between them for a moment, with Wood just staring down at it. Then she took it in her hand and the deed was done.

"I can't believe you're actually giving this to me."

"I'm sure you'll put it to good use." Sim forced a smile. She didn't want to talk about it anymore. She took her book and opened to the page she'd marked. Saffron and Pulchrina were obviously into each other, obviously perfect for each other, but they were from warring nations and forbidden to love each other. At this point in the story, they were both doing all they could to hide their feelings; Saffron thinking that Pulchrina couldn't possibly be interested in him, and Pulchrina thinking the exact same thing. A wild thunderstorm had them stuck alone together in a cave, and Sim thought she knew exactly where things were going.

Wood looked up at her with a glint in her eyes. Her smile held a touch of playful mischief.

"What?" Sim asked.

"When do you have to go into work?"

Sim glanced at the multi-dialed watch that she'd built for herself at the Incubator. "I have about an hour." Really she had a half hour. She figured Azzer wouldn't care too much if she came in a little late. Things were always slow at the beginning of the day.

"Want to give me that spell-casting lesson now?"

"Here?" Sim looked around the nearly full café.

"No, Sim," Wood said with an amused roll of her eyes. "We can do it at the wall. I know a place where no one ever goes."

Sim drew her lips to the corner of her mouth and put on a thinking face.

"Please, Sim," Wood said, folding her hands in front of her and leaning closer.

"Okay, okay." Sim gave in, though of course she'd planned on doing it all along. She took a mason jar out of her bag and sloshed the rest of her coffee into it. "We'll be needing this," she said, holding it up. "I'm starting you with my favorite little trick."

Wood smiled so that her eyes shone and Sim's heart skipped a beat. "Sounds great," Wood said, and they both stood, bundled their books into their bags, and headed across the street and through the green tunnel of vines and weeds that led to the Old Wall.

"You have to concentrate," Sim said for the third time. Wood was getting frustrated. She wasn't good at this, not at all. Nothing was happening. Sim had turned her coffee from hot to cold to hot to cold so many times that she was afraid that she'd shatter her mason jar. She rubbed her shoulder and stifled a grimace. The spot where she had landed on the car was starting to throb steadily and give her a headache.

"I can't do it," Wood said, throwing out her arms.

"You can. Just concentrate and try again."

Wood crossed her arms over her chest and glared off into the distance.

"Maybe you should just read the book," Sim offered.

Wood met Sim's eyes with a sharp scowl. "Maybe I should just wait for classes to start and then a real teacher can show me how to do it."

Sim blinked and Wood looked back to the wall.

"You have to be getting to work anyway, don't you?" Wood asked.

Sim jerked her wrist up to look at her watch. An hour and a half had passed. She hadn't even thought of keeping track of time. "Crap. Yes."

Sim wished she could do something—anything—to make Wood feel better. "It took me a really long time to get it," Sim lied. "I had to practice a lot before anything happened. You just have to stick with it."

"Right," Wood said, pressing her lips together.

"You can do this, Wood. I know you can."

That had to be the energy she felt every time they were close to each other; some sort of magical ability that they held in common. If she had to lie to Wood to get her to tap into that energy and develop it, then she'd lie. If she had to step back and make herself seem less capable of magicweaving than she really was, she could swallow her pride and do that. A slippery confusion riddled Sim's mind. She wasn't used to thinking like this; she didn't know why she was acting this way.

"I have to get to work," Sim said. "But I'll see you soon. And then you can heat up my cold coffee at Stein's." The comment fell flat. It was out of place, meant to encourage Wood when all it did was highlight her lack of ability. Sim turned away and went back to their bikes, feeling sadder than she had reason to. Wood followed behind her in silence and waved a demure hand when they parted.

That day Azzer expressed his discontent with Sim's lateness through silence peppered with disgusted, berating comments. "What a dumb idea," he said down to the counter when he nearly knocked off the mason jar she'd left there. When Sim forgot to let the glue dry on a broken-soled boot before sealing it with a waterproofing spell, Azzer snatched it out of her hands and took it to his workshop without even explaining himself. Halfway through the day he brought up the goggles and Sim had to admit that she hadn't had a chance to test them yet. She'd been too distracted by the wand and Wood, though of course she couldn't say so.

"Working hard?" he said when he caught her staring out the window for a moment. After that she worked extra quickly on the repairs, but he was still silent or quick-spoken when the day was over. At the time it had felt like the obvious choice to be late for work so that she could teach Wood how to spell cast. And even now that Sim realized how crazy she'd acted, she still knew that she'd do it again if she had the chance. After work she turned her bike away from Stein's and headed toward the bridge. She felt like Wood wouldn't want to see her, and a part of her was happy to wallow in the pseudo heartbreak gnawing at her chest. It was a new feeling—soft and throbbing like a toothache. And everything would be so much easier if Wood would only start to hate her.

VII

It was early. From the bathroom window, Kai's herb spirals looked like fuzzy corkscrews haloed in soft morning light. Sim could barely spare them a glance. She hardly noticed the chill in the air or the calming scent of lavender coming through the open window or the pixie dragons that were just beginning to sing their tribute to the new day. She'd lain awake the entire night before, thinking about what she could say to make Wood stop being mad at her. Then she started to think about how Wood talked a little faster when she was nervous, as if she was afraid that she wouldn't get all of her words out. She thought about Wood's goofy smile and the nerdiness that hardly anyone but Sim ever got to see. When Sim closed her sleepless lids all she could picture were the amber eyes that sent her stomach reeling whenever she looked into them. She thought about the look on Wood's face when she'd offered her the wand, and went back to conversations they'd had, imagining what she could have said to make herself sound smarter. When Sim finally arose, she slipped out of bed an hour earlier than she needed to, just so that she could get to Stein's before she went to work, in case Wood came in for a morning coffee.

And now Sim stood at the mirror, realizing that she couldn't deny it any longer. The whirling in her stomach, the fire in her veins, the way her throat closed at Wood's slightest touch: These were not just feelings of friendship. She was in love; completely, head over heels in love in a way that she had never imagined to be possible. An endless yearning to be with Wood, to hold her, to touch her, throbbed through Sim's body with a constant, painful-yet-pleasant ache. She'd been telling herself that this was just because they were really great friends, but she'd always known in her heart that it wasn't true. Sim frowned into the bathroom mirror, looking for something to show that she was diseased, or demonic. She was in love with a girl. Another girl. And so much that she wanted all of it to just go away, but she couldn't keep ignoring the feelings that she'd been denying for so long.

A shudder rocked her body. She didn't want this. She covered her face with her hands. She perched her elbows on the edge of the sink and leaned forward onto them. Tears burned at her eyelids. Inhaling deeply, she switched on the sink and splashed cold water onto her face, again and again. She would not cry about this. Sim sat on the edge of the tub and threw her towel onto the toothpaste-stained faucet. The worn wooden floor swam under her gaze, and she demanded to know why she couldn't be satisfied with what she had: talking with Wood and laughing with her and just hanging out.

A storm of emotions pushed Sim's mind to its stretching point: relief at not having to suppress her feelings anymore; guilt, because she knew those feelings were wrong; anger, when she realized with an iron determination that no, she couldn't be wrong. She couldn't be damned for something that she had no control over. And then there was only the anger: anger at the world for telling her she shouldn't be who she was, anger at the priests who proclaimed she'd burn for eternity just like those who chose to steal and murder, anger at the mind-healers who insisted that loving someone of the same gender was an insanity and were looking for a potion to cure it. Well, they might as well join the alchemists in their search for gold. Because Sim wasn't wrong, she wasn't evil, and she wasn't insane. She was just herself—or trying to be, finally.

But what would Kai say? Or Cader? Or Azzer? Or Pru? Even Pru would start to look at her differently once she found out. That's what scared Sim more than anything: that she would somehow be changed in the eyes of her friends. She could never tell Wood, but eventually she might realize too and then...Sim stood, too quickly. Black dots swirled before her eyes. She held onto the sink so that she wouldn't fall, washed her face again, tried to compose herself. She could figure this out later. No one needed to know about it. She forced the thoughts to go away, made her mind go blank. Sim brushed her teeth, spit into the sink, put away the toothpaste, shut the cabinet, and there was her reflection again. Normal, except for the reddish tinge to her eyes and cheeks.

Cader came into the kitchen while Sim was sipping at a coffee and reading the paper. His morning meditation had left a fuzzy, calm look on his face. He was wearing tightish jeans that were cut off just above his knees and a pair of worn boatsman's shoes. A brown leather vest covered an old flannel button-down with the sleeves cut off, and his leather questing pouch hung from his belt. Sim looked up and frowned at his clothes.

"I gotta look the part," he said with a shrug.

"For what?"

"I convinced Azzer to hire me." Cader smiled. "I'm going to help him find those stones he likes to use in his gadgets. They're tough to come by, but I can do it. We're going to be coworkers."

"Oh, great," Sim said with a roll of her eyes. She could act normal, she realized with a shot of relief, she could act just as she always had. Nothing had changed. She squinted at Cader and added, "Wasn't it one of your philosophers who said to watch out for endeavors that require new clothes?"

"Whatever." He shrugged. "The clothes don't make the man."

"The Mondrans are really going to hate you," she said, looking at his bare arms and knees.

"They can deal with it. How's that shoulder?"

"All healed," Sim said with a smile, rubbing it. "Thanks for that, by the way, whatever it was you did." It seemed like he had just hovered his hands over her body for half an hour.

"I didn't do anything," he said with a smirk as they walked out to the backyard. "It was the universe."

"Right." Sim hopped down the steps and grabbed her cruiser. "Well, at least I can still go to the Battle House this Veldindy. Once a week is already hardly enough for me to make any improvement."

"You should come more often."

"Maybe once I at least get the archery down. The other days are so intense." And she usually spent them hanging out with Wood, though she'd never admit that. "You're going to be so tired if you skate there," Sim said, noticing the board under his arm.

"Not me."

Sim laughed. "Okay." She started toward the street and smiled back at him. "It's going to be so great to have you there."

"I know." Cader cruised beside her. "And we get to keep all of the awesome gadgets for ourselves."

"If Azzer lets us."

"Oh, he will. I dig his ideals. Gadgets to the people, magic to the people. We're going to make it happen." Cader jumped his board over a pothole and kicked hard, speeding forward and leading the way.

Green, sprawling fields stretched away from the Old Wall and ended at the sudden ascent of the Dragon Spine Mountains. If she squinted, Sim could see a fringe of dense forest twenty miles away. She did her best to stay in the moment, to focus on her surroundings, but all she could think about was whether or not Wood was going to be at Stein's later. The sun was hot, but the breeze made it bearable—more bearable than sitting in the stuffy Incubator. Sim turned away from the rolling green landscape. The other side of the wall was lined with dingy abandoned factories that nature refused to reclaim. To their left, the Bikeway Narrows was a green splash of life among the ruins. Cader was out there somewhere, looking for parts on a list that Azzer had given to him as soon as they got into the shop. Sim wondered what time it was, so that she could count the hours left until she'd be off work and able to maybe see Wood again.

"Okay, calibrate the goggles," Azzer said. The wind pushed his graying hair forward and over his lenses. He turned to Sim with a curt nod and calibrated his own.

The world filled with color and Sim didn't know where to set her eyes. There were the ancient, silvery protection spells glowing dimly along the Old Wall, the glow-stick skyscrapers rising above the Brigantine River, the long-distance charms streaming through buildings like fairies playing a lightning-paced game of tag.

"There," Azzer said, pointing to one of the buildings off to the right. "The one with the high fence. Focus on that factory and zoom in."

Sim closed her eyes to shut out the light.

"Zoom in?" she asked, feeling a headache coming on.

"Intention, Sim. It's all about intention. Focus on your center and zoom in."

She gathered energy into her chest and imagined her vision becoming stronger. The world whooshed toward her in a sickening rush. Everything slid away and the factory rose before her eyes so that it was all she could see.

"Woah." Sim steadied herself, worried for a moment that she might loose her balance and stumble forward.

"I told you to play around with them. Now, notice anything strange about that factory?"

"It's glowing."

One of the metal doors opened and a line of dwarves filed outside.

"Right on schedule," Azzer said with a self-satisfied hum. "Break time."

The dwarves congregated in little groups, stretched, and talked. Some pulled out brown paper bags and started eating sandwiches.

"What are they doing in there?"

"Follow the lines. The dust's being channeled through pipes that run underground. You have to focus."

Now that Azzer had mentioned them, Sim noticed the bright tubes, shaded a few hues darker by the earth. Millions of them stretched from this factory and the factories nearby and disappeared into the Brigantine.

"Is that magic dust?"

"Exactly. Exactly. Power plants. That's what's going on out here. And those dwarves—I'll bet you anything that they don't have working papers. They're the ones living in the abandoned apartments. Someone with a lot of money, or a lot of magical ability—probably both—is keeping this secret. It seems like this place is abandoned, to the naked eye. No one looks. See that shimmering pink wall, just after the Incubator's block?"

"Yeah, I see it."

"Cloaking spell. Incredibly strong. Makes people look away, much in the same way that advertisement charms will draw your attention."

"But why would anyone want to hide—"

"Look back to the factory. What else do you notice?"

Sim frowned and scanned the building. "Black smoke, coming from those smokestacks. That must have a cloaking spell on it, too."

"You're right about the cloaking spell, but that isn't smoke. Take off the goggles. Decalibrate them. There are some things you should know. The sun's too hot to stay out here any longer."

They sat on the steps leading back to the street, next to each other but not touching.

"They moved them away, you know, all of the people who used to live here, back before the dwarves came," Azzer said, staring off.

"Why?"

"Because when you have a gigantic factory turning magic dust into magical potential, some of that charged magic escapes instead of being used in the spell." He glanced at Sim to see if she understood and, apparently deciding that she didn't, he continued, now speaking a little slower. "You have to understand how these things work." He held his hands before him as if there were a miniature power plant floating in the air in front of his chest. His eyebrows were drawn together and his lips were curled in an expression of disgust. "They take the magic dust out of nature—from mines, from trees, from the earth—and transport it to a converter, a factory. There, workers run machines that change the magic dust into magical potential—pure energy—so that it can be pumped into the grid. That's those bright lines you saw running under the ground. If you don't pour magic dust straight into a gadget, like you do for carriages, then it'll have to plug into the grid. Unless it runs off the magic stones I use."

"But how does the dust get here?" Sim interrupted.

"I don't know." Azzer waved his hand. "It's not that difficult to cast a transportation spell, and with those cloaking spells, it's not all that surprising. It's all being transported in from the Hinterlands, probably. Or, worse: They're taking the magic out of the air right here in the city. I don't know. I can't tell. It doesn't really matter. We need it, and that's why this is happening. I'm sure some people in the city government know about all of this, but we need the magic to power the city's millions of gadgets—the air coolers, the coffeemakers, the ovens, the carriages, the lights. Everything. That's how we got here, slaves to those who stole what was always ours. And we let them steal it; we idolized them for it."

His eyes were wide and wild. He looked at Sim for some sort of affirmation, waiting for her to nod and agree with him. She caught herself and frowned. His passion made his words sound true, but they weren't making sense.

"But what's wrong with that?" she said, her voice slightly more shallow than she'd wanted it to be. She coughed and continued, "You said yourself that gadgets set people free. Dust is mined and available to anyone who's willing to work hard for it. Now magicweavers in the upper class aren't the only ones who can manipulate magic to make their lives easier. Carriages allow people to go wherever they want. Women don't have to spend five hours a day washing clothes now, because they can use a charmed washer. Instead of trapping fairies in orbs to light our streets, we can use charmed light posts. How is that a bad thing?"

Her words ended, but the moment hung in time for an instant longer. It was important: Sim had never stood up to Azzer before, not about his ideals or anything else. A blip of fear flashed in her chest, but she held her ground. She wasn't going to let herself be a pushover. She'd wanted to point out that the things he made could never replace all of the gadgets people used. They were too expensive. The stones were too rare. Sim could see it, but she couldn't point it out to him. It was a line that she still couldn't cross, and perhaps one that she shouldn't.

Intense anger, almost as directionless as the charged magic he was talking about, pulsated out of Azzer's chest. His arms were open wide and his voice was starting to sound angry. "The workers, the people living around the plants, the people using the crap they make." He counted them off on his fingers. "We're all being exposed to this charged, volatile magic. There's no way of predicting what it will do. It just does. You see it coming off truck pipes sometimes. That black stuff, that unused burnt-out magic dust is poisonous to our magical selves. In small quantities you don't even notice it. You can't track it back to the source. But when you're living right next to a plant, there's so much black magic being pumped into the air that it's all so obvious. That's why they moved everyone away, years ago when the factories first opened here—and then the workers started to get sick. The lucky ones packed up and left before they could become affected. And the rest of them...They were left here to die, to kill each other off like monsters. Striges. That's why the plants around here are supposed to be shut down now—all of the weird shit that happens to people around them can't happen to us, at least not in a way we can track back to the magic-dust plants, or there'd be a revolution.

The people would tear them down! But put the plants in the Hinterlands and those ignorant barbarians are too dumb to even realize what's happening. Man the factories with dwarves, let the dwarves get sick, and no one cares. That's what's happening now. And we're all falling for it."

"Striges?" Sim said with a frown, catching the word.

"Strix in the singular. It's what people become when the dark magic eats away at their life energy. A strix won't die right away, but it'll have to absorb other people's energy in order to stay alive. The damn things would have taken over the whole city if the questers hadn't come in and taken care of them."

Sim gave him a questioning look.

"First the Guard tore down the carriage bridge leading over here, and then the questers killed the Striges off. They had to. Don't you see, Sim? There are consequences to the lives we lead. People slave away at work to buy their pre-charmed trinkets, and for what? So that they can push a button instead of heating their food over a fire? So that they can zoom around in those damned charmed carriages instead of journeying to where they need to go? So that they can wear long sleeves in the summer, sitting in magically cooled air instead of bearing the heat? We are destroying ourselves without even realizing it, and Nogron is puppeteering us along to our final demise. I'm sure it's Nogron who's behind this. Bad times loom ahead."

Sim fought a sigh. "So what do we do?" she asked.

Azzer paused, stared off, and lifted his eyebrows a little. For a moment his eyes were like shallow puddles: clear, blue, empty. Without changing his expression, he said, "I don't know." And then he pressed his lips together and turned his face toward the ground. "Volatile magic isn't an issue when gadgets are made on a small scale, like we do at the Incubator. But it's impossible to sell handmade gadgets when factory-made ones are so much cheaper. I have to try to sell people on the uniqueness of a piece. That's all that's keeping the shop alive. That and those crazy bikers who, for whatever reason, have decided that they like to get their things mended instead of just buying something new. Thank the heavens for that." He sighed. His energy was draining away. Sim felt it seeping out of the air, like coming down off a caffeine high. He continued, his voice hardly clearer than a mumble, "I can barely figure out how to get people here to take control of their own lives. But I'm starting to see that it's all pointless, maybe. Like putting on flying shoes in a cage." He slapped the step lightly, shrugged, and stood. "I think that's enough of this for today," he said, heading back toward their bikes. "I just thought you ought to know. I'm not sure anyone else will believe it, unless they can see it with their own eyes."

* * *

The mechanics of brewing absorbed Sim's attention until there was nothing left to do but stare at the beer streaming out of the decanter's spigot. Her mind wandered to Wood, and Sim forced herself to think about other things. She wrapped her heart in cement. This was for the best; this way they could still be friends. She wouldn't have to worry that her feelings for Wood were incredibly obvious to everyone, or if Wood could possibly feel the same way about her. And, so long as she battled with her obsession, she was able to forget all that Azzer had told her that day, able to push it far back into her mind where her thoughts couldn't reach.

The smell of curry and cumin spiced the kitchen when Sim came up from the basement. Carrots, eggplant, and onions, still wearing the dirt that birthed them, were piled on the counter near the sink. Kai stood at her cutting board, humming quietly.

"You're in a really good mood today," Sim said, almost thinking out loud. She could almost feel the lift in the air, and though it was mostly because of the sunlight streaming through the kitchen window, everything seemed to have a golden tinge around its edges.

"Haven't you noticed?" Kai said, pausing her chopping and motioning around the kitchen. "I got the whole thing cleaned today. Finally. A tidy kitchen is all I need."

"Makes sense. Can I help with something?" Sim asked.

"Absolutely." Kai grabbed a handful of carrots and handed them to Sim with a smile. "Just make sure you wash them first," she added before going back to the herbs she'd been chopping. She started to quietly sing a song that Sim sensed she'd learned at Veldindor devotional.

"You know, you have a really pretty voice, Kai," Sim said after a moment.

Kai stopped abruptly and glanced over at Sim. "Oh. Thanks." She turned away. "I was thinking of joining the choir at devotional, actually."

"You should definitely do it."

"Maybe. I'm not sure I have enough time. There's so much to be done to keep up the garden. And the people who sing in the choir are really good."

"So are you. You should go for it."

"There's actually this one priest who keeps trying to convince me to join, but..." She smiled and shook her head. "I think he's just being nice. He's nice to all of the girls who go to devotional as much as I do."

"Go for it," Sim said again, focusing on the carrots in order to hide a frown. She was probably imagining it, but she could've sworn that Kai had a crush on the priest from the way she was talking about him.

"Thanks, Sim," Kai said with another smile. They went back to their work, and Kai continued singing, though a little quieter now.

Prudence came in through the back door just as Sim finished scrubbing the tubers. "Hey guys," she mumbled, and went to the kitchen table to drop her bag on one of its chairs.

Sim waved her peeler at Pru in greeting and started to slice off the carrots' spotted skins. Kai looked up from chopping an onion and gazed down at the floor, where little clumps of dirt marked a path from the door to the table.

"How did you manage to get mud all over your shoes like that?" Kai said, gazing down at Pru's feet.

Pru shrugged and went to the sink to wash her hands. The heat of the day had Pru wearing a sleeveless T-shirt, showing off the tattoos on her tanned arms. Her tank was black and hung just above a studded belt that held up her low, dark cutoffs. She worked a bar of white soap in her hands, creating a sudsy lather that climbed up her forearms and shrouded the tattoo of a nautical compass that colored the skin above her right wrist.

"Couldn't you take them off before you came in?" Kai asked.

Pru craned her neck to look back at the dirt. "I'll clean it up."

Kai turned away, picked up her knife, put it back down, and turned back to face them.

"Prudence, why can't you act more like a girl?" she blurted.

Pru's eyes went up to the wall behind the sink. The bar of soap was suddenly motionless. She frowned. A muscle in her jaw tightened.

"What the hell is that supposed to mean?" She looked over at Kai, who was leaning back against the counter.

Kai took a deep breath. "You dress like a boy. Your hair is always a mess. For whatever reason you even make your voice sound like a man's. I'm just saying, maybe boys would notice you if you were a little more feminine."

Sim felt her eyes widen.

"I don't even know how to respond to that," Pru said. Steam started to waft off the water running from the faucet.

Kai continued, "I'm just saying—You're a girl. It wouldn't be that hard to act—"

"Look, Kai." Prudence dropped the bar of soap into the sink with a clunk. "Not that it's your business, but I don't make my voice sound like anything." As she continued, Pru stuck her hands under the scalding water and stripped off the soapy foam clinging to her skin. "And I dress the way I want to." She shoved back the sink handles with such force that Sim was surprised they didn't snap off. "And I'm not interested in attracting men because I like to fuck women."

Pru turned to face Kai, one hand on the edge of the sink and the other soaking the part of her shirt that covered her hip. "Have any thoughts on that?"

Sim stole a glance past Pru's back and over her shoulder. Kai's face fell. Her mouth hung open. Her eyes kept blinking. She turned back to her onions. "That's wrong." She breathed. And then she continued chopping.

"Fuck you." And at that, Prudence stormed upstairs.

Sim peeled the carrots in silence, and slowly, so that she wouldn't have to ask Kai for another thing to do. When she was finished, she took the raw orange sticks over to Kai's cutting board and left them there.

"Mince this," Kai said, and dropped a handful of garlic cloves onto the counter. She turned on the stove's magic-dust dispenser and snapped her fingers over the burner, starting the ignition charm that created a ring of blue flames.

"Did you know about Pru?" she asked suddenly.

"I thought you did, too."

Sim wanted to stick up for Pru, to tell Kai that she shouldn't have said those things and that she should go upstairs and apologize. But she couldn't do it. It was as if there was a stopper in her throat, and to explain it Sim told herself that it wasn't her place to step in. She was lying to herself and pretending that she wasn't. Sim knew the real reason she kept her mouth shut was because she didn't want Kai to guess that she liked girls, too.

Kai snorted in response. "Why would I think something like that?" The onions sizzled at the bottom of the pot. "Hurry up with that garlic."

"Throw it in," Kai said when Sim was finished. "And don't expect this to be good tonight. I can't stop all of this negative energy from curdling the food. Not literally, of course. But it just won't be the same."

"That's okay," Sim said. She wanted to go upstairs and hide in her room. But she didn't. She continued to help Kai cook and did her best to act normal.

"What if she likes one of us?" Kai said. "I can't imagine why she would want to... with a girl. It isn't normal. It's just so wrong—"

"Are you okay on your own for now?" Sim asked. She couldn't listen anymore.

"Yeah, I got it," Kai said with a wave.

Up in the shower, steam sheathed Sim in a hot, wet cocoon. Her back heaved but her lips were pressed together so tightly that no cry could escape them. Love wouldn't just happen. The universe wasn't going to just throw some perfect relationship into her lap. Now that she'd finally, finally found someone who set her heart on fire, she couldn't even be with her. Water pattered onto the back of Sim's drooping head and mixed with the warm tears streaming down her cheeks. Her soul ached with the desire to let Wood know how much she cared about her, to see if Wood could possibly feel the same way. Nothing would ever happen if Sim just continued to act like her friend. But she couldn't stand the thought of telling her and losing her. The possibility of pushing Wood away by sharing her feelings scared Sim more than anything ever had. She would rather they be friends than nothing at all. She was crazy. Crazy. Her awareness of this made everything that much worse, because there was absolutely nothing she could do about it, because she had no clue why she felt this way, no clue what she'd done to deserve this. She hunched low into the tub, pulled her legs up into her chest, and stayed like that until the water cooled and the steam disappeared.

VIII

Wood's hair was pulled back, tied with a piece of twine so that her loose curls spilled over one shoulder. She was sitting alone at the end of the communal table, her attention absorbed in a thick book. Sim took a step toward her, hesitated, and turned toward a table near the bookshelves where Wood could see her when she looked up from her reading. Sim took out *Saffron and Pulchrina* and did her best to pretend that Wood wasn't there. But she couldn't stop herself from glancing across the café every time she took a sip of coffee. Wood's gaze was fixed downward. She seemed to be off in another world, completely oblivious to anything happening around her. Sim was about to get up and go over to her, before Wood could notice that she'd already been sitting alone, but it was too late. She'd look ridiculous. Sim stayed anchored to her seat. The memory of their fight kept running through her head. Sim should have known better than to think that she could teach anyone to spell cast. A sick feeling hovered just above her stomach, and Sim had the keen sense that her whole world was about to fall into shambles. A part of her knew that she was being crazy, that their fight really hadn't been that bad. But that wasn't enough to change the way she felt. Out of the corner of her eye, Sim saw Wood launch her arms above her head in a stretch. Her eyes brushed over Sim for a moment and went back to her book. She'd seen her. She wasn't going to come over. They'd ignore each other now; they'd stop being friends just like that. Sim had overreacted to everything and ruined it all.

Eventually Wood stood and started toward her, and Sim felt yet another confusing rush of emotions. She felt both relieved and dreadful, both happy and afraid. Everything started to happen in too much of a rush.

"I'm sorry about yesterday." Wood slid into the chair across from Sim and frowned down at the table. "Are you mad at me?" Her voice was quiet and vulnerable in a way that Sim had never heard before.

Sim took a moment to respond. "It seemed like you were mad at me," she said, finally.

Wood shook her head. "I just—" She sighed and looked away. "I have a hard time with not being good at things. I'm sorry."

"It's okay."

"I really hate it when I get like that." Wood frowned and closed her eyes against a scrim of tears. "I know exactly what I can say to hurt someone, and I say it. I shouldn't, I know that I shouldn't, but I still do it. I'm just jealous, I guess, because all of this magic stuff comes to you so easily."

"You're jealous of me?" Sim asked with a little laugh.

"It shouldn't be that surprising. You're really talented, Sim. And I, clearly, can't even cast the simplest of spells."

"I'm not." Sim shook her head.

"No, Sim. You are. You're awesome." Wood tried to meet her eyes and Sim looked away. "But for some reason you can't seem to see it. Questers who can't do half of the things you can strut around here like pompous assholes, and you just keep it all to yourself. That's one of the nicest things to do for a person; to teach them something. You've been really great, Sim. Don't think I haven't noticed."

"I shouldn't have pushed you."

"You didn't push me. Don't try to take the blame. I was a total bitch."

Sim frowned and nodded. "Maybe a little."

"Thanks for being honest." Wood pushed herself away from the table. "Friends again?"

Sim forced a smile in return. "Of course."

"Good." Wood narrowed her eyes and then went up to the beast-man at the counter.

Sim stared down at her coffee. Friends, they were friends, she reminded herself. This changed nothing. Just because Wood thought it was important to apologize didn't mean that she shared Sim's feelings. Those things she'd said, they were only words of friendship.

"I think I just need to try it by myself for a little," Wood said when she got back. She pushed an oversized cookie toward Sim. "Once I get the hang of the basics, then I'll be at a point where you can teach me more."

"Whatever you want." Sim broke the cookie in half and slid the plate back toward Wood.

"So, anyway, I have to tell you about this customer who came in today," Wood said. "He was such a pain in the ass..."

Eventually Wood said that she was tired and had to head home, but Sim stayed and read through the last chapter of *Saffron and Pulchrina*. Every few minutes Sim would stop and forget the story and bask for a moment in the glowing feeling that

96

encompassed her whenever she thought about Wood. They were going to be okay. And it was enough for her, to have this feeling all to herself. They could be friends. Sim closed the paperback and shoved it into the bookshelf. Wood had been right: It was a great story. But the ending left her cold. Saffron and Pulchrina got together at last, founded the nation of Pulchra through showing their people that they shouldn't be enemies. They lived happily ever after. Sim wasn't a fan of all that. Real life never worked out that way.

The next morning Sim lounged on a couch in the living room, thinking up an excuse to go to the Narrows, just in case she might run into Wood. It would be crazy for her to go all the way out there when she'd have to come back to go to the Battle House that night. But the temptation was there. It was always there. She was pretty sure Wood had Veldindys off too, though, so Sim shoved the thought aside and went back to the new book she'd started to read.

"Anyone want coffee?" Pru called from the kitchen. "Or that herbal tea crap?"

"Coffee, if there's enough in the press," Sim yelled back. There always was. Even though Kai thought that coffee was "black poison that rotted your body from the inside out," she still filled the press for them every morning, once everyone was up and in the living room.

Cader frowned into a book by a Munian spiritual leader called Sage Kokoro. "No, thanks," he said without looking up from the book, just loud enough for Pru to hear him. Drangs was curled up against Sim's thigh, breathing hot breaths into her brown trousers. She ran her fingers over his soft turquoise fur and thought about her conversation with Wood the day before.

After the quick patter of cabinets opening and closing, Prudence strode into the living room with toast hanging from her mouth, two steaming mugs in her hands, and a thick novel wedged under her arm. She was wearing the black linen yoga pants that Cader had given her. She refused to wear them outside of the house. Or to do yoga. But they had become her Veldindy morning uniform. A drip of milky coffee tumbled over the rim of Sim's mug as Pru slapped it onto the table. She mumbled an apology and settled into the fraying armchair with a sigh that led into a deep, raspy cough. Her back arched as a fit of coughing seized her. Pru shook her head, choked back the coughs, and took a long sip of her coffee.

"I can heal that for you," Cader said while still focusing on his book. He blinked and looked up at Pru with an eyebrow raised.

"Nah." She swallowed more coffee and then tried to stifle another fit.

"It would be easy." Cader was trying to sound like he didn't care about Pru's decision.

Times were tough for healers: People were beginning to doubt that traditional healing magic actually worked, and were opting to buy mass-produced potions instead. Cader hated this in a way that hovered just below the surface of his practiced indifference, even though he himself dealt in the potions business. The potions that Kai made were different, he'd said, since they were tailored to each individual and made on such a small scale.

Prudence put her half-eaten toast on the table next to her chair and opened her book. She leaned back and rested her left ankle on her right knee. "I'm not going to make you heal something I do to myself. It wouldn't be right." She flicked open her reading glasses, slid them over her ears, and frowned down at her plain-covered paperback.

Cader stared at her, his jaw jutting out the way it did when he disagreed with something but was trying to let it go. His clear gaze looked over at Sim, who responded by drawing her lips to a corner of her mouth and shrugging. He took a long, deep breath that would have been unnoticeable if Sim hadn't been looking for it, and went back to Sage Kokoro's writings.

The tension in the room eased as they all went back to their books. Sim rested her mug on her thigh and sipped at it occasionally. Her coffee was just about finished when the front door creaked open and then clicked shut. Kai scanned the living room, took two canvas bags full of groceries to the kitchen, and came back with a plate clutched in her hand. She grabbed the toast, held it between her index finger and thumb for a moment, and dropped it onto the plate. She gave Pru a reprimanding look, which Pru returned with an emotionless stare, and went back to the kitchen without saying a word.

"We should probably help," Sim said.

Pru shrugged. "You can if you want."

"I'll help," Cader said. He hurried to the kitchen, ever eager to keep the peace.

"How was fighting school?" Kai asked with a slightly judgmental edge, and Sim wondered at Cader's ability to put up with her mood.

"You know I don't go until later on Veldindy," he said calmly.

Sim stared down at her book without reading the words. Cader and Kai were busy putting away the groceries. This was the perfect moment to bring up Wood, to see what Pru thought. It wasn't even Pru's advice that she wanted so much as to say it out loud; that she was in love with a girl. Sim wondered if it would be more real to her after she said it. She stole a glance up at Pru and then decided that she didn't want to bother her. Besides, even if she was quiet, Cader and Kai might overhear her, and she definitely wasn't ready for them to know.

Pru sighed, folded down the corner of her page, and dropped her book into her lap. She crossed her arms and looked at Sim over the tops of her reading glasses. "What's up, Sim?"

Nervous energy flooded Sim's chest. She opened her mouth, and then closed it again. She felt her face get hot. "Nothing," she said.

Pru was wearing the same emotionless stare that she'd just had on for Kai. "Okay," she said, threw her book onto the coffee table, and stood up into a stretch. She disappeared into the kitchen without saying anything else, and Sim was left alone to glare down at her book. If she could just figure out why it was so hard for her to talk about Wood, if she could just make it make sense, maybe she'd finally be able to say the words that had been bottling up in her chest for so long. She just had to do it, she knew she had to. But now another chance had been lost.

"Hey, Sim," Cader called from the kitchen. "We need your help with something."

Sim took a deep breath and waited until she was composed again before pulling Drangs off her lap and padding over to the kitchen. Acheron was there, leaning against the counter and talking softly to Prudence. "Oh, hey," Sim said. She hadn't heard her come in. After finishing whatever she was saying to Pru, Acheron looked over at Sim and nodded.

"So do you think you can help me out with a transportation spell?" Acheron asked. "I want to move a bigger batch today."

Kai snorted from her seat at the kitchen table, with holly and buchu herbs scattered in front of her; ingredients for sleeping potions.

"Shut up," Pru snapped.

Kai raised her eyebrows, gave Acheron a disapproving look, and said, "Just don't ask for my help when you all get caught."

"You shouldn't even joke about that, Kai," Sim said quietly.

Kai shrugged, dropped a handful of holly leaves into a mortar, and began to grind them with quick, angry strokes of her pestle. Sim turned away from the scratching stone-on-stone sound. "I've never done a spell like that before," she said to Acheron. "But if you tell me what to do, I'll try."

"Okay, guys, it's ready," Cader yelled from down in the basement.

"Good," Acheron said. She took off her leather vest, hung it on the doorknob of the broom closet, and descended the steps. "You just have to add to my energy," she said over her shoulder to Sim. "You don't actually have to cast the spell; I'll do that."

Ten brewing boxes were stacked in a pyramid in the middle of the basement. Pru hoisted herself up onto the workbench to watch, and Cader went to stand beside her. Sim stayed by the steps, waiting to be told what to do, while Acheron circled the pyramid, letting salt spill from a satchel she held lightly in her hand. From the top of the stairs, Drangs mewed and poked his head down to see what they were doing.

"You stay up there," Sim said, pointing a finger at him.

"Okay." Acheron rubbed her hands together. "I think I have it. Sim, just stand here next to me and when you feel the spell start, add your energy to it. Does that make sense?"

"Yeah," Sim said, rubbing her hands together the way Acheron just had. For a moment she wished she had her goggles, but soon she realized that they weren't necessary. A tingling feeling buzzed at the edges of Sim's mind. She closed her eyes and reached out to it with her consciousness. The energy at the center of her chest grew hot and bright as Sim built it up. In one burst, she released it all into Acheron's spell.

"Holy shit, Sim." Acheron breathed.

Sim opened her eyes to see Acheron stumbling back, her hands held over her heart. A three-foot hole scarred the basement floor where the boxes of Kaianide had just been.

"That was way more juice than was necessary."

"I'm sorry, I didn't know—"

"No, it's okay." Acheron shook her head and took a deep breath. "It's just a good thing I cast that barrier circle, or you would have dragged half of the basement along with those beers. Veldindor." She took another deep breath, sighed it out, and composed herself. She looked up at Cader and Pru. "You'd better get this girl a mentor. I'm sure someone would take her on as an apprentice."

"I've been trying to tell her," Cader said with a shrug.

"Well, try again. I have to get going. I'll be at the Dragon Spine tonight if you feel like hanging."

"Cool," Cader said as he followed her and Pru up the steps.

"Maybe I'll stop by," Pru added.

"I doubt it," Acheron said with a laugh. She glanced over at Pru as she slipped her vest back on. "I know you have your places."

Pru grinned. "Get outta here. You have important business to be taking care of." She opened the back door for her. "I'll talk to you more about that quest later, okay?"

"Sure thing, Prudence." Acheron paused and looked past her toward Sim. "Hey, thanks for the help, Sim."

"No problem."

"Just watch yourself, okay? A talent like that could attract a lot of unwanted attention."

"Yeah, I will."

Acheron mounted her track bike and sped out toward the street.

"I don't want that girl coming over here," Kai said, still grinding the holly.

"Why not?" Cader asked, surprised.

"I just don't trust her."

"But you don't even know her."

"I don't want to."

Pru clenched her fists, and for a moment Sim was afraid that she was going to step over to Kai and slap her. Instead, she stormed out of the kitchen and into the backyard.

Kai looked from Cader to Sim. "I mean, am I wrong?"

"I think you need to have a talk with Prudence," Cader said.

"I already tried to."

She looked to Sim for some sort of affirmation, but Sim just shrugged and walked away, back to the living room and her book. Cader joined her a moment later, giving her an almost apologetic look. "They'll work it out," he said. "Just don't let Kai drag you into the argument when you have nothing to do with it."

Sim looked at him with a small smile and a nod. He was wrong. It had everything to do with her. She just didn't know how to say so yet. After ten minutes of trying to read, Sim dropped her book and went to the garden with the intention of weeding. Pru was still there, to Sim's surprise, sitting on Kai's meditation rock and smoking what looked like a cigarette, but was really tobacco sprinkled with pixie pollen. She could tell by its earthy sweet smell.

"Want some?" Pru asked, holding the smoke out toward Sim.

"No, thanks."

Pru nodded, took another drag, and held the pollen in her lungs. "I'm going to the Geraldine tonight if you want to come. You could go to the Battle House tomorrow night instead." She exhaled, and then glanced up at Sim to wait for her response.

The haze of alcohol helped Sim forget her problems. So did the haven of the Geraldine. Sim was surrounded by its graffitied walls and tattooed women nearly every night for the next week. She would hang out with Wood at Stein's and, when Wood inevitably left to meet up with some guy, Sim would sit there and wait for Pru to come in and get her.

As they pedaled away from Stein's the following Remidy, the muscles on the side of Pru's arm caught definition in the moonlight. Slight shadows distorted the moon goddess inked onto her upper right bicep. A fierce wind whipped Pru's hair out of her face. Her brows were drawn down and her charcoal-lined eyes scanned the street.

"You should get a sword," she said after swerving around a pothole. She glanced at

Sim and added, "I'll bring you one next time. Things are going to get worse here soon. I can feel it."

"Worse how?"

In silence they glided past the darkened windows of an old factory and crossed an empty intersection. Old scaffolding formed a dark tunnel along the side of the block that led to the Geraldine. Bikes were leaned up against the graffiti-covered plywood and rusted poles. Sim knew that when girls slipped out of the Geraldine together, they were usually going to hide in one of the construction tunnel's nooks. Sim had heard their moans of pleasure, and had watched them emerge, sometimes holding hands, sometimes blushing. Sim guessed that the factory workers used to live here. The Geraldine had probably been their bar before it was taken over by the women of the Bikeway Narrows.

"Worse how?" Sim asked again. She hated how Pru would sometimes just ignore her when she asked a question that Pru didn't want to answer.

Pru glanced at her. "It's just a feeling, Sim," she said. "Don't worry about it. I'll bring that sword for you next time. You can never be too careful. That's all."

The special that night was pixie papayas, a sweet drink that Candace liked to make strong because the papaya juice masked the bitter pixie nectar so well. Sim got one for herself and Pru ordered a Bongo Tree.

"That girl's here alone," Sim said to Pru, frowning down at the other side of the bar. The girl was sitting where the bar met the wall, with a Kaianide clutched in her hands and her arms resting on the counter. She was exchanging a few words with Grimms, a regular who was at the Geraldine every night. Pru knew her. Grimms turned away and acted as if the other girl wasn't there.

"So?" Pru said, looking down the bar.

Sim pressed her lips together and frowned down at her drink.

"She's cruising, Sim," Pru said and took a sip of her Bongo Tree. "A lot of girls come here alone." She raised an eyebrow. "Actually, I saw her checking you out just a few minutes ago."

"Me? I doubt it. She was probably looking at you."

Pru shrugged. Sim noticed that the girl didn't try to talk to Grimms again. In five minutes she finished her beer and then left.

"Come on, girls," Candace said, walking up to Pru and Sim. "Still on your first drinks? The night's nearly over already." She dropped three shot glasses onto the bar and turned over a bottle of moon glow, filling the glasses quickly.

"Thanks, Candace," Sim said with a smile, and handed one of the shots to Pru.

"Drink up," Candace said. She threw back her shot and then added, "You know, I have to say, those Kaianides are getting to be pretty popular. It would be great if we could manage to get enough of them so that we didn't run out two hours before closing every night."

"Would it be?" Pru said, giving Candace a harsh look.

"Well, maybe you'll be getting more then," Sim said.

"Now, that's what I like to hear." Without even looking at the short-haired girl who had just come up to the bar, Candace smiled at Sim, poured a pixie papaya, and pushed it toward the girl's wrists, which were covered in bike-chain bracelets.

"Two sols," Candace said. She glanced at the girl, and then turned back to Pru and Sim. "It's like family here. We have to take care of each other."

"Thanks, C," the girl said, putting her money on the counter and taking her drink back to her friends. They were crowded around the jukebox, pouring in their magic dust and taking turns deciding which song to put on next.

"Be right back," Candace said to Sim and Pru when she noticed a girl who had been waiting for her at the other end of the bar.

Sim sipped at her pixie papaya, thinking about what Candace had said. Maybe she was right: If nothing else, the Geraldine girls could relate to Sim in a way that Cader and Kai would never be able to. She didn't have to wonder at whether they accepted her despite her sexuality. They were the same as she was, even if they didn't know it just yet.

Sim glanced at Pru, who was scanning the crowd. She wanted to bring up Wood. Now was the time; there was nothing else to talk about. But again the words caught in the back of her throat and hooked themselves there.

"I'm going to smoke," Pru said. "You coming?"

They navigated through the sea of wifebeaters and tank tops. The bar was packed, and moving anywhere was a challenge. One wifebeater-clad girl refused to move out of their way, just to try to be tough. Pru shoved her with her shoulder so that she stumbled into the girl behind her.

"What the hell?" the wifebeater girl demanded. A wet trail of beer stained the front of her shirt. But Pru had already moved past her. The girl glared at Sim, who looked away and continued on. Fights seemed exciting and they were fun to talk about sometimes, but she wasn't about to get into one if she could help it.

When they got outside Sim scanned the crowd and tried to figure out who it was that Pru had spotted. This was a typical thing for her to do: She'd see someone she was interested in, wait for her to go outside to smoke, and then a minute later would casually follow. The girl had long black hair and green eyes. After sitting for a minute, Pru approached her and asked for a light. Their eyes held as Pru thanked her. Then she turned toward Sim and forgot about the girl, or acted like she did.

"What's bothering you, Sim?" she asked, taking a long drag and leaning against the planter. "It's not Kai, is it?"

It wasn't Kai, but Sim nodded.

Pru narrowed her eyes at her, as if she had just thought of something. She took her pack of cigarettes back out of her pocket and held it open to Sim.

"No, thanks," Sim said, in spite of the fact that she was tempted to try one. Pru's deep, raspy cough and everyone else's complaints about addiction were enough to make her decide otherwise.

"It just doesn't make sense to me," she said, as Pru tucked the pack back into her pocket. "None of it makes sense to me. I don't see why anyone would care who you're attracted to." One of the girls glanced over at Sim and she sensed that she was touching on a taboo topic, but she didn't care. No one at the Geraldine ever acknowledged that they were there because they weren't welcome anywhere else, not unless they pretended to be something that they weren't.

"Ah, don't let it get to you," Pru said. "A lot of people think it's wrong for girls to like girls or guys to like guys. And the whole conversation ends there, because that's what their parents and everyone else has been telling them since they were little: that it's strange, or dark, or unnatural. Even if they don't talk about it outright, that's still the accepted mindset."

"Yeah, it was the same where I grew up. But that's not what I think."

"Exactly. Some people are open-minded—people who are sane and can think for themselves. Those are the only people who matter, anyway. Those are the people who you can be completely yourself with, because you know they won't judge you."

Pru looked at Sim as if she were waiting for her to say something.

"R-right," Sim stuttered. "That's why we come to the Narrows, because we're all a little different."

"Right," Pru repeated, seemingly unsatisfied by the conversation. She stood, threw her cigarette into the street, and went back inside.

It wasn't long before she was talking to the green-eyed girl, in a corner where no one would bother them. Sim took a shot with Grimms and some of the other regulars. She still didn't remember most of their names. Whatever they were talking about blurred into a meaningless haze. But there was laughter. And dancing. Pru came back from the corner and joined the others while her girl waited on a stool, watching her. Pru grinned at Sim. This was her favorite game, and she was extraordinarily good at it. Usually. She lifted her hand to Candace to order another beer, and paused. The green-eyed girl was dancing with someone else.

"We should go," Pru said, not mad but frustrated. She finished off her beer in one long swig.

"Not so soon?" Candace said, setting down three Kaianides and taking money off the bar.

"I'll see you later this week," Pru said. She gave Sim a look and jerked her head toward the door. Sim didn't want to go yet. But the expression on Pru's face was enough to push her to follow without questioning.

Pru grabbed Sim's hand and pulled her through the dancers toward the door. Sim left a trail of apologies behind her as they made their way up to the alley where their bikes were hidden.

"What's the rush?" Sim asked.

A garbage bag caught on Sim's pedal and tore open as Prudence ripped it off the bike.

"Dammit." She turned to Sim. "Will you help me instead of just standing there?"

"Sure." Sim rushed to her bike, kicked off another one of the bags, and lifted the frame upright. She shook off a few dirty napkins and old french fries and turned it around so that she could wheel it out of the alley.

The night was chilly, but Sim didn't feel cold at all. Adrenaline flooded her veins, heightened her senses. Her legs pumped her cruiser as fast as it would go. Squat, dark factories zipped past her. The Narrows Bridge, its high arch reflecting the moonlight, rose into view. A moment later Pru was beside her. Her sword was in her hand, her face set into a look of staunch determination.

"What's wrong, Pru?" Sim yelled over to her.

"Keep your eyes on the street," Pru snapped. "Stay close to me. Make sure you keep up."

Dark potholes scarred the road like land mines in the inky night. Pru wove through the nicks with a quick and fluid grace, etching a pathway for Sim to follow. With every moment that passed Pru pulled farther ahead. She slipped under the arch to the Narrows Bridge and climbed her bike up the ramp. With as much concentration as she could manage, Sim pulled magic from the air and channeled it through her palms and into her handlebars. She pictured it flowing down into her cruiser's hubs, forcing them to spin faster.

The bike shot forward, but even with the speed spell the climb was still hard, and Sim had to stand and pump her pedals to keep up with Pru. Sweat dripped down the sides of her face and her tobacco-clogged lungs refused to take in more than short gasps of air. Pru glanced back, saw that Sim was behind her, and rushed into her descent. They weren't using their brakes at all, going so fast that the bridge supports blinked by in a blur. Sim's handlebars started to clatter and shake from the speed, but she clenched her biceps to keep the wheel straight and struggled to quell the drunkenness softening her mind from the pixie papayas she'd had at the Geraldine.

There was no time to wonder why Pru was standing up tall on her pedals. She reached up her left hand, grabbed a crossbeam that stretched horizontally over the bike path, and flung her bike in front of her. The frame flew through the air and collided with a dark figure. Sim yanked on her breaks. Pru swung her body forward as someone jumped from the shadows and tried to grab her. She swung her arm back and sunk her blade into his skull.

Sim couldn't stop. She swerved to the left of Pru's dangling legs and collided with something huge and soft. Her body hit the bike path in a shock of pain and skidded along the concrete. She rolled over, her knees and forearms on fire, ready to defend herself. A guy with long white hair and impossibly pale skin was scrambling into a squat. His sky blue irises glared in the moonlight. His teeth were pointed like needles. Just as he shifted his body to move toward her, his jaw fell open and his eyes widened. He stopped. An expression of painful surprise crumpled his features. A blade protruded from the middle of his chest before he slid off it and fell to the ground in a heap. Pru stood tall behind him, her sword dripping blood. Without giving him another glance, she climbed onto the railing and leaned forward over the river, one hand wrapped around a bridge support for balance.

"I think there were only three," she said, jumping back onto the path.

Sim was still sitting in the middle of the bikeway, unable to think, unable to move. She stared at the white-skinned creature lying dead in front of her. His mouth gaped so that his sharpened incisors tilted up toward the bridge's spider-web support beams. Pru stepped over to him and used the creature's black tunic to wipe his blood off of her sword. The other two lay dead just beyond him.

"What are they?" Sim asked.

"It doesn't matter." Pru scanned the bridge again. "Here, help me." She wrapped one hand around the thing's forearm and the other around its ankle.

"What are you doing?"

"We're going to throw them into the river."

"What?"

"We're going to throw them into the river."

"We should tell someone—"

"Tell who?" Pru asked, dropping his limbs and standing up straight.

"But what if there's more?"

"Then we'll deal with it. Look, Sim, I want to get the hell out of here. We can talk about this somewhere else. Not on the bridge. Not now." Pru grabbed the body again and looked up at Sim expectantly.

Sim gritted her teeth and grabbed the creature's chilled skin. He hadn't been dead long enough for his body to be this cold already. His face was lifeless, his impossibly light eyes staring out at nothing at all. Sim had never seen a dead body before. The right thing to do would have been to close his eyes, but before she knew it Pru was counting to three and they were hoisting him up and over the railing, with Pru carrying most of the weight. The body tumbled through the air, around and around, and then splashed into the gleaming, moonlit river. They did the same to the other two before Pru went to her bike and inspected it.

"Still rideable," she said. "How's yours?"

"Handlebars are bent." Sim tried to force them back into place, but they wouldn't budge. "But I can manage to get home."

"You go first this time," Pru said. "I'll watch our backs."

Sim set off quickly so that Pru wouldn't yell at her to go faster, and because more than ever before she yearned for the safe haven of Kailash. In her mind all she could see was the creature's snarling face. Had Pru been a heartbeat slower, Sim was sure that it would be her body at the bottom of the river, instead of his.

"Slowly now," Pru said, riding up next to her as they approached Kailash. "Stop here. Just wait."

Sim stood with her back against a tree, scanning the empty street, waiting for someone to jump out from behind one of the parked carriages. Pru strode back to her, her bike left behind, her palms open at her sides and ready to draw her sword in a flash. She stopped in front of Sim, met her eyes for just a moment, and said, "Come on, it's fine."

"What's going on, Pru?"

She opened her mouth, closed it, and looked away. "I don't know."

IX

The Bikeway Narrows was quiet this early in the morning. The sky was still a pinkish blue and the empty streets were filled with rustling leaves and birdsong. Sim sat cross-legged on the sidewalk with her back leaned up against the Incubator's locked door. Warm coffee heat bled through the mason jar cupped between her palms, warming her skin against the chill hanging in the air. Azzer's shadow glided down the street as he approached the Incubator on his clunky step-through cruiser. With the grace of an acrobat, he guided the bike up onto the sidewalk and swung his left leg over its leather saddle while the wheels were still moving. He hopped to the ground.

"Maybe I should get you a key," he said. Azzer didn't trust magic alone to guard his shop. Sim herself could probably break the locking charm he kept on the door.

"Sure," Sim said, even though she knew he'd never get around to doing it. That was just Azzer's way.

"What happened to your arms?" he asked, noticing her bandages.

"Bike accident. I got doored in Greater Terresin."

A worried look widened Azzer's eyes. "Are you okay?"

"Yeah, I'm fine."

Azzer gave her a look as if he wasn't sure if he should believe her, but then nodded and stepped up to unlock the door. As he entered the shop, he walked slowly toward the center of the room, as if he couldn't decide where he wanted to go, and then grabbed a stool and placed it across from the counter. The wood creaked as he hooked his heels on its middle rung and stared out the window. Sim waited for him to say something. Azzer hadn't brought up the dark magic since he'd taken her up to the Old Wall. She had the feeling that he might want to talk about it again.

"Do you care if I play this in the shop today?" Sim held up an album that a friendly guy with light blond hair and fuzzy muttonchops had dropped off the day before. He had a warm glow to his words and the happy glint in his eyes that Sim was beginning to recognize in those people who did what they loved in life. "I haven't listened to it yet," Sim admitted. "But if it's bad I can put on something else. It's a good idea to have music playing, I think. Especially now that I've fixed that Victrola. Maybe this way someone will buy it."

"Okay," Azzer said with a nod. "Good thinking."

Sim pulled the record out of its cardboard case, put it on the turntable, and started to crank the Victrola's winding key. To make the turntable spin again, she'd had to take the whole thing to pieces and pinpoint exactly which part needed to be replaced. It hadn't been easy, but she'd done it. And now she turned the winding key with the sort of satisfaction that could only come from puzzling over a thing for an hour and then finally figuring it out. Sim watched the record spin for a moment and then placed the needle onto its oil-black surface. Staticky guitar music filled the room, grew smooth, and was soon accompanied by a quick drum beat.

"Not bad," Azzer said with a raised eyebrow. The guy's voice was nasally and rich. He sang about not being able to sleep at night. He was waiting for his lover to come home, to lie beside him again, and all he could do was stare into the darkness and feel the seconds drawing on like miniature eternities.

They listened to the music for a while until the next song came on, an instrumental that let the guitar do the singing, and Sim felt the need to say something. It was strange to see Azzer just sitting there when he would usually rush to his workshop and get straight to work.

"If you could invent anything, what would it be?" she asked, feeling awkward.

Azzer smiled. "A time machine."

"Really?"

"I wouldn't want to go back and change anything big. Just those moments when you let something slip by you, when you realize that you had a chance to have something amazing, but the chance is gone and now that you see it, it's too late."

"Do you think it's possible?" Sim wanted to ask what opportunity Azzer thought he'd missed, but she wasn't comfortable asking about his personal life—or hearing about it.

"Anything's possible." Azzer blinked and sat up straighter. "It's just a matter of what you're willing to give up in order to achieve it. I would have to spend my entire life working on a time-traveling device. Just think of all the other things that I could invent in the meantime and all of the opportunities I'd miss while making it. It would be a tragic irony."

The front door swung open. A tall girl with mirrored aviators struggled to pull her bike into the shop. Azzer strode over to her and flipped down the kickstand doorstop.

"I have a flat," the girl said quickly, and pushed her bike toward Azzer. Her hands free, she pulled her hair off her shoulders to tie it at the back of her head in a messy bun.

"I'll have this finished in ten minutes," Azzer said, wheeling the bike to his workshop.

"Yeah, okay. I'll just wait for it."

The biker unbuckled an old leather belt that held her messenger bag across her chest and dropped the bag next to the door. She hung her sunglasses on the neckline of her black tank top and cast her catlike blue eyes toward Sim, who immediately pretended to be absorbed in the silencing gadget she'd been working on. Sim didn't bother trying to start a conversation with her; she'd had enough interactions with these types of people to know that they were all the same. Their sole purpose in life was to make other people feel unworthy of their presence. They were all judgmental and cold and pretentious, and she didn't like them. Sim could tell this by the clothes the girl wore, by the way she held herself. Pretty girls like her were never nice. The biker's thin legs moved around the shop gracefully, as if her steps were a dance. Had they been at the Geraldine, Sim might have considered approaching her. She might have tried to meet her eyes and give the girl a look that said she was interested, to see if the attraction was mutual. But Sim knew that even at the Geraldine she probably would have been too self-conscious to do anything but look away. Sim started to pull her goggles over her eyes when the girl turned to face her.

"I love rockabilly," she said.

"Huh?" Sim frowned up at her.

She waved an arm toward the Victrola. "Who is this?"

"The album cover's right there," Sim said, not remembering. She put on her goggles and started on the gadget, while the girl went over to the record and then studied the bookcases while she waited for Azzer. When the flat was fixed and she came to the counter to pay, Sim took her money without looking at her. The girl thanked Azzer, strapped her bag over her chest, and took her bike back out to the street. As she pedaled off, Sim realized that she should have offered to teach her how to fix flats. Almost everyone in the Narrows was able to do it themselves. The repair was easy, and the Incubator sold the tire levers and patch kits.

"Just wait until you see what I have for you to play with," Azzer said, grabbing Sim's attention and ending her moment of contemplation. He rubbed his hands together as he went back to his workshop.

Sim went to the Victrola to turn the record over and crank the key.

"Here they are," Azzer said, holding out two identical palm-sized metal notepads.

One was open, showing a small sheaf of plain paper. A metal stylus held the other one shut, keeping the coppery case closed against a spring in the binding. A tiny stone was set into the center of each one.

"What do they do?" Sim pulled out the stylus and opened the notebook he'd slid onto the counter in front of her.

"Watch, watch," Azzer said as he twisted his stylus so that a quill tip descended from one end. Azzer scribbled something into his notebook, blew on the ink for it to dry, and shut it with a snap.

As if an invisible hand was writing the words in front of her, *Isn't this great?* appeared on Sim's paper in capital letters. Sim frowned up at Azzer, grabbed a pen, and wrote under his message, *So how do these work?*

"You have to close it," Azzer said, waving a hand at her when she looked up at him.

"Oh." Sim dropped the cover over the parchment.

Azzer turned his book to Sim. Both messages were on his parchment. He looked back at her note with a smile.

After spending most of the day tweaking the tablets so that they would work over long distances, Azzer gave Sim the notebooks and sent her off with them. "Give one to a friend and let me know if there are any problems," he said.

He let Sim off early and she rushed over to the bookshop with them, since it would be another twenty minutes until Wood was finished working and Sim couldn't bear to wait around for her at Stein's.

"Hey, Sim," Wood said with a smile when she walked into the small store with its book-must smell. The walls were covered with bookshelves, and a counter trailed along the back of the room. Sim's boots creaked on the old wooden floor as she headed toward the counter, where a charmed fan made Wood's long hair dance around her shoulders. She was hunched over, sorting a pile of softcovers into alphabetical order by author so that she could shelve them.

"You have to check this out," Sim said, getting straight to the point because she didn't want Wood to think she was bothering her at work just to chat. Sim put one of the notepads in front of her and demonstrated the gadget in the same way that Azzer had.

"Azzer invented these? How did he do it?" Wood asked.

"No idea."

Wood smiled, scribbled something into her notebook, and closed the cover. A drawing of a unicat appeared under Sim's note.

"You want to keep it?" Sim asked with a laugh. "I need someone to help me test them out."

"Are you kidding me? That would be so awesome."

Wood's boss glanced up at her from where he was sitting and reading a book. "Whatcha got there?" he asked.

He stood and went close behind her to look over her shoulder at the page. Sim inspected him; she had been in the bookshop before, but never when he had been working. He wore thick, black-framed glasses and had longish hair that hung in his eyes. He was thin and bookish-looking, but handsome, and seemed to wear his glasses and old cardigan as an attempt to cover up his attractiveness. This had to be the bookshop guy that Wood was always running off to see. Sim frowned to cover any emotions that might betray her feelings, and looked away.

"Pretty awesome," he said.

"It's from that little fix-it shop off of Christiania, the one with the gadgets that don't need magic dust. Sim works there," she explained, motioning to her. "Sim, this is Daryl."

"Nice to meet you, Sim," he said with a grin. "That's a pretty cool gadget."

"It's in the beta version, but I guess we'll be selling them soon."

"Let me know when you do?"

"Sure thing."

Daryl nodded, looked at the pile of books in front of Wood, and went back to his stool and his reading.

"I have to finish sorting these," Wood said, catching the hint.

"Stein's later?"

"I have plans." Wood grinned and raised an eyebrow. Her eyes shifted toward Daryl.

"Okay," Sim said with a forced shrug. "I'll see you around then."

"You'll be hearing from me." Wood tapped the top of the notepad and put it into her bag. "I'm glad that you asked me to help with this. Thanks, Sim."

"Who else am I going to write secret messages to?" Sim laughed. She waved and left, going toward her bike because she no longer felt like going to Stein's.

Thoughts of Wood buzzed through Sim's mind throughout her whole ride home, to the point where she was starting to feel like she was going crazy. It wasn't right to continue pretending that she just wanted to be friends with Wood when she knew now that she'd always want more than that. But she couldn't just stop being friends with her. She couldn't stop seeing her.

A soft, persistent feeling of guilt was starting to haunt her conscience. Sim hopped off her bike and led it to the back of Kailash. She noticed that the vegetables in Kai's garden were just about to reach the height of their ripeness and went to the tomatoes, pinching off the suckers where the branches split so that the fruit would grow big and full. An old barrel filled to the brim with rainwater chilled her hands when she plunged a watering can down to her elbows. For a moment she stayed still and embraced the coolness, before going back to the plants and the distractions that made everything seem okay for a little while. The vegetable scent of earth and summer clung to her hands as she went into the kitchen and pulled the notebook out of her bag to see if Wood had written anything to her yet. The parchment under the drawing of the unicat was white and empty. Sim sighed, snapped the notebook shut, and climbed the steps.

"New gadget?" Kai asked, glancing up at her from a big bowl of blueberries. She'd been making jam all week and lining the basement shelves with her sweet concoctions.

"Yeah. It's—"

"Oh! I almost forgot," Kai said suddenly, and ran into the foyer.

"What is it?" Sim asked when Kai came back with a bag swaying in her fingers.

Smiling so broadly that her cheeks pushed up the bottoms of her glasses, she pulled a light-blue dress out of the paper bag. A fringe of flowers rimmed the low-cut neckline. Sim had been surrounded by Jaylenik Nogron's designer clothes for most of her adolescence; she could tell by looking at it that this dress wasn't cheap.

"That's really cute, Kai. What's the occasion?"

"It's not for me, Sim." Kai rolled her eyes. "It's for Prudence. She'll be home any minute now. I can't wait to give it to her."

The dress would come just to the middle of Pru's thighs, swoop just above her small breasts.

"It's a peace offering," Kai explained. "I realized that I should try to be helpful instead of judgmental. Whatever Pru did in the past doesn't mean—"

"You can't give her that." Sim cut her off.

"Why not?"

"You know Pru would never wear that."

"Well that's the problem, isn't it?"

Sim sighed and looked at the wall. She sucked on her upper lip and bit it hard with her bottom teeth. Everything she'd ever held back from saying to Kai suddenly welled up in her chest and hovered in the hollow space just below her throat.

"Once Prudence pretties up a little, she'll get more attention from boys and then she won't have to look to women for affection," Kai continued. "She just needs some help, and as her friend it's my duty to help her. I'm trying to save her soul, Sim. It's—"

"Are you listening to yourself?" The words snapped out of Sim's mouth. "Prudence doesn't want to date men. She told you that. She likes women. Why can't you accept that?"

Kai held her ground with a laugh. "She doesn't really like women, Sim. It just...It goes against nature—"

Sim held up her hand and interrupted. "What do you even know about love, Kai? You just stay inside here all day and hide away from the world. The only time you ever leave is to go to devotional or to the market. And even if you did try to find someone, I doubt they would have you. You don't care about anyone but yourself and your close-minded beliefs."

"I don't—" Kai began. But now that she'd started, Sim couldn't stop.

"Here's the truth, Kai: Somewhere along the line you got it into your head that you live on some high pedestal where you get to decide what's right and wrong in the world and then make everyone else follow your rules. But you're not better than anyone else and your rules are bullshit. These aren't Veldindor's laws; they're yours. They're idiotic and ignorant. And I know that a woman can love another woman. Because I'm in love with one. And you go right ahead and try to tell me that's wrong. Try to tell me that, Kai. Look me in the fucking eyes and tell me that I'm going to burn in hell because of something that I have absolutely no control over. Go ahead and do it."

Kai's jaw shifted up and down in speechless shock. She looked away and shook her head, blinked tears down her cheeks, and shifted her long black hair so that she could hide behind it.

"Say it to my face," Sim said through clenched teeth.

"I do not make up Veldindor's laws," Kai said quietly. She put her hands up to her eyes. Breathing deeply, but not quite sobbing, Kai rushed past her and out into the garden. The screen door slammed behind her.

"All of that over a dress?" Prudence slipped into the kitchen from the foyer.

Sim wiped at her eyes and tried to compose herself. "What did you hear?"

"Everything." Pru pulled the dress out of the bag, shook her head, and dropped it. "You didn't have to do that."

"I did."

Pru nodded. "That's what you've been wanting to talk to me about. I figured, but I didn't think it was this serious. Well, who is she?"

Sim looked up at her. She wasn't sure she could say the words out loud.

Pru shrugged. "I mean, you don't have to—"

"It's Wood. I'm in love with Wood."

"The bookshop girl." Pru frowned. "Love's a strong word," she said slowly.

"I've never felt like this about anyone before." The tears came to Sim's eyes again, and she hated herself for it. She was glad that Prudence wasn't looking at her. "There's no other word to explain it. I'm head over heels in love with her and she doesn't even know it."

"Do you think she might be interested?"

"I don't know. I think she's kind of seeing this guy."

Pru sighed through her nose. "Sim, there are plenty of other girls in this city."

"I can't think about anyone but her. I wish it weren't the truth. I've tried to forget about it. I can't."

After a moment of thought, Pru went to the fridge and pulled out two Kaianides. She clattered around inside of a drawer and scanned the countertops for a bottle opener. Pressing her lips together, Pru rested the edge of the cap on the corner of the counter and slapped the heel of her palm down onto it. The cap fell to the floor. She handed the Kaianide to Sim and opened her own beer the same way before turning and leaning against the counter with her arms crossed over her chest.

"So what are you going to do?" she asked.

Sim sipped at the lager. "What do you mean?"

"You can't keep walking around dreaming about someone. It's not good for you. You have to do something."

"You think I should tell her?"

Pru shook her head. "This is all on you. Tell her, stop seeing her, or date other people. You have to figure it out. But you have to do something."

"I tried to stop seeing her and I can't." Sim sighed.

"So then maybe you should tell her. You don't know for sure how she feels. Maybe she's really into you. But don't just leap into this, Sim. There's something to be said for treading carefully."

Sim took a long swig of her beer and waited for Pru to say something more, but she didn't.

"I should just talk to her," Sim said. "Then when she tells me she doesn't feel the same way, at least I might be able to move on."

"You're such a masochist," Pru said with a short laugh and a shake of her head. She tilted the bottom of her bottle toward Sim. "So how does it feel to have finally said it?"

Sim tapped the bottom of her own bottle against Pru's and took a long drink. She was glad that Pru was trying to keep things light. "Feels good, I guess," she said with a little smile. And it did. The feeling that had been pressing in on her chest for the past couple of months eased up enough for Sim to imagine that it wasn't even there anymore. Even though she was starting to feel guilty for what she'd said to Kai, and she still had to figure out what to do about Wood, she felt better than she had in a long time.

"Porch?" Pru asked.

Sim nodded and followed her out of the house. They talked while Pru smoked and made fun of Wood to make Sim feel better. She could easily find a girl who was a lot less self-absorbed, Pru said, and who didn't go home at eight every night when she wasn't hooking up with some dude. Mostly they just watched the people going by.

Her beer finished, Pru stood and headed for the house. "Let me know if you decide to try the dating thing." Pru threw Sim a grin over her shoulder. "That I can help you with."

"Yeah, I will." But the idea of going on a date made Sim's heart seize up. She couldn't date. She didn't know the first thing about going out with girls. Or with anyone at all. She gulped down the rest of her Kaianide and headed for her bike.

Pausing next to her cruiser, Sim took out the notepad again. Still blank. *Have fun on your date?* Sim wrote, partly because she couldn't think of anything else, but mostly because she wanted Wood to say that it hadn't been a date. She snapped the notepad shut and put it into her bag. Maybe things weren't better now that she'd told Pru and Kai that she liked a girl.

Sim headed down Kailash Street toward Lower Terresin, wondering if she'd maybe bump into Wood on her way home. Another biker passed her, going the wrong way down the street, but it was some girl that Sim didn't recognize. As she biked to clear her mind, Sim vacillated between basking in a wonderful, fuzzy, in-love feeling and imagining the horror of Wood's imminent rejection.

She'd tell her to stop at the bottom of the bridge on their way back, or at the wall where they kept their bikes. Playing it all by ear seemed to be the best option. Standing outside of Stein's, Sim checked the notebook one more time. Wood had never responded to her message. That was a bad sign. Sim threw the gadget back into her bag and went into the café, which was full of people and chatter—even more full than usual for that time of day. All of the seats at the communal table were taken except for one that Wood had saved for Sim with her bag. Adrenaline coursed through Sim's limbs as soon as she saw Wood. Her hands started to shake. She hoped no one would notice, and went up to the beast-man to order her coffee. By the time she went to sit next to Wood, she'd calmed herself enough to act normal.

"Sim!" Wood smiled. "How was work?"

"Same as always. You?"

"Really busy, actually. Everyone wants to read books all of a sudden. I'm sorry I never got a chance to answer you with the notebook thing, by the way. I ended up going back to Daryl's place. I told myself that I would absolutely not sleep with him after the first date but...." She grinned. "You know how it goes. But I promise I'll write something tonight."

"Whenever," Sim said with a shrug. "I'm glad the thing with Daryl went well. So you're dating, then?"

Wood frowned. "No," she said with a short laugh. "It's hardly that serious. I mean, he's really cool but I doubt that he'd even want a relationship."

Relief calmed Sim's nerves; she still had a chance. She could still tell Wood how she felt. But not just yet; not in Stein's. Wood changed the subject to revolution and how necessary it was and how they could make it happen.

"We all need to band together," Wood said. She'd just finished a book called *The Revolutionary's Manifesto*, about how manipulative and sinister the government was and how they were all just slaves to the system. Wood slapped her palms down onto the table. "We can't stand for this: for the oppression of our own people, for the racism that rules everything, for this vile, unjust war."

"So what do we do about it?" Sim asked. Half of her mind listened to what Wood was saying while the other half continued to recite the profession of love she'd decided to deliver. She had to make it clear that she didn't expect Wood to feel the same way; that was the only way she wouldn't totally freak her out.

"The press." Wood held up an old copy of the *Candle*. "And demonstrations. We can block the streets. We can have sit-ins, hunger strikes."

"Azzer's talked about this before," Sim said. "The governors are elected democratically, right? So we just have to get enough people for them to be worried about keeping their offices, and then we can push through whatever changes we want."

Wood shook her head impatiently. "It's more than that, Sim. Sometimes you have to be destructive in order to get your message across. Sometimes destruction is warranted. Daryl was saying this earlier today and I think he's absolutely right."

Daryl. Sim shifted in her seat. She'd never heard Wood talk like this before. "I guess so," Sim said, though she didn't entirely agree with her. It felt wrong, to try to end hatred with hatred. And she wasn't sure exactly what it was that Wood was so outraged about.

The conversation went on, with Sim listening and Wood ranting, until before she knew it Wood was stuffing her things into her bag. "You staying?" she asked.

Sim nodded and stayed frozen in her seat. Tomorrow. She'd talk to her tomorrow.

"Okay. I have to go home and read more. Classes start in two weeks. I have to be ready."

"Good luck. See you," Sim said. Her stomach sank at the thought of Wood going back to school. Sim wondered if they'd still hang out, once Wood didn't come to the Narrows anymore.

* * *

The loud music and dim lights of the Geraldine greeted Sim like an old friend. The girls were already buzzed on dragon-nectar sours, even though the sky had hardly begun to darken. One couple was making out against the back wall. Another two girls slipped into the bathroom, giggling. Brooke, the blonde girl who had been bothering Pru the first time Sim had come to the Geraldine, hoisted herself onto the bar to let Grimms take a body shot off her stomach. She rolled up her shirt to the bottom of her lacy black bra and leaned back onto her elbows. Candace poured moon glow into her navel and stepped back with a laugh. Afraid that she'd be asked to do it next, Sim kept her eyes clear of the bartender.

"No more Bongo Trees," Candace said when Pru tried to order.

"You're already out? It's not even ten yet."

"I mean no more ever." Candace raised her eyebrows and wiped down the counter as if she were indifferent to the whole thing. But her voice was a notch higher than usual, and her movements just slightly quicker. She shrugged and threw the rag behind the bar. "They've been busted."

"Busted?" Sim's heart jumped.

"Damn," Pru grumbled. "I really liked that beer."

"What do you mean they've been busted?" Sim asked again.

"It's a risk we all take," Candace said, meeting Sim's eyes. "The Bikeway Narrows is probably one of the safest places for violators of the prohibition law, but even here we can get caught."

"What happened?"

"The Guard found their distributor and he ratted them out. Three other brewers went down, too."

"And now—"

"They're in the work camps." Candace finished for her. "That's what I've heard, at least."

"So what's good now, then?" Pru asked.

"Kaianide's been hotter than ever."

Pru glared at her. "What else?"

"I don't know." Candace sighed. "You can try Lewd Lager. It's a dirty brown."

Prudence sighed deeply and looked at Sim. "You want to come out while I have a cigarette?"

"Sure."

"Oh, come on, girls," Candace said. "Lighten up. Here, have a shot of dragon nectar on me before you head out."

When we come back," Pru said, already halfway to the door.

Sim followed, her arms crossed over her chest and worry knotting up her shoulders. "I can't believe Bongo Tree got caught," Sim said softly, even though they were the only ones on the sidewalk.

"Acheron's not sloppy," Pru said. "And neither is Cader. Don't worry about it. You'll be fine."

"I don't know, Pru. I'm not sure it's worth it—"

"Can we talk about something else? If anything, it's your mouth that's going to get everyone in trouble."

"Fine. What do you want to talk about then?"

"Anything. See anyone you like?"

"I don't know. Not really. I was going to talk to Wood today, but I chickened out."

"Do it tomorrow. Find someone else for tonight."

"Maybe." Sim gulped away the fear that Pru would actively try to find someone for her. She started to talk about how there needed to be an uprising, a revolution fueled by those who went to the Narrows, so that the government would finally listen to them.

"Where is this coming from?" Pru frowned at her.

"Wood was talking about the war today. It's all over magic dust, you know."

Pru frowned up at the fire cage, the orange light swimming over her features, and then stared across the street.

"I don't think it's that simple."

"It is simple," Sim said, even though Pru didn't seem to be in the mood for a discussion. "The war is wrong. We need to do whatever we can to stop it."

"Don't fool yourself, Sim." The end of Pru's cigarette glowed as she took a long drag. "No one gives a shit about what we think."

"They'll listen to us. Once everyone hears the truth they'll have to. There's black magic coming off the factories, you know. I've seen it with my own eyes. With Azzer's goggles."

Prudence laughed, deep and cynical. "A lot of people know about that. Anyone who reads a legitimate newspaper knows about it, just like they know that the war's not really about us preventing an ogre invasion. They already know the truth. And they're pretending not to."

"I don't believe that."

"Then you're just as deluded as they are." Pru threw her cigarette into the street. "That girl is filling your head with bullshit. People believe what they want to."

"Well, it's not fair."

"So?"

"How can you sit there knowing that Siccorians are being killed every day, in your own country, and not even care?"

"Look, Sim, it's nice to talk about these things—it's nice to rant about them in the Candle or at Stein's—but let's be realistic: There's nothing we can do."

"That's a pretty pathetic excuse."

"I've tried." Pru's voice was growing angry. "It's bigger than we are. The world is fucked and no matter how hard anyone tries to unfuck it, there's absolutely nothing we can do about it."

Sim was quiet. She stared forward with angry tears burning her eyes.

"It's not really anything to cry over." Pru glanced at her uncomfortably and looked away. "You okay?"

Sim didn't answer.

Pru pulled two cigarettes out of the pack in her pocket and held one out to Sim, who paused but then took it. The soft filter compressed a little between Sim's lips while she waited for Pru's fire. "Inhale," Pru said, holding her thumb at the edge of Sim's tobacco. Sim breathed in a cloud of smoke and coughed. Her lungs felt scratchy and her head light and fuzzy.

"You'll get used to it," Pru said, taking a drag of her own.

"You really think there's nothing we can do about it?" Sim asked. "The black magic, I mean. And the war."

"Who are we to try to change anything?"

"But you're a quester. You're one of the good guys."

Pru sat and hugged her legs to her chest. "I do that for the money. It's not always good." She took a drag of her cigarette. "I just want to mind my own business and get by, that's all. It's useless, trying to save the world. Only crazy people fight a battle that they know they'll loose. Took me long enough to figure that one out." She took another long drag of her tobacco and closed her eyes as she exhaled. She opened them and glanced at Sim. "You good?"

"Yeah." Sim put out her cigarette on the edge of the planter and threw it to the roots. "Let's try that Lewd Lager."

"Absolutely not."

Sim gave her a questioning look.

"I'm not drinking something with a name that stupid."

She and Pru had a few dragon-nectar sours, and then Pru started to dance with a girl Sim hadn't seen there before. She had long blonde hair, bright green eyes, and nimble fingers that were starting to wrap around Pru's neck, wind in her hair. Sim could have gone to talk with Grimms and the other Geraldine girls, but she didn't feel like it. Slightly tipsy and incredibly drained, she went to the alley for her bike. Sim rode back alone, swearing that she'd never have another cigarette when she started up the bridge's ramp and could barely get a lungful of air. Somehow she made it to the top and sped down toward the Mondran Quarter, almost wishing that the creatures would appear on the bridge again so that there would be an end to all of this.

X

The next morning Sim sat alone in the kitchen, eating cold cereal, trying to read the newspaper. It was Veldindy, but Pru still hadn't come back from the night before and Cader had gone off somewhere early that morning. Sim glanced up at the glass cabinets that held Kai's potions. She wondered if Kai had any love potions in there, or if she had a book with instructions on how to make one. Even as the thought ran through Sim's mind, she assured herself that she would never actually use a love potion on Wood, or an anti-love potion on herself. She knew that would be a horrible idea. But it couldn't hurt to know if Kai had one. Just as Sim was getting up to check, quick footsteps pounded up the staircase in the foyer. Kai burst into the kitchen, threw her wallet and keys into her purse, and ran back into the other room.

"What is it?" Sim asked, rushing after her. "Kai, what's wrong?"

The thin laces of Kai's boots slipped from her fingers as she tried to tie them. She jerked up and looked at Sim, her eyes wide behind her glasses.

"Pru's in the hospital," she said as she grabbed her purse off the floor.

"What? Is she okay?"

"I don't know. A pigeon brought this to my window. Pru must have spelled it to carry the message." Kai pushed a rolled-up piece of paper into Sim's hand. It was a note in Pru's handwriting, saying that she was in Veldindor Health Center and the nurses wouldn't let her leave. She was somewhere on the second floor and she needed them to help her get out.

"Why does she need our help?" Sim asked, frowning down at the note.

"I don't know, Sim. Does it really matter? But, I mean, Pru isn't Pulchran, you know. She doesn't have the papers she needs to stay here legally."

Sim's heart dropped. "They'll deport her."

"They might do worse than that."

"Where is it? I'm going."

When she got her bike onto the street, all of the possibilities of what could have happened to Pru started to flash through Sim's mind: She could have gotten into a fight, could have gotten hit by a carriage on the bike ride back, could have been attacked by one of those creatures. Sim imagined Prudence lying on a hospital bed, bloody and riddled with bite marks from their fangs. She cast a speed spell on her cruiser. Her hair whipped behind her. A horn blared. Sim stuck up her middle finger and focused on not getting caught between stopped cars.

The waiting room of Veldindor Health Center greeted Sim with a welcome shock of icy air. Goosebumps ran up her arms. She scanned the occupied chairs, the stacks of old magazines, and the fake plants greening the corners where translucent dividers sectioned off waiting areas. The whole place smelled of sour cleaning potions. The receptionist was an older lady with glasses that drew up into points at both ends. Gum snapped between her teeth. She glanced up at Sim, who was standing a few feet away, and scanned her eyes disapprovingly over Sim's tank top, her tight black jeans, and the goggles on her forehead.

"Uh, where's the restroom?" Sim asked. The receptionist looked away and pointed to a door just down the hallway to her left.

"Thanks," Sim mumbled, but the receptionist's attention was back on the paperwork in front of her. Her pen scratched across the parchment. Sim glanced at her once more before slipping past the restroom door and trotting lightly down the long, gleaming hallway.

The stairwell hadn't been too difficult to find. Sim squatted on the landing of the second floor and pushed her hair out of her face. A bold "Authorized Personnel Only" sign was tacked above the door's handle, where a locking charm glowed in a bright red halo. She directed her attention toward the charm's brightest points and shot energy out from her center. The charm broke in a thousand droplets of red light, bursting into a tiny firework that evaporated around Sim's knees. She decalibrated her goggles with a tired sigh, pulled open the door, and stepped into a hallway that seemed to be deserted. She turned right, went to the closest door, and squinted through its gated window.

The room was small and dark. Long curtains formed rings around each of the beds. When she was sure there were no nurses or healers inside, Sim stepped inside and shut the door gently behind her. The air smelled rank, like urine and something rotting. As Sim approached one of the bed stalls, the long tube that flickered dim florescent light onto the walkway between the curtains buzzed and went out. For three breaths Sim stood perfectly still, blind in the darkness. The light flicked back on. Sim inhaled. The curtain was thick and rough in her hand. Her heart pattered and Sim silently scolded herself for being so frightened. She pulled the curtain open, just a few inches, enough so that she could see if Pru was in there, and stifled a gasp.

Tubes ran from a large glass cylinder, channeled a pulsing green liquid at the rate of a heartbeat to where it disappeared into the pale inner forearm of the person lying on the bed. He was almost human, but not quite. The light flickered again and shadows danced across the thing's face. One side of its mouth peeled down into its cheek, showing a few yellowed teeth jutting out from pale gums. The thing was thin, emaciated. Light, mucus-laced snores came from deep in its chest. A dark blood stain ran down the length of one side of the bedding, where it looked like the creature—or person; Sim didn't know what to call it—had bled out from the tubes. The thing's wrists were wrapped with thick metal cuffs, chained to the bed with a padlock so that it was trapped in its stall.

Sim stepped back. She thought for a moment that she was going to be sick, but in a blink the feeling was overtaken by an irresistible urge to run. Rotting skin, like a compost heap amplified a hundredfold: That had to be the rancid smell that Sim could nearly taste on her tongue. She shut her eyes tight and swallowed hard. She had to focus; she had to find Pru. Leaving the first curtain open, Sim went to the stall on the other side of the walkway, only to find a similar creature with the same glass cylinder and tubes running into its arms. This one was womanish, slightly more human looking, also bald except for a few stubborn hairs clinging to her scalp. Her breasts formed twin bumps under the sheet, her nipples hard from the room's cold air. Sores dotted one side of her face and her shoulders were hunched up to her ears. Sim had seen enough. Pru couldn't be in this room.

A loud clank came from a few stalls down. Sim scanned the walkway. Her heart was pounding hard enough to hear it in her ears. The curtain of the first stall was still open. Sim went to close it and froze. The creature gazed at her with milky blue eyes. Moaning, it tried to lift its hands, but couldn't—not because of the chains but because its arms weren't strong enough. It was trying to say something. Water. It was asking for water. Sim looked away from the thing, locked up to a bed, left alone in that horrible blinking darkness. She went to the sink, found a glass there, and filled it.

It slipped out of her hand and shattered when she turned back. One of the creatures was on its hands and knees, only a few feet away. All she could see of its dark outline was sticklike arms, an arched back, legs that were impossibly long. It crawled toward her, its long knotted hair dragging on the floor. It moaned loudly, crying like a child. An ancient hand, its knuckles swollen and arthritic, reached toward Sim's leg. She imagined the hand wrapping around her ankle, imagined the creature infecting her with whatever disease it had. Sim turned, wrenched the door open, and sprinted to the steps. There was no time to think. She closed the stairwell door behind her and watched through the window as a nurse appeared, walking quickly down to the room. Sim wanted to go back to the bathroom on the first floor, hide in one of the stalls, and stay there. But she had to find Pru. She had to get her out of this place.

"How did you get out of your bed?" she heard the nurse yell, muffled behind the room's closed door. "I'll have to give you an injection now. How do you like that? You know you're supposed to stay in bed."

The creature's wail came from the room, followed by a sharp slap. "I don't want to hear it," the nurse snarled. "Shut up." The thing moaned again and then broke out in raspy sobs. Another slap followed. "Shut up, I said! Didn't you hear me? Shut up!"

Sim couldn't listen anymore. She crept from the stairwell toward the door that the nurse had left open and slipped into a room that was full of light from two big windows on its far side. Sim peeked into each of the curtained stalls, meeting the eyes of a yellow-skinned junkie in one and an angry-looking, red-mohawked punk in another, until she got to the third stall from the last. There was no body cast, no bite marks. There was just Prudence, lying on a cot with her arms crossed over her chest and her head tilted to the side. Dark makeup ringed her closed eyes and slight snores escaped her open mouth. Sim slid the curtain closed behind her and sat in the one chair that was across from the bed.

Pru's eyes opened slowly. She glanced at Sim and then looked away. "I had to spell a pigeon," she mumbled. She looked exhausted. "I hate spelling animals. It's horrible. Barbaric."

"Whatever, you had to," Sim said quickly. Spelling a pigeon hardly seemed barbaric compared to what she had just seen. She whispered, "We have to get you out of here. I don't know how we're going to sneak you past the nurse."

"That spell really drained me, Sim," Pru said.

"I'll help you."

"Sorry you had to come." Pru's voice choked a little as she spoke, like she was holding back tears. "They wouldn't let me out."

"What happened?" Sim asked, ignoring the apology.

Pru shook her head and frowned. "I was dumb. Had one too many shots of moon glow. I left the Geraldine with a girl, but I don't remember anything after that. A cop found me sleeping on the subway platform and made me come here. I got lost somehow. I think I was trying to make my way back. I have no idea where my bike is. I have no idea where that girl is, or if she's okay."

"But you're okay?"

Pru nodded. "Just incredibly hungover."

A hangover. All that Sim had been through in the past hour had been for a hangover. Her mind told her that she should be angry, but she wasn't. She couldn't be.

"As long as you're safe, that's all that matters," Sim said. "It's a good thing they found you. Those people who are in the subway late at night...But you're okay. You're lucky."

"Yeah, I guess." Pru sniffed. "But that girl...I think I left her. I gave the night patrol a hard time when they found me. That much I do remember. I really didn't want to go with them, but I had to or they would've arrested me. And then when I woke up here and tried to leave, they wouldn't let me."

The figure crawling on the floor flashed into Sim's mind. She blinked. Pru sat up, crossed her legs, and buried her head in her hands.

"I can't believe this happened. I can't keep doing this. This is it. And I let you go home by yourself again. Anything could have happened to you. I can't believe I did that." Pru looked up. Her eyes were full of tears. Sim had never seen her so close to crying. "I'm so sorry, Sim."

"It's okay. I was fine getting back by myself. I'm just glad that nothing bad happened to you."

"A lot of bad things happened. This was the worst...." She clenched her jaw and frowned against her tears. "But I deserve all of it."

Before Sim could respond, Kai slipped open the curtain and stepped inside.

"Pru! Thank Veldindor," she whispered. "There are two Guard members out there asking about you. I was just barely able to slip past them."

"How did you—" Sim started, but Kai waved a hand to quiet her.

"They're at the other end of the room filling out paperwork," Kai said, peering through the gap in the curtains. "We have five minutes maybe. I can't tell. Did they get your information?"

"I wouldn't give it to them. And they couldn't find it. I lost my wallet."

"Good. Then we just need to sneak out." Kai said, and looked at Sim.

"Don't look at me," Sim said. "I don't know how the hell we're going to do that."

"Well, you two better think of something." Kai glanced out at the Guards again.

"I can distract them," Sim said.

"You're going to have to decharm the lock on the bathroom window," Pru said. "Kai will have to distract them and then walk out the front door."

They looked to Kai. She nodded and said, "Okay. What do I have to do?"

"I want to see my boyfriend now!" Kai shouted. "I was told that he was in this room, and I want to see him now."

"I'm telling you, you're on the wrong floor," the nurse snapped.

"I'm not some idiot. I know I have rights. You had better start respecting them, or I'll get my father over here and..."

Sim could tell by the sound of her voice that tears were running down Kai's cheeks. She peeked out of the stall to see Kai stomping her foot and trying to grab the nurse's clipboard.

"I have a right to see him. I'll check every stall again if I have to—"

"Ma'am, I told you, he's not here. You're not even supposed to be on this floor. Now if you don't calm down—"

Kai turned to the guards. "Do something!"

"Now," Sim said, and hurried to the bathroom across from the bed stall. Pru crept behind her, the blanket wrapped around her upper body and head to hide her unmistakable hair and clothes.

"Crap," Sim muttered under her breath as she fumbled with the knob. She knocked on the door.

"Just a minute!" someone called from inside.

"Can you hurry?" Sim asked. "It's an emergency."

"There's another bathroom out in the hallway."

"Hurry the hell up," Pru growled at the door.

"There a time limit on taking a dump now?"

"Awesome," Pru said, and glanced around. The windows were open but barred, and in full view of the door. Sim slipped on her goggles and blinked until her eyes adjusted to the burst of colors.

"I'm not fucking going to jail," Pru said. She cupped her hand around the bathroom doorknob and cast a de-locking spell. The knob turned bright red just before the lock clicked out of the door. Pru dipped from fatigue, but without a breath to wait she pushed the door open and went to the toilet. Her hand wrapped around the collar of the old man who was crouched there. She yanked him to his feet and flung him into the main room, where he tripped over the pants bunched around his ankles.

"So much for being discrete," Sim mumbled as she closed the door behind her, locked it, and turned to the window.

"Hurry," Pru said, switching places with Sim and leaning her weight against the door.

The window had both an alarm charm and a lock charm: One cast bright-red bars across the glass and the other outlined it in green. Sim knelt before the window, tapped into the energy of the red bars, and tried to break it with her own. They were too strong.

The magic dust in the air was thinner than usual from all of the spells and charms streaming through the hospital. Sim pushed as hard as she could, but the red bars wouldn't give. She severed the connection to the lock charm and put her hands on her knees. She gasped for air. A fuzzy blanket of exhaustion wrapped around her and her thoughts became short and muddled.

"Sim? What's wrong?" Pru asked.

"I can't do it."

"What?"

"Hello?" There was a knock on the door. "Hello? Ma'am? Can you open the door please?" It was one of the Guards.

"Yeah, just hold on," Pru said. She paused and then added, "I have my period."

"Ma'am, we need you to come out here right now."

"I will! Just wait a second!"

Sim looked around the bathroom for something to break the window with. Her eyes caught on a bright-blue bottle at the base of the toilet. Magic dust. It must have fallen out of the man's pocket when Pru grabbed him.

"Ma'am, we're going to have to break down the door if you don't let us in."

"Just hold on," Pru said, watching Sim. "I've made a mess of myself. I'll be out in a minute."

Sim poured the dust into her palm. It looked like liquid light behind the lenses of her goggles. At Sim's direction, the light rose out of her hand and went to the red bars. Like creeping ivy, blue tendrils of magic wound around the red lock charm. When Sim felt that there was enough blue magic, she sent out a burst of energy, making the lock charm evaporate into a sprinkling purple rain. The alarm spell still glowed green along the edges of the windowpane. Sim sent out the tiny bit of dust she had left and then poured her own white light out of herself, intensified the blue magic, and, with one burst of force like that last knock-out punch, she drove her will at the alarm charm.

"You open it," she whispered to Pru. She pulled the goggles past her nose and let them hang around her neck.

The door kicked open. Without hesitating, Pru pulled back her arm, punched the Guard in the face, and kicked him back out into the room, where the nurse and the other guard were screaming. Pru slammed the door shut and in the next moment she was hoisting herself up onto the windowsill and sliding outside. She stood on a concrete ledge that was just high enough for her to still be able to see into the bathroom.

"Hurry, Sim!"

She'd sent out too much of her energy. Her legs were too heavy to lift. Sim stuck her head and shoulders out the window and looked down at Pru.

"I can't do it. You have to run. My bike's near the front."

"I'm not leaving you." Pru glared at her. "Now get your ass out onto this ledge."

"I'll try."

"Hurry the fuck up."

Somehow Sim was able to get her right foot up onto the windowsill and start to edge outside. It wasn't a terribly long fall, but without a doubt she'd break her leg if she jumped from that high. Pru wrapped her hands around Sim's waist and steadied her.

"Don't worry, you won't fall," Pru said, her voice now calm. "I've got you, I promise."

Sim slid forward, her eyes closed, her teeth clenched, ready to slip and tumble off the ledge. But Pru's strength guided her until she felt her boots meet the ledge with a solid clunk. She opened her eyes. Pru's hands were on her arms now, still holding her up. She crouched down a little to Sim's height so that she could look her straight in the eyes.

"Can you stand on your own?"

Sim grasped the window ledge and nodded. The Guard's partner ran into the bathroom.

"Don't look at him," Pru said. "Don't let him see your face."

Pru turned, took three strides along the ledge, and hoisted herself onto a fire escape. Sim pulled up her goggles to hide her eyes and followed. The ladder clicked down with a loud creak when Pru jumped onto it, and stopped three feet above a closed dumpster. Without hesitating, Pru dropped the rest of the way, hopped down into the alley, and ran to get Sim's bike. The Guard was climbing out onto the ledge but was struggling. Sim couldn't help but glance back. His enormous stomach made it too difficult for him to lift his leg over the windowsill.

"Stop or I'll shoot!" he yelled.

Sim had to hope that he was bluffing. She hopped onto the fire escape and climbed down the ladder, keeping her face toward the ground so that he wouldn't see it. Her knees gave out from the small jump onto the dumpster's lid and she tumbled to the ground next to Pru, who had just sped back into the alley. Sim's bike rested against the back of Pru's legs as she pulled Sim to her feet.

"You have to sit on the seat and hold onto me," she said. "Don't think about how tired you are. Just do it."

Pru held the bike steady as Sim hopped up onto the saddle and splayed her feet outward so that they wouldn't get in the way of Pru's pedaling legs. An immense feeling of helplessness tightened Sim's muscles. She grasped Pru's shoulders.

"You ready?" Pru asked, but she didn't wait for Sim to answer. She stepped onto a pedal and sped toward the street. The second Guard came running through the hospital's sliding-glass doors just as Pru jetted by them. There was a gun in his hand— Sim saw it out of the corner of her eye: a black metal pistol that caught the afternoon sunlight with a sickening gleam.

"Hurry, Pru," Sim said, wrapping her arms tight around Pru's waist and trying not to throw her off balance.

A shot went off behind them and shattered the rear window of the carriage they'd just passed. "Shit," Pru mumbled, but she didn't seem scared. She kept her pace quick and steady and tried to stay in front of a carriage so that it would block them from the Guard's shots. The pistol went off again somewhere behind them. Two shots. Both missed. They were lucky. They made it back to Kailash.

Sim slipped off Pru's saddle and sank onto the front steps. Pru brought the bike up to the porch and sat next to her, resting her head on her knees. Neither of them said anything. Eventually Kai came back and sat between them.

"Well, that was interesting," she said after a minute. "Glad to see you're both still alive."

Sim couldn't speak. Her mind wasn't quite working yet.

Pru took a deep breath, let it out slowly, and turned to Kai with a grin. "I didn't know you had such great acting skills," she said.

Kai huffed, sat up straight, and started to pull her hair into a high ponytail. "I did what I had to." She got to her feet. "Don't think I'm not mad about all of this."

Pru nodded, her face becoming serious again. "Yeah, you should be. But thanks."

"Don't thank me. Sim's the one who got you out of there. Look at her, she's practically in shock."

"I'm not," Sim said quickly. "I'm fine."

"You sure?" Pru studied her with a frown.

"It's not the first time I've been shot at."

Pru smiled, but it was shallow, forced. She looked up at Kai. "See? She's tough. She'll be all right."

"You should be glad you're not in jail," Kai said. "You're lucky to have a second chance, Pru. Don't waste it." And at that she stomped into the house and shut the door hard behind her.

XI

aphazard piles of weeds—the leftovers from Prudence's attempt at morning chores—dotted the periphery of the wooden planters. The brussels sprouts, potatoes, and kale had ripened, and Sim had spent the last two days harvesting them under Kai's careful instruction. Pru had been helping for the past few days too, since she'd stopped going out after the hospital incident and had more free time than she knew what to do with.

"Is Prudence back yet?" Kai asked when Sim creaked open the door and stepped into the battling scents of the drying house: lavender, purslane, rosemary, tamarind, so many others that she still didn't know the names of.

"I haven't seen her."

"She's been gone for over an hour now. I knew I should have just gone to the market myself. If only there weren't so many freaking stalks to tie up." Kai yanked on the ends of a piece of twine, binding a bunch of lavender together. She threw it on top of a pile and glanced over at Sim. "Just leave that mint there. I need you to hang these for me. You're taller."

"Sure thing."

"Just a second, though. I need to charge them first." Kai squatted down by the pile and held her hands just above it without quite touching the stalks.

"Hello?" someone called from the backyard. "Is there anyone back here?"

Kai's eyes snapped open. Sim had never heard the voice before. It was a girl's, with a strange accent that she couldn't quite catch.

"Did you invite anyone over?" Kai asked.

"No, of course not." Strangers never came to Kailash; there was too much they could see, too much that they all had to hide. Kai jumped to her feet, but Sim was already rushing toward the drying house door. She slipped around one of the herb spirals and halted. A girl wearing an ivory dress and shiny white pumps was standing next to the back steps, her hand resting on the saddle of a black track bike. Her eyes were wide and nervous, giving her an almost childlike look, but she had to be in her early twenties. She was tall, with perfect posture and silky brown hair that was long for a Mondran woman.

"I think you have the wrong house," Sim said.

Kai peeked out from behind a spiral and jerked her head back. Sim gave her a look and hoped that she wouldn't act weird.

"Wait," Sim said, cutting the girl off just as she was about to speak again. "Where did you get that bike?"

"That's why I'm here." Her voice shook. "I've come to return it. Is Prudence here?"

"How do you know Prudence?" Kai stepped out to stand next to Sim.

"I met her a few nights ago. I said I'd bring it back for her, but I wasn't able to get away until now."

"Remidy night?" Sim asked.

The girl nodded. "I tried to get her to stay with me, but it was all I could do to convince her she was too messed up to bike home—"

In the kitchen, Prudence clunked the groceries onto the table and went to the door. "I'm never going back to that market again," she called out to the yard. "There's so many idiots just standing in the way—" She pushed the screen open and let it hang in her hand. She stepped outside and stared down at the Mondran, letting the screen door slam shut behind her.

"That's my bike," she said, glaring at the girl.

In two steps Pru was on the walkway and snatching the handlebars. The girl took a step back. Pru lifted the frame and leaned it against the house, on the other side of the steps.

"Prudence?" the girl said. "You don't—don't you remember me?"

Still turned toward the house, Pru glanced back at her with a deep frown.

"It was three nights ago," the girl continued. "I'm Audrae. You fell off your bike after you came over the bridge, when you were going through the Mondran Quarter. We sat together for about twenty minutes and then you were going to ride off again but I convinced you to leave your bike with me. I tried to tell you to stay, but you wouldn't."

Pru ran a hand through her hair and looked away. "I don't remember any of that."

"You were pretty drunk."

Pru searched for something to say. "You kept my bike for me?"

"I told you I'd bring it back. I meant to come sooner, but I had to help my family with their bakery. You don't remember anything at all?"

"No." Pru sniffed, crossed her arms over her chest, and turned to Audrae. She studied her face. "I don't remember you. But thanks."

"You're welcome." Audrae opened her mouth and closed it, as if there was something else she wanted to say but then thought better of it. She sighed, shook her head, and stared off. A thoughtful frown crept across her face. "Is that rosemary?" she asked, looking over Sim's shoulder.

"Yeah," Sim said, glancing at the herbs next to her. "We grow it on these spirals."

Kai snorted. "We?"

Seeming to forget the awkwardness of the bike situation, Audrae went to the spiral and ran her fingers over the leaves, brought one of the stalks up to her nose, and inhaled its scent. She looked at the three of them. "Can I buy some from you?"

"Buy some?" Kai echoed.

"For our bakery. It's really hard to find good herbs in the city. Especially rosemary."

"We don't sell—" Kai started.

"You can have as much as you want," Pru interrupted, and glared at Kai when she began to protest.

"Really?" The girl blinked with disbelief at Pru's sudden kindness.

"I owe you," Pru said with a shrug. "Just let us know what you need."

"Okay." Audrae smiled and then brought the corners of her lips back down. "Well, I can't take it now; I'll have to come back for it."

"That's fine."

Audrae nodded and went to the side of the house to leave. She turned and glanced back at Pru. "Well. I'll see you later this week, then."

"Okay," Pru said.

Audrae smiled once more and disappeared toward the street.

A moment later Sim exchanged a glance with Kai, and then Pru. "Well, that was weird," she said. She looked back at Kai. "Come on, we have work to do."

"But—"

"Come on, Kai. We have to do it now or I'm not helping." Sim went back toward the drying house and pulled Kai along with her, worried that she'd start asking questions that would throw Pru into the sour mood that possessed her whenever she dwelled on the night that had ended in the emergency room.

"Fine," Kai said. She yelled back to Pru, "You could at least put away those groceries."

Pru didn't acknowledge that she had heard her. A deep sigh coursed down her spine. Sim let go of Kai's arm and took a step toward the house.

"I'll be right back," Sim said.

"Fine. Whatever." Kai waved her away.

When Sim got into the kitchen Pru was opening the cabinets and emptying the market bags with sloppy movements that betrayed the emotionless expression on her face.

"Want to go to the Geraldine later?" Sim asked, thinking it might make Prudence feel better.

Pru dropped a bunch of carrots into the refrigerator, closed it, and looked up at Sim. "I think I need to stop drinking for a while."

"That makes sense."

"I don't even remember leaving the girl I left the bar with," Pru said, focusing on the bears' milk and butter she slipped into the fridge. "For all I know I could've made a fool of myself. And I—I was trying to stop hooking up with random girls. I told you that, remember? It's all so fucking self-destructive. I feel like shit."

"So no more Geraldine?"

"Not a chance." Pru threw the empty canvas bags under the sink and slammed the cabinet door. "I'm sick of that place. I'm not going there anymore. I have more important things to focus on. Cader and I are going to the Battle House tonight. You should come. Once a week there isn't enough for you to improve."

"Yeah, I'll come." Sim pushed away the blip of inexplicable dread that pulsed in her chest whenever she thought about the Battle House, and hurried upstairs to get changed into the one questing outfit she owned.

An arrow whipped through the air, seeming to defy gravity for a breath before it plunged into a red bull's-eye, next to three other shafts. Four out of six, so far. Sim reached behind her left shoulder to pull another arrow from the quiver strapped to her back. She notched it onto her bowstring and cleared her mind. Her left arm was straight and strong. Her right pulled back on the string and bent the bow into a deep curve. Sim inhaled slowly as she eyed her mark and released the arrow with her breath. The arrow sailed forward and sunk into the canvas target, two inches outside of the bull's-eye. Four out of seven. If she made the next one she'd be in the clear; five out of ten wasn't so bad. Sim pulled out another arrow and tried to breathe away her nervousness.

"Sim!" Cader's voice called from across the Battle House. He jogged toward her in his brown leather armor, a longsword strapped across his back. He must have just come from the orb room. Even though she'd been coming to the Battle House for a few months now, Sim still wasn't allowed to go near the battle simulations.

"What's up?" she asked when Cader got close, and glanced down the line of archers to make sure that Master Videria was still occupied with a swordster who kept missing his target entirely and sinking arrows into the wall.

Cader eyed Sim's target with a grin. "Someone's improving."

"Yeah, I guess."

"Keisenheart and Pru are about to duel," he said. "You're gonna want to see it. Trust me."

"I have to finish—"

"Videria won't care." Cader waved a hand at her. He grabbed Sim's bow and took it over to the wall. "Pru's one of the best swordsters in the house," Cader said. "You can learn a lot from watching her fight someone with experience." Sim dropped the rest of her arrows into a bin and hung her quiver next to it. "Keisenheart will probably win, though," Cader added.

Half of the questers in the house were crowded around the center ring. Cader pushed through, heading to the front. Sim kept her eyes fixed on the ground and hurried behind him. She stopped behind the front line of people and stepped on her tiptoes to get a better look.

Pru stood in one corner of the ring, examining the edge of her blade with a slight frown. She seemed not to notice the excitement building around her, or the smug grin on Master Keisenheart's face. She swung her sword in long arcs, loosening the muscles in her right arm, tossed the blade to her left hand, and then did the same again. Not once did she look at the other questers. Her attention was focused completely now on Keisenheart, her features solid and stoic. She looked neither afraid nor confident, neither bored nor excited.

"Let's get this started," Master Throop said in his gravelly voice. He stood at the ring's center and looked from one dueler to the other. Pru and Keisenheart stepped toward each other, holding their blades out and stopping when the points touched. Both pulled their weapons back and stood in an attack stance. Throop stepped backward a few paces and stopped just in front of Cader and Sim. Sim craned her neck to the left to look past his height.

"Okay, on the count of three," Throop said.

Pru's breathing was calm and even.

"One..."

Keisenheart's grin deepened.

"Two..."

The slightest frown line appeared between Pru's brows, either in determination or due to a past grievance.

"Three."

Keisenheart's blade flashed like a fish in the shallow part of a stream. But Pru was ready for him. As soon as Keisenheart moved, she shifted into a defense stance and blocked his swipe. They were lunging at each other with fluid grace, quickly exchanging blocks and attacks and then stepping away, heaving slightly, circling each other to see who would make the next move. Pru jumped forward as if to swipe at Keisenheart's head, but ducked down at the last moment and kicked at his feet. The entire weight of his body clunked to the ground. The questers were silent. Pru could've ended it right there; she could've put her blade to his throat and won the match. But she stepped back and waited for him to stand.

Humiliated, Keisenheart grew angry. His jaw was set and his eyes flashing. He went at Pru with his brute strength. She was fast, nimble, more like a dancer than a fighter. She blocked some attacks and deferred others with her own jabs. But Pru couldn't match Keisenheart's muscles. Every time one of his blows landed on her sword, Pru would stumble a little from the impact. She was getting tired. Keisenheart seemed to just be getting started.

And then it was over—so quickly that Sim wasn't even sure how it had happened. Pru went to block an attack, her sword slipped, and then Keisenheart had his arm wrapped under her shoulders, holding her back to his chest and resting the length of his blade against her neck. Master Throop raised his sword, signaling the end of the match.

Pru wrenched his arm off her and spun to face him. She shook his hand, as they were supposed to do at the end of every match. Keisenheart towered over her, standing close and staring down at her. Pru refused to step away. His knuckles were white around Pru's fingers, but she didn't show any sign of being in pain.

"Show off like that again and I'll have you doing drills for a month," Keisenheart said tightly, right there in front of everyone.

"I wasn't showing off."

"Don't mouth back at me." He pressed his finger into the center of Pru's chest, right where her ribs met.

She slapped his hand away. "It was a fair fight."

"This is my house: It's fair if I say it's fair."

Sim frowned over at Cader, but Cader didn't notice her; his attention was fixed on the center ring, a scowl curling his lips. Pru looked like she might continue arguing. Instead, she stepped back and tried to pull her hand away. Keisenheart held it tightly for a moment longer, causing Pru to stumble back when he released her.

"Fine," Pru muttered under her breath. She threw her sword into the case next to the ring and shook her hand to get the blood flowing into it again.

"Laps for the attitude," Keisenheart snapped. "Around the entire house. Fifty of them. Or you won't set foot in here again."

"You've got to be kidding—"

"It'll be double that if you don't shut your mouth and start moving."

Pru's nostrils flared, but she didn't say another word. She went to the running track and started to jog. The questers were filing back to their stations, some working at swords, others at the target range, others following Master Throop to work on their axe handling.

"You," Keisenheart growled.

Sim looked over at him in surprise. He was looking directly at her.

"Yes, you. Come here." He pointed to the ground next to him, a slight snarl on his face.

Sim took two steps forward and stopped, leaving a good four feet between them.

"You're working on swords today," Keisenheart said. "You've done enough archery. You can't just waltz in here and do whatever you want." Sim had been trying to avoid Keisenheart's drills whenever she came to the Battle House, but she'd been convinced he hadn't noticed. Sim nodded and headed toward the armor.

"Stop shuffling your feet like an invalid," Keisenheart yelled at her back. "Hustle, girl. I swear, I have a house full of idiots here."

Sim hurried to find armor and took down the same flimsy sword that Keisenheart had chosen for her on her first day at the house. As soon as she joined the line, he ripped the weapon from her hand and flung it at the wall. The metal clattered on the ground. "Not that one," he said. He shoved a heavier blade into her hand. "I'm sick of these shortcuts that everyone's been taking. It has to stop. Now into your battle stances. Drill one. Start."

Prudence was smoldering, Cader quiet and thoughtful. Usually when they walked back to Kailash from the Battle House Pru and Cader would recount what had happened in the orb room and argue over which questers would be the next to get coveted assignments.

"I can barely lift my arms." Sim groaned in an attempt to break the silence.

"You did better this time, though," Cader offered.

Sim laughed. "Right."

"I can't believe he's picking on you because he's pissed at me," Pru said. "You'll never learn swordhandling with him screaming at you like that."

"It's kind of humiliating," Sim admitted.

"Don't take it personally," Cader said. "Keisenheart's just like that. He's a great teacher if you're one of his favorites. He'll take you under his wing and teach you everything he knows. But if he has a reason not to like you, then you have to deal with all of his bullshit."

"It's a power thing," Pru explained. "He has to be in control. He's just picking on you because he knows I could have beaten him in the ring today."

"So why didn't you?"

Pru snorted. "Everything would be so much worse if I'd won. Look at how pissed he was just because I came close."

"He should want you to beat him."

"No," Cader answered. "The only thing Keisenheart cares about is having a reputation as one of the best battle house Masters. Patrons will go to him with what they want done and pay him to put together a team of the best questers. The point is for him to train fighters who will get him paying quests."

"He told me I have to keep doing sword practice." Sim moaned. "But I'm so bad at it. I don't understand why I can't just do archery." Sim shuffled her feet, weighed down by the knowledge of her lack of ability. She couldn't even be mad at Keisenheart for yelling at her throughout the drills. She wasn't good with swords. She didn't belong in a battle house. She deserved his anger.

"I'll help you," Pru said. "We'll just go a little earlier. There's more to it than drills. You have to get into the ring to get better."

"Prudence used to be one of Keisenheart's favorites," Cader said with a raised eyebrow. "One of the only girls he actually ever noticed. But I guess now she's gotten to be too good."

"Bullshit," Pru grumbled. "He knows I can pack up and go to any other house in this city. I only stay because he has such great connections. He'll never kick any of us out. He seems like an oaf, but he's not that dumb. Anyway, don't worry about it, Sim. You'll get better at swords. You just have to keep at it."

Two girls roamed the Incubator, checking out the gadgets. Sim could tell they weren't going to buy anything, so she let them be. A quester with a shiny compass watch eyed Azzer's compressor sheathes and slid his sword into each of them. Sim let him be, too. Azzer was out on an errand and Cader had just come into the shop, so they could stand around and talk without getting yelled at for being idle.

"What's up with Pru?" Cader asked. He leaned back against the counter. "She's been acting kind of weird lately."

"The hospital thing really shook her, I guess."

"She's been through way worse than that, though," he said in a thoughtful mumble.

"Don't know what else it could be," Sim said.

The door jangled open. Sim remembered the guy who strode in, wearing tight black jeans and a striped T-shirt. He was a musician who had brought in a guitar for Sim to repair. His hair stuck out at odd, sharp angles. The only gadget he wore was a silver ring on his index finger. It allowed him to write invisible notes in the air and then magically replicate them onto parchment whenever he wanted. At first Sim couldn't decide whether she should admire him or scorn him; whether he was legitimately being himself or if he wore the ring just as a pose. But he was nice, and in the end that was all that mattered. He walked up to the counter with long strides and his back held straight. Confidence hovered around him like a bright aura. Flush with an admiring jealousy, Sim wondered how he had gotten to this point, where he seemed to accept exactly who he was.

"Awesome," he said with a little bend of his knees when Sim grabbed his guitar from a stand next to the counter and laid it down in front of her. He slid off his sunglasses and danced his fingers over the strings. "May I?" he asked, glancing up at her.

"Of course."

He switched on the guitar, threw the strap over his head, and started to play a quick riff. The shop filled with an impressive slur of magically amplified notes. The quester and the two girls stopped what they were doing and looked over at him. The guy was good, practiced, as comfortable with his instrument as he was with himself. Before Sim had fixed it, the sound charm on the guitar had been all torn apart and it refused to play in more than a whisper. Now a glowing blue light pulsed beneath the guitar's strings, where the magic dust turned the strings' vibrations into amplified sound waves.

"Excellent," he said, silencing the gadget.

"I intensified the charm so that it should be able to play louder now," Sim said. "But don't push it this time. That's what tore the old charm. You were playing too loud." She wasn't positive that this was the case, but her goggles had shown the amplifying center to be all torn up, so she assumed that had to be it.

"Can't get too loud," he said with a laugh. "Okay, though. I get it. I'll take it easy."

"Twenty sols," Sim said, when he asked about the price.

"Seriously? That's it? I only have magic dust to pay you."

"It didn't take me that long. Dust is fine; it's all the same." Sim put an empty twenty-gram jar onto the counter.

"Hell." He hunched over to measure the reddish sand he poured into the shop's jar. "Well, I'll tell you what. You like punk rock?"

"Sure," Sim said, even though she wasn't exactly sure what it was.

"I'm playing a show tonight. That's why I told you that there was such a rush on the guitar. It's awesome that you fixed it so quick. Here's the address." He wrote it in the air with his finger and then swiped his hand down at the used repair tag that Sim slid toward him. Two street names and a warehouse number appeared on the paper in dark ink. "And you can bring whoever you want. You're obviously invited, too," he said to Cader. "The more the merrier."

"Cool," Cader said. "Maybe we'll see you later then."

"Yeah, see you," Sim said, raising her hand.

The guy smiled at her, pushed on his sunglasses, and strode his heavy boots out of the shop. Sim looked over at Cader once he was gone.

"That guy is one of the best guitarists in the Narrows," Cader said, watching him leave.

"Is he? Do you think we can convince Pru to come?"

Cader made a face. "No way will this 'not going out' thing last."

"It's not the Geraldine," Sim agreed. The quester headed toward the counter with the sheath he'd finally chosen.

"I gotta run and pick up some things," Cader said. He slapped his hand onto the counter. "But I'll be back later. We can head to the show together. Yeah, Pru'll definitely come."

Pru was waiting for them outside when they got off work. She was sitting on the ground with her back against the apartment building across the street. The crumbling brick wall behind her highlighted the arch of Pru's neck and the frown weighing at the corners of her mouth. Aviators hid her eyes, but she seemed to be gazing down at the sidewalk, lost in thought.

"Hey," Cader said, stopping just in front of her. She looked up at him.

"I figured we could all ride home together," she said, to explain why she was there.

"There's this warehouse show on the way back," Cader said. "Sort of toward the west. We should go."

"It's in the west?" Pru asked, deepening her frown. Hardly anyone went west, toward the gray streets and looming factories where Sim had first met Lilith.

"Guess things are moving over there," Cader said. "The music will be great."

"Yeah, sure," Pru said, pulling herself to her feet.

"Should we get some beer on the way?" Sim asked, even though she knew that Pru was trying not to drink. It made her uncomfortable, the idea of a Prudence who didn't drink or go out at night. It wasn't Pru.

"Definitely," Pru said, to Sim's relief.

"I know a place on the way where we can get it for really cheap," Cader said.

"No Kaianide." Pru made a face. "I'm sick of always drinking that stuff." She glanced at Sim. "Not that it's bad. I just can't stand to drink the same thing all the time."

"We can get whatever." Cader glanced at his watch. "But it's still early."

"So let's hang at the Blue Carnation for a bit," Pru said. She was standing now, swinging her leg over her bike, itching to move.

"The Blue Carnation it is." Cader grinned and glanced at Sim as if to say "I told you so." He swung his skateboard onto the street, ran to it, and leaped onto the board to add extra force. By the time either Pru or Sim even stepped on a pedal he was already halfway down the block.

XII

The self-analyzing, politically correct bikers who liked to go to Stein's couldn't be bothered to frequent the Blue Carnation. Nor did Blue Carnation patrons tend to venture three doors down to the bike-laden fence of Sim's favorite café. The two venues shared the same old-world woodwork aesthetic and the close-knit atmosphere of a hangout space, but the similarities ended there. The Carnation was thoroughly a whiskey well, where customers tended to drink their ways to fistfights or oblivion. The bartenders liked to leave their posts and come out to drink with their friends, sometimes finishing the good bourbon before the late-night customers could even get any. There was no complaining about it, except by those who were willing to back up their curses with their fists. When the atmosphere turned especially rowdy, shouts from friendly, pointless tussles and loud cracks of laughter would bubble up above the bluegrass music streaming from the old jukebox. Sim had never been inside the Carnation, even though it was on her way to Stein's from the Incubator. She'd glanced inside before while biking by, wondering at the strange people who were a part of another subworld of this small universe of bikers and boarders.

Cader shoved open the bar's patchwork wooden door and Sim followed him inside. The air smelled sweet with alcohol and the floor was already coated with a film of spilled whiskey and dirt. Banjo music came from the jukebox and candles melted into mason jars shed an extra glow onto each table. Even though the sky was still light, the bar would have been as dim as midnight without the old, sooty oil lamps strewn around—two on top of a piano with a few of its keys missing, one hanging from an iron hook on the wall, another on the blackened mantle of an empty fireplace. Cader went straight to the bar, where a guy in a striped shirt, suspenders, and a black bow tie was shaking a mixer with vigorous arms that seemed a mismatch for the calm expression on his face.

"James," Cader said with a smile. He stuck up his hand for a high five, and the bartender paused his mixing to slap Cader's palm.

"Hey, man," James said. "Hey, Pru." He poured the cocktail into two mason jars and pushed them toward the couple sitting on the barstools next to them. "What can I get you?"

"A Windsor on ice," Pru said, her eyes still on the whiskey bottles.

"Same," Cader said with a nod.

James shifted his gaze to Sim.

"Whiskey sour," Cader said for her, sensing her uncertainty. Sim hated him for it even though she knew he was just trying to make her feel more comfortable. She could order her own damn drinks. Just because she was a few years younger didn't mean that she didn't know how a whiskey bar worked. And even if she hadn't, she could have figured it out on her own.

"Actually, I'll just have a whiskey with soda and the house bitters," Sim said, just to spite him. Cader glanced at her and shrugged, but she knew it'd bothered him and she was glad for it.

"Sure thing." James turned away from them and started on the drinks.

"We should try distilling," Cader mused.

"Seems like you have your hands full as it is," Pru said.

"Not if Sim quits her job at the Incubator." Cader looked over at Sim and added, "Think about it, Sim. You'd make so much more money."

"I like fixing things."

"We could hire someone else," Cader said, rubbing his stubble.

"It sounds like you're about ready to be questing again," Pru said. James put Windsor whiskies in front of her and Cader. Pru thanked him, took a sip, and continued. "It's not like you to stay in one place for so long."

"I don't know about that," Cader said. "It might be nice to settle down for a bit."

Pru shook her head. "You really don't want to get caught, Cader. Get too successful and the Guard will be on your asses in a heartbeat. You'll spend the rest of your lives in jail. That's what happened to the Bongo Tree guys. Stay small and they don't care. But you know you're not the type of guy to stay small and be content. Even if that spiritual bullshit of yours says you should."

Cader drank his whiskey with a thoughtful expression. "Whatever." He waved the thought away. "I'll quest if something good comes my way. Who needs whiskey, anyway?"

James glanced at Cader, seemingly not amused, and then laughed.

"That's right James, you heard me," Cader said. "You whiskey boys take yourselves way too seriously."

"Guess we do," James said into the glass he was working on. He poured just the right amount of bitters in the bottom of it and added another ice cube.

"The quests in the east keep paying better," Pru said. "That Ogbond quest has me set for a while now."

"Yeah, they're paying better because questers keep dying off over there. I don't want to get wrapped up in the ogre war. No way am I messing around with those things."

"It's not so bad."

"Maybe for you it isn't. I'm not nearly as good with a sword."

Sim stared down at her drink, wondering if Cader and Pru would care if she ran to Stein's. Wood had sent a message to her notepad earlier that day saying that she was planning to go after work. But Sim knew it would be silly for her to leave. The light laughter and crooning music of the Carnation was calm and welcoming. Cader and Pru were inviting her into their world. Sim was living the life she wanted to live. But it wasn't enough.

"What about you, Sim?" Cader asked.

She blinked and looked up at him. "What? Sorry, I've been so spacey lately."

"Ever think about questing?"

She had. Of course she had. Questers had no boss, no one to answer to. They only had their missions, and their teammates if they had any, and money to be earned after the job was done. Questers were respected.

"Cader and I were just talking about an easier quest that's coming up in a few weeks," Pru explained. "It would be a good one for you to start with, if you're interested."

"I don't know. I think it might be nice to settle in the city for a while, like Cader was saying. I'm not sure I'm cut out for questing. You've seen me at the Battle House."

"That's why we'd be with you," Cader said. "It's a team job, and we'd need a magicweaver. You'd need a wand in the Hinterlands, but you already have one so you'd be set."

Sim's heart dropped to her stomach. The last time she'd used her wand was when she was running away from Locklawn. She couldn't bring herself to tell Cader that she'd given her wand away. "I'm not really a magicweaver," she mumbled.

"Veldindor, Sim." Pru slapped her glass onto the bar. Anger colored her voice and crumpled her face. "Stop trying to be so humble. It's not becoming. You're a magicweaver; live up to it."

"I don't know anything about magicweaving," Sim shot back. Most of her drink was gone and the whiskey in her veins was making her brave. "I can chill beers and calibrate and pick locks, but I don't know how I do anything else. I don't know how I made the wind blow the glass off the bridge and I'm not even sure I could do it again. I'm not a magicweaver."

"Fine. I don't give a fuck. Stay at the Incubator for the rest of your life, then."

"Watch the cussing, ladies," James called from down the bar, without giving them a glance, as if he'd said it to thousands of patrons thousands of times before. Sim glared down at him. Either the whiskey or the atmosphere of the Carnation was bringing out a latent rowdiness inside of her. Nothing was off limits. Nothing was unspeakable. She was going to be honest and real and she didn't care if she hurt anyone's feelings or said anything embarrassing.

"You'd need to get a teacher," Cader said levelly, trying to keep the peace.

"You know I can't afford that."

"Forget it, Cader," Pru said. "Anyone here would be glad to start questing. I'm not going to try to talk her into it. We can do something that pays more without her."

"True," Cader said with a shrug. "Acheron could still distribute for us while we're gone."

"Maybe." Pru clinked the ice around in her empty glass. She frowned deeply and changed the subject. "One more before we head out?"

"Can't say no to free whiskey." Cader grinned but the air was still taut with anger and irritation. He looked at Sim. "Same drink?"

"I'm actually going to grab a coffee," Sim said, standing and pulling on her bag. "I need some caffeine before this concert."

"Going to Stein's?" Pru asked casually.

"Stein's is closest," Sim said, meeting Pru's gaze. "I'll meet you back here."

"Okay," Cader said, looking confused. "I mean, don't worry about the questing thing, Sim. You don't have to do it if you don't want—"

"It's not that. Honestly I just need to feed this caffeine addiction."

"I hear ya."

"You want me to bring you anything?"

"Nah, one addiction at a time is enough for me."

Sim glanced down at Pru, who shook her head, more in disgust than to say no. She turned to get James's attention.

"Be right back," Sim said. She did her best not to rush out of the bar.

The late summer air was cooling as night approached. A crumple of old, dirty papers danced in the wind along the curb, until they were caught in the brambly arms of an overgrown weed. Questers with their brown leather and punks with their dark colors and bohemians with their splashy accessories mixed together on Christiania's sidewalks. They weren't as easy to segregate and label as Sim had thought when she'd first started coming to the Narrows. These people were the sane few who weren't trapped in the vicious cycle of fashion that consumed Greater Terresin, where the shopping district pulsed with people who bought new clothes almost as often as they washed their old ones. Those who came to the Narrows tended to imbue the things they owned with a deep sense of themselves. Sim wore her loose button-down, thick leather belt, and tight black jeans at least three times a week. She had one pair of boots that she loved and refused to replace. Prudence's bronze-buttoned military jacket was thoroughly her. Cader would have looked strange without his leather wristbands. They couldn't afford to shop all the time, but they didn't want to. They were giving meaning to things, instead of just using them thoughtlessly and throwing them away into some invisible abyss. They used things, but in a way that fit the meaning of their lives instead of controlling them.

Stein's stone dragon greeted Sim with its frozen snarl, and now that she was at the café she had to confront the absurdity of what she was doing. She should have just stayed at the Carnation, should have forced herself to forget about Wood and have a good time. She wasn't even sure exactly how she had ended up here, standing in line for a coffee, glancing around the tables until she spotted Wood in the jean jacket she'd started wearing now that it was getting cooler at night.

Sim stared at the counter display of brambleberry cookies and gut-warming brownies. She was ready to tell Wood everything. She was in the perfect mindset for it. But now wasn't the time; not with Cader and Pru waiting for her. Sim used the refuge of the line to calm herself. She was here now. She couldn't just turn around and leave. These people knew her. She couldn't make a fool of herself. She'd be fine. She'd done this a hundred times before. She was just grabbing a coffee with a friend. That was all.

"Hey." Sim sat at Wood's table and perched on the edge of her seat. Adrenaline shot out of her heart and tingled at the back of her head, just behind her ears. She placed the back of her hand on her face and hoped that she wasn't blushing.

"Sim," Wood said with an endearing croon that Sim hated because she didn't know how the hell to interpret it. "It's good to see you. I thought you might not end up coming today."

"I actually can't stay long," Sim said. "I'm going to this show in the west with Prudence and Cader. Just needed a coffee before we headed out."

"Sounds exciting."

"It should be fun," Sim said with a shrug. "You can come if you want. They're over at the Blue Carnation now."

"Really? I've been wanting to do something like that before I go back to school and classes consume my life."

"So come then."

Wood thought for a moment, chewed on her lip—one of the many expressions that Sim had fallen in love with. The urgency of spilling her heart hit Sim like a thunderclap. She should ask Wood to go for a walk so that they could talk. Cader and Pru could wait. This was more important than the show.

Wood looked her honey-moss eyes up at the wall behind Sim and said, "I don't know, maybe next time. I have a date with this guy tonight. He's from school." She smiled and raised an eyebrow. "We used to hook up in the library, hiding between the shelves where no one went. In the Covish literature section. Awesome sex."

Sim's heart sank. Her mouth opened and the words she'd prepared balanced on her lips. *We need to talk.* That was all she had to say. Instead she shrugged and mumbled, "Yeah, maybe next time." And the words slipped back down her throat, settling into the hole in her stomach where all of the things she couldn't say collected and festered like rotting flesh.

"I have to get back to Pru and Cader," Sim said. She stood, a little too quickly, and hoped that Wood hadn't noticed her agitation.

"Are you sure you don't want to just stay and finish your coffee?"

"I should really get back." Sim shrugged. "Don't want to keep them waiting."

"Okay. See you tomorrow, then."

"Yeah, maybe." After a breath, Sim looked down at Wood with a grin and added, "Have fun tonight, girl," just like she knew a good friend should.

"Hopefully," Wood said with a little laugh.

Sim felt her face crumple as she turned away. Her eyebrows and lips drew together, clinching to hold in the anguish coursing through her body with a chemical heat. She did her best to look calm, to leave all thoughts of Wood behind her right then and there. On her way in from a smoke break, the edgy girl barista pulled open the door and stood to the side so that Sim could get out.

"Thanks," Sim mumbled as she passed her, and looked away so that she didn't have to meet the girl's eyes.

"Yeah, no problem." The girl's voice was soft and light. She frowned at Sim with the same worried expression that Cader had just given her.

Sim rushed to the doorway niche of an abandoned storefront and hid from the people walking on Christiania. She slid to the filthy ground and forced back the tears stinging behind her eyelids. She had no right to be upset, no right to be angry that Wood was going on a date. A vile, irrational jealousy churned her insides, set her head on fire, blurred her thoughts. It didn't make sense for her to feel so viscerally upset. She couldn't understand it. All Sim knew was that her hands were shaking again and her chest was on the verge of a dry heave and her eyes were nearly bursting with the desire to cry. Wood was going on a date: Not with Daryl, who she just liked to mess around with, but with a guy she genuinely seemed to like.

Deep breaths were the only way she could calm herself. Sim made her face relax, she put on a mask of normalcy, and pulled herself off the stoop. When no one was looking, she sloshed the rest of her coffee into an overgrown planter outside of the Carnation and pushed through swinging doors into the cacophony of the bar. Sim slowed and listened to the lyrics streaming from the jukebox: *I don't want you but I need you, don't want to kiss you but I need to...* She was feeling bad enough for herself as it was without hearing these dumb love songs. She blocked it out. Cader had saved her barstool with his bag, but three plaid-shirted guys were huddled around it, trying to order drinks. Sim stood behind them, waiting for them to order so that she could get to her seat.

Pru glanced over at her. "Hey, get out of the way," she said, glaring at the guys.

"Huh?" The one closest to the bar glanced back at Sim and looked like he was about to tell Pru to piss off. Rubbing his bearded chin, he looked back to Pru, seemed to think better of it, and moved to the side.

Sim mumbled an ignored "Thanks," and pushed her coffee mug toward James. "It's from Stein's," Sim said when he came to take it. He nodded and threw it into a dirty-dish bin behind the counter.

"You awake now?" Cader asked.

"Yep. That was just what I needed."

"Shots before we leave?" Pru suggested, eyeing Sim.

"Shots and a beer," Cader agreed. "Then beers from the corner and we'll get to the warehouse just as the first band is finishing up."

"Shots and beers," Sim said with a nod.

They took their whiskey at the bar and brought the beers outside, inviting James to come with them and have a cigarette.

"Looks like you're doing pretty good business here," Cader said, motioning to the Carnation.

"Yeah, it's all right." James pulled out a wooden matchbox and lit up. "Keeps me busy. Keeps the bills paid."

"How's the art coming?" Pru asked, taking the box from him when he offered it. The pungent smell of sulfur tinged the air as she struck a match instead of casting the flame spell she usually used.

James shook his head and shrugged. "No time for it. I work here all night, get home, and I'm exhausted. I need to start painting again. I want to."

Something crashed inside the bar, followed by the sound of a glass breaking. James stood up on his toes and looked through the window.

"Aw, crap." He rested his fresh cigarette on the windowsill. "I have to check on that," he grumbled and rushed into the bar.

"Maybe we should help him...." Cader frowned through the window, gauging the fight.

"James can handle it." Pru pulled her bike out in one quick motion and looked up at the darkening sky. "Let's go get that beer before the place closes."

Wind howled through the spaces between the factories. Sim's hair blew in a mess around her face until she pulled it back with the black shoelace she always kept tied around her wrist, just in case she needed it for something. Scampering rats scraped their nails along the edges of the street. The full moon dripped an eerie glow over the faceless buildings and made the long night-shadows seem darker than ever.

"Are you sure this is it?" Prudence asked, eyeing the blackened windows.

"Has to be." Cader said. "They must be using a silencing gadget."

The factory rose straight up from the sidewalk. There was no fence, no lock on the thick metal door. Sim looked down at the address on the crumpled repair tag, and looked up at the building. The numbers matched. "But where are the bikes?"

"Probably hidden, which is what we should do, too," Pru said. "Come on, let's find a good spot."

They walked two blocks down, along a crumbling concrete sidewalk. Sim thought this might be the area where she'd first met Lilith, but she couldn't be sure. The factories and warehouses all looked the same to her.

"Here," Cader said, handing Sim a flask that James had filled for him before they left the Carnation.

She made a face as she swallowed the straight whiskey.

"So how exactly did you get your bike back?" Cader asked, looking over at Pru with a grin.

Pru took the flask from Sim and glanced at him. "Don't worry about it."

"Not worried. Just curious."

Sim threw Cader a look. Pru was already pissed off enough as it was, and she was well on her way to becoming drunk. She wished he'd stop provoking her.

"This alley should be fine." Pru turned down a small space between two warehouses and walked about halfway in. She leaned her bike against the wall. "They should be fine without the spell," she said, stepping back so that Cader and Sim could put their bikes against hers.

"Are you sure?" Sim asked. "We can wait—"

"Cast it yourself if you want," Pru snapped. After another shot of the whiskey, she gave the flask back to Cader and started out of the alley.

"You never showed me how to," Sim said, following. She was starting to feel dizzy and warm with bourbon. Their boots clicked on the sidewalk from their long, quick strides.

"I'm not showing you anything. You said it yourself: You're not a magicweaver. Why should I waste my time?"

"Cut it out, Pru," Cader said and handed her back the flask.

"Why should I? No one, no one turns down an offer to become a quester. Do you even realize that, Sim? Do you realize how many people wait around for years just to be invited on their first quest? Do you realize how rude it is to just brush something like that off, as if we're asking you to come and play fucking hopscotch?"

"I didn't know," Sim said, her voice sounding more hollow than she'd intended.

"Well that's too bad, because it isn't going to happen again." Pru took a swig and gave the flask back to Cader, who passed it straight to Sim.

They walked the rest of the way to the warehouse without saying anything. Even Cader was quietly frowning down at the ground, but Sim didn't think that it had anything to do with Pru's temper. He was wearing the same mask she'd seen when they'd met Acheron at the Dragon Spine. Cader had morphed into the tough guy who didn't seem to care about anything and couldn't be bothered.

They got to the warehouse just as a bear of a guy in a studded leather vest shoved open the door to get inside. He was with a girl whose head was shaved except for a patch of long hair that streamed down from the top of her neck. The shaved part was died in rainbow colors, and when the girl glanced at them Sim tried not to stare at her pierced pink eyebrows. They were followed by a few others from another group: pretty girls with long, straight hair and dark makeup. They wore torn jean shorts with torn tights beneath them, and scowls to make themselves look tough.

Cader handed Sim and Pru each two beers, threw the empty box on the ground next to the double doors, and followed the girls into a dark hallway. A few glow sticks hung from the ceiling and grew denser as they went farther in, so that the walkway was bright enough to see the graffiti covering the dingy cream walls, shaded blue and green in the strange light. Cader snapped the top off his beer bottle and handed his opener to Sim. A steady bass beat vibrated through Sim's chest and betrayed the border of the silencing gadget, which ended abruptly in a burst of drums and guitars, just where the glow sticks were at their thickest. Smokers hung out against the walls, talking and eying everyone who walked by. Screechy punk music bled into the hallway and joined the heartbeat bass. Sim stepped around the shredded boots of a girl who was sitting on the floor and followed Cader into a dark room where the air was hot and moist with evaporated sweat. A high-pitched guitar riff tore at Sim's ears. They were immediately thrust into a crowd of people. Someone jabbed his elbows into Sim's back. She wriggled away from him, fighting an urge to grab the back of Cader's shirt as he pushed to the front.

There was no stage, and the crowd bled toward the musicians and pulled back like ocean waves. The guitarist from the Incubator played to the right of the singer, whose eyebrows were arched into angry peaks, his face etched with anger lines. The front man screamed so that his teeth showed. Sweat soaked his forehead and bare chest. Sim couldn't understand what he was saying. He was pissed off. It didn't matter why. The guitarist stomped on a pedal next to his microphone and pulled his instrument into a long, quickly paced wail. He rushed into the crowd and fell to his knees, tipped back his head as if praying. The guitar notes became higher and faster. His fingers bounced over his fretboard, and then slowed as everyone pushed apart so that he could crawl back to the stage. Sim got shoved into Cader as a circle opened in the middle of the crowd. People jumped in, thrashing wildly to the music, kicking, punching, slipping to the floor because it was covered in a wet slick of spilled beer. A girl's feet flung out from underneath her and she landed hard on her back. Two guys on the periphery of the circle grabbed her arms, pulled her up, and pushed her back in.

"You coming?" Cader yelled into Sim's ear.

Sim shook her head. He waited a moment for her to change her mind, shrugged when she didn't, and followed Pru into the mosh pit. Sim watched, wanting to join them, working up her nerve. She drank her beer quickly, watching as a brawny guy knocked Cader to the ground. Pru grabbed him by the elbow to yank him back up to his feet. The music continued, loud and fast.

Someone grabbed Sim's arm from behind. Her beer slipped from her hand and dropped to the floor. Sim spun around to face Lilith's wide, flashing eyes. She pointed to the door and Sim allowed herself to be pulled out, through the dirty hallway and into an empty room. The whiskey and beer buzzed in her temples, but her thoughts were still clear.

Lilith walked over to a broken window and looked out at the moon. "They wanted to warn you," she blurted.

"What?"

"They wanted to warn you and you fucking killed them."

Sim was silent. She felt the blood drain from her face. "Wait, what?" she asked again.

"On the bridge," Lilith added.

"I didn't—"

"Listen. It's not as simple as you think. Not all of us give in to the hunger. Some of us don't want...We don't want anyone else to change."

"You aren't making any sense," Sim said. Her heart was still pumping wildly from the music. She looked back to the door, but didn't move toward it.

"The magic-dust factories," Lilith explained. "They were shut down, so it's not as bad now. But the dwarves started them up again, and you idiots keep moving closer. There is a reason that no one comes this far west. Now it's only a matter of time."

"Until what?"

"Until you become like us," Lilith snapped. She looked away and crossed her arms over her chest, hugging herself. "Even if people aren't attacked by a strix, even if they don't have the magic sucked out of them so that they themselves become monsters, the black magic from the factories will change them anyway. That's why we put the glass on the bridge: to keep you out. To warn you."

"Oh. That was you?" Sim swallowed and frowned down at the floor. The black magic. What Azzer had been talking about. That's what it did. Sim felt slightly overwhelmed. "But what exactly...are you?"

Lilith grunted in frustration. "You should understand better than anyone else. Magicweavers can naturally connect with the energy source of the world, they're born intuitively knowing how to connect with magic. Everyone else can do it, too, but they have to learn how. Striges can't connect with anything, no matter how they try. We're dead, Sim. Worse than dead. We live in sorrow, estranged from the universe. Only through sapping the magic from a living soul can we feel alive again. It's like a drug to us. But it comes at a price. The person whose spirit we steal becomes a strix themselves unless we kill them out of mercy. And the high never lasts. It always fades away as their spirit leaves us and returns to the ether." Lilith paused and frowned down at the ground. "I'm surprised Prudence hasn't told you any of this."

"How do you know Prudence?" Sim noticed the tattoos of a sword, on her inner forearm, and a colorful compass rose, on her shoulder, similar to the ones that Pru and Acheron and so many of the people at the Battle House had.

"We're old friends."

"She said the striges were killed off."

Lilith looked away again. "Some survived. The ones who gave in to the soul lust got killed by the questers. Those who knew enough to lay low live on, confined to the shadows. With all of you bikers running around, though, they'll start killing again. And even if they don't, the black magic will turn you all into striges anyway." Lilith stared at Sim for a moment, and then continued. "You won't be able to cast spells anymore. You'll loose your ability to weave magic."

Sim searched for something to say. "No one's going to stop coming here. There's nowhere else for us to go."

Lilith shrugged. "Then you're all idiots." With that she pushed past Sim, out into the cigarette smoke and the loud chatter. Sim rushed to catch up with her. She wanted more answers, but the right questions wouldn't come to her mind. Her hand caught Lilith above the elbow. In a breath, she had Sim pinned against the wall. Her fingers gripped Sim's throat and her face was inches from Sim's nose. "Don't you understand? I could kill you in an instant. And you—you're worse than all of them. Your life source would keep a strix alive for years. You aggravate the soul lust more than anyone else. Stop coming here. There's nothing else to understand."

"Aw, man, there's gonna be a chick fight!" A guy standing near them giggled drunkenly. He slapped his friend's arm and pointed over to Lilith and Sim.

Lilith glared at him. She pushed Sim away and strode down the hallway.

"Hey, wait!" Sim started to follow her.

"Sim?"

She turned back to see Cader, who had just come out of the room where the show was, and looked back toward Lilith again, but she was already gone.

"You okay?" Cader asked, looking worried.

Prudence pushed out into the hallway. Her hair was plastered to her forehead with sweat and her dark makeup smudged around her eyes. She gave them both a questioning look.

"I—" Sim shook her head, remembering the conversation she'd already tried to have with them about striges. "Yeah. I was just hanging out."

Pru lit up and they hung out in the hallway while she smoked. Sim was glad to go back into the dark room with the loud music, where no one would notice her. She pretended to be focused on the music when really Lilith's words kept playing over in her head. Cader kept glancing at her with a worried expression when they left the warehouse and went back to their bikes. But they rode back in silence.

A crystal ball with a blue stone set into its center hovered three feet in front of Cader and washed a pale light over the street. Azzer had made the gadget for him, after Cader had complained about not wanting to carry a light in his hand while he was skating. A few people joined them when they got to the street that led up to the Narrows Bridge, and they all rode together, following Cader's quick lead. They were connected, all of them. Even if they didn't know one another, they all knew about a place that was different from anywhere else in the city. The Narrows connected them. Sim knew already that she'd ignore all that Lilith had told her. Maybe she'd start to carry a sword around, like she'd been meaning to, in case another strix tried to attack her. But she wouldn't quit her job and she wouldn't stop going to the Geraldine or

Stein's. Maybe it was worth it, to lose her spell-casting abilities. Besides, it had to take time, for the black magic to have an affect on her. She'd have to notice it happening. She could continue to go to the Narrows while she figured out what was the best thing to do. But she knew she could never stay away, just like Pru couldn't stop smoking her cigarettes even though she knew that they were killing her. She knew it. The Narrows might kill her. But she didn't care.

XIII

Bursts of lightning struck every few days now, and the sky streamed with rain almost always. Sim's clothes would be soaked through by the time she got to the Incubator. She'd cast an anti-wet spell on her goggles just so that she could see while riding to work. Eventually, when they became old news, stories of lightning strikes disappeared from the headlines and were buried in the back pages of the papers. Some people who worked in the Narrows had started to sleep in abandoned apartments so that they wouldn't have to bike through the rain all the time. Sim heard them talking about it in Stein's and wanted to tell them that they shouldn't stay overnight, that they couldn't spend all of their time there without the risk of becoming...soulless. They would think she was crazy. So Sim kept her mouth shut and went to work and tried not to listen to Azzer's grumblings about an imminent apocalypse.

One day, when Wood hadn't been at Stein's, she rushed home from the Incubator and put her bike in the drying house instead of its usual spot near the back door, so that the rain wouldn't rust her breaks. That was probably why Pru assumed that she was still in the Narrows, and not down in the basement with the brewing machine.

"I'm telling you, she's the one."

Sim recognized Acheron's voice and paused halfway up the staircase. She stared up at the basement door, her heart accelerating because she knew instantly that she was listening to a conversation she wasn't meant to hear.

"No. She's nothing special, Acheron." That was Pru, sounding frustrated. "Cader never should have brought her here."

"You can't brew without her."

"Forget about the beer. Quests are more important. Especially this one. You don't want to end up looking like an idiot."

"Sounds like you're trying to protect her."

Prudence laughed. "Right."

"You're sleeping with her, aren't you?"

"What? No. She just keeps hanging around me. Listen, I'm telling you, she's not a magicweaver."

"I don't know, Pru, I've seen her—"

"Yeah, I have too. She can calibrate. Barely. That's it. And even that she had to learn from the gadget-master she works for."

"And the transportation spell?" Acheron asked.

"I don't know. There's a lot of magical energy around Kailash. It's why Kai's herbs are so potent."

"She have a wand?"

"Is this a fucking interrogation? No. She only got into the Battle House because Cader demanded a space for her. Ask anyone and they'll tell you she doesn't belong there. Do what you want, Acheron, I really don't care. I'm just watching your back."

"I guess you're right," Acheron grumbled.

There was a pause. Sim held her breath, praying that the basement steps wouldn't creak.

"Anyway, you need to take this quest then." Acheron changed the subject. "It's our only lead."

"I'm not going back to Ogbond."

"You owe me, Prudence."

There was a pause again.

"Fine. But no one else can know about it. Not even Cader. Especially not him. Sim reminds him of his sister, I think."

"That girl still missing?"

There was a pause. "Yeah. He's finally stopped looking for her."

"Good. I'll get the details for the quest tonight."

"Fine."

Sim stayed on the steps for five minutes after she heard them leave the kitchen and go out the back door. When she was sure they were gone, she ran up to her room and pulled out her notepad.

What are you doing? Sim wrote. *I need to talk to you.* To make sure that the message had been sent, Sim put on her goggles and watched the stones draw magic dust out of the air in a tiny blue swirl. The translucent shimmer of Sim's writing rose out of the notebook and flitted off through her bedroom wall in the direction of Wood's apartment. But before she had even sent the message she'd known that Wood wouldn't respond. She was hanging out with some guy again. Sim had no one to talk to. No one.

Drangs jumped up onto her bed, seeming to sense Sim's distress, and rubbed his soft face against her knees. Sim lay there and held him and thought about how Pru thought she was worthless and about how Wood didn't care about her at all, about how she was just another boring person, nothing special. And then she just stared off and dwelled in her loneliness until she sank into sleep.

Each swipe of Sim's sword was more forceful than it had to be, meant to hurt and kill. She knew Cader could handle the sloppy swipes of her blade, so she struck at him again and again, releasing some of the anger in her stomach with each clash of metal against metal.

"What the hell, Sim?" Cader breathed. His body was wet with sweat and his chest heaved from the fight. "Take it easy."

"I need to get better." Sim gasped for air. Her arms were tired, but she lifted her sword. "Let's keep going."

She'd never told Cader or Pru about seeing Lilith. They wouldn't have believed her anyway, and maybe Pru was right: Lilith was just some crazy chick. She'd have to steer clear of her. Sim had other things to worry about.

"You need a break," Cader said, looking worried.

"I need to push myself. Come on." Now that she knew what Pru really thought of her, Sim boiled with the need to prove her wrong.

Cader didn't argue. When Sim swung at him, he hit her sword away and nearly knocked it out of her hand. He parried three more times before Sim fell to the ground after her legs gave out from blocking one of his blows.

"Working hard, girl?" Master Keisenheart frowned down at her on his way to a more advanced ring. He couldn't remember Sim's name, no matter how many times she tried to remind him. "Get up and get out," he said, looking back at her. "You're taking up space. Laps before you leave. That'll build up your endurance."

Keisenheart had never paid her so much attention. Sim almost felt happy about the endurance guidance. Cader pulled her up and they went to the edge of the room, behind three girls who were shooting arrows across the warehouse. Master Videria stood a few yards away, with her cold eagle-eyes darting between the girls and their targets. She frowned and turned from the archers to continue restringing a cedar longbow. Sim slid to the floor. Her legs were stretched out in front of her and her back leaned up against the wall. A numb feeling tingled her muscles; a happy endorphin buzz encased her mind.

"I'd swear you were going off to war," Cader said, handing her a water bottle. "Are you sure you're okay, Sim?"

"It's the lightning," Sim lied. "I'm just worried that something's going to happen. I want to be prepared."

"A sword's not going to help you against lightning." Cader studied Sim with a clear gaze. He was crouching with one knee on the ground and the other bent before him. His attention was focused on her completely.

"Obviously." Sim gulped at the water. "It's more than just the lightning," she explained. "It's a sign of what's to come. It's not natural."

"You're starting to sound like Azzer." Cader frowned.

The twang of a taught string sounded a few paces away from them. Master Videria hung the bow and moved on to another.

"You're a spiritual guy." Sim opened her arms and looked upward. "Don't you feel this sense of impending doom?"

Cader rested an elbow on his bent knee and rubbed his scruffy chin. "I don't know. Sometimes I wonder if I'm projecting my own problems onto the world."

"What does that even mean?"

Prudence walked over to them, a jump rope hanging from her hand. She looked from Cader to Sim, seeming to realize that she was interrupting something. "Can I get some of that water?" she asked.

Sim threw the bottle at her.

"You can only find answers by looking within," Cader said.

Pru frowned down at the both of them, but didn't say anything.

"I can show you," Cader offered, "if you want to try meditating. It's not difficult."

"Yeah, maybe."

"Just ask." Cader stood and turned to Pru. "You should see this one in the ring now," he said with a smile.

"I saw." Pru nodded. She looked down at Sim and continued, "Just don't forget that things take time. You develop as you practice. Burning yourself out isn't going to get you anywhere."

"I know that."

Pru crouched beside her. She seemed to be picking up on Sim's frustration but completely misinterpreting it. "Anyway, check out those new girls," she said, jerking her head forward toward the archers. "Anyone you're interested in? I bet that one on the right would totally be into it."

Sim glanced at the girl, with her long black ponytail and toned arms, and started to respond, but before she could, she became intensely aware of a presence beside them. Master Videria towered above them, glaring down with angry eyes.

"I'll have none of that vulgarity in my battle house," she snapped. The girl with the black hair looked back to see what was going on. Master Videria put her hands on her hips and added, "If you must talk about such things, take it outside and keep it to yourselves." She glared at Prudence and then back at Sim, with an expression meant to convey her seriousness. Sim threw Pru a dirty look and then locked her eyes on the floor.

Master Videria's boots clipped away from them. "Stop staring," she yelled at the archers. She threw the newly strung bows at their feet and stomped off in the direction of Master Keisenheart. The archers frowned and huddled together to whisper.

"Fuck her," Pru said, glaring at Master Videria's back.

Sim frowned and nodded, squirted some water into her hands, and splashed it on her face to cool her burning blush. Master Videria knew now. She realized with a jolt that Cader already had. Kai must have said something to him.

"Let's go." Cader snapped to a standing position and grabbed his things. "They're lucky to have us here. We don't have to put up with this."

"No, it's fine—" Sim started, but Prudence interrupted her.

"You have to learn to stand up for who you are, Sim. Otherwise you'll live your whole life with people pushing you around."

Sim kept her eyes on the ground. She had to stand up for herself—she said this over and over again in her head as she gathered her things together. But a part of her thought that Master Videria was right: She was a vulgarity. And no matter how badly she didn't want to think this way, it wasn't something she could just change. They left the clanging metal and twanging bowstrings behind them, emerged onto Central Terresin's busy streets with their blaring carriages and shouts and murmurs, and headed toward the haven of the Bikeway Narrows. The bridge's towering arches were blanketed with a fog that made the rusted metal look like a crumbling staircase to the heavens, where they were no longer delinquents but god-gifted prophets of a time to come.

"Anemone for protection," Cader said the next morning, and threw a pinch of dried petals onto the burning coals. "And uva ursa to awaken the psyche." He added a handful of crushed green leaves to the mix. "Bracken for healing." He glanced up at Sim. "And, for you, chicory, to remove obstacles." The white powder smoked as it met the coals and burned.

Cader's meditation room was clean and bright. A few cushions were stacked up against the wall next to three rolled yoga mats. Cader and Sim were sitting on pillows in the middle of the floor, on either side of a bronze incense bowl. A bookcase on the wall behind Cader held large mason jars full of the herbs he burned to induce a meditative state. He also had singing bowls of all different sizes and the wooden mallets he trailed around their circumferences so that they would vibrate at healing pitches. A few crystals and stones were on the top of the shelf, but Cader hardly used them. He preferred the herbs for healing.

"Now just close your eyes," he said, adjusting his spine so that he was sitting up perfectly straight.

Sim had only agreed to meditate with Cader so that he'd stop bothering her about it. Thick incense pricked at her nose and melted away the anxiety that usually knotted up her shoulders. Something about the room made her feel quiet inside. But she still resisted believing that the peace washing over her had anything to do with Cader's spiritual practices.

"Now just picture that your mind is an ocean and your thoughts are waves," Cader said softly. "Your thoughts come in and that's okay, but just let them go back out into the sea. Just let the waves slip away."

Almost on its own, her mind went back to the day when she and Wood had been sitting on the wall and their arms were pushed together and Wood didn't pull away.

"Just let your thoughts drift off," Cader said. "Acknowledge them and then let them go."

The way Wood had apologized after Sim had given her that magicweaving lesson. The book that Wood had gotten for her. All of those times Wood had waited outside of the Incubator for Sim to get off work. Wood's foot pressing against Sim's shin under the table at Stein's. There was proof; there were reasons for Sim to believe that maybe Wood liked her back. She couldn't be imagining things.

Cader stopped talking and they sat there for twenty minutes until he played the singing bowl. Sim opened her eyes.

"How'd it go?" Cader asked. A sharp, clear look made his face seem like it was glowing. Sim could sense that his energy had grown stronger. It buzzed in her temples, similar to how she felt when she was about to cast a spell.

"Really well," Sim lied. "I feel better already."

"Did the herbs help?"

"I think they did."

"Let's go get some food." Cader stood and stretched. "It'll help to ground us."

Prudence was already in the kitchen making herself a sandwich. "Super vibey now?" she asked Sim with a grin.

"Sure."

Pru frowned at Sim's short response, shrugged, and looked up at Cader. "Did you get those herbs together for me?"

"There's a bag behind the jar of nettles, where Kai wouldn't find it."

"It's ridiculous that she won't sell her rosemary," Pru said, going to the cabinet. "I don't get it."

"You're usually the one who doesn't like to let people come here," Cader said.

"Look, this chick saved my bike. I owe her."

"Is that really why you're so eager to help her out?"

Pru turned to Cader with a frown. "Yes, that's why."

"Okay." Cader shrugged.

"I'm not trying to get in her pants."

"I didn't say you were."

The doorbell rang. Pru pointed a warning finger at him and dropped the bag on the table as she left the kitchen.

"You said it, not me," he called after her.

Pru turned back and gave him a warning look.

"Oh, hey," she said a moment later. "Come on in. Your stuff's in the kitchen."

Audrae stopped in the doorway from the foyer and stayed there, watching Pru. Her cardigan and dress were impeccably white. Though Mondran women usually wore bonnets, her head was bare and her hair hung free like it had the last time she'd come to Kailash. Audrae crossed her arms over her chest, moved her hands to her sides, and then wrung them in front of her.

Pru paused in the middle of the kitchen. "This is Cader," she said, motioning to him. "You already met Sim."

Audrae took a step in and waved at them. "I'm Audrae."

"Nice to meet you, Audrae." Cader smiled. "It's good to see that maybe bikers and Mondrans aren't born hating each other, like so many people seem to think."

"Mondrans really do hate bikers," Audrae said with a laugh. "To the point of it being ridiculous, actually. I think they're all just looking for something to complain about. It's the men mostly, of course."

"Of course," Cader repeated with an apologetic shrug. "Well, as a peace offering, it's the least we can do to invite you to stay for dinner. Pru can show you around the garden while we wait for our roommate Kai to come back. She's a great cook."

"Really?" Audrae asked. "I'd love to get a good look at those herbs."

Pru looked from her to Cader. "Yeah, sure," she said.

"That would be so great."

"Cool." Pru paused, stumbling in a way that Sim had never seen before. Pru smiled to cover it up and went to the back door. "I really don't know that much about the plants, to be honest, but I try to help out," she mumbled. "You probably know more about them than I do."

"I doubt it." Audrae laughed.

Cader grinned at Sim once they were outside. "Don't say I never do anything for you girls."

Sim glanced out the window to see Pru and Audrae standing close together, laughing about something. Audrae touched her hand to Pru's elbow and then put it up to her mouth as if to hold back a giggle.

When Pru came in through the back door, she grabbed the bag of herbs and handed them to Audrae almost as if she was in a rush to see her leave. "Anyway, here you go."

"I really wish I could stay."

"Yeah, maybe another time," Pru said, shrugging and not meeting her eyes.

"Definitely." Audrae beamed. "It's so suffocating being surrounded by my family all the time. I need to get out more."

Pru nodded. "Well, we can figure it out when I bring you more rosemary."

Audrae smiled, nodded once, and turned toward the door. She hesitated and turned back. "Thank you so much for this. I know I've already said it, but it's really going to help."

"No prob—"

Audrae cut Pru off by wrapping her in a quick, unexpected hug. For a moment Pru left her arms at her sides and then brought them up lightly to Audrae's back. They held each other a few moments longer than was appropriate for acquaintances, before Audrae pulled away, her face pink, and went toward the front door. "I'll see you in a few days then," she said without looking at Pru.

"Yeah," Pru said, following her and scratching her head. Sim heard the door open and then close. A minute later Pru trotted up the steps in the foyer and shut her bedroom door behind her.

Azzer was storming around the shop in a rage. Sim stood frozen in place. She was exhausted from trying not to have any feelings for Wood, exhausted from wondering why Pru had told Acheron that she wasn't good enough to quest with her, exhausted from Lilith's black magic crap. Whatever it was that Azzer was mad about, she didn't want to hear it. She was just barely able to deal with her own problems. To cope, Sim had started going to the Geraldine alone every night, hanging out with Grimms even though she didn't really like her, and drinking too much even though she knew she shouldn't.

"Can you believe this?" Azzer slapped a newspaper onto the counter. "They're writing about it as if it's actually news to anyone. What did they think would happen

162

once they started burning up tons and tons of magic dust?" He grabbed a silencing box that Sim had been working on and flung it against the wall. The gadget shattered and fell to the floor in pieces. "Of course the lightning storms are from that. Anyone who knows how magic works can see it. Anyone with a shred of sense can see it."

Azzer threw the newspaper across the room and put a hand on the counter to steady himself.

"The lightning storms are caused by magic dust?" Sim was almost afraid to ask. She'd never seen Azzer like this before.

"Some people say they are." Azzer sneered. "And some people say they aren't. Who cares that the three magicweavers denying the whole thing are in Nogron's pocket? In the name of objectivity the papers are saying it's inconclusive. Inconclusive! Well, good. Now everyone can convince themselves otherwise and go on driving their carriages and cooling their air and consuming more and more dust from the factories. We're poisoning ourselves." Azzer pounded his fist on the counter, making Sim jump. He grabbed one of the light orbs and flung it against the wall so that it exploded with a flash and a loud crack. Sim stepped away, back toward the door. He threw another and split it in half against a bike, another at the bookcase, and another at the map of the world. Glass was strewn across the Incubator's wooden floor in glittering heaps.

"I should be happy," Azzer yelled. "I should be happy that people will finally be forced to see the truth. But they won't. They don't want to. Nogron will plant his little seeds of doubt and they'll all just convince themselves that everything is fine."

"Well, what do you expect people to do?"

"Exactly what they won't do. No one's going to stop driving, no one's going to turn off their air-cooling charms, no one's going to change how they act. They'll say that it doesn't make a difference. And I don't know, maybe they it doesn't. It's too big, Sim. It's just too big." As if a flip had been switched, Azzer crumpled onto a stool and stared at the floor. "Sorry about the silencing gadget," he mumbled, flinging his hand toward it. "I'm going to my workshop. Call me if you need me."

"Okay." Sim nodded. "Azzer?" she said as he pushed aside the curtain. He paused and Sim continued. "We are making a difference here, I think. Maybe we just can't see it."

"I hope you're right, Sim," Azzer said with a sigh. "But I really don't think that we are." And with that, he pushed aside the curtain and disappeared behind it.

Sim grabbed the newspaper off the floor and sifted through the pages until she found the headline. The overuse of magic dust had been linked to changing weather patterns. Some magicweavers believed that the storms were going to become more frequent and more violent as more magic dust was consumed, but others insisted that there was no real proof of this connection; the lightning storms would be happening no matter how much dust Pulchrans used. Cader came in and Sim showed him the article.

"I wouldn't go back there," she said. "Azzer's in one of the worst moods I've ever seen."

Cader scanned the story and handed the paper back to Sim. "It's hard, I guess, when you take the whole weight of the world on your shoulders like he does."

"No one's asking him to." Sim went to the broken silencer and started to gather up the parts.

"True." Cader restocked the shelves with some of Kai's potions and glanced at the broken bits of glass from the light orbs. "I have to scrounge up more of those stones, or I'd help you clean up. I just wanted to come here and check in with him first."

"It's fine; I can handle it. I'll tell Azzer you were here."

"Well, drinks after work?"

"For sure."

They got their drinks from the Blue Carnation and took them outside, sitting on a bench that someone had dragged onto the sidewalk. The air was still warm, but autumn was undeniably approaching. Cader leaned back against the worn brick exterior of the bar and rested his left ankle on his right knee. He took a long swig of his whiskey and sighed.

"Long day?"

"When isn't it?"

"But you got the stones."

Cader nodded. "I did. But it's never easy."

A guy named Ralph, one of the regulars who would come into the Incubator weekly to get something mended, biked by at a slow cruise. He looked over at Sim from behind his large, round glasses and seemed unsure if he should acknowledge her. Sim lifted a hand. He beamed, waved back, and biked on.

"It's weird not having Prudence around," Sim said, wondering if she should bring up the conversation she had overheard between Pru and Acheron.

"This is good for her, though. It seems like she really likes Audrae. The last girl Pru was serious with—the only girl she was ever serious with, actually—was a quester like us. She was killed when they were on a mission together."

"How—"

"Striges. Not here. They were both called into a city in Eridos because they were known for being great at hunting the monsters down. Don't let Pru know I told you this, though. She'd be really pissed."

"Is that why Pru's so…"

"What?"

"I don't know. Evasive. Noncommittal. Detached."

Cader snorted. "Nah, that's just Pru. It's in her nature. She doesn't fall often, but when she does she falls hard. I get it. I'm kind of the same way, I guess."

"Really?"

Cader looked at her with a grin and a raised eyebrow. "I was head over heels for this girl. Stopped hanging out with my friends because I just wanted to be with her all the time." He shrugged. "But she wasn't so into it. Broke up with me about a year ago. I'm still getting over it, but whatever; I will." He glanced at Sim. "What about you?"

Sim scanned the street to see if anyone was listening. "Yeah," she said. The whiskey sitting in her empty stomach had relaxed her enough so that she felt able to speak freely, but she still felt guarded. She wasn't used to talking about these things. "There's this girl who I'm good friends with," she continued. "I don't think she knows how I feel about her."

"It's really hard to be friends with someone you have strong feelings for." Cader glanced at her with a frown. "You going to talk to her about it?"

"I don't know if I can," Sim said. "You think I should?"

"Yeah, I think you should."

Cader changed the subject. The sky got dark and he had potions to deliver. It was time to go. "Heading to Stein's?" he asked, standing with a stretch.

"The Geraldine."

"Alone again? Are you sure that's a good idea?"

"No." Sim laughed. "But I'm going anyway."

Candace kept brushing her bangs out of her eyes, holding her palm to her forehead, looking out the window. The girl who always wore aviators yelled at her for making her mixed drink too weak. Candace ignored her and went to the next customer.

"Still no Prudence?" Candace leaned forward on the bar, toward Sim. Her long blonde hair draped over the bangles on her wrists.

"Pru's all wrapped up in some chick."

Candace's eyebrows shot up. "Really? Prudence?"

"That's what I thought, too."

"Must be a real winner to make Pru settle down."

"Haven't met her," Sim said before taking a drink. She knew by now that it was better to err on the side of secrecy whenever Pru was involved.

"Eh, well, we'll see if it lasts."

The front door shoved open and everyone turned to see Grimms enter the bar.

"She'll be fine," Grimms said, shaking her head and glancing at Candace. She came over and slid onto the stool next to Sim.

"I left her in front of a Mondran hospital," Grimms said to Candace. "It was all I could do. I had to leave or I would've gotten into trouble, too."

"At least she'll be okay," Candace said, the tension in her shoulders melting away. "I don't want a death hanging over my head."

"What happened?" Sim looked from Grimms to Candace.

"It was Brooke," Grimms said. "She was puking everywhere and then looked like she was about to pass out. Couldn't even tell me what her name was. Took her to the hospital. I had to. Hopefully they'll let her off easy."

"Brooke? She'll get sent to—"

"I know," Grimms interrupted. "There's nothing we can do about it, though. Better at the work camps than dead."

"Were you sure she couldn't just sleep it off?"

"Obviously," Grimms snapped. She sighed and stared down at the bar for a moment, then looked up at Candace. "Get me a beer?"

"Yeah, of course." Candace looked down at Sim's empty glass. "Another?"

"Why not?" Sim forced a smile and sat there, sipping at her drink, laughing with Candace as if the whole thing had never happened, just like everyone else was. Brooke was gone. She wouldn't be coming back. And no one seemed to care enough to go and try to get her out of the hospital before the Guard came, as Sim had done for Pru. It could have been any of them, though. They all had their nights when they drank too much.

A girl slid into the empty space next to Sim and waved to get Candace's attention. "Any Kaianide left?" she asked.

Candace kept her eyes fixed on the bar and shook her head once. "Kaianide's no more, dear. You'll have to get something else."

At first Sim thought that she'd heard her wrong. Her dragon nectar paused halfway to her lips. Sim took a quick drink and acted like everything was normal. She turned to Grimms and pretended to be listening to whatever she was saying.

"They got nabbed?" the girl behind her asked, surprised. "Did the Guard catch another distributor?"

"Yep, that's right," Candace said. "So what'll it be then?"

Grimms was talking about the next tattoo she was going to get; a shark on her forearm, or a rabid cat on her bicep. Something dumb. Some new girl was hanging on her every word, telling her how awesome her idea was.

"I can't believe Kaianide got—"

"How about a dragon nectar?"

"Yeah." The girl stumbled, finally realizing that Candace didn't want to talk about it. "I'll have a dragon nectar."

The girl left and Sim spun on her barstool. She met Candace's gaze and held it.

"I'm sorry, Sim," Candace said, looking away. "I wasn't going to bring it up—"

"When?"

"What?"

"When did it happen?"

"Don't you know?"

Sim stared at her, waiting for an answer.

"Three days ago." Candace faltered. She started wiping down the bar again. "I'm surprised you didn't know," she mumbled.

"So am I."

The dragon nectar was heavy in Sim's hand. She didn't feel like drinking it. She became painfully aware of the dueling desires inside of her: The impulse to leave because she hated being there and the urge to stay, just in case someone might approach her or she might be able to forget Wood for long enough to approach someone herself.

"Time for shots, girls!" Candace yelled, pretending to be joyful. She looked at Sim with a grin and a raised eyebrow. "You'll have one, won't you? Fire whiskey. Only the best for my favorite ladies."

"Maybe next time." Sim grabbed her bag and, before they could protest, eased through the crowd and out the front door.

They weren't really her friends. The precious time spent where love could be found was not to be wasted on genuine friendships. But the Geraldine girls didn't know how to love, or maybe just Sim didn't know how to love. They were victims, each and every one of them, of a society that insisted they should not be who they really were, and only through the haze of alcohol-induced drunkenness could Sim ignore the negative energy permeating the place.

Sim got on her bike and rode to the apex of the Narrows Bridge, where the bikeway flattened and the railing curved outward into a niche. She rested her cruiser away from the bike path and climbed into the bridge's framework, just like she used to climb the branches of ancient oak trees when she worked at Nogron Mansion and needed to run away for a while. The iron beam was hard and cold beneath her thighs. Her legs dangled above the churning Brigantine. Sim gazed outward at the skyline of Terresin, a city that knew nothing of the dark's calm peace. Its towers shone with magical lights that reflected their twinkles in the river—a city person's stars. A deep and lonely longing for the woods of her childhood washed over her like the rising tide.

Sim sat there for what felt like an hour, thinking calmly about how easy it would be to just slide forward. That was all she would have to do; give herself a little push, and then her body would somersault into the river, just like those striges had two months before when she and Pru had thrown them off the bridge. For a few beautiful moments it would be like she was flying, weightless, until the water hit her and it would all be over: her endless, crazy infatuation with Wood, the incessant worry that people would hate her for who she was, the dread sitting at the bottom of her stomach, promising that she would forever be alone. No one would love her, not ever.

And then it was time to go. Sim hoisted herself to her feet and hopped back onto the bike path. There was more to the world than what she knew. Only that thought, that one comforting thought—that she could maybe search and find some answers—gave her hope. For a moment her bike was solid beneath her, and then she was flying down the ramp and back toward the Mondran Quarter, back to Kailash.

XIV

ai's trimmed-down herb spirals shook in the shifting air, adding to a symphony of shuffling leaves and snapping branches. Sim was sprawled on a frayed rug, gazing up at a crack in her bedroom ceiling, listening to the soft sound of rain falling outside, waiting for the last possible minute that she could start to get ready for work without being late. It was a moment of calm, a pause before the chaos she sensed hovering in her near future. Sim stood with a groan. She pulled on her dirty black jeans, buttoned up her shirt, slid her side pouch onto her belt, and secured the buckle tight around her waist; the tiny motions that she had repeated so many times, the meaningless things that gave structure to her life.

Sim scanned the newspaper as she ate her cereal, but there was nothing worth reading, just the same rehashed stories. She cleaned out her bowl and dried it with a quick spell.

"You could have just put it on the drying rack," Kai said, glancing up from the international section.

"I need to practice."

"It's wasteful."

Sim threw out her arms. She couldn't win. Cader and Pru kept saying that she should work on her spell casting, or that she wasn't good enough at it, and now here was Kai saying she shouldn't do it at all.

"Do you know if Cader will be back soon?" Sim asked.

"Do I ever?" Kai turned the page and scanned the next one. "Be careful with this talent of yours, Sim. You should have a teacher, and not Azzer. He's a gadget-master, but I'm sure he doesn't know anything about magicweaving. You should go to Munia and find a master there. Ask Cader or Pru about it."

"Yeah, I will." But there were other things she had to talk to Cader about. He must have known that Acheron had been caught. She couldn't believe that he'd kept that from her.

"Anyway, I'm heading to work," Sim said, raising her hand.

"See you." Kai didn't seem to want to talk more about it anyway; her eyes were locked on the thick potions book she'd gotten in the mail earlier that week.

Sim gazed upward as she went to get her cruiser from the drying house. The rain had stopped but the sky held the promise of more lightning storms. She walked her bike out to the street and pedaled slowly down the smooth asphalt, not really caring if she was late to the Incubator. She mulled over Kai's advice. Maybe it was time for her to leave Terresin, to move on and develop her magicweaving skills. Every day she took these same streets, guided her bike on the same path through Greater Terresin and the Mondran Quarter, over the bridge and then to work. A change could be good for her. She could travel, carry everything she needed on her back, climb the great Acinom Mountains, walk Munia's curving golden wall, sail through the Maria Islands. There was a whole world out there, and nothing to stop her from seeing it.

As Sim biked she watched the Brigantine flow black below the Narrows Bridge. She stopped at the top of the bikeway and looked north into the depths of the gray skies. An incredible downpour had to be drenching the magic-dust mines in the Dragon Spine Mountains, to wash down enough waste rock from the mountains to turn the river to ink. The air was heavy; the whole sky was pressing in on her. Sim wondered if she should go back to Kailash. Whatever storm was brewing would not be a slight one.

It would be fine, she decided in the end. The rain had never hurt her.

The door to the Incubator rattled as Sim pulled and pushed on the handle. Azzer should have gotten her that key. She slapped her palm onto the glass and scanned the street with a sigh. She'd just have to wait for him. A dwarf cruised by on a mountain bike with thick, knobby tires that weren't good for smooth pavement, but made sense for some of the Narrows' crumpled streets. He glanced at Sim with a whistle and a wink. She glared back at him, waited for him to bike on, and went to pull a book out of her bag, when she noticed a white envelope leaning against the bottom of the door.

The envelope was blank, and whoever had left it there hadn't sealed it. A sheaf of sols was tucked behind a folded sheet of parchment. Sim paused for a moment, figuring that the letter was probably for Azzer, and then took out the note. She recognized the blocky handwriting immediately. Azzer had only written two sentences: *SIM, I APOLOGIZE FOR THE SHORT NOTICE, BUT I MUST CLOSE THE INCUBATOR. I WISH YOU THE BEST, A.* Sim read the note two more times before pulling herself to her feet and peering through the front window. Everything was just how she'd left it the day before. She pulled on the door again, but she knew it was useless to try to get inside. The stack of sols was thick between her fingers. Azzer had left her two weeks worth of wages. Five hundred sols. She threw the money into her bag and grabbed her bike.

Most of the shops were closed in anticipation of the brewing storm, but a few bikes fringed the street and happy laughter crackled behind the Blue Carnation's gated windows. Sim leaned her cruiser against Stein's front fence and entered the glow of flickering candles and warm torches that made the café feel like a womb against the cold, windy streets of the Narrows. *The Revolutionary's Manifesto* was in her bag, waiting for a brighter day when Sim could handle reading about impossible utopias and how messed up everything was. Instead, she read a book about a quester who was destined to be a great hero, and all the troubles he overcame to fulfill his destiny, and the beautiful girl who just fell into his lap like a gift from the heavens—a girl whom he loved and who fell in love with him.

"I was hoping you'd be here," Wood said, arriving when Sim was a few pages in. She put a steaming mug onto the table.

The first thing Sim felt was relief. Now that Wood was here with her, she wouldn't be distracted by thinking about her all the time. She could actually register the words she read. For a moment she could settle back into herself, and be calm and centered. Wood was her best friend now. She couldn't ruin that.

"I forgot the book you gave me at home," Sim lied. "Had to pull this crap off the shelf." She waved the novel in front of her. The cover showed the muscled hero flexing his bicep in a sword-drawn battle stance. Behind him stood his lover, her long hair blowing wildly in the wind, her breasts about to burst out of her cuirass. And then there was the old wise wizard, the man with all the answers, standing tall in the back with his magical staff. The three were perched atop a rock, fierce, confident, ready to save the world. Wood flicked her bangs out of her eyes and glanced at it with a small smile.

"Better than nothing," she said. "And the manifesto won't get wet this way. The weather's crazy." She pulled out a copy of the *Terresin Daily*. "I really hope we don't get caught in the rain."

Wood started to read the paper and Sim went to the bathroom, where writing and lewd drawings spanned across the walls in permanent marker. She stared at the door before leaving, reading the words printed there: *You will never find another like her*. A sign, Sim was sure of it.

There were prettier girls in the Narrows, prettier girls who went to the Geraldine. Maybe there was someone who would actually like her back. But Sim didn't care. Her relationship with Wood was special, fated. She could feel it. When Sim came back, Wood looked up and slipped into a rant about the corrupt Pulchran government, triggered by something she'd just read. Sim nodded along with Wood's assertions, but barely heard her words. If it wasn't the government, it was the corporations, the media, the mindless masses. Wood had to vent her angry energy somehow, and Sim was always willing to listen. And to pretend that she agreed with Wood's simplified, sometimes paranoid views even when she really didn't agree with them at all. Sim was beginning to wonder why she still put up with it, while another part of her itched to just spit out a proclamation of love, so that she could receive her inevitable rejection and get on with her life.

"The world's just so messed up," Wood said. No plan on how to make the world better, no consideration of the other side of the issue. "We have to do something about it."

"Like what?"

Wood paused and frowned off. "Revolution. We need a revolution. That's the only way."

"A revolution?"

"Yes. An uprising. We have to band together with the dwarves and help them liberate themselves. It's wrong, Sim. It's wrong that people in the Hinterlands are suffering so that Pulchrans can buy cheap clothes, cheap gadgets, cheap everything. It's wrong that dwarves who are Pulchran citizens are pushed to the fringes of society just because of their race. People complain about them, say that they're overrunning our country, and yet they're the ones doing all of the crappy underpaid jobs that no one else wants to do." Tears blurred Wood's eyes and her fists were clenched.

"You're right," Sim said with a nod, because she couldn't bring herself to ask how, exactly, a revolution would change any of that.

They got more coffee and Wood changed the topic of conversation from social ills to her latest sexual infatuation. Any talk of revolution seemed to be forgotten. Sim shifted in her seat and did her best to make sure she didn't seem jealous.

"I just don't know what to do," Wood started. "There's Daryl, and he's really hot and really into me and the sex is great, but he's kind of a psycho. And then there's Adrian, the guy from the bar down the street who plays in that rock band. He's a complete asshole but sometimes he's cool and maybe things could work out with him if he gets his act together. But then there's Rudd, this guy I know from school, who has a great family and a great future ahead of him and wants to bring me home to his parents for the holidays. But he's also seeing this other girl and the sex isn't all that great anyway.... At least Brian's out of the picture. He keeps trying to hang out but..." She shrugged and raised her eyebrows. "It was just for fun. And he started hooking up with this girl I work with, so forget that. Not that I care. But I'm not going to be sleeping with him while he's about to run off with one of my friends."

Sim smiled a little and shrugged. "You'll figure it out," she said. But it was obvious what Wood was going to do: She'd juggle them all, suck the attention and energy out of each of them, and bask in the feeling of being wanted by so many people. Sim knew she didn't fit into the picture, but this wasn't the picture she wanted to fit into, anyway. She didn't want to be just another name on Wood's list of admirers, another person Wood could chalk off on her people-who-want-to-fuck-me list.

"We should go," Wood said, finally. "Before this storm hits. I should've stayed home—I have so much laundry to do, I'm on my last clean pair of underwear—but I was just so frustrated with the idiots in my classes that I needed a break from it all."

You will never find another like her. Sim's heart started to race.

"I forgot to ask you how that was going. It can't be that bad," Sim said as she pulled on her jacket.

"You have no idea. They're all so idiotic and close-minded. I don't even want to get into it. Let's just get on our bikes and head home. I'll ride over the bridge with you."

A thick fog hung over Terresin's spiraling towers as they plowed through the storm. The city lights reflected off the clouds in a dull orange gray, making the sky look like a teeming, dirty sea. "We never should have come this way," Wood mumbled, and Sim grunted in agreement. Her mind was elsewhere. The words she'd rehearsed hundreds of times were still refusing to come out of her mouth. When her hands started to shake she wrapped them tight around her handlebar grips and clenched her jaw to keep it from chattering. Rain splashed onto her chalky knuckles and beads of moisture clung to her leather jacket. Wood mumbled a curse. She was hunched over her road bike and squinting against the weather.

"You want my goggles?" Sim asked.

"No, I'll be fine."

A gust of cold air whipped Sim's hair out of her face and ran chills down her back. The rain fell in a quick and violent burst.

"This is getting really bad," Wood yelled over the rain's patter. "Maybe we should stop somewhere and wait it out."

A string of lightning crackled above them, turning the sky into a giant strobe light. For a breath all was calm except for the rain, and then a rumble of thunder loud enough to make the ground shake boomed above the factories. They were nearing the Geraldine.

"I know where we can go," Sim said, though she was barely able to work up the nerve. "Follow me."

Wood frowned, confused, as they passed the scaffolding tunnels and abandoned apartments that led up to the bar. "You know about the Geraldine?" she asked.

"Prudence and I hang out here sometimes. It's the closest place I know."

Wood's gaze was on the street again. "The Geraldine is fine. I've just never been there before. I didn't know you went there."

Filth washed out of the alley in a gray stream. Sim stepped over the sludge and glanced back to make sure Wood was following. "Our bikes should be fine here," Sim called, leaning her cruiser against a brick wall. Rain dripped off Wood's hair and caught in her eyelashes, making her look like a beautiful, lost sea creature. They stood next to their bikes, inches away from each other, Wood looking at Sim as if she wanted to say something and Sim waiting for her to say it.

"We should go inside," Wood said finally, and turned back toward the street.

The Geraldine was only half full, but Sim liked it better that way, anyway. There was more room to move around. Wood's eyes were everywhere: on the walls, on the bar, on the girls, on Candace.

Water streamed to the floor from her sopping jacket. She hung it on the back of a stool and twisted the front of her T-shirt together to wring some of the rain out. Sim glanced up at Wood with a questioning look. "Want a drink?"

For a moment she was sure that Wood was going to say no, but then she nodded. "I'll just have whatever you are."

Dragon nectars. If they'd still served Kaianide, Sim could have ordered that and told Wood that she brewed the beer. At least now she didn't have to worry about showing off.

Grimms and a brunette were whispering with Candace at the other end of the bar. A few other girls shot curious glances over at Wood. They were all wondering who this new girl was, and with so few girls in the Geraldine, Wood was hardly able to blend in. Sim had heard the conversations before: They were trying to figure out if Wood liked girls, if she was with Sim or up for grabs.

"They play really great music here," Wood said with a smile, relaxing and nodding to a rock song. She glanced at the walls. "And the art's pretty awesome."

"Now, Sim," Candace said, pretending to be offended while she poured them shots of moon glow. "You haven't even introduced me to your friend."

"Oh, sorry. This is Wood. She works at the bookstore on Christiania."

"Candace," she said and shook Wood's hand. She went straight to talking about the weather and complaining about how it was keeping business away. "But we're going to have a good time of it anyway," she said. "You can sleep in the back if you want. We don't want anyone getting struck by that damn lightning. Now, drink up. These are on me."

Candace pushed the shots toward them and gave Grimms more magic dust to put into the jukebox. A whiney girl-rock song came on, followed by another by the same band, before the machine groaned and stopped running.

Candace left her post behind the bar and kicked it with a bang. "Shit!" She slapped it with her palm.

"It wasn't me." Grimms threw up her arms in a shrug. "I don't know what happened."

Wood put her hand on Sim's arm and said, "Can't you can fix it?"

"What's that?" Candace snapped her gaze toward Sim and Wood.

"I've never—"

"Get your arse over here and try," Candace said with a wave.

The rubber eyepieces of Sim's goggles pressed wetly into her cheeks and nose. She crouched down in front of the jukebox, put her fingers to her temples, and sent out her energy. When she opened her eyes, the box was a mix of dimly lit colors, more than she'd ever seen in a gadget. "Someone give me magic dust," Sim said and stuck out her hand. She wasn't about to pull magic out of the air with that storm raging outside. Candace took a jar of purple dust from under the counter.

"Will this do it?"

"That's more than enough."

Even slightly buzzed, Sim was able to navigate the color lines that would make the jukebox run. She directed the magic dust into the box until the colors blinked and became bright like tubes of neon. Moving her hands in front of her as if she was actually touching the magic, Sim directed the color lines to attach and detach from one another until the jukebox glowed bright violet and the rock song burst out of the speakers again.

"That's my girl," Candace said, slapping her on the back. "Everything's on the house tonight."

Some girls put on some poppy electronic music and danced wildly in the empty space between the bar and the bathroom doors. It was as if the Geraldine had become a whole new place. Sim and Wood switched to fire whiskey mixed with a syrupy soda and the joined the dancers. Both swayed their hips with a newfound abandon, and Sim wondered how she could have lived for so long without ever dancing like this.

"I know what we need!" Wood said, tipsy with whiskey and elated with dance. She went to the jukebox, scanned through the records, and came back to Sim with a mischievous grin on her face.

The music changed abruptly from electronic funk to a swingy old-time soul song. The dancing stopped, but Wood smiled confidently. Sim felt a blip of fear, sure that none of the Geraldine girls would be into the music. But the moment passed in a snap, with one of the girls yelling in approval, and the dancing started again, different this time but everyone still threw their whole bodies into it. The song stopped and switched to another of the same genre and Sim sat down, taking a break and ordering a drink. Wood joined her and nodded when Candace offered her another.

"I actually kind of like this music," Sim said, raising an eyebrow.

"I know. It's awesome."

"Thanks, Candace," Sim said when she put down their drinks. The bartender nodded, then rushed out to the dance floor, suddenly deciding to join the other girls.

"You know, Sim, for whatever reason I feel like I can talk to you about anything." Wood was leaning on the bar, crouched forward toward Sim. Their knees pressed together, but Sim had already drunk enough so that it didn't make her nervous.

"Really?"

"I don't know why." Wood shrugged. "You're just—everyone else is so judgmental. I feel like you actually listen to me when I talk."

"Of course I do," Sim said with a laugh.

"Well, I'm glad we found each other."

"Me, too." Sim downed the rest of her drink and slapped the empty glass onto the counter. She turned to Grimms. "Can I bum a cigarette?"

"Since when do you smoke?" Grimms asked, but still pulled out her pack.

"I smoke sometimes," Sim lied. There was something pressing in on her. She needed to go outside, get away from the Geraldine for a minute. Smoking was the perfect excuse. Grimms glanced at Wood and handed Sim two of her menthols.

"Thanks, lady," Sim said with a grin. She tucked the cigarettes into an inner pocket of her jacket and stood to leave.

"I'll come out with you," Wood said.

"No, you don't have to. You'll get soaked."

Wood smiled. "Race you to the scaffolding." And then she was gone, the barstool nearly falling out from under her. Without hesitating, Sim dodged between Grimms and some girl, shoved the door, and burst out into the street. A million little fountains were dancing on the concrete around the Geraldine. Steam rose in tendrils from the fire cages. In two breaths, Sim's clothes were soaked through again and her boots were filled with puddle sludge. She dashed into the scaffolding cave of old wood and steel pipes.

"Wood?" Sim's voice echoed down the sidewalk. Rain made a dull, pinging sound on the corrugated tin roofing. The fire cages lit the entrance of the tunnel, but darkness shrouded most of the walkway. Sim shivered, took another step in, and called for Wood again.

Someone grabbed Sim from behind and covered her eyes with their hands. She was about to kick back hard at where the person's knee should have been, just like she'd learned to do at the Battle House, but the hands slipped away. Sim turned around to find herself face to face with Wood. Her beautiful gaze looked into Sim's eyes and heat flooded through her body, made stronger by the alcoholic haze clouding her mind. Sim was about to lean down and kiss her, but she took a step back. It was time. "I've been meaning to talk to you about this," she said.

"About what?" Wood frowned.

The words she'd been holding back for so long spilled out of her mouth: "I know you probably don't feel the same way, but I'm kind of in love with you. I think I always have been."

Sim held her breath. The sound of rain filled the tunnel. Wood blinked and laughed. "What?"

"You heard me," Sim said with a smile; a big fake smile because that was all she could manage.

Wood laughed again, as if the whole thing was a joke. "I don't know what to say to that."

"Well, you'd better say something."

Icy panic seized Sim's throat. The expression on Wood's face made everything clear. She shook her head and looked up at Sim. "Are you sure?" Wood asked.

"I'm sure."

"But we're friends."

Sim looked away and nodded. She got the picture.

"I don't hear the thunder anymore," Wood said, glancing beyond the scaffolding. "I should get back....I really have to do that laundry. Can we talk about this later?"

Sim nodded again, still looking at the ground. This was what she'd expected, after all. She didn't even feel disappointed. She felt nothing. Not upset, not relieved, just numb on a meaningless adrenaline high.

Wood wrapped her in a light, unexpected hug. "I love you, Sim," she said, but Sim couldn't bring herself to repeat the words. Wood turned to leave, awkwardly, and then stopped just at the mouth of the tunnel. "You're going to be okay getting home?"

"Yeah, I'll be fine."

And then she left, becoming nothing more than a silhouette in the light of the Geraldine's fire. Sim sat on the stoop to one of the apartments next door, not wanting to go back into the Geraldine but wanting to let Wood get a head start toward the bridge. She pulled the cigarettes out of her pocket and flung them into the gutter. She had been a fool, to think that a girl like Wood could ever be interested in her. But now she knew; at least now she knew for sure that all of those little signs that might have pointed to Wood liking her weren't really signs at all. It had all meant nothing.

But it wasn't fair. It didn't make sense. Sim couldn't figure out how she could love Wood so much when Wood felt nothing for her at all. The universe shouldn't work that way. Wood had to feel something for her. She had to.

Sim forced herself to stop dwelling on it and went back out into the cold rain. As she pedaled over the bridge she saw that damage from the storm was worse than it had ever been. The Brigantine had swollen beyond its edges. Trees were strewn across the streets like wooden barricades. Sim jumped her bike up onto the sidewalk and did her best to avoid the wide pools of flood that were nearly impossible to bike through. Lightning marks charred the occasional building's facade like charcoal scars, and Sim prayed to the godless universe that no one she knew had died.

By the time Sim got home, her drunkenness was starting to ebb and her head was pounding steadily. She went straight to the shower, now her favorite place to cry, and found her eyes surprisingly empty. After all, she'd gotten the rejection she'd been looking for. Sim put her hand against the ceramic-tile wall and rested her hairline on her forearm. For a moment all she knew was the sharp, almost painful feeling of scalding water on chilled skin. There was no cathartic release. There was nothing at all. She still cared about Wood, still wanted to be with her. She should have kissed her. She should have just kissed her instead of saying that she loved her. She never, ever should have said that. Sim punched the wall with the side of her fist and buried her fingers in her sopping hair. Nothing had changed.

XV

With no reason to go to the Narrows, Sim stayed at Kailash for the entirety of the next day, lying in bed and wallowing in her loneliness. She tried to distract herself with a quick-paced adventure novel, but after every few pages she'd put down the book and stare off at nothing at all, thinking about how she could have approached Wood differently, about what she should have said instead. She promised herself that she would never again tell someone that she loved them, not like that. She'd never been more embarrassed in her life, not even by all of those humiliating things that Jaylenik had made her do when they were younger.

Sim's attention shifted to Azzer's letter, crumpled on her dresser, next to the envelope full of money that would last her a week or two if she was lucky. There was a knock on the door downstairs. Sim stared at the ceiling and waited for someone else to answer. Then there was knocking again, a minute later, louder this time. Sim sighed, pulled on a pair of jeans, and made her way down to the foyer.

"Hey," Sim said with a frown when she opened the door. It was Audrae. The evening sunlight illuminated the street behind the willowy Mondran. Dust motes hung in the air. Sim had only seen her a few times with Pru, in passing, since that day when she had come to Kailash for rosemary, and not at all for at least a week. They'd never really talked. Audrae stood a good step away from the door, biting her lip and clutching her cream bag in front of her like a shield.

"What's up?" Sim asked.

"Maybe I shouldn't be..." She looked away, stared down the distance of the street, took a deep breath, and looked back to Sim. "Have you seen Prudence recently?"

"I haven't," Sim said, realizing it only now that Audrae had asked. "I figured she was hanging out with you." Sim looked at Audrae again. "When was the last time you saw her?"

"Just over a week ago."

Sim remembered the conversation she'd overheard between Pru and Acheron. "Maybe Kai knows," she said. She waved Audrae into the house and led her out into the backyard.

"Kai!" Sim yelled.

Kai appeared from behind one of the spirals, clutching a bundle of dried herbs in each hand. "What is it?" she asked. "I'm kind of busy."

Sim stopped just in front of her. "Have you seen Pru?"

Kai stared at Sim for four full seconds before she rolled her eyes and turned back to the drying house. "She's locked herself in her room," she said over her shoulder.

"What?"

"Locked herself in her room?" Audrae followed Kai into the garden. Sim stayed close behind. She glanced up at Pru's bedroom window. A dark curtain hung behind the glass, blocking out the sunlight.

"It took you long enough to notice," Kai said. "She's been in there for forever."

"Did she say why?" Audrae asked.

Kai sighed and turned to them. "All I know is that on last Monidy she came through the garden with this strange look on her face and she said that she was going to her room and not to bother her."

"And she hasn't come out in a week?" Audrae said.

"Look, I'm sure you don't want to hear this, but Prudence isn't exactly the relationship type. You should have known better than to get involved with her."

"Kai!" Sim said, not believing what she'd just heard.

"What?" Audrae snapped. Her hands were on her hips and anger shone in her eyes. "You heard me."

Sim blinked. She turned to Audrae, who seemed to be speechless. "Come on—" Sim began. She was about to suggest that they go inside, but Audrae was already on her way in. Her fists were clenched at her sides, her brow furrowed, her jaw just slightly jutted out. Her long hair billowed out behind her in a plume as she stomped up the back steps and threw open the door to the kitchen. Sim waited a breath, looked back at Kai, who seemed genuinely not to care about any of it, and followed Audrae inside.

By the time Sim got to the foyer, Audrae was upstairs and pounding on Pru's door. The sound was loud and angry—five quick raps, followed by five more. Sim stayed at the bottom of the stairs, wondering how she had known which room was Pru's.

"I thought you were dead!" Audrae's voice was approaching a scream. "Prudence!" she yelled. There was silence. Pru's door didn't open. Her voice didn't come from behind it.

"At least tell me why you're doing this. You just disappeared. What am I supposed to do? Sit around and wait for you? Prudence!" She kicked the door. A moment later

Audrae came down the steps. Her eyes were swollen and red.

"Wouldn't answer?" Sim asked, only because it would have been more awkward to say nothing at all.

Audrae composed her face in an emotionless expression. Her head was tipped up. "When Prudence decides to come out, tell her that I don't ever want to see her again, and that if she tries to approach me I'll refuse to talk to her."

Sim opened her mouth. Audrae waited for an answer, but then her mask crumbled. She blinked rapidly and looked away.

"Are you okay?" Sim asked.

But it was the wrong question. Audrae suddenly seemed pathetic, another victim of Pru's old love tirades. Broken.

"Just tell her that," Audrae said.

She crept down the front steps and left without looking back.

Sim refused to help with dinner. She stayed up in her room, trying to read, frowning up at the cracks in the ceiling, watching the daylight fade away, until Kai yelled up to her and told her to come eat. Their dinners were more elaborate now that Kai's garden was at its peak, but Sim barely noticed the food she piled onto her plate. She stole a few glances at Cader, but mostly frowned down at the table, trying to decide if she was going to bring up Acheron's arrest or if she should wait to see how long it would take for him to tell her about it.

"What's wrong, Sim?" Kai asked.

"Nothing."

"You're not mad about Pru, are you?"

"Pru can do whatever she wants."

"Azzer's closed the Incubator," Cader explained with his mouth still full. He didn't seem too bothered about it.

"Did he leave you a note, too?"

"Told me the night before when I went back to bring him more stones. You'd already left."

"So why didn't you tell me?"

Cader looked up at her with a slight frown. "Because I figured he'd want to tell you himself."

Sim looked away and then glared back at him. "Well, there's always the Kaianide, right?" she said, trying not to sound too sarcastic. "We can just brew more beer. No need to worry."

Cader blinked. "Right." He paused and used his food as an excuse not to look at her.

"But you should probably look for a new job, too. Just to be safe."

The Kaianide was starting to pile up in the basement while Cader must have been looking for a new distributor. He was avoiding her, Sim could tell. Pru was still locked up in her room, or off on that quest. It didn't really matter which was the truth. Sim kept biking to the Narrows every day to sit in Stein's, even though she didn't have to go to the Incubator for work anymore. She sat alone for a week until Wood finally came in again.

"Can I sit with you?" Wood asked. It was the first thing she'd said to Sim since that night at the Geraldine.

"Sure." Sim glanced up at Wood and then looked away.

A dragon steamed whiteflower milk into foam. People laughed. Mugs clanked. Wood perched on the edge of her seat and stirred her coffee while Sim frowned down at the table. A numbing silence hung in the air between them.

"Sorry I've been so MIA lately," Wood said, finally. Her voice shook, just a little.

Sim looked up.

"Everything got crazy with school," she explained.

"Whatever." Sim shrugged. She didn't want to let Wood know that she cared.

Wood grinned with one side of her mouth. "I miss our talks, though," she said. "All of that studying and memorization I have to do for my classes—it's all vapid and meaningless."

A month ago, Sim would have clung to that phrase as evidence that Wood had feelings for her. She knew better now. "I missed them, too," she said carefully.

Wood nodded and looked away. "You really mean a lot to me, Sim. You know that, right?"

"Yeah."

"No, Sim, I mean it. You're an amazing, amazing person. I just—" Wood sighed and looked back at Sim again. "I'm just not in a place where I can think about—"

"I get it." Sim frowned and brushed away a tear. "Look, you're making me cry," she said with a laugh, trying to lighten the mood by looking down at her hand as if she were surprised to see the moisture there. It was a good thing she'd chosen a seat in the corner, where no one would notice them. Sim forced herself to look calm and smiled across the table.

Wood put her hand to Sim's face and rubbed her thumb from her nose to her cheekbone, to wipe away the tears that Sim had missed. "I don't ever want to make you cry," Wood said softly.

Sim pulled away, nodded, and frowned at the ground. This wasn't helping. This wouldn't help at all. This would only make Sim like her more. This would definitely make things worse. Sim asked Wood what her classes were like, and so it went on, each of them saying things they'd normally say and both of them ignoring the secret Sim had let slip out of her mouth. By the time Wood's coffee was finished, it was almost as if the whole thing had never happened.

"Want to bike to the bridge?" Wood asked, after returning her mug to the counter. "Seems like a shame not to take advantage of this awesome weather."

"Sure thing," Sim replied with a light smile.

Wood seemed happy, elated almost, as they biked together to the Narrows Bridge. Sim realized with a soft shock that they were going to act as though her confession had never occurred. They wouldn't be lovers. But they also wouldn't have the catastrophic-yet-satisfying fight that Sim had pictured in her head so many times.

"I've only been gone for a week and everything feels so different here," Wood said. The dying sunlight caught on her cheekbones and in the soft highlights in her hair. She looked over at Sim with a smile as the sun streamed into her eyes, turning them brazen. "The more the merrier, I guess," she added, and her smile shifted into a small grin, the one that always made Sim's chest feel like it was charged with electricity.

"It is changing," Sim agreed.

"I absolutely love this time of day," Wood whispered, looking around at the long shadows and the factory windows glowing dusky red gold. Amid the graffiti, a blocky metallic BEAUTY stood out from the rest of the dark spray paint. Even the Brigantine looked like it was capped with molten metal.

Sim's heart lifted for a moment and then fell. Wood was here with her again. And yet, just as the evening sun cast golden highlights across the landscape, Sim knew that the two of them riding together in seeming harmony was only half of the story. It was the shadows that defined them, just as they always had.

The flannel blanket Sim kept at the bottom of her bed was pulled tightly around her shoulders. Her legs were hugged into her chest and her back leaned against the wall. It was late, at least a few hours past midnight, but she couldn't fall asleep. Her desk lamp was lit, eating up magic dust in a steady, invisible stream. Sim gazed over at it, remembering the lightning storms, and shut it off with a click. She snorted and hugged her legs again. As if one lamp would make a difference. It wouldn't, she knew it wouldn't, but at least she felt a little better about herself now, sitting there in the darkness like a martyr.

The front door opened and closed. At first Sim took in the noise indifferently, but then she remembered that Cader and Kai had already gone to bed. She pulled herself to her feet and tiptoed to the railing. Prudence stood in the foyer, a sword hanging from her waist, her shirt smeared with dirt and blood stains. She stumbled into the kitchen with her shoulders hunched forward and her boots dragging.

The sink turned on and Sim used the cover of the noise to creep down the stairs. She stopped at the kitchen table and waited. Pru shifted her feet into a battle stance and then glanced at Sim through her greasy bangs. A deep, scabbed cut ran down the left side of her face like a frozen lightning bolt. A fresher gash tore through the moon goddess tattoo on her right bicep.

"Hey, Sim." Pru released her grasp on the hilt of her sword and relaxed into a normal posture.

"You look terrible."

Pru just stared back at her, looking at Sim as if she was seeing her for the first time. She gulped down a glass of water.

"How'd the quest go?" Sim asked, her face neutral and emotionless.

"I don't know what you're talking about." Pru turned back to the sink and turned the tap back on.

"I heard you and Acheron talking before you left."

The glass froze in Pru's hand, halfway to the faucet, and then continued forward. "I don't know what you're talking about," she said again.

"Like hell you don't."

Pru took a long sip of the water, left the glass on the counter, and went to push past Sim.

"What are you hiding?" Sim demanded between gritted teeth. "Why don't you want Cader to know about the quest you took?" Sim grabbed Pru's sleeve as she passed her and pulled her back toward the kitchen.

Pru's lips were pressed together, her nostrils flared. She ripped her arm away and pushed her finger into Sim's chest. "I don't have to tell you shit." Pru turned toward the steps and then spun back to face Sim. "You're the one who's been keeping things from everyone. You're the one who's been putting us all in danger."

"What are you talking about?"

"You know what I'm talking about." Pru sneered. "Nogron, Sim. I'm talking about Nogron. You should have told us you were running from him."

Sim blinked. "I worked for him, that's all."

"You're lying."

Sim set her jaw. "I was a maid for his daughter. It was horrible. She would mess with my head, pretend to be my friend and then humiliate me. If I did anything wrong, or even if I just made Jaylenik mad, Nogron would dock my pay, and my mother, she would get furious. She'd kick me out. I'd have to sleep in this old, abandoned house, even in the middle of the winter. I couldn't stay there anymore. I ran away. I had to."

Pru was on the bottom step. She crossed her arms over her chest. "But that's still not the whole story, is it?"

"What do you mean—?"

"What's going on?" Cader came onto the landing, sleepy-eyed and looking confused. "Pru, what happened to you? I thought—"

"She was on a quest," Sim said. "She didn't want you to know about it."

Pru and Cader exchanged a glance.

"I did know about it," Cader said carefully.

"So you were just going to let me think that she'd locked herself in her room?"

"It's not your business," Prudence said, sounding tired.

"Oh, really? And what about the Kaianide?" Sim glared up at Cader. "When were you going to tell me that Acheron had been caught? Or is that not my business, either?"

Crickets were chirping outside. A clank came from one of the old radiators.

"It was safer for you not to know," Cader said softly.

Hot anger flooded Sim's head and rung in her ears. "Why won't anyone ever tell me anything?" Sim shouted. "And if you wanted to know what I had to do with Nogron, then why the hell didn't you just ask me?" Sim was struck by a moment of clarity. Her heart dropped. "You work for him, don't you? This whole time...You've been waiting to hand me over to him."

Prudence met Sim's eyes with a hurt expression. "Is that really what you think, Sim?"

"Just tell her the truth, Pru," Cader said.

All of a sudden Sim got the sense that she was acting incredibly immaturely. But after the scene she'd just made it was too late to turn back. She crossed her arms over her chest and waited.

Pru looked at Sim with a blank, even stare. "There's a quest out for you. I've known about it since just before you cleared the glass off the bridge: When I saw that I was sure you were the girl everyone was after. The only reason you haven't been caught yet is because you were smart enough to lie low. And hardly anyone expects you to be hiding in Terresin. But Acheron was starting to piece things together. I tried to convince her that it wasn't you he was after—that's probably what you overheard—but I could tell that she wasn't buying it. So I tipped off the Guard about her beer distribution. It was the only way to stop her."

"You turned her in?"

"I had to."

"It's that wand you stole, Sim," Cader said. "Do you know whose it was?"

She frowned up at him. "It was given to me."

Cader sighed and shook his head.

"She's telling the truth," Pru said. "You didn't quite steal it, did you Sim?" She met Sim's eyes.

"It was given to me," Sim repeated.

"It belonged to Leonidas Lightshield. And Nogron wanted you to take it from him, because he knew that you were the only person other than Lightshield who would be able to touch it."

Sim stared back at her. "Governor Lightshield made me keep it."

"Because you touched the wand and broke the spell. Now anyone can take it and use it," Pru said. "But did you ever wonder why Nogron might want it? Did you ever think about why you could touch it when no one else could?"

"It doesn't matter."

"It does. Nogron wants you and the wand, and he'll pay anything to get what he wants. Anything. That's how important it is to him. You broke the spell because it was your mother who cast it. Because he's her brother, Leonidas was able to carry it. But he could never use it."

"So it's true then?" Cader asked.

Pru nodded.

"Why didn't you tell me about this sooner?" Sim demanded.

"Because we wanted to make sure it was you, and we didn't want to freak you out. That wand is the key to bringing Nogron down," Pru said. "That's what I found out on this quest. A wand tracks every spell it casts, and remembers who did the casting. It would be irrefutable evidence against Nogron in a court of law."

"What did he do?" Sim asked.

"I don't know." Pru shook her head. "But it must have been something horrible. He must have had the wand at some point while your mother was still alive, before she cast the spell that would allow only her direct descendants to use it, and only those with her blood in their veins to touch it. I don't know. There's still so much that doesn't make sense."

"The wand is yours by blood right, Sim," Cader cut in. "You should be the one who figures out its secrets. But if you're not willing to do that, then you should give it to someone else who is."

The two of them stared at her, waiting for her to answer. Sim stared at the ground, finally accepting the thought that she'd been pushing away since the night when she'd met Governor Lightshield at Nogron Mansion: The woman who had raised her, the woman she'd called her mother for her entire life, wasn't really her mother at all. Sim's entire past suddenly became slightly surreal. She closed her eyes tight and pushed the thoughts away again. For now it was enough to accept the truth. She could search for answers later. There were more pressing things to be dealt with first. Sim swallowed hard and looked back up at Cader and Pru with what she hoped was an apologetic expression. She closed her eyes so that she wouldn't see their reactions. "I don't have it. I gave the wand away."

The sharp scent of spearmint, persimmon, and mesquite hung around Pru wherever she went. Every few hours she would take out a tub of Cader's healing ointment and lather oily lotion over the deep cuts on her face and bicep before reaching under her shirt and attending to hidden wounds. A slight rain fell from the overcast sky and people walked by with quick steps and large black umbrellas, as if they were all running from a funeral. Sim and Pru were sitting on the porch the next afternoon with a bucket of Kaianides between them, Pru hunched low in her chair and healing, and Sim watching her words so that she could avoid the topic of her having given the wand to Wood. Whenever it came up, Pru would scowl at her and grumble about how Sim had to go to the Narrows and get the wand back from "that dumb chick" as soon as possible. But Sim wasn't ready; not yet. First she had to figure out what she'd say. So she'd decided to avoid both the Narrows and the topic.

"So you can't talk about the quest?" Sim asked.

Pru coughed and grimaced. She touched her fingertips gently to her chest and groaned. "I really need to quit smoking." Cader had said that she'd broken two ribs and was lucky that whatever had cut her face hadn't taken out an eye. There would be a scar, but Pru didn't seem to mind. She took a long draw of her beer, glanced at Sim, and said, "It's best if I don't tell you. No need to get other people wrapped up in it. It's not a big deal, really. Not even worth talking about."

"Was it ogres?" Sim asked.

Pru laughed and then clenched her teeth. "You just don't give up, do you? Okay. I can tell you this: Those things are the nastiest, most disgusting creatures I've ever seen. And man can they can fight." She took another swig of her beer. "They're strong and fast and they have this thick skin that makes you have to jab twice as hard to get a sword through them. This quest was a rough one."

"Was it in Ogbond?"

"Enough questions," Pru said with a wave of her hand. "You really need to get that wand back, Sim."

"But I can't—"

"Just do it. This girl's obviously a bitch. I don't know why the hell you gave it to her in the first place."

"I like her."

"Well, then you should be that much more eager to get it back, before she gets kidnapped and taken to Nogron. Not all questers are nice, Sim. Even once they find out that she's not the right girl, that doesn't mean they're just going to let her go."

Sim chewed on her lip. "Do you really think they'll kidnap Wood?"

Pru snorted and rolled her eyes. "I don't know. Maybe we'll get lucky and someone'll grab her after you get the wand back."

Sim sighed. She knew that Pru was just being protective of her, and saying things like that because she knew how much Wood had hurt her. But she still hated to hear anyone talk about Wood that way. "Well, what do you plan to do about Audrae?" she asked.

There was a pause. Pru frowned. "What do you mean?"

"She came here, about a week and a half ago, and was really pissed that you just fell off the face of the earth without saying anything. That's a really messed up thing to do, you know—to just stop talking to someone and not even tell them why."

The pain on Pru's face made Sim instantly regret what she'd said. But she couldn't take it back. "I'm—"

"What did she say?" Pru interrupted.

"That she never wanted to see you again."

Pru nodded slowly, but stayed silent.

"So you're just going to forget about it?"

"It was never going to work out anyway."

"You could make it work."

"Not sure if it's worth it." Pru frowned and stared off. "I think I'm going to head inside. Take a nap. See you at dinner, I guess."

"Okay," Sim said, already starting to feel guilty. She stayed on the porch, reading her book and watching the rainy day turn warm and bright.

Pru rushed back outside a half hour later. "Are you busy?"

Sim shook her head.

"Get your bike," Pru said, going around to the back of the house. "We're going to the Mondran Quarter."

"The Mondran Quarter?" Sim asked, following her. "What if someone sees me?"

"You'll be fine. You haven't been caught yet, and you can't hide out in Kailash for the rest of your life. Come on. I'm going to get Audrae back. I need you there in case one of her brothers catches me."

* * *

They rode fast like they always did. Sim and Pru wove through carriages and pedestrians, not stopping for anything. It was one great, fluid dance through the city streets. Audrae lived in a duplex in a three-story purplestone building with a small courtyard at the back of it. No one was around. At Pru's direction, Sim climbed up into a tree that hung over the courtyard. A thick branch swayed under Sim's weight but was strong enough to hold her, and leafy enough to shroud her from anyone who might walk by.

Pru pulled herself over the alley's wall and jumped into Audrae's courtyard. After pausing for a moment to wait for the pain in her ribs to pass, she grabbed a pebble from a pile of rocks next to a pansy garden and threw it at a window on the second story. There was nothing. Pru sighed visibly, grabbed another handful of pebbles, and started throwing them again. Sim held her breath. After a minute the window opened and Audrae's face appeared, looking distressed.

"What do you want?"

Pru shoved her hands in her pockets, hunched up her shoulders, and stood on her toes. "I just want to talk to you," she said. "I want to explain—"

"I don't want to hear it." Audrae shut the window with a snap.

"Audrae!" Pru yelled up to her. "Come on, Audrae! Just come down for five minutes, and then if you tell me you never want to see me again, I promise I'll leave you alone."

There was silence. The window was blank. Pru sighed and ran her hands through her hair. She walked around in a circle, glancing at the wall and then back up at the window. There didn't seem to be anyone else home. Sim sat hovering above the whole thing, surprised that Pru wasn't just accepting Audrae's demand that they never see each other again, ready to move on to someone else the way she always did.

"Please, Audrae!" Pru yelled up. The back door opened and Audrae came stomping out. She walked right up to Pru and punched her in the shoulder, hard. Pru grimaced.

"Why would you do that to me?" Audrae said. "Lock yourself in your room like that without even—"

"I didn't lock myself in my room," Pru said quickly. "I don't want to lie to you. I want to tell you the truth, or as much of it as I can."

Audrae blinked and frowned. "Kai said that you'd locked yourself in your room."

"Because that's what I told her. I was on a quest. I couldn't tell anyone. I still shouldn't talk about it. But I can't stand to lie to you."

Audrae reached her hand up to Pru's face and pushed away her hair to look at the cut that ran from her temple to her jawline. Her face softened. She moved her fingers to the gash on Pru's bicep, and the deep purple bruise below it.

"I thought that you were avoiding me, and then I was worried you might be dead," she said, almost in a whisper. "It looks like I wasn't so far off."

"I'm fine." Prudence took a step closer to her.

"It'll happen again, won't it? You'll just leave and I won't know when you'll be back, or if you ever will."

"Probably."

Pru's head was tilted down toward Audrae, who was looking at the ground. A sound came from inside the house. Audrae glanced back and then pulled Pru over to a corner of the garden, where they were hidden by a cluster of high bushes.

"Look at me," Pru said. Audrae's back was against the stone wall just below Sim. "I think I love you, Audrae. We haven't even known each other for a month." Pru laughed and grinned with a shrug. "But that's how I feel." Her face sobered back into a mild frown. "I never should have disappeared like that without telling you why. I'm sorry. I can't stand the thought of not having you in my life."

A sort of calm settled onto Pru. Her words hung in the air between them. In a sudden burst, Audrae flung herself at Pru and wrapped her arms around her, hugging her so tightly that Pru couldn't help but gasp from her injured ribs being disturbed.

"Oh, sorry!" Audrae said, pulling away. But Pru pulled her back and kissed her and they held each other until any sense of pain slipped away and was replaced by a growing desire for sheer closeness.

"Come back with me," Pru whispered. Their foreheads were pressed together. Audrae pushed Pru's hair out of her face and looked her in the eyes. She smiled.

"I want to," Audrae said, and kissed her again. "Tonight. I can't get away right now. My mother will suspect something."

Pru nodded. "Tonight," she said. They kissed again, for so long that Sim thought Audrae might change her mind, but then, without another word, Pru pulled away and clambered up the wall without looking back. Before Sim could even process what was happening, Pru was standing at the bottom of the tree. Her dark eyes looked up at Sim. They weren't happy, as Sim expected them to be. They were guarded. The mask was up again. Pru tilted her head to the side, motioning to where their bikes were. Sim silently slid down the branch, and didn't dare say a word on the entire bike ride back to Kailash.

XVI

Broccoli Rabe was a slightly upscale restaurant hidden away on one of the quiet side streets adjacent to the main stretch of shops and eateries that ran through Central Terresin. It was nicer than any place Sim had ever eaten in, though hardly as fancy as some of the gourmet restaurants that Jaylenik Nogron used to brag about frequenting. A tea candle set into a terrarium splashed light onto the table between them. Audrae had spent the last three nights at Kailash, and now Pru was treating her and Sim to a dinner at Broccoli Rabe, since she'd made so much dust on her last quest. A bar serving fresh-squeezed juices ran long against the other side of the walkway, where waitresses in pressed white button-downs strode back and forth with heavy trays of food. The hostess at the door had barely agreed to seat them. After openly judging their offbeat clothing and squinting her eyes at Pru's tattoos, she told them to wait just a moment and then strutted off in her black stilettos to go find the manager. Audrae was the only one who managed to project a semblance of normalcy, with her hair partly pulled back and her lips just slightly rouged. She'd traded her Mondran whites for a purple skirt from Kai and one of Pru's old button-downs. Only her cream slat-heeled shoes gave away her ethnicity.

The hostess had come back, pulling down on her well-tailored dress shirt and looking at Pru with a slight scowl. She had put them at a table near the back, across from the juice bar and just in front of the restrooms.

Audrae didn't seem to notice. Pru bristled with agitation, but stifled it, probably for Audrae's sake. The whole thing was soon forgotten when they ordered their food and Audrae began to explain the details of Mondran culture to Sim. It was considered impolite for a man to even look at a woman who wasn't his wife, and it was a Mondran custom to keep most of your skin covered. The bare arms of someone like Prudence riding through their neighborhood had caused some of the children to start asking questions about why they had to dress so properly.

"But it's ridiculous," Audrae said. "The times are changing and we need to embrace them."

"It's your culture," Pru said with a shrug.

Raising her eyebrows, Audrae turned to Pru. "My culture also says that I shouldn't ever see you, that I shouldn't—"

"I get it," Pru interrupted. She glanced around.

Audrae nodded and turned back to her salad. Sim wished she hadn't agreed to come. They'd only asked her so that it wouldn't look like they were on a date. Sim could see that now. The guys in the restaurant all wore collared shirts, dress pants, and cardigans. The women wore perfectly pleated dresses that stopped just below their knees, and ribbons in their hair. Sim wondered why on earth Pru would ever want to come here.

Pru sighed and inched closer to Audrae. Their hands were probably intertwined under the table, tucked away where no one could see. "Your culture is important," Pru said. Sim took a careful interest in the condensation that had formed on the side of her water glass. Two girls in swaying skirts walked by. Sim looked up and met the gaze of one of them. The girl snapped her eyes away.

"My culture forbids me to be with the girl I love," Audrae said.

Sim glanced around. A young soldier at the juice bar across from them sat up straighter and tensed his shoulders after the comment. But Sim wasn't sure if he'd actually heard it.

"I don't see why it has to be all or nothing," Pru said. "You should be able to have both."

"I agree," Audrae said with a light laugh. "But that's not how the world works, Prudence. The Mondrans are an all-or-nothing sort of people. I shouldn't have to follow their rules just because I was born to Mondran parents. My entire life I've been told that if I wear anything but white, I'm disrespecting Mondra; if I let my hair fall below my shoulders, I'm disrespecting Mondra; if I don't kneel for an hour every day and insist that I deserve nothing good, I'm disrespecting Mondra. I'm finished with it."

"Does everyone follow all of those rules?" Sim asked. She glanced again at Audrae's long hair, her lightly made up face, her colored clothes.

"Some more than others. My parents are really strict. My brothers are almost militant about following Mondra's dictates. It's suffocating. But I love them. They're my family, you know?"

Sim nodded, even though she didn't know. She didn't know anything at all about her family. So much of her childhood had been spent wondering why her mother hated her so much, why she made her work at the Nogron Mansion even though Sim told her how horribly she was treated there. But it didn't matter. She had a new life now.

Pru and Cader and Kai were her family. The waitress came with their food and Sim was relieved to be distracted from her thoughts.

"At least you can come out with us," Sim said to Audrae. "You can be whoever you want outside of the Mondran Quarter."

Audrae smiled and dug into her pasta. "And I get to sort through all of Prudence's ridiculous clothing," she said.

Pru pretended to sound insulted. "How are my clothes ridiculous?"

"There are metal bits and useless loops on your pants. Your shoes are so heavy, and everything's black."

Pru snorted. "Borrow Sim's clothes then."

Audrae tickled Pru's side. Pru squirmed away and grabbed her hands so that she couldn't get to her sensitive skin, and Audrae gave up with a sigh. Pru smiled. Her eyes shone. Sim could tell that she wanted to wrap her arm around Audrae's shoulders, to hold her close. Instead she paused and looked away. Audrae looked as if she wasn't sure what she should do—if she should continue to flirt with Pru or act more chastely. She chose to be chaste. They ate and talked about various things; the Battle House, why Azzer might have closed the Incubator on such short notice, Audrae's new take on the city now that she had the bike Pru had found for her. When they were just about finished, Audrae looked at her watch, and then checked it again as if she hadn't believed what she'd seen.

"I didn't realize it was this late. It's nearly ten. I need to get back," she said.

"I'll come with you to get your bike," Pru said, sliding out of the booth as she looked up at Sim.

"I'll wait here for the check."

"Cool." Prudence slid on her jacket and held Audrae's out to her. "I'll pay when I get back."

They left the restaurant with their arms pressed together and their pinky fingers lightly grazing each other. Sim signaled the waitress and then noticed the soldier at the juice bar again, sitting with his jaw clenched and his eyes glaring out the front window. She followed his gaze to where Prudence and Audrae were laughing with each other, standing close.

"Thanks," Sim said to the waitress when she placed the bill on the table. Her attention went back to the sharp profile of the soldier at the bar. She could almost feel his anger, but it didn't make any sense—neither Pru nor Audrae had said anything to him all night—unless he recognized Pru from somewhere.

Outside of the restaurant, Pru leaned in and kissed Audrae quickly on the lips, then tilted her head down as if she wanted to kiss her again, really kiss her. But she only touched her shoulder, stepped back, and waved. Audrae's light hair flowed behind her as she biked away on her new cruiser. Pru stood where she was, watching her leave. The soldier's stool scraped on the floor as he pushed himself away from the bar. Pru headed away from the restaurant, probably going back to get their bikes. With his fists clenched, the soldier strode toward the front door.

Sim's palms were sweaty as she fumbled in her pockets for some sols and left the last of the money Azzer had given her on the table. She pulled on her jacket and rushed past the hostess into the cold night air. Prudence was standing in front of the soldier, two buildings down from the restaurant, where no one sitting inside would be able to see them.

"What did you say?" she demanded. Sim hurried closer, nearly running.

"I said that you and that fucking bitch are sick." The soldier spat onto the ground. "I don't know who the hell you think you are, pulling that shit out in public—"

"Why don't you mind your own fucking business?"

"I'll mind my business when you're not throwing yours in my face. Now, I like this place and I'm going to keep coming here, but I'm warning you, I'd better never see you in here again."

Sim stopped just behind the man, but Pru didn't look at her. Her attention was focused on the soldier. They stood eye to eye, both in each others' faces.

"Yeah? Or what?"

"Try it and you'll find out."

"Fuck off," Pru said, turning away from him and going toward where their bikes were.

"Fuck off?" The soldier spat. "Fuck off? I'll tell you what I'm gonna fuck. I'm gonna go on down to the Mondran Quarter, find that chick, and fuck her." Pru froze. The soldier continued, "I'll show her what a man can do for her."

Prudence spun on her heel, took two steps toward the soldier, pulled back her arm, and planted her knuckles into the center of his face. He stumbled backward with his hands up to his nose, looked up at Pru, and charged at her. Sim forced a deep breath into her lungs and glanced back at the restaurant. A second soldier, tall, muscled, and blonde, had just stepped out of Broccoli Rabe and was searching for his friend with a confused frown. His eyes settled onto the other soldier and Pru, and then he was rushing toward them. Sim stayed frozen in place. It only took him a second to take stock of what was happening. He ran past Sim and grabbed Pru from behind, wrapped his muscled arms under Pru's armpits, and cupped the back of her neck. A grunt escaped Pru's lungs as the shorter man drove his fist into her stomach.

Sim ran at them. Her thoughts shut off and she moved as if in a vivid trance, driven by instinct and adrenaline. She swooped down to pick up a two-by-four that had been left out for the trash. With her hands wrapped tight around it, Sim swung the broad side of the board at the back of the blond man's head, just as she would have done with a sword at the Battle House.

He raised his arm just in time, warned by the look of surprise on his friend's face. The board flew out of Sim's hands. Without a moment's hesitation, the soldier smacked Sim on the side of her head. The world went dark. A moment later Sim realized she was on the ground. She scrambled to get to her feet. Then there was the board, coming at her so fast that she only had enough time to put her arms up to her face to stop it from crushing her skull. Something sharp tore at her forearm, where she'd ripped the skin off when the striges had attacked them on the bridge. A warm, sticky liquid ran across her wrist.

The bigger guy landed on the ground beside her, and Sim scrambled away. Anger pumped through her veins and tapped into something deep inside her. The seventeen years that she had served at the Nogron Mansion, berated by Jaylenik Nogron, shunned by the other maids, beaten by Nogron: In a flash, all of these memories came to her again, forced to the surface by the fury that was already seizing her stomach. Pru kicked the board with its rusty nails out of the smaller guy's hands and then blocked one of his punches. Sim's left arm had gone numb, but there was no time to think about it. The bigger soldier was getting up, glaring at Pru and about to charge at her.

Without wasting a breath, Sim sprinted at him and jumped onto his back. She realized almost immediately the mistake that she'd made. The soldier was twice her size, and trained to fight. He reached his massive hand behind him, pulled Sim off, and pushed her down hard onto the street. The air rushed out of Sim's lungs with a whoosh. She thought she was going to suffocate. The soldier's hand wrapped around her throat.

"Sim!" Pru called, but it sounded more like an echo. All Sim could see was the soldier's angry face leering down into hers. His lips were contorted into a snarl, his eyes strangely calm. And then he was gone, and Sim fought to fill her lungs with air. Pru's face appeared above hers. She slapped Sim's cheeks. The air flooded back into Sim's chest. She gasped and sat up. A puddle of cherry-red blood was pooled on the street next to her, but she didn't know whose it was. She'd had no idea that blood could be so bright red.

"Careful, Sim, careful," Pru said.

"I'm fine." Sim pushed her away and scrambled to her feet. The anger was still inside of her, deep and wordless, but bubbling to the surface like magma. Sim stumbled over to the blond soldier, who was on his knees and trying to get up, and planted her foot into his stomach as hard as she could. She gritted her teeth and kicked him again. His hands went up to his face to protect it, but she kicked through them, springing at the knee as Master Throop had taught her. Sim was ready to turn around and kick the other soldier, but he was lying on the sidewalk. Someone put a hand on her shoulder. It was Pru. She met Sim's eyes.

"Stop, Sim."

Sim blinked.

"Are you okay?" Pru asked.

"Yeah, I'm fine," Sim mumbled.

"Where's all of this blood coming from?" Pru started to pull up Sim's sleeve. "Is that from your arm?"

"Yeah, I think so," Sim said as Pru peeled away her wet shirt. "It kind of hurts." Her head was in a daze, as if everything going on around her wasn't really happening.

"Shit, Sim." Pru jerked away. Sim looked down to see a steady flow of blood streaming out of her arm, pulsing a little with each beat of her heart. There was a deep puncture in the middle of her forearm, where the nail must have entered, and a gash running nearly to her wrist below it. The skin around the cut was deep purple and her wrist already swollen to twice its size.

"Better my arm than my face." Sim raised her eyebrows at Pru and chuckled.

"You're in shock." Pru's right eye was severely bruised and nearly swollen closed, but other than that she moved just as well as she ever had. "What else hurts?" she asked.

"Nothing," Sim said. "I'm fine. It's just a little cut."

"Sim. I can see it. You're loosing a lot of—here, keep your shirt on it. We gotta get out of here." Pru glanced over at one of the soldiers, hurried over to him, and put two of her fingers to his neck to check his pulse. Sim looked back to the man she had just been kicking. The fingers he held up to his face were sticking out at strange angles. He was groaning and rocking back and forth, not even making an effort to get up. Sim realized in a flash what she'd done.

"Is he...?" Sim asked, unable to finish her sentence.

"Still breathing," Pru said. "But we have to get out of here before anyone notices. Come on."

Sim looked back at the soldier with the broken fingers. He was lying in the middle of the street.

"Come on, Sim," Pru said.

"Shouldn't we help them?"

"Do you really want to go to prison for them? Now, I'm not gonna say it again: We have to get out of here before someone comes. You won't be able to run."

"Okay, let's go. I think I can bike."

"Are you sure?"

Sim nodded. "I just want to get back. Walking will take too long. I'll be fine."

The foyer was washed in dark blue. Their hurried steps and deep breaths sounded out of place in Kailash's nighttime silence. In her haste, Pru caught her foot on an armchair and scraped it across the wooden floor.

"We're going to wake up Cader and Kai," Sim mumbled. "Cader said he was going to the Battle House at six in the morning tomorrow."

"Don't worry about it. Here, come to the sink." Pru's hand was strong under Sim's arm, supporting her and drawing her forward. Sim grabbed the edge of the counter. Pain. It filled her all at once, like a mumbling in the back of her mind that burst into a scream. Sim gasped in agony as Pru ran the faucet over her cut. Her entire body started to shake. "Shit, Sim," Pru said. "This is really bad. What else happened?"

Sim shrugged. "T-threw me onto the ground," she said between chattering teeth. "Got the wind knocked out of me I think."

"Did you hit your head?"

"Maybe." Her thoughts were slippery, so hard to grasp. She was going to die, that was all she could think about. She'd wanted to die, that night when she had thought about jumping off the Narrows Bridge, and now she was actually going to; her blood would pool out of her body right there in Kailash's kitchen and she'd be nothing but a lifeless corpse.

"I can't get this bleeding to stop," Pru said. She seemed calm, though her movements were quick and anxious. "I'm waking Cader up. Try not to move."

Sim nodded, and then grimaced. She couldn't stop shaking, no matter how hard she tried.

"Don't look at it," Pru commanded, and then she was gone for what felt like an eternity. Sim's eyelids drooped down and then snapped up, only to droop down again. It was all she could do to stay slumped over the sink, the water diluting her blood to tomato juice. Bleed to death. She was going to die, and whatever emptiness or afterlife awaited her, she was certain it would not be pleasant. She'd done nothing for the world, nothing for anyone, nothing for herself, even.

Sim heard Cader's sleepy voice ask Pru what was wrong. They were coming down the steps. "Your face—what happened?" he asked from a million miles away. An echo of a question.

"Sim's worse. She's in the kitchen."

Cader's chest was bare and his legs were covered in flannel pajama bottoms that hung low on his waist. He flipped on the kitchen light and Sim squinted against the sudden brightness.

"Turn it off!" Sim said, putting her good arm in front of her eyes. The light sent a sharp pain through her head, making her feel like she was going to pass out. Pru flicked the switch and the kitchen was shrouded in darkness again.

"What the hell happened?" Cader demanded, now wide awake. He went over to Sim and started to inspect her arm in the moonlight streaming through the kitchen window.

"We had a run-in with some soldiers," Pru said. "They weren't happy about our choice of clothing."

"Right." Cader stepped back. "I'm sure that's all it was." He looked to Sim and said, "You're going to have to take your shirt off so that I can get at that cut." And then, back to Prudence, "Maybe you should start taking a little more shit and a few less punches." He sighed at Sim's fumbling attempt to pull her shirt over her head, and turned to Pru. "Help me out, will you?"

Pru pulled herself from the wall and went to Sim. "Here, just lift up your arms," she said softly. Big, gentle hands, Cader's hands, cupped Sim's elbows and lifted them above her head. Her shirt came up easily and then plopped onto the floor, heavy and blood-soaked.

"Now the potions," Cader said, and Pru went to the cabinet.

With his eyes closed, Cader cupped the sides of Sim's head with his palms. A light, fuzzy, almost drunken feeling filled her head. He frowned deeply and stayed like that for a while before pulling a chair out from the table and motioning for Sim to sit in it. Colorful bottles, labeled in Kai's neat handwriting, dotted the edge of the table. Cader snatched up a few of them and started to pour drops from each into a large stone bowl. Pru leaned against the wall again, watching Cader work.

"This is what happens, Pru," Cader said, glancing up at her but waving a hand at Sim. His voice was angry now. He sprinkled some dried leaves and chunks of a chalky stone into the bowl and started to grind the mixture together with quick, strong movements. He continued, "You went and picked a fight and Sim got dragged into it. We're lucky she's awake right now, with the injury to her head. It'll be days before she heals from it. Hopefully there's no memory loss. Hopefully her arm won't catch infection."

"I didn't pick a fight."

"Like hell you didn't." Cader went to Sim with the pasty mixture and turned the sink on again. "Okay, come back here, Sim." Sim gasped when he gently pulled her arm under the water and rinsed off the fresh blood that was running down her arm.

"Hand me that iodine," Cader said, and Pru grabbed one of the bigger bottles off the table.

"We were defending ourselves," Pru said.

Cader turned to her. "Really? And who threw the first punch?"

Pru frowned and looked away.

"I know you, Prudence. I wasn't even there and I bet I know exactly what happened: Some guys said something offensive and you lashed back with your fists."

"What the hell was I supposed to do?" Pru said, her anger showing now. "The things they said about Audrae...I couldn't just let it go."

"You could have. You have to. Do you think those guys are going to be any different now that you've beaten the shit out of them?" Shaking his head, Cader turned back to Sim. He rinsed more blood off and held the bottle of iodine in his hand. "Now this is going to hurt, so get ready."

Sim nodded once and clenched her teeth. The cool liquid tickled the top of her arm and then ran down into the gash like molten iron. She refused to cry out. The hand of her good arm grasped the edge of the counter so tightly that it dug into her fingers. A sick feeling filled her stomach. Her consciousness swayed toward the oblivion of passing out. Her whole body shivered and for a moment dark specks flashed in front of her eyes. Nothing existed but her arm and the cut and the pain that seemed like it would last forever. She tried to think about nothing but her breathing. In and out, smoothly. Then Cader rubbed the cool paste into the cut and Sim realized that her eyes were closed. She opened them. The sharp pain receded, replaced by a sore, throbbing numbness.

"I take shit all the time, Cader, and you know it," Pru said.

Cader wrapped a gauzy bandage around Sim's arm to keep the paste on. It had stopped the bleeding.

"You have to learn to deal with your anger, Prudence," Cader said without looking at her. He was focused on making sure Sim's bandage was perfect.

"I'm not doing that meditation crap."

"Do what you want. Maybe next time you'll get someone killed instead of just bloodied up."

Sim frowned up at him, finally realizing what he was suggesting. "This wasn't Pru's fault," she said. "I jumped in. It was my own choice. I would have done the same thing if I were her."

Cader put his hands on either side of her head again and told Sim to shut her eyes. The fuzzy feeling came back and Sim fell into it; a dizzy, beautiful abyss. She started to doze off, but Cader shook her shoulder.

"Drink this," he said, handing her one of the vials.

"That's worse than Kai's tea." Sim made a face. Cader grinned.

"She can't go to sleep," he said to Pru. "She has to stay awake at least for an hour or two. You should get some rest, I'll—"

"I'll stay up with her," Pru said.

"No," Sim said. "I'll be okay. Just let me go to bed. I'll be fine."

Cader and Pru exchanged a glance. "I'll make sure she stays up," Pru said.

"Fine. I'll be upstairs if you need me."

The living room was dim and somber. Just the one table lamp was lit, behind where Sim was reclining against the arm of the couch. Cader had gotten her a big T-shirt to wear, and Pru covered her in a fuzzy blue blanket. Drangs, who had been at the edge of the kitchen the entire time, watching the whole confusing event with wide eyes, mewed and jumped up onto the couch with Sim. He nuzzled his body between her and the back of the couch, vibrating steady purrs into Sim's side. She absentmindedly stroked his head as her eyelids drooped. Pru moved to the table and sat across from her.

"Feel any better?" Pru asked.

"Numb." Sim didn't move or change her expression. "I can't believe those guys would do something like that."

Pru sighed deeply, as she did when she was annoyed, closed her eyes, and opened them again. "Don't be so naive, Sim. What happened tonight is normal, not the exception. People hate us."

"I don't think—"

"They do. Because they can. Most people aren't good. I've told you that before."

"People can change."

"Change?" Pru laughed, short and sarcastic. "Hell will freeze over before that ever happens."

And then Pru was silent and the void between them was filled with only the sounds of Kailash's old wooden framework settling into place: creaking wood, clicking pipes, congealing mortar. A gust of wind howled outside, across the porch and through the tree branches.

"So then we just don't do anything?" Sim mumbled, because it was too hard to force herself to speak clearly.

"We recognize that there's nothing we can do. And we live our lives the best we can."

"That can't be the answer."

"There's no hope for us, Sim. But look at it this way; we're definitely better off than all of those people who convince themselves that they love people they're not even attracted to. They live a lie because they think it's easier. At least we're true to ourselves."

"At least we're true to ourselves," Sim repeated. She let her eyes shut.

"No sleeping," Pru said, leaning forward and shaking Sim's shoulder to wake her.

"Talk to me about something."

"Like what?"

"I don't know; anything."

Sim took a deep breath. "Actually, there has been this one thing that I've been meaning to bring up for a while now. Since that day at the hospital."

Pru's frown was darkened by the deep eggplant bruise swelling around her eye. She was a mess, with the scabbed-up cut on one side of her face and the black eye on the other, her knotted hair framing the whole thing. A slouch softened her shoulders, made her look as if she was about to break. The dizziness in Sim's head, the potion-induced softness at the edges of her consciousness, made her feel as if she was someone else, separate from the girl lying on the old, fraying couch surrounded by bookcases and strange things collected from Cader and Pru's quests. The chalky skull of a small animal stared its blank eye sockets at Sim, watching the whole scene silently, waiting to see if she would bring up what she'd seen that day or let it remain just a thought, something not quite real. To talk about it would give it reality. Words changed things. To admit what she'd seen would mean that she'd have to do something about it. It wasn't fair to bring Pru into it. Then she'd have to do something about it, too, and Pru already seemed so fragile, so very close to breaking. If Sim was a good friend, she'd let it go. If she cared at all about living a simple, carefree life, she'd let it go. The skull waited.

"What is it?" Pru asked and Sim realized that she was already too far into it to go back. She had to tell her. The potions helped; separate from herself, all of the reasons for not speaking, all of the consequences, were distant and trivial. Pru sat forward, attentive.

"At the hospital, before I found you on the second floor, there was...There was this other room I checked first." As she began to speak, Sim realized that she didn't quite know how to put what she'd seen into words. Her words came out slower than usual, full of thoughts and hesitation. "The people in it, I think they were doing experiments on them. I don't know what it was. They were human, but not really. They were so small. Maybe they were dwarves. They reminded me of those creatures we saw on the bridge, the striges. I know you said they're not striges, but they are, I just know they are and those people in the hospital, they were almost the same. More ill. Dying. There were these tubes—feeding tubes I think. One was trying to escape, but they were all locked in there and the nurse was so mad when she found the woman trying to get out. She hit the thing. Hard. And I just left them there, left them all there, and ran away."

The expression on Pru's face was unreadable, as always. She stared ahead, not trying to hide her emotions but processing what Sim had just said. The skull was laughing at them. The lampshade cast a dark grinning shadow over the smooth surface of the table.

Laughing. Sim wondered if she'd regret this later, when she was more awake.

"What else did you see?" Pru asked, looking at her again.

"It was dark. It smelled really bad. That whole place was creepy. Had to break a charm to get in. I don't know. They were all really sick looking. Just bones and skin. Gray, disgusting skin. Some of it was already rotted away."

Prudence was silent and Sim couldn't stand it. "What do you think it is?" Sim asked; the obvious question.

"I don't know."

"I think they're doing experiments. They must be."

"I don't know, Sim."

"Or they were all quarantined. But that was over a month ago and I'm still normal, still fine. I don't think they infected me. But they could have."

Pru looked up and met her eyes. "They didn't. You're obviously not infected with anything."

"We have to go back."

"And do what?"

"Break them free, Pru. They were tied down, chained to those beds so that they couldn't move. We can't stand for it. Can't let them just—"

"And how are we going to break them free?"

"I don't know, but—"

"And even if we do, what would we do then?"

"I don't know."

"Now's not the time for this," Pru said with a sigh. "Let's talk about something else. Did I ever tell you how I got to be a quester?"

"No."

"Okay, well I'll tell you about that then. You just have to listen and stay awake."

Sim barely heard Pru's words, and when she woke late the next morning, she couldn't recall anything that Pru had said about her life. All she could remember was Pru's soothing, raspy voice and staring for hours at that grinning skull.

XVII

tein's was full, but Wood was nowhere to be seen. Pru slouched low into one of the worn couches, a scowl darkening her face. She was doing her best to focus on the book she'd brought to read. Sim shifted nervously, glancing at the door every few minutes and doing her best not to dwell on how Wood might react when she asked for the wand back. Pru had insisted on coming along, even though she hated Stein's: She didn't trust Sim to get the wand back on her own. Sim scratched at the bandage on her right arm. In three days the gash had transformed into a gnarled scab that had to be lathered in ointments and wrapped every morning.

"Any word from your questing contacts about what I saw at the hospital?" Sim asked, hoping to distract Pru from Wood's absence.

Pru looked at her for a moment and then sat forward. "They could have just been sick people, Sim. They were probably chained down because they're clinically insane. I asked around, but I'm telling you, there's probably nothing to find out."

Somehow Sim knew this wasn't true. But she couldn't explain why, so she just nodded and dropped the subject.

"And what about the other thing?"

Pru frowned at her and blinked when she realized that Sim was asking about the quest out for her head. "Don't worry about that. That's why we're here."

The table behind them had started to argue about the war. "Those ogres are probably just pissed that we're taking all of their magic dust. You really can't blame them for that."

"We're not taking anything—we're paying for it..."

"I don't know how much more of this place I can stand," Pru said under her breath. She glanced around again. "Where the hell is this chick? I thought you said she comes here every day?"

"I don't know. I haven't been here as much lately. She used to—"

The door swung open. Wood walked in, pushing her bangs out of her eyes and frowning at the lack of empty tables. Sim felt her heart drop. The couch creaked as Pru shifted to follow Sim's gaze.

"Finally." Pru leaned back and opened her book. "Don't take forever."

"I won't," Sim said with a nod. She glanced over again and caught Wood's eye without meaning to. Wood smiled a little—it was obviously forced—and raised her hand. Her eyes went to Pru and she turned toward the barista to order a coffee. She took it to a table on the other side of the cafe.

"Go," Pru said.

Sim nodded.

"Go now or I'll do it myself." Pru's stare held Sim's.

"Fine."

Sim stood and wiped her sweaty palms on her pants. Her heart felt like it was going to burst out of her chest. The calming café sounds—chatter, ruffling fire dragons, pens scratching on parchment—faded away, and all Sim could hear was a deep blood-beat drumming in her ears. She focused on calming her breath as she walked awkwardly to the edge of Wood's table.

"Hey," Sim said.

"Hey." Wood looked up at her with her beautiful siren eyes and waited for Sim to say something. "What happened to your arm?" she asked, when Sim stayed silent.

"It's nothing. I need the wand back," Sim blurted.

"What?"

"The wand I gave you. I need it back."

Wood laughed and raised an eyebrow. It was the expression she wore when she was ready to get in an argument, but it had never been directed toward Sim before. "You're kidding, right? You know I need it for my class."

Sim shoved her hands into her pockets and glanced over at Pru, whose back was to her. She didn't know what to do. Wood shifted to see what she had been looking at and then turned back to Sim. Her expression was hostile. "You said I could have it."

"It was a mistake."

A hurt look darkened Wood's eyes, and Sim could see that she'd misinterpreted her, that now she thought Sim had only given her the wand because she'd had a crush on her.

"You don't need the wand," Sim said, trying to make up for it. "You're talented enough to spell cast without it."

"So then why did you even give it to me?"

"Because you weren't going to take that class unless I did."

"What?"

"You wanted to take that class," Sim tried to explain. "And you said you wouldn't without the wand—"

"So you figured that you needed to lie to me to get me to do what was best for myself?" Wood's voice was getting louder. Sim was starting to get angry, because she knew that she deserved none of this.

"That's not what I said. I was just trying to—why are you being such a bitch?"

"I'm being a bitch?" Wood said, loudly enough to attract a few glances from the people near them. "You're the one who tried to get me drunk and then seduce me."

The breath gasped out of Sim's lungs. Her throat muscles seized and choked her. Heat rushed up into her cheeks. "That's not true at all," Sim croaked.

Wood shrugged and looked away. The baristas, standing nearby, tried to pretend that they were wrapped up in their work and not paying attention. A girl at the table next to Wood's glanced up at Sim.

The anger that Sim had been repressing—from all the time she'd wasted thinking about Wood, from Wood never actually acknowledging Sim's feelings when she'd said they'd talk about it, from Wood not liking her back—boiled to the surface. Sim felt her face burn with a flush.

"You used me," Sim said, her own voice getting louder. "You only hung out with me because I would listen to your vapid, shallow, self-involved—"

"Please, Sim. Stop being so dramatic."

"Dramatic? Well, I guess you would know. You're the one who sleeps around all the time and then complains when guys won't take you seriously. You're too dumb to see that they only want you for sex."

Sim's heart dropped. She didn't realize the weight of her words until they'd already spilled out of her mouth. Everything paused for a moment as icy regret cut through the irrational anger that had been possessing her. She was left with a sense of vertigo, awash with intense emotions that didn't quite make sense.

"Wow, Sim." Wood choked, and looked away with tears in her eyes.

Sim tried to apologize, but found that she couldn't. "I wouldn't ask for the wand back if it weren't important," she said instead. "Please just give it to me."

"Why should I?"

Sim's voice was firm, but quieter now. "I don't have to tell you why. It's mine. I let you borrow it and now I want it back."

Wood shrugged and looked away. The baristas, standing nearby, tried to pretend that they were wrapped up in their work and not paying attention. A girl at the table next to Wood's glanced up at Sim. Suddenly Sim didn't care who was watching, she didn't care what these people thought of her. "Fine," she said through gritted teeth.

Before Wood could react, Sim grabbed her bag and tore it open.

"What the hell?" Wood demanded, springing to her feet. "Don't touch—"

"Try and stop me." Sim turned from her and dumped the contents of the bag onto the table. Paperbacks, pens, and notebooks fell out, but the wand wasn't there.

"Do you really think I'm dumb enough to keep it in there?"

Sim threw the empty bag at Wood's chest, grunted in frustration, and stomped out of the café. Wood followed her, grabbing at her arm. Sim flung her grasp off, shoving her into the stone dragon next to the door.

"You gave it to me, Sim. I'm not giving it back to you. Just stay away from me."

"You're the one following me, asshole."

Wood stepped back, shook her head, and looked away. "This is it, Sim. We're done. We can't be friends anymore."

"Fine by me." Sim laughed, short and sarcastic. "You were a pretty shitty friend, anyway."

Pru rushed outside, carrying their things. She met Sim's eyes and started to turn to Wood but then seemed to think better of it.

"Time to go," Pru said, putting her hand on Sim's back and leading her toward the Blue Carnation. Sim glanced back at Wood, whose face was bright red. She shook her head and disappeared back into Stein's.

"Way to be subtle," Pru said as they dodged through the people walking down the sidewalk. She pushed through the Carnation's swinging doors and gave Sim a look that affirmed her sense of embarrassment. The whole coffee shop had seen their outburst. Heat rushed to Sim's cheeks.

"She wouldn't give it back to me! And the things she said—"

"I heard. Everyone heard." Pru went up to the bar and ordered them each a shot. "You okay?"

Sim nodded. She felt exhausted and numb, but she'd be okay.

"I thought we were going to the Geraldine," Sim said with a frown. "And what about the wand?"

"We'll have to think of a way to be more persuasive. But we can worry about that later." Pru grinned. "I have a surprise for you."

A tattoo gun buzzed to life in a back room of the Blue Carnation. Prudence insisted that the artists at the shop two doors down were subpar and that the small room behind the bar was the best place to get inked. "I know the girl," she'd said. "She's way better, and she won't overcharge us. It's only by appointment and someone just cancelled yesterday, so if you don't do it now who knows how long you'll have to wait?"

Sim wasn't sure if she would have gone through with it if Pru hadn't insisted that she go immediately. The idea of something being on her body forever made her inclined to avoid the situation. But she wanted the tattoo, she was sure she did.

A guy who had snakes covering his biceps and thumb-sized gauges in his ears lay on a wooden table in the middle of the small room, staring up at the ceiling. Helena, the artist, was inking letters into his chest with a buzzing needle. Her long dreadlocks hung in front of her face and her body was in a pose of perfect concentration. A tattoo of a longsword ran down the back of her right arm, and a thistle marked her left shoulder blade. Her calves held snarling dragons, facing each other as if they were about to duel. Rock music played from the portable speaker she'd set up in a corner of the room. The buzzing stopped and Helena pulled away to dip her needle gun into a brass bowl of ink. Black-red blood oozed from the outline of the words "End Times," written below the guy's clavicle in an old-world script. Helena rubbed away the blood with a wet cloth and went back to filling in the letters, the gun buzzing to life when she leaned in to work and going silent when she paused to inspect her progress.

The music dimmed and then ran out. "I got it," Pru said, pulling a jar of magic dust out of her side pouch. She opened the top of the box and poured in three sols worth of dust. A green light pulsed to life behind the speaker and the rock song continued where it had left off.

"Thanks, Pru," Helena said without looking at her. The gun hummed and the guy grimaced when it met the soft skin next to his nipple. He stood when Helena said she was finished, and inspected the art in a mirror that ran vertically along the wall across from the table.

"Awesome," he said with a nod, and raised his arms for Helena to wrap him in a protection charm, so that no dirt would get into the fresh wound.

"You know the drill," she said as she removed the needle from the gun and threw it into a rusty trash can. "Need any ointment?"

"Nah, I still have a tub of it from the last one."

"Cool. Just come find me if there are any issues."

"Sure thing. Thanks again, Helena. A hundred, right?" He put a small jar of silver magic dust on the edge of the table he'd been lying on.

"That's right."

They said their goodbyes and then guy was gone, leaving Sim with only moments to consider backing out.

"Your turn," Helena said, meeting Sim's eyes with a smile. "Still going for the sword?"

Sim nodded. "Between my elbow and my wrist," she said. "Wherever you think will look best."

"There's no turning back after this," Helena added. "You'll have chosen the path of the quester."

"I'm sure," Sim said, meeting Helena's eyes to assure her. She jumped up onto the table and watched as Helena packed some dust into her tattoo gun and dispersed the protection charm encasing a new needle.

"Put the heel of your palm on the end of the table here," Helena directed. "Yeah, that's right, just wrap your fingers underneath. Okay, cool. So I always work freehand, but here's the sketch I drew up, from what Pru said you'd want."

The blade was long and narrow, the hilt wide and detailed. It had a bike wheel at its center—a symbol for the Narrows, Helena explained—and arrows on either side. The base held four symbols that Sim had never seen before. "The four elements," Helena said. "The mark of a magicweaver."

"Is that a good idea?" Sim asked, looking at Pru.

"It's what you are," Pru said. "It's an honor to wear that mark. And no one who would recognize it will mess with you. If anything they'll protect you."

"Okay." Sim trusted her. She could have been putting a bull's-eye permanently on her body, but she knew that Pru would never do that to her.

"You want the point down by your wrist?" Helena asked.

Sim nodded.

"Cool." Helena squatted on a stool next to the table and looked up at Sim. "Now it's not going to hurt as much as you think, but it will sting. Whatever you do, don't flinch. And let me know if you need a break."

"Okay," Sim said with a nod. She stared at the wall across from her and tried to focus on the music. The gun buzzed to life. Sim breathed in as Helena placed the edge of her hand on the back of Sim's uninjured forearm and then bit the needle into the skin just below her elbow. Sim exhaled. The feeling of her skin ripping apart was strange and slightly painful, but she could handle it. She glanced over at Pru, who smiled back at her, and then closed her eyes.

"You good?" Helena asked.

"Yep."

The constant pain drove all other thoughts from Sim's mind, and she wondered if this was what meditation might be like for Cader. The procedure was methodical: cut, rub the ink away with burning strokes of a cloth, and inspect. The cleaning part felt the worst, like scratching at an open wound.

"Okay, you're done," Helena said, sooner than Sim had expected to hear it. "Go check it out and let me know if there's anything you want me to change."

Sim stood sideways in front of the mirror, turning her arm inward a little so that she could see the sword. The lines were black and stark against her pink, agitated skin. She felt powerful somehow, knowing that this image was now a part of her forever, that this moment in her life would always have its place on her body. She let the thought wash over her, and then turned to Helena with a smile. "I love it."

Pru paid the hundred grams of magic dust, Helena wrapped Sim up, and they made their way out to the bar, where Cader was already halfway through his first glass of bourbon. Sim waved at him with a smile and twisted her arm so he could see the sword through the clear protection charm.

"Welcome to the club," Cader said, grinning and slapping Sim on the back. "Looks great."

James brought their drinks and Cader and Pru started to talk about Atif, who had just been awarded a really well-paying quest. Sim frowned down at her new tattoo as she thought about the last time the three of them had been at the Carnation together. Her heart started to race as something clicked in her mind and everything suddenly fell together.

"Uh, Pru?" Sim stammered and took a swig of her whiskey sour.

"What?" Pru frowned at Sim with a concerned expression, seeming to pick up on her anxiety. Cader leaned his elbow on the bar and glanced past Pru with the same look.

"I—uh, I—that girl I told you about, who came up to me in the alley next to the Geraldine a few months ago." Sim lowered her voice so that only Pru and Cader could hear. "The one who told me that she was a...a strix. Well, I saw her again, that night we went to the concert in the west. And she said she knew you, Pru."

Cader's frown deepened, but Pru's expression remained constant. She looked around to see if anyone was listening. "Really?" she said, and Sim knew that she was dangerously close to setting Pru off. Under any other circumstances she wouldn't dare bring up striges or Pru's quests in public.

"Well, there's something more, though." Sim glanced at Cader.

Pru blinked. "What?" She wasn't even trying to hide how annoyed she was.

"The girl, the strix, she—" Sim swallowed. "She had a sword tattoo like this one. She was a quester."

Pru's expression shifted into an emotionless mask. Her eyes jumped back and forth as they scanned Sim's face. "Did she say what her name was?" Pru asked casually.

Sim bit her lip and wished she'd never brought it up. "Her name's Lilith."

Pru turned away from her and faced the back of the bar. She stared straight forward for a heartbeat, and then she pushed her chair away and was stomping toward the door.

"Pru, wait!" Cader jumped up to follow her. Sim rushed behind them, wondering what Pru might do, but she just stormed out and leaned against the dirty brick of an abandoned apartment two doors down. She slid into a squat and buried her head in her hands.

"We don't know if it's her," Cader said, glancing at Sim and pacing back and forth.

"It's her." Pru's voice was muffled by her hands.

"We can't be sure," Cader insisted. "Lilly died, Pru. You saw it with your own eyes."

Pru shook her head and snapped her attention to Sim. "Thin, medium height, pale skin, reddish hair, dark eyes?"

Sim nodded, just once, and Pru looked to Cader with a scowl. "There's no use denying it. I'd assumed they'd killed her. She looked like she was dead. There's every possibility that she came back."

"But why would she hide from you?" Cader said. "Why would she approach Sim? It doesn't make any sense."

"It doesn't have to." Pru sprang to her feet. She looked angrier than Sim had ever seen her. "I'm going to find her." She headed in the direction of her bike.

"Wait," Sim said, rushing again to catch up with her. "It's useless. She could be anywhere."

"Fuck off, Sim. I'm still gonna try. You can't stop me."

"I want to help you."

Pru stopped and frowned down at her. "How?"

Weeks had passed since Sim had last biked down the Incubator's weedy street. She looked at the crooked trees and crumbling curbs with new eyes. Everything seemed different, somehow. Long end-of-the-day shadows stretched between the buildings, and pixie dragons flitted between the trees, getting ready to say good-bye to the sun. It was just about the time when Sim used to get off work and head over to Stein's.

They didn't even have to break in. When they'd dropped their bikes in front of the store and Sim started to warn Pru that she wasn't sure she could break the lock, Cader pulled his chain off his belt loop and held up a padlock key. "Nabbed this extra one just in case I'd ever need it," he said with a grin. "Azzer never even noticed that it was missing." Then Sim had her goggles over her eyes, and was dispersing the two booby-trap spells that Azzer had placed on the window and front door. After the spells' magic fell to the ground in a sprinkling of colorful light, Sim decalibrated her goggles and pulled them up onto her forehead. She turned to Cader and Pru.

"Let's go in," she said, feeling bad for breaking in but knowing that it was necessary.

Light came in through the front window and illuminated the shop's gray surfaces. Everything was covered in dust.

"Ugh. It smells gross in here," Pru said.

"Cat must've gotten in and died." Cader scrunched up his nose.

Sim scanned the dusty bikes and Victrola. Everything was just as she'd left it on her last day of work. "Looks like he hasn't even been in here," she mumbled.

"Must have left the city," Cader agreed.

"So where is this thing?" Pru's boots creaked over the floor as she looked around the shop for the compass.

"Maybe it's back in his workshop," Sim said. "The last place I saw it was right here next to these maps."

Pru paused in her pacing. "Well, are you gonna get it or what?"

Sim hesitated. She'd never gone back into Azzer's workshop, never had a reason to. He'd never deemed it off-limits, but it had been almost an unspoken rule. She headed toward the gap between the bookshelves. The room behind the maroon curtain was neater and brighter than Sim had expected it to be. Two clean windows looked out on a rectangular, overgrown courtyard that all of the buildings on the block shared. The tools on Azzer's workbench were organized and perfectly orderly: Wrenches hung on nails, starting with the smallest and growing diagonally to the largest. Three pairs of goggles hung next to them. Attached to the bench was a crank for holding metal in place. An anvil with a heavy hammer was pushed up against the wall. The compass was on top of it, looking like it was waiting to be smashed. Sim hurried forward and grabbed it, eager to get out of this forbidden place and away from the smell that was even worse in the back room than it had been in the front of the shop.

She turned to leave but then froze in place. At first Sim didn't quite register what she saw. She'd never noticed that Azzer wore brown leather saddle shoes. The light from the window shone dully on their rounded toes, which were slanted down toward the ground. His tool belt was fastened tightly around his waist, just as always, with the black cotton apron he wore underneath it to keep grease off his clothes. Sim gasped and looked away before her eyes could move up to Azzer's face.

"Sim?" Cader said, pushing aside the curtain and coming in just at the right moment, because she wasn't sure she would have been able to yell for him, wasn't sure she would have been able to move. He looked from Sim to the other side of the workshop, where Azzer was hanging from a thick knotted rope. "Oh, shit," he said. And then he was next to Sim, wrapping his arms around her, pulling her back to the front of the shop.

"Awesome. You found it," Pru said, looking at the compass in Sim's hand. Her face fell. "What's wrong?"

Sim held the compass out to her, but she didn't take it. "What's wrong?" Pru asked again. She made a move toward the workshop.

"No, don't." Cader stopped her. "It's Azzer. He's hanged himself."

"What?"

Cader shook his head and took the compass from Sim's hand, still stretched out toward Pru. "Take Sim outside. I'll get him down. He must've done it just a few days ago."

"I should've come back," Sim mumbled as Pru grabbed her hand and pulled her out to the street. She let Sim go and searched her pockets for her cigarettes.

"The last time I saw him, he was in such a horrible mood. And I didn't do anything, didn't even try to comfort him," Sim continued. "I should've known, when I got that note, that something was wrong. I should have tried to get in and see if he was okay. I was too wrapped up in my own problems to notice—"

"Sim, stop." Pru held her shoulders and looked her in the eyes. "There was nothing you could've done, okay?" She stepped away, clicked a flame up from her firestarter, and lit her cigarette. She inhaled deeply and sighed out a plume of smoke.

Sim shook her head. "He was trying to get me to help him but I didn't want to listen. I saw it, with the goggles. I saw the black magic. And Lilith, she said the same thing. That we'd all become soulless if we stayed here, that we'd loose our ability to spell cast."

Pru blinked and then frowned. "What?"

"Nogron's factories are turning people into striges. I've been trying to tell you. Those things in the hospital, that has to do with the black magic, too. It has to."

Pru ran a hand through her hair and looked back to the shop as Cader pushed out of the door, carrying one of Azzer's worn leather bags. "Three days probably," he said. He scanned the street, as if he didn't know where to set his eyes. The sky was growing dark blue. "I took a quick look around," he continued, "and I found this." Cader unrolled a long parchment with a map drawn onto it. "It's the factories in the west," he explained. "It looks like he mapped out which ones are running again."

"Why would he do that?" Pru asked, her eyes falling onto the bag.

Cader pulled out a squat gadget with a glass dome set into its center. The dome was filled with a handful of the stones that Cader had been finding for Azzer. "It's a pretty powerful bomb. He was going to blow up the factories. There are five of them. I should've known that all those stones I got for him weren't just for ordinary gadgets."

Sim stared down at the sidewalk, trying to figure out what she was feeling. But she couldn't. All she could do was picture Azzer's toes, pointing toward the ground, and his limp, limp legs. "But why would he do all of this planning and then just..."

"I don't know. I took his journal, but I haven't looked at any of it yet. He's probably put a spell on it."

"Well, what now?" Pru said. She peered into the compass, trying to figure out how it worked.

"Now we find Lilith," Sim said. "We can come back for Azzer. We'll have to bury him. No one else will. But we can do that later."

"Are you sure?"

"I'm sure. Let's find Lilith. It's even more important that we do now. She lives out in the factories, I think. Maybe she knows why Azzer didn't go through with blowing up the factories. We can use the compass to find her."

"Oh, please. As if that silly gadget could ever track me down." The three of them spun to face the alley between the Incubator and the building next door. Lilith stepped out of it and stopped just at the edge of the sidewalk, her arms crossed over her chest, looking annoyed.

"Lilith," Pru breathed.

"Hello, Prudence." Lilith pressed her lips together in frustration and then added, "I was hoping you wouldn't have to see me. Hello, Cader."

"Hey," he said, looking just as shocked as Pru.

Pru stepped closer to her. "I thought you were dead."

"I might as well be."

"How did you know that we were here?" Cader asked.

"I've been following the magicweaver. Someone had to protect her. Do you realize how many times I had to get different questers off her trail? We're lucky she hasn't been caught yet. We'll need her tonight, when we use those bombs to finish what the gadget-master started. I've been watching him, too. He had a change of heart in the end, maybe. He thought his bombs wouldn't make a difference."

"What are you talking about?" Pru asked.

"Ugh, don't you see, Prudence?" At first Lilith looked angry, but then her eyes grew sad. She pulled her hair off her delicate shoulders and looked away. Her arms were still crossed over her chest, as if to hold in her emotions. "It all started with us, and we were blind to it. All of those quests we took to kill off the striges, to slaughter them—we're the murderers."

"No," Pru snorted. "I've seen striges grab people and suck the souls straight out of them. They're monsters."

"Not every strix is a cold-hearted killer. We killed innocent beings; we did it for Nogron when all along he was the one we should have been fighting. He was the one causing the change in people."

"No."

"It's the truth, Prudence. You know it is. What he does is wrong," Lilith continued. "It goes against the laws of nature. We should have seen that, Pru, but we didn't. And now that the gadget-master has failed, people will continue to come here. They'll become striges. But for me this is about more than that: It's about revenge. I'm going to hunt Nogron down. I'm going to destroy everything he's created, even if it kills the little part of me that's left. And you should want to do the same. The magic is leaving you, Prudence, I can feel it." Lilith stepped up to Pru and placed her hand on her chest. Instead of pulling back, Pru stepped closer. Lilith stepped away. "Your life source is so low. You can't spell cast anymore, can you? That's why you've been using a firestarter."

"You're not—you're not a strix," Pru stammered. "And neither am I."

"You're not; not yet. But you will be, and so will everyone else if you don't destroy those factories." Lilith held Pru's gaze.

Pru propped herself against the outside of the Incubator and slid down to the sidewalk until she was sitting on the ground. Her firestarter was in her hand. She clicked a flame to life, put it out, and clicked one to life again. A jolt of fear hit Sim's chest when she saw the glimmer of insanity in Pru's eyes. Her brow furrowed and her nostrils flared and her breathing became short and fast. Her anger was building with each passing moment.

"Nogron did this," Pru said, more to herself than to anyone else.

"We have to warn everyone," Sim said. "We have to tell them to leave the Narrows—"

"No," Pru snapped. "It's too late for that." Fury was lighting up her eyes. "Lilith's right. And I should have listened to you from the beginning. Those factories are turning people into monsters, turning them into whatever the hell it was that you saw at Veldindor Health Center, and I'm going to put a stop to it right here and now. That fucking asshole manipulated me, made me..." Pru trailed off. She sprang to her feet.

"What are you going to do?" Cader said, looking worried. Pru snatched the bag from his hands.

"I'm going to blow up the fucking things myself."

"But—"

"You'll need the magicweaver, to grow the flames once the bombs have been set off." Lilith said, looking from Pru to Sim. "The bombs alone won't be strong enough."

They were all quiet, everyone's attention fixed on Sim.

"She's a strix, Pru," Cader said. "This won't bring her back."

Lilith glared at him.

"I don't care," Pru said with a wave of her hand. "This is bigger than that."

"I'll get you the wand back," Lilith said, her eyes fixed on Sim. "I'll convince the girl to give it back to you before it gets her kidnapped."

Sim's heart skipped a beat, and she wondered just how much Lilith had seen while she'd been trailing her. Wood could get kidnapped. This could stop it. This could make it so that they could all go to the Narrows and not have to worry about becoming striges. But it felt wrong, to burn down the factories. It was crazy, insane. Those factories belonged to Sir Nogad Nogron. Pru had to have a death wish. At least Sim already had a price on her head. She had little to loose. But still, it probably wasn't a good idea to do anything that would bring attention to herself.

"My mind's made up." Pru turned away and grabbed her bike. "I'll do this with or without you."

This was definitely wrong, Sim was sure of it. But she couldn't let Pru do it alone. Sim paused for a moment longer.

"Wait," she said, grabbing her own bike. "I'm going to help you."

"Are you sure?"

"I'm coming with you. Someone needs to make sure you don't get yourself killed."

"I am, too," Cader said, looking confident in his decision. "This is incredibly, incredibly dumb, Prudence. But I've got your back."

Pru nodded. "Help me and Lilith put these bombs in place then. Sim, meet me at the wall. We'll be faster alone at first, but we'll need you from there."

Sim nodded, a feeling of aching dread washing over her, and started to pedal toward Christiania.

XVIII

A sharp wind iced the air at the top of the Old Wall. Sim pulled her jacket around her, waiting alone for Prudence and Cader and Lilith to show, with nothing to think about but how crazy this whole thing was. But maybe it would be worth it, if it meant that everyone could keep going to the Narrows without getting sick. Thunder rumbled in the sky and Sim's thoughts shifted to how high up she was, jutting out above the wall like a soft-bodied lightning rod. She took a deep breath in through her nose, smelling the air.

"I'll need you to conjure some wind," Lilith said from behind her, making Sim jump.

"I didn't even hear you coming."

"First I have to ignite the fires," Pru said, following behind Lilith.

Cader came last, and they all stood around Sim. Pru started to rub her hands together. Her eyes were closed and her expression calm except for the angry knot tying her brow. "Lilith was right about me losing my ability to spell cast. I'm not sure I'll be able to do more than spark them, so once you can see the fires, help them grow and then shoot some wind at the factories."

"I'm going to give Pru some of my energy," Cader said. "I'm not sure I'll have enough to heal you if you push yourself too far, so watch it."

"Okay." Sim pulled on her goggles and tried to center herself. When the connection to the goggles was strong, she opened her eyes to see Pru's arms stretched out toward the factories. Red magic flowed from each of her palms, breaking apart and running like strings of glowing yarn to each of the spells she'd set. Popping sounds echoed up to the wall and then explosions flashed red in five of the factories' windows. A handful of small fires sprang up and grew stronger as Pru poured her energy into them. Cader drew magic out of the air so that it looked like Pru was haloed by a bright yellow light. The glow intensified with each of his breaths. He seemed to pause, just for a moment, and drove the force outward in one harsh exhale. The flames exploded at his addition of magical energy. Tongues of fire licked up at the sky in flashing red tendrils. But the factories were too big. The flames weren't spreading. Pru's red magic dimmed and blinked out. She collapsed to the ground.

"That's all I've got," she croaked. "It's all you now, Sim."

Sim glanced at her. The goggles made Pru seem dimmer now, closer to black and white, closer to the hue of Lilith's skin. Sim closed her eyes again, felt the wind ruffling her hair and chilling her neck. She grabbed it, just as she had that day when she'd blown the glass off the Narrows Bridge. This time she grabbed more, tethered it with fistfuls of breezes. A feeling of pure, natural power coursed through her entire body.

"Hold on tight," Sim whispered, and then let the wind loose. It sprang forward in hurricane gusts, swirled Sim's hair away from her head, but didn't cause her to lose her footing. She opened her eyes and directed the wind magic to join with the flashing fires. Pru cowered at her feet, pressed up against the lip in the stonework and digging her fingers into cracks between the stones. Lilith had her hands wrapped around Pru's bicep, her face pressed against Pru's arm. Cader was next to them, his arms in front of his eyes to block out the wind. In two breaths the flames had tripled in size and inky smoke was forming dark pillows in the night sky.

Sim inhaled deeply, and then decalibrated the goggles as she exhaled. She opened her eyes and let the magic finish its work. The sound of cracking flames and howling wind reached all the way up to the Old Wall.

Down near the factories little dark figures were streaming out into the streets. Dwarves. Sim had forgotten about the dwarves. A lattice of lightning crackled in the sky above them. "Shit," Sim said, looking up. "We need to get out of here."

Cader pulled Pru to her feet. She shoved him off and turned to Lilith. "I want to go with you," she said. "We can fight Nogron together."

"You need to fight for yourself before you can fight anyone else," Lilith snapped. She glanced at Sim. "I'll be seeing you, magicweaver."

"Lilith, wait." Pru stepped toward her.

"I don't want to be with you, Prudence." Lilith looked her straight in the eyes.

Pru laughed in disbelief. "I don't believe you."

"That's because you can't possibly understand. Don't be deluded; I'm here to stop Nogron, not to see you." Lilith paused for a moment, and her firm expression changed to one that was almost apologetic. But instead of saying anything more, she turned on her heel, ran to the ledge, and dove over it, into the alleys that ran along the base of the Old Wall.

Pru sprinted to the edge of the stonework and leaned over as far as she could without falling. "I don't see her anywhere. I don't know how she could have..." She looked up at Sim and Cader. "She's gone." Her expression was empty. Not masked anymore, but emotionless. This time she didn't push Cader off when he helped her down to the street where their bikes were. He made her hold his skateboard and sit on her handlebars while he pedaled her bike, fast, toward the Narrows Bridge.

Poisonous sulfur smells inundated the Bikeway Narrows and followed them during the whole ride to the bridge's upramp, where they stopped at the top to look back at the progress of their work. The factory fires rose into the night like burning pillars. The city's massive dragons were flying over them, their riders releasing gallons and gallons of water over the flames, but it didn't seem to be helping.

"We'll have burned down the whole Bikeway Narrows." Sim's stomach did a somersault. "We never warned anyone—"

Cader shook his head. "Azzer designed those bombs with protection charms, so that only the factories would burn. But we have to go. They'll have the Guard at the exit of the bridge any minute now."

"I'm okay to bike," Pru insisted. She handed Cader his board and jumped onto the saddle of her single-speed. "Let's get out of here," she said, and darted down toward the Mondran Quarter.

Sim glanced back, hoping that the dwarves would be okay. She followed Cader and Prudence, having a feeling that this would be the last time they rode together, and that this phase of their friendship was now approaching its end. Pru slowed as they passed Audrae's house, and glanced over at the dark-windowed building. Sim waited to see what she would do, and then stood on her pedals to catch up with Pru as she shook her head and bolted past.

They got back to Kailash and the three of them just stood in the empty kitchen. Sim looked at Kai's neat arrangement of herbs, and then at the spotless counters and tables.

"I'm leaving," Pru said, breaking the silence. "I have to get out of this city, figure things out for myself. I can't be here anymore."

Cader nodded, a deep frown set onto his face. "You're going to look for Lilith?"

"No. I don't know what I'm looking for. I just have to leave."

"It'll be good to disappear for a while. Nogron will probably be after all of us now."

"He'll probably track those bombs back to Azzer. But you're right." She looked at Sim. "It would be good for all of us to lay low now. Anyway, will one of you go wake up Kai? I'm just going to grab some things together and then you can see me off. I don't know that I'll be coming back again."

Cader nodded. "I'll get some potions together for you to take."

Kai was not happy about being awoken in the middle of the night, but once Sim whispered that Pru was leaving for good, Kai was out of bed and heading down toward the foyer. "What do you mean leaving for good?" she asked, shoving her glasses on.

"She said she might not be coming back."

"Not ever?"

"I guess not."

"Veldindor. What did you three do?" she demanded, fierce though sleepy-eyed. Cader was in the foyer, holding a satchel of potions.

"Nothing," Cader assured her.

"Yeah, right." She glared at him, and then turned her attention to the top of the steps, to Pru, who was dressed in her questing suit, with her sword strapped to her waist and a duffle bag across her back. She looked just like she had when Sim had first met her. She dropped the bag to the floor and wrapped Cader in a tight hug, holding him for a good ten seconds. "You know how to find me if you need me," she said into his shoulder.

Cader nodded. "Take care of yourself, okay?"

"Always do," Pru said with a small grin.

"And if you hear any word of my sister—"

"I'll let you know right away." Pru slapped his arm and turned to Kai. "You stay out of trouble, lady."

"Come here." Kai opened her arms and hugged Pru.

And finally Pru turned to Sim. "I hate good-byes," Pru mumbled before wrapping her in a quick hug. "Watch out for yourself, okay?"

"Pru, I'm sorry—"

"Cut that out. There's nothing for you to be sorry about. Tonight was your first quest and you nailed it. You had my back tonight. I'll never forget that. You can use my bike if you want, while I'm gone. Just don't mess it up."

"Okay," Sim said quietly.

"Watch your back."

"I will."

"And Lilith's always good on her word. You'll get that wand back. Just wait for her."

"Okay."

And at that Pru drew her lips into a smirk, waved to Cader and Kai, and made her way across the front porch and into the night. By the time the city put out the factory fires late the next morning, she was miles and mountains away.

Three days had passed since Prudence had left and the air enveloping Kailash was soft and sad. Its wooden floors reflected a dull, quiet gleam. Drangs snored lightly on an armchair with his face curled up into his body as if to shut himself off from the world. Sim took a new book from the shelves and the newspaper from the front table. Without looking at either, she retreated back upstairs to her room, where no one would bother her.

Word in the Bikeway Narrows, according to Cader, was that the dwarves had been responsible for the fires, though no one could really figure out why they'd do it. He'd taken care of Azzer's body and told Sim not to worry about it. He said he'd try to find out if Azzer had any family and let them know.

Sim sat cross-legged on her bed, staring down at the front page of the newspaper. The headline read: "Nogron to Build Condos on Factory Burn Site, Revitalize Forgotten Neighborhood." Sim read it again, and then again. She laughed, because there was nothing else she could do, and remembered the night that she and Pru had been arguing about the war outside the Geraldine. "Only crazy people fight a battle they know they can't win," Pru had said. And then she remembered Azzer's dangling feet, and thought about how maybe Azzer had been right about everything being hopeless. Sim put the paper down and dwelled on the anger simmering deep in her stomach. They'd won: There would be no more factories spewing black magic in the Narrows. But the magic dust would have to come from somewhere. The city needed to be lit and people needed to power their gadgets. Nogron would just build new factories somewhere else, and now the Narrows would never be the same.

Sim picked up her book and threw it against the wall with all of her strength. It fell to the floor crooked, its spine broken. Things had always seemed simple up until then, up until she'd found the Bikeway Narrows and the Incubator and Wood and the Geraldine. She had to leave; she could feel it in her bones. She had to figure out who she was and then maybe she could figure out what was right and wrong in the world, what was worth fighting for.

The doorbell rang. It was Audrae, probably, coming to see Pru. Sim dreaded having to tell her that Pru had run off again without saying goodbye. She pretended she didn't hear the knocking, and decided to let Kai deal with it.

"Sim! There's someone here to see you," Kai yelled a moment later. Sim stomped to the railing, her anger about the factories still festering. Wood was standing just outside, on the porch. She glanced up at Sim and then looked down at Drangs, who had just emerged from the kitchen.

"Hi, sweetie," Wood said with a smile. She crouched down and petted the fur growing around his horn. She was trying to act normal, and Sim wasn't in the mood for it.

"What do you want?" Sim asked, still standing at the railing. Kai looked up at her with a surprised expression, then widened her eyes as if to say she didn't care and slipped into the kitchen.

"I wanted to talk to you," Wood said, standing up straight and looking up at Sim. "Please?"

"Okay, well, come in then," Sim said, starting down the steps.

"No, that's okay. I just—it won't be long."

"Fine," Sim said throwing her arms out to either side of her in an exaggerated shrug. She leaned against a table next to the door and crossed her arms. Wood took a step in so that she could face Sim directly.

"I wanted to give this back to you." Wood brought a hand out from behind her back, pointing the base of the worn wand toward Sim. "Your friend Lilith, she...she explained everything. Thanks for letting me borrow it, but you should have just told me—"

"You're welcome." Sim grabbed the wand and tossed it onto the table. "Is that it?"

Wood bit her lip, frowned, and looked away. She opened her mouth, then closed it again. "Did you see the paper today?"

"I did."

"We need to fight this. The Narrows is our place."

In a flash Sim realized that this was her chance, her opportunity to become good friends with Wood again. They could work together, fight together. But she wasn't sure that was what she wanted anymore.

Sim laughed and shook her head. "Why bother? Nogron is going to build those high-rises. If there are protests, he'll quiet them. If there are sit-ins, he'll move people away. If there are hunger strikes, he'll let everyone starve. We can't stop him."

"We have to try. If we can just get enough people—"

"No one cares, Wood. You read the article. They're happy about this. People want this."

"It's wrong and you know it."

"No, I don't."

"You yourself have said that we have to stand up and fight for what we believe in, that revolution is the answer, that we can't stand to let a few old white men rule our lives."

"No, Wood. You've said that. And even if I did believe that once, I don't believe it anymore. There's nothing we can do. There's nothing at all that we can do. So it's useless to try."

"That's really cynical, Sim."

"It's the truth."

Wood frowned. Her teeth were clenched and tears shone in her eyes. "I won't sit around and let this happen while I know it's wrong. I won't see a place that I love be destroyed. We have to change the way things—"

Sim shrugged. "So then go fight for it. Maybe it'll make you feel better about yourself. But do you really think you'll have enough time, with classes and everything?"

"Wow, Sim." Wood laughed and looked away. "That's really nice."

"You should go." Sim motioned toward the door.

"Yeah, I guess I should."

Their eyes locked, for just a few moments, just long enough for all of the unsaid things, all of the unsayable things, to become acknowledged. Sim realized with a strange surge of relief that now she could move forward. She could learn who she was, accept who she was. She could stand up for herself. She didn't have to believe the things that Azzer did, or that Wood did, or that Pru did. There had to be another way, something besides hatred of everything civilized, or a blind call toward revolution, or icy apathy. There had to be something more, and Sim was determined to find it.

An awkward silence tensed up the air between them. Wood drew her lips into her forced smile, the one where she didn't show her teeth, and, after a moment's hesitation, she turned back to the porch and hurried down the steps. Sim watched her leave before closing the door and wandering into the kitchen.

"That was the girl?" Kai asked, looking up from her potions.

"That was," Sim said.

"Hmm." Kai face was thoughtful. "She's pretty but you'll find someone better for you." She shook her head. "Definitely not her."

"Thanks, Kai," Sim said. She headed toward the basement without looking at her, and hurried down the steps.

In the days following, Kailash's dark, dusky netherworld became a safe refuge, a place where Sim could lose herself in the methodical mechanics of her hands and not have to think about what lay in the bright, glaring world above her. Random gadget parts rescued from trash cans littered the tool bench, strewn among the useful things that Cader had found and brought home for her now that she'd started sculpting. Sim used her magic to braze them together, never knowing what it was that she was trying to make, never bothering to slip on her goggles and attempt to calibrate her Frankenstein gadgets. It was art, mostly. Useless. The twisted, gnarled structures mirrored her inner turmoil. They were her sole outlet for the emotions that were still too hard to face. Kai loved them. She tied two of them to high poles and stuck them in her garden to scare away the pixie dragons.

Now that she had no reason to go to the Narrows, Sim was torn between wanting to go just to hang out at Stein's and knowing that she shouldn't. She needed to be away from Wood, but she still wanted to be around her, even if they didn't talk. She didn't go. But she didn't know how long she'd be able to stay away.

Sim calibrated her goggles and started to sculpt the blade of a saber with a fissure down its center that Cader had found at the new battle house he'd joined. Sim never knew what she was going to make right when she started out. Something docile, earthy with this one; she could feel that much. Thoughts of wildflowers and thick-trunked trees and gurgling streams filled her mind for what seemed like hours. Time became soft and hazy when she was sculpting. But even as Sim worked on the sword, focusing intently on the tiny details she curved into the metal, dark thoughts nagged at the back of her mind. She pulled off her goggles, sighed deeply, and let her eyes slip down to the end of the workbench, where Azzer's journal lay, untouched since she'd thrown it there over a week ago. Cader had given it to her, saying that she should break the spell on it and read it. But she wouldn't.

Sim put her work on the center of the bench and climbed the steps to the kitchen, where Kai was busy cooking. She seemed absorbed in her chopping, even more so than usual. Cader had come home and was sitting at the table, frowning down at a letter. Its torn-open envelope had fallen to the floor near his feet. His eyes snapped up to Sim and she saw that they were swollen with tears before he was able to look away and stretch up the neckline of his T-shirt to dry his cheeks.

"What's wrong?" Sim asked, and held her breath. Her mind went straight to Prudence. Nogron couldn't have traced the factory fires back to her, and even if he had, he couldn't have tracked her down so quickly....

"Bad news, Sim. Bad news for the both of us," Cader choked out. His eyebrows were knitted together, his fist clenched so tightly that she could see the bones through his skin. Sim pulled out a chair and sat across from him. He glanced at her again, looked away, and continued, "Wood's been kidnapped."

Sim's heart stopped for a moment and then pumped wildly, as if to make up for the missed beats. She swallowed, not quite comprehending what she'd heard. "What?" she croaked.

"Acheron. She got out of prison by striking a deal with the Guard and ratting someone else out. She knows that Pru and I turned her in. She knows that you're the magicweaver Nogron's after. She would never face you in Terresin, where you can just tap into the magic that occurs here naturally, so she's out in the Hinterlands, where you won't be able to use your magicweaving against her. Unless you figure out how to do it with your wand, but that takes years of training—"

"Why would she take Wood?"

"I don't know. Maybe she thought that Wood still had the wand. Acheron has a lot of friends around the Narrows."

Sim swallowed. "And what's your bad news?"

"She says she has my sister, too. She knew where she was this whole time." Cader slammed his fist onto the table so hard that he made the salt shaker jump and spill over. "She kept it from me, knowing she could use it against me if she ever had to."

"How do you know she really has them?"

A disgusted expression stretched across Cader's lips as he scooped the envelope off the floor. He turned it sideways so that two locks of hair, tied together with black ribbon, slipped out and fell onto the table. One was the deep auburn that Sim knew so well, and the other a dark bluish-black, the same color as Cader's. "I know Acheron," Cader said. "She definitely has Wood, and my sister too if she's actually found her."

"So what does she want?"

Cader laughed, short and shallow, and looked over at Sim. "Your wand. And a duel to the death with Prudence."

"So what do we do?"

Cader frowned his eyes shut. "I can't go."

Sim waited for him to take a deep breath and then explain.

"Pru and I, we're hired by Kai's father to protect her. Someone has to be here with her. The last quest I went on—the one I was coming back from when you met me—the guy who was covering for us left just a few days before that. Even that could have broken our contract if Kai's father had found out. But that guy's not around anymore and it'll be at least a month until I find an adequate replacement. It'll probably take just as long to track down Pru, anyway."

"So I'll go," Sim said, not really thinking about what she was saying, but knowing that she'd be bound by her words. "I'll find Pru and convince her to help me save Wood and your sister."

"You'd do that?"

"I have to." And in that moment Sim knew that this was what she was meant to do, that the past week she'd spend alone in the basement was nothing more than a pause between everything that had happened to her since she had come to Terresin and the vast unknown that now lay before her. She was meant to leave, meant to go on this quest. Knowing this cast a calm sense of peace over Sim, so that she was able to look Cader straight in the eyes and let him know that she meant what she said. "I'm going to do this."

"I know a guy who has a ship," Cader said. "He'll even give you free passage to Branium if you promise to deal with any trouble that arises on the journey. You know—

pirates, mutiny, that sort of thing. I doubt that he'll actually run into pirates. And we both know that you can kick ass when you have to." He leaned back in his chair and frowned off. "Half of being a quester is just acting the part. Act like a quester and everyone will be fooled into thinking that you are one. And then, before you know it, you'll even be admitting it to yourself."

"You should head toward Munia," Kai said, still looking down at the stove. Sim turned to face her. She'd nearly forgotten that Kai was there.

"Just stay away from the northern part," Kai continued, "Because they're having ogre attacks. And definitely avoid Ogbond and Sangua. You can go the whole way by ship, or by land through Branium and Elm and Coveland."

"Thanks, Kai." Sim paused, and then continued. "Why...Why do you need someone here to—?"

"Don't worry about it," Kai snapped.

Sim frowned, decided to let the subject drop, and turned back to Cader. "Would it really be free?"

"Yep," Cader said. "It's the best way to do it. That'll get you on your way to Eridos, where Prudence is. I can get you a map and show you the way. There're a few other things you'll need to get, too. I can help you out. The world beyond Terresin is an incredibly different place, though, Sim. Things aren't so safe out there: bandits, pirates, wild dragons. You always have to watch your back, trust no one....You sure you want to go through with this?"

Sim had grown up hearing stories about the lands without magic, where fights were settled with swords and sharp-toothed creatures lurked in the shadows. She nodded, feeling the answer even as she said it. "I'm sure."

The wooden deck shifted under Sim's boots. A steady breeze blew at the back of her head and caught in a plump sail that stretched away from the ship's high mast. The towers of Terresin's downtown slipped by as the ship approached the Narrows Bridge. The mast would just clear its highest point.

It had taken only three days for Sim to get everything she needed: wand, goggles, sword, compass, bow. And Azzer's journal, tucked away deep in her knapsack for when she was ready to read it. A happy nervousness buzzed in Sim's chest, but she was careful to keep her face emotionless. She didn't want the crew to think she was a pushover. Whenever she caught them studying her with curious, uncertain eyes, she would meet their gaze with a scowl, trying to perfect the look she'd seen Prudence wear so many times.

The Narrows Bridge passed over them like a dark shadow. Sim gazed up at its iron underbelly and then over at the factories that eventually gave way to Christiania Street. She'd never gone back to the Narrows after that night when the fires had burned. She'd felt no need to say good-bye to the place she'd grown to love, the place that had pushed her to cast away the normal-girl skin she'd been painting over her soul for her entire life. Everything she'd known had been burned down to its ashes. With each sway of the ship Sim felt as if she were finally squirming out of a cocoon that she'd long ago outgrown.

A sailor walked by her, shoving hard into her shoulder with his. Sim frowned back at him, waited for him to pass her again, and stuck out her foot just before he did. He fell onto his face and scrambled to his feet with a scowl. He looked like he was about to swing at her.

"Try it," Sim said evenly, her hand on her sword. Her heart was pounding wildly, but she kept her face calm and relaxed.

The sailor paused, grumbled under his breath, and sauntered back to his post. A few others stared at her for a moment longer before going back to their work. They were starting to be afraid of her. Good. Sim crossed her arms over her chest and grinned as the ship cleared the Old Wall.